Melting

SCEPTRE

Also by Anna Davis

The Dinner

'Anna Davis's debut is as sharp and sparkling as breaking glass, and very funny while the laughter lasts . . .'

Jill Paton Walsh

'Davis describes a hard, cynical world filled with lies, deceit, loneliness and vacuum – dark alleyways through which to wander. Simple and fluid words poignantly reveal society's shallowness and frivolity . . . Davis has carved out a smooth if bitter path. Easy to read, harder to digest.'

The Times

'This is a stylish tale, told with sensitivity and relish. None of the guests reveal themselves quite as one would expect and easy clichés are avoided like the plague. It is a well-written, well-structured and satisfying read, which is crying out to be made into a film.'

The Guardian

'Sharply individual. A brilliant clever idea'

Rachel Billington

'. . . a brilliant first novel, wittily describing the dinner party from hell'

Amanda Craig in The Times

Melting

ANNA DAVIS

SCEPTRE

First published in 2000 by Hodder and Stoughton
A division of Hodder Headline
A Sceptre book

10 9 8 7 6 5 4 3 2 1

A CIP catalogue record for this title is available
from the British Library

ISBN 0 340 71843 9

Typeset by Palimpsest Book Production Limited,
Polmont, Stirlingshire
Printed and bound in Great Britain by
Clays Ltd, St Ives plc

Hodder and Stoughton
A division of Hodder Headline
338 Euston Road
London NW1 3BH

For Simon

Melting

5

The Train

The man sitting opposite was peeling a lychee with long pointy fingernails. He worked at the fruit with great care, concentrating so hard that he didn't seem to know his mouth was slightly open, his tongue absently stroking the lower lip. The inside of his mouth was amazingly red, as though he'd just popped a capsule of stage blood. He raised the egg-like fruit to his lips and slipped it inside. He was still sucking on it as he took out another from the paper bag on his lap; melting it down and smiling to himself. 'Try one?' he asked, as the train went into a tunnel. 'It's like eating pearls.'

'Thanks.' Samantha noticed, as she reached for the lychee, that the nails on his left hand were clipped short. 'Do you play the guitar?'

'How clever of you.' His grin revealed a chipped tooth. 'I bet you're a solicitor or a journalist – some occupation requiring keen observation.'

'I like bird-watching. Does that count?' The pressure in her ears made her voice distant, as though it were not her own. The train came out of the tunnel. An expression spread over his face that was somehow sleazy. He might have been about to say that he enjoyed a spot of bird-watching himself. Samantha shivered and turned her attention out of the window. The clustering twinkling lights reminded her of her aunt's old pin cushion. 'Do you know where we are?'

'I think it must be Stoke-on-Trent,' he said. 'Where are you headed for?'

'Manchester.' She bit into the lychee, and her mouth was

flooded with cloying sweetness. There was no freshness in this fruit.

'Me too.' He placed the bag on the table between them. 'Just help yourself.'

Actually she was having trouble swallowing this one. She felt as though she were chewing raw human flesh.

Samantha supposed many women would find this man attractive; women who enjoy a predator – the kind of predator that doesn't even bother to pretend to be anything else. She knew there were such women, had even been one herself when she was younger and naive. It was a mistake to believe you could hold your own with a man like this, an even bigger mistake to think you could change him. And that of course was the challenge this kind of man dangles like the proverbial carrot, while the poor foolish girl donkeys her way towards it, braying and snorting as it remains out of reach. Samantha had long ago concluded the pursuit of this carrot was pointless – more than that, it was dull.

She guessed he was about thirty-two or thirty-three, old enough to have left a great deal of wreckage in his wake, but not old enough to have grown out of wrecking as a hobby. The thin blond hair flopped over his collar and stuck out around his ears – the sort you would like to ruffle and would love to take a pair of scissors to. He had coat-hanger shoulders and a wiry body that was too thin to make clothes look good. She suspected his baggy linen suit was expensive, but the overall effect was cheap. His trump cards were his baby blue eyes.

'I've never known this train so quiet,' she said, looking around her. There were only four other people in the carriage. An old woman knitted feverishly a couple of seats away, while a fat man snored with mouth wide open – his false teeth had slipped out of position. A drawn-looking mother was sucking butterscotch and turning the pages of a battered Mills & Boon. Her sulking adolescent son had his Walkman turned up loud so that the tinny hissing and ticking was pestering Samantha's ear drums like a persistent insect.

'Do you make this journey often?' asked the man, in a phrase too irritatingly close to the old cliché.

'Now and again,' said Samantha, reluctant to give too much away.

'Do you know, I've never been to Manchester before,' he said. 'Isn't that silly! The second or third biggest city in England and I've never once visited. We live in this tiny pocket handkerchief of a country and yet we hardly venture beyond our own front doors.'

'So what takes you to Manchester now?'

'Oh, just business, you know.' He shrugged the word away. 'What about you? No, let me guess.' He sat forward in his seat and looked her up and down, seeming to assess. 'You live and work in Manchester. Maybe you're a teacher – no, no, you're too smart for that—'

She gave a sort of half nod.

'Perhaps you're an accountant or a management consultant . . .'

She wrinkled her nose in disgust.

'Television producer?'

As far back down the track as Milton Keynes, Jason Shoe had noticed the *Lancet* and the *British Medical Journal* peeping from Samantha's half-open satchel. He noted the dark shadows under her eyes, the way she kept rubbing them. House officer, he thought – those nasty long shifts – senior house officer, perhaps. He'd also spotted the Mercedes symbol on her bunch of keys, and he strongly suspected her cute little earrings were real diamonds.

'Architect?' he asked as he reached for another lychee. 'Museum curator? University lecturer?'

Anthony Shepperton took a sip of Scotch and stole a covert glance over his lap-top at the woman opposite. She looked rather like his ex-wife; all straight lines and sharp corners, relentless but sexy. Big nose. He'd always liked cold, hard women. A few years ago he might have had a bit of a go, but not now. These days he was a mere browser in the library of womankind – he'd done all his borrowing and returning, seen plenty of tarnished pages and dubious stains, experienced enough disappointing conclusions. It was all too exhausting a prospect for a man of sixty-five on the verge of blissful retirement and grandfatherdom.

He jiggled his ice cubes and returned his attention to the lap-top. He was tempted to click out of his spreadsheet and have a quick game of computer solitaire, but no, he must get this finished. If only he didn't feel so weary, so . . . his thought was interrupted by a hippopotamus-scale yawn. Perhaps he would just lay down his glasses, tilt his head back and doze his way to Stockport.

What was she writing, that spiky woman opposite? She was busily scratching away with a biro in a small, leather-bound notebook, her head bent low so that her glossy bobbed hair hung down like a curtain. If only *he* could be so industrious. He leaned forward slightly to try to get a glimpse, but some instinct made her look up at that moment, and she darted him the steeliest of glares. Abashed, he returned to his screen and his Scotch.

Fifteen minutes later his glass was empty. But, ah, here came the man with the trolley, whistling and rattling up the aisle. Surely one shouldn't have to put up with such tunelessness when one travelled first class – whistling should be done well or not at all. 'Scotch, please, with ice,' he ordered. The attendant bent and searched on his trolley for another Bell's miniature.

'Better make it two,' said Shepperton. The woman's head jerked up and she eyed him suspiciously over her witchy nose.

'I've got one Bell's and one Grant's,' said the attendant, with a horribly liquid sniff.

'Yes, yes, that will do.' Shepperton opened the briefcase that lay on the seat beside him, and rifled about in his wallet for a ten pound note, aware that the woman was still watching him with an expression of angular disapproval. What was she, some sort of school mistress? He looked her straight in the eye with defiance as the attendant handed him his change.

'I'll have a gin-and-tonic, please.' Her voice was surprisingly deep. He had been wrong about the disapproval – she'd simply been debating whether or not to buy a drink. His sense of embarrassment drove him back to the spreadsheet.

The ice cubes had melted away into the dregs of Grant's and Bell's at the bottom of Anthony Shepperton's glass. His eyelids were like concrete blocks pressing down to shut over his eyes. All those numbers, digits, letters. They were swimming together in Egyptian hieroglyphics on his screen. It was all he could do to save, exit the program and close the lid. Oh, the sheer bliss of sleep.

Fran Pelt laid down her notebook as the train eased into the station at Stoke-on-Trent, and tried to assess how deeply the elderly businessman was sleeping. He hadn't stirred when the attendant and his trolley had clattered past again. He didn't even twitch when the guard announced they were arriving at Stoke. She coughed loudly and watched his face for any sign of waking. Nothing.

Slowly, smoothly, she slipped on her jacket and put the notebook and pen into the inside pocket. Careful now to avoid sudden movements and sounds, she began to bend from the waist, arching her back and contorting herself under the table, holding its edge with one hand to keep her balance. Avoiding his sprawling legs, she extended her right arm beneath the table to reach for the briefcase that lay on the seat beside him, stretching further, touching, grasping for the handle . . .

A piercing trill from inside the case shattered the silence. Fran bashed her head hard on the under side of the table as she jerked up and pulled back. The trill rang out again, and the businessman cursed incoherently as he lurched into semi-consciousness and grabbed at his case. He rubbed his bleary eyes and fumbled with the clips. 'Damn thing,' he muttered, as he reached in to switch off his mobile phone.

Fran breathed deeply and pretended to examine her left shoe. The man snapped his case shut and slid back in his seat, closing his eyes once more as the train pulled out of Stoke-on-Trent and began to gather speed.

A girl was counting out a pitiful pile of coins onto the buffet bar under the eye of an impatient steward. 'Forty-five, fifty, fifty-five, fifty-seven, fifty-eight . . .' She groped about in her grubby cloth purse for further pennies, producing one more. 'Fifty-nine . . .' She laid it with the others.

The steward folded his arms, waiting for the inevitable. A nerve twitched in his cheek. Jill Foster, next in the queue, thought his expression was overly austere, unnecessarily haughty. How she hated these jumped-up Hitlers. Now he was trying to catch her eye, raising an eyebrow in bemusement. No, she would not be drawn into sympathy with him.

The girl was shaking the purse in her desperation. A Yale key, a safety pin and a length of cotton fell out onto the bar but no more money. 'How much am I short?' she asked in a small voice.

'One pound and one penny,' replied the steward, merciless, exacting. He was already reaching to take back the plastic cup of coffee that sat between them on the bar.

'Oh, God.' The girl was checking the pockets of her jeans, no doubt praying for one of those golden moments when you discover a forgotten five pound note. But had this girl ever experienced one of those moments?

'This isn't fair,' the girl muttered, irrelevantly. 'I know I've got some more somewhere.' She pulled an ancient tissue from a back pocket.

'Does this buffet look like a charity to you? Does it?' The steward was all puffed up like a proud cockerel. The queue was becoming restless.

'I'm not asking for your charity.' She stuffed the tissue back in her pocket, dropped the key and the safety pin back in the purse. 'I just forgot to go to the cash point, that's all. It's a mistake, a stupid mistake.'

Her face wore a look of injured pride, but Jill knew she was lying about the cash point, and so, apparently, did the steward. He flapped his feathers and clucked. 'A cup of coffee costs one pound and sixty pence.'

If Marcus was here, he would tell her to stay well out of it. *Don't get involved, Jill,* he'd say. *It isn't your problem. You always let yourself get sucked into other people's messes. It's a question of boundaries.* If only she could draw her boundaries as clearly as Marcus, then life would be a whole lot simpler.

'I'm not a beggar,' said the girl. 'This has never happened to me before.'

'No, of *course* it hasn't.' The steward's voice was loaded with sarcasm. 'Now, would you kindly get out of the way. I've got a queue of people waiting who can actually *pay* for their coffee.'

She couldn't be more than about twenty-two, younger than Andrea. What was she thinking of, travelling half way across the country with only fifty-nine pence in her purse! Jill noticed the darning on the faded shirt, the threadbare patches on the jeans, the dirt under the fingernails – she didn't really look any more scruffy than your average student, but it all added up to something else in this girl.

'What would you like, madam?' The girl still stood in front of the steward, but now he simply talked over her, or through her. She no longer existed.

'Give her the coffee.' Jill opened her purse and slapped a pound coin on the buffet.

The steward's face was sour and annoyed. He clearly felt his authority undermined. 'There's no need for that, madam, really there's not.' He spoke in a low, constrained voice, as though this would prevent the girl from overhearing. 'The situation is entirely under control.'

'Go on. Take your pound of flesh.' Jill pushed the coin towards him.

The girl was looking up at Jill with big, confused eyes.

'But, madam—'

'I said take it. Give her the coffee.'

The warty old lady behind Jill was tugging at her sleeve. 'What a kind, Christian gesture,' she gushed, with a whiff of halitosis. 'You're like the good Samaritan.'

Jill thought of remarking that in fact she was Jewish, but decided against it and smiled weakly instead.

White with anger, the steward cleared his throat. 'Haven't you forgotten something?'

'What?'

The girl was actually very like Andrea; small and delicate, but darker, and wounded, obviously wounded.

'One penny, please,' said the steward, withholding the coffee. 'You're still a penny short.'

'Here you are,' said the old lady, wanting a slice of the action. 'Now let the poor child have her cup of coffee.'

'I'm not a child,' said Eileen Locket. She looked the steward straight in the eye as she reached for her coffee, knowing full well that he wouldn't be able to meet her gaze. Even cats couldn't stare Eileen out. 'What's your name?' she asked.

'My name?'

'Your name.'

Rather than deigning to speak to her again, he merely held his badge out for her to see.

'Thanks, Derek,' said Eileen.

She turned to smile at the tall woman in the cashmere coat. 'Thank you,' she said.

At the sight of that smile, Jill Foster felt herself melting inside.

'It must be nice to do a job that's really worthwhile, where you can actually make a difference.' Jason took the last lychee from the bag.

Samantha wrinkled her nose. 'It's exhausting.'

'But to save people's lives, to heal people . . .'

'People have very romantic ideas about what it's like being a doctor,' said Samantha, world-weary. 'You don't want to get me started, really you don't.'

Jason shrugged. 'OK, then, Dr Derby. It's your turn to guess.'

Samantha brightened, keen to change the subject. She looked at his hands again. Pale and soft with long, thin fingers and those ridiculous nails. Her mother always said you could tell a lot about a man from looking at his hands. Samantha didn't entirely agree, but she did subscribe to the theory that the size and shape of the hands bore a direct relation to the size and shape of the penis – by which rule this man would have a pencil dick. 'We've established that you play the guitar,' she said, trying to rid herself of thoughts of his penis, 'but I don't think you're a professional musician.'

'Why not?' He looked hurt.

'If you were a musician, you would have already told me at great length all about your current band or project, and then proceeded to give me a blow by blow account of your career to date, why your views on music are so much more profound than anyone else's and how you've been fucked about by umpteen people who've grabbed your rightful place in the hall of fame. You'd have given me complimentary tickets to your next gig and offered me private lessons. Need I go on?'

He was clearly impressed with this analysis. 'I take it you've known a few musicians, then.'

'One or two.' The old woman sitting nearby was knitting more ferociously than ever. Was she giving Samantha the evil eye over her needles?

'I think you're an actor,' said Samantha, suddenly inspired.

'Really, why's that?' He looked alarmed.

Samantha felt rather pleased with herself. 'Quite honestly there's something stagy about you,' she said, watching his reactions carefully. 'Something false. I get the feeling you're performing for me right now. Playing some sort of role.'

His smile seemed fixed. 'My, my, who's a clever girl, then.'

'So am I right?' She was delighted.

But now his face relaxed again. He popped the last lychee into his mouth. 'About me being an actor? No, no, completely wrong. But I *am* doing my best to charm you, honey. I suppose that's a kind of performance.'

'Yuk.' Samantha looked away from him and out at the dark shapes of trees and pylons rushing by outside. A motorway snaked into view, a ceaseless stream of pulsing light.

'So the charm isn't working,' he said, a slightly forlorn note in his voice.

'You won't impress me with a few corny lines.'

His baby blue eyes were big with disappointment and an unexpected innocence. 'What does impress you, then, Samantha?'

Suddenly Samantha could see nothing but images of Greg – Greg in the kitchen cooking aubergine soufflé, Greg bringing her a hot water bottle and stroking her forehead when she lay ill in bed, Greg laughing at a bad joke, Greg picking her up from the station in the car, Greg touching her breasts – and for a moment the memories threatened to overwhelm her, to make her scream and howl for what she had lost. But of course she didn't scream or howl, and as the stream of light snaked on and on outside the train, Samantha Derby did her best to send the memories away.

'I'm not easily impressed,' she said quietly. 'I don't particularly want to be impressed.'

Jason shrugged. 'So I can't wow you with my business card, then?' He whipped from his inside pocket a metallic silver card, rather plain and stylish with one small line of white writing.

'Independent financial adviser,' read Samantha. 'Not at all what I'd have expected.'

'I like to surprise.'

'So what does that really mean?'

'Oh, pensions, savings, investments. Mostly investments,' said Jason, with a dismissive wave of the hand.

'What should I invest in, then? Assuming I had something to invest?'

He shook his head with a smile. 'Oh, no, Dr Derby. If you were to hire me I'd give you my advice. I don't offer advice for free.'

'How much do you cost?'

'More than you could possibly afford. I work on the principle that people value most what they have to pay dearly for.'

Samantha laughed lightly. 'I don't think we live in the same world.' She made to hand back the card.

'Well, for a while at least we're going to be living in the same city. Keep the card.'

'Thanks . . .' Samantha looked at the card for help, 'Robert.'

'Call me Robbie,' said Jason. 'All my friends do.'

If Anthony Shepperton had got a look at what Fran Pelt was frenziedly jotting in her notebook, he would have seen something remarkably similar to the spreadsheet he was working on. There were several columns of figures, to which Fran was adding further figures at great speed. Every so often, she would pause in her scribbling to quickly tot up the totals. She would subtract the total of the furthest left column from the furthest right column and write one final figure at the bottom right of the page. Then she would move on to a fresh page and an entirely new set of columns.

Fran looked up from her notebook every couple of minutes to check on the businessman. He appeared to be sleeping soundly now, occasionally muttering in his sleep. Mostly she couldn't make out what he was saying, but once or twice she thought she caught the word 'suffocate'. Or was it 'Saturday'? She hoped for his sake that it was the latter, since she didn't wish nightmares on the poor old chap. Besides, nightmares might wake him up.

The train was slowing down and the guard announced that they were now approaching Macclesfield. The announcement was made at a high volume – Fran imagined the guard bellowing into his microphone, not realising that technology meant he didn't have to shout in order to be heard. Miraculously, the elderly gent didn't even twitch.

Once again, Fran contorted herself under the table and reached for his briefcase. She grasped the smooth leather handle and eased it towards her.

'The train is now approaching Macclesfield . . .' Christ, he was off again, and louder than before. Fran froze. The case was heavier than she might have expected.

'. . . Macclesfield will be our next station stop. Please remember to take all your belongings with you. We hope you have enjoyed your journey, and we apologise for the slight delay at Milton Keynes, which was due to signalling problems . . .'

Fran's palm was sweating. The case felt like a ton weight and the handle was slipping in her hand. She didn't dare move. She glanced at the businessman's shiny shoes, checking for any sign of movement. She could feel the panic in her throat.

'. . . Thank you for travelling with us, and do make sure you have all your belongings with you when you leave the train . . .'

The case fell with a thump to the floor, narrowly missing the man's feet. Fran suppressed a nervous squeal. She held her breath and waited. Surely the businessman would wake up now. And yet somehow his feet and legs remained still.

'. . . This train will then stop at Stockport before terminating at Manchester . . .' Was there no stopping this man's verbal diarrhoea? Did he really love the sound of his own voice that much?

'. . . Macclesfield – I repeat Macclesfield will be our next station stop.'

And finally, he was done.

Still watching her victim's feet, Fran found her grip on the handle of the briefcase again, and slowly, surely, brought it out from under the table, as though it were a bomb set to explode at the slightest knock.

She moved quickly now, slipping the notebook into her jacket pocket, slinging her bag over her shoulder and grabbing the old vanity case she had stowed on the overhead luggage rack. Almost as an afterthought, she stooped to pick up the abandoned lap-top by its clever little built-in handle.

Seconds later she was stepping off the train, mindful as ever of 'the gap', and hurrying down the platform towards the taxi rank, never once looking back.

'Manchester, please,' she told the ageing cab driver, who scratched his head in puzzlement.

'But haven't you just got off the Manchester train, miss?'

'Just drive me to Manchester.' Fran's voice was cold, forbidding. The driver shrugged, and drove.

'So, what do you study?' asked Jill.

Eileen couldn't reply for a moment – her mouth was full of crisps. Jill had offered one and the girl took a handful, which she consumed voraciously. Jill surrendered the rest of the packet without a word.

'Study?' she said at last, wiping her mouth on the back of her hand.

'At university? In London?' Jill prompted.

'Oh, yes, sorry. I've got things on my mind.'

This was far from convincing, and still Eileen didn't answer the question. 'My daughter, Andrea, did French and Business Studies,' said Jill, sitting back in her seat and folding her arms. 'She finished a couple of years ago. She's in Paris at the moment, working.' Jill could hear and feel the pride in her voice, but perhaps she should stop talking about Andrea. Eileen looked sulky. She was sticking her chin out and sucking at her upper lip as a small child might. 'So, what about you?' Jill tried again.

Eileen seemed to revive. 'Maths. I do maths.' She was folding the empty crisp packet into triangles, smaller and smaller.

'Really? What kind?'

Eileen frowned her confusion. She had transformed the crisp packet into the tiniest possible triangle and had tucked it inside itself so that it couldn't spring back to full size. 'Just maths. You know.'

'You'll have to help me a little here,' said Jill. 'I don't know much about mathematics – when you say "just maths", do you mean pure maths, applied maths or what?'

'Oh, right.' Eileen dropped the crisp packet in her empty coffee cup. 'Pure. I do pure maths.'

Jill felt she should drop the subject, but something drove her on. 'I have a friend who's a mathematician,' she said. 'She says that pure maths is actually closer to philosophy than it is to the kind of maths we did at school. Would you agree?'

'Mm.' Eileen snapped her plastic coffee stirrer in two, and then started breaking the two halves into tiny pieces.

She was so childlike; impatient and petulant. There was something of the spoilt brat in her behaviour, and yet Jill didn't feel this could be the explanation. Eileen's small frame was loaded with damage – you could almost see it settling on her shoulders, weighing them down. What was the shape of her life? She was no student of pure mathematics, so what was her story?

Don't get involved, Jill, came Marcus's voice in her head. *You've children of your own to worry about.*

Halitosis woman was ambling down the aisle carrying a can of lager. She almost fell in Eileen's lap as the train lurched.

'Sorry, dear,' she muttered, seemingly without recognising Eileen and Jill from the incident in the buffet car.

'She's an alcy, that one,' whispered Eileen, as the woman regained her balance and staggered on.

And what exactly are you? thought Jill. What she actually said was, 'So what takes you to Manchester?'

'My grandmother's sick,' said Eileen. 'I'm going up to look after her for a bit. She's having trouble managing things. You know, shopping and all that.'

'I'm sorry to hear that,' said Jill. 'Where does she live?'

'Oh . . . south Manchester.' Eileen darted Jill a look of suspicion.

'Really? So do I. Perhaps I can give you a lift to your grandmother's house. My car's at the station. Whereabouts in south Manchester?'

Eileen was squirming visibly. 'There's no need, Mrs Foster, really. I'll be fine, thanks.'

'Call me Jill. It's no trouble at all. Where did you say she lives? Anywhere near Didsbury?'

'No, it's farther out than that. Quite a long way, in fact. I'll be fine, honestly. I'll get a cab.'

'But you don't have any money.'

'I'll go to a cash point.'

There was clearly discernible panic in Eileen's voice now. How much further could she be pushed?

'Look, as long as your grandmother doesn't live right out in Copple Park or something, I'd be happy to drive you.'

'Copple Park, that's the place!' Eileen looked up at Jill with big innocent eyes. 'That's where granny lives.'

'Oh.' Jill tried not to smile. It would be cruel to smile at such a moment. 'Are you sure?'

'Of course I'm sure.'

'The train will shortly arrive at Stockport,' cut in the guard over the tannoy. 'But before it does so we must appeal for your help. Would any passenger who has seen a tall woman with red hair and a grey suit, carrying a leather briefcase and a lap-top computer, please make your way to the guard's van at the rear of the train? We believe, but are not certain that this woman left the train at Macclesfield. We appreciate your help in what may become a criminal investigation. Thank you for your attention, ladies and gentlemen.'

'How bizarre,' said Eileen, excited. 'What do you think is going on?'

'Eileen,' said Jill, quietly, 'there's no such place as Copple Park. I made it up.'

Samantha had always found it rather irritating when men offered to carry her bags on occasions when she could manage perfectly well herself, and even though they frequently seemed to be struggling under the weight of their own bags as it was. She supposed she ought to try to see it as chivalrous and polite, but instead she thought they did it because they wanted to soften you up, to make you grateful, to show themselves to be gentlemen. And anyway, they never seemed to offer when you genuinely *couldn't* manage. She knew people would consider this opinion churlish at best, rampantly and ungraciously feminist at worst – but still she felt uncomfortable at the thought of being in a man's debt.

'It's really sweet of you, Robbie, but I can manage perfectly well myself, thank you. It isn't at all heavy.'

'Are you sure?' Jason was puffing along the platform behind her, trying to keep pace although somewhat encumbered by a large suitcase and bulky, matching leather overnight bag.

'Quite sure, thank you.'

It was a fine April night, clear and fresh, even taking into account the grubby air quality of central Manchester. Samantha was glad to be out of the fusty atmosphere of the train and reluctant to go straight back to her room in the hospital accommodation block.

'Shall we go for a drink?' He seemed to have read her thoughts, but she wasn't sure she wanted to share her last few hours of freedom with him.

'I can't, I'm afraid. Lots to do before tomorrow morning.'

'Pity. Are you getting a cab?'

'Yes.'

'Well, let me see you to the rank.'

How absurd – as though she couldn't walk to the taxi point by herself! But she could hardly say this, and after all she supposed that she had enjoyed talking to him – in a way. He *had* made the journey pass quickly.

The station was busy with students returning from the Easter break, humping their huge rucksacks around like snails. The cab rank was quiet though – the students were mostly heading off for the bus station.

'Where to, love?' asked the fat side-burned cabby at the front of the line of black cabs.

'Manchester Royal Infirmary, please,' said Samantha, as Jason opened the door for her. 'Where are you going?' she asked him.

'Me? Oh, I'm staying centrally. The Portland Thistle down the road at Piccadilly. Won't take me five minutes to walk over there.' He grinned, flashing his chipped tooth. Why didn't he get it fixed? He could surely afford to.

'Hop in if you like,' she offered. 'We can drive past the Portland.'

'No, thanks. I fancy the walk.' But he lingered on. She noticed for the first time how small his ears were – like tiny shells on either side of his head. Her mother had always told her that large ears were a sign of intelligence – it followed therefore that small ears signified stupidity.

'Well—' she said, holding out her hand for him to shake. 'Bye, then.'

Instead of shaking the hand, he held it firmly in his, and raised it to his lips. Samantha recoiled.

'Will I see you again?' he asked, with an expression of distress.

She shrugged. 'Manchester's not such a big place.'

The cabby cleared his throat loudly and impatiently.

'I'd prefer not to leave it to chance,' said Jason.

Samantha wished he would just go. 'Look, Robbie, it's been nice meeting you, but I've got a lot on right now. I'm about to do three weeks of night shifts and I have an exam in six weeks, an important one.'

Now he was annoyed. 'I'm just talking about going for a drink,' he said. 'A harmless little drink. You're the only person I know in Manchester. And you're lonely.'

'I'm putting the meter on, love,' said the cabby. 'I can't just sit here all night.'

'OK, I'm almost ready.' She turned back to Jason. 'It's difficult for me right now,' she said, softly.

He straightened, pulled out of the cab. She'd bruised his ego, she could see that. He wasn't used to rejection.

'You have my card, Samantha,' he said, coldly. 'There's a mobile number on it. Call me if you change your mind.'

As the taxi pulled away to join the traffic, Jason smiled to himself. 'About a week, I'd say.' He began to walk slowly out of the station into the bustle of hooting trams, rowdy drunks and speeding traffic, and down to merge with the crowd in Piccadilly Plaza, where a tawdry funfair was tootling and humming – business was booming on this sweet, April night.

Jill took pleasure in the sight of Eileen's face as the waiter set an enormous plate of spaghetti puttanesca in front of her.

'Fazzioli's has been going for years and years,' she said, watching Eileen's futile attempt to twirl the pasta around her fork. Eventually she gave in and started shovelling it up and sucking it in. 'I used to come here as a student. I've never had a bad meal here. It's a family-run place. They're always the best of course.'

'Why?' Eileen said through a mouthful of spaghetti.

'Why what?'

'Why are family-run places always the best? What is it about families?'

'Well, I don't know, really.' Jill cut a piece of her pollo al limone. 'I suppose it's because of the continuity and the intimacy.

Recipes passed down from generation to generation, a sense of tradition and the personal touch; the kind of love and care you only get at home.'

Eileen took another huge forkful. 'God help us if my family ever took to running a restaurant!'

'What are your family like, Eileen?'

Eileen swallowed heavily. 'Sorry, I shouldn't have mentioned them.' She took a sip of wine. 'It's really nice of you to buy me dinner. You shouldn't have to hear about my shitty childhood. The deal is one-sided enough as it is.'

'But I want to know.'

Eileen's long hair was dangling down in front of her face, almost trailing in her pasta sauce. Jill could have reached over and smoothed it back behind her ear, but this would obviously transgress all boundaries. She imagined how it would have been if Eileen were her little girl – how she would have brushed that hair every morning and every night and put it into long, silky plaits. *I want Rapunzel hair, Mummy,* that's what Andrea used to say. But somehow Andrea's hair never got beyond shoulder length.

'Do you know what spaghetti puttanesca is in English?' said Eileen.

'No. What is it?'

Eileen leaned forward conspiratorially, and whispered, 'Whore's pasta.'

Jill tried to laugh, confused, searching Eileen's face for a clue.

Now Eileen was laughing, a strange laugh with no trill, no resonance – as though she were able to suck her voice out of it; a laugh like the crackling of a wood fire.

Jill was wrong-footed. She reached for her wine glass and cleared her throat nervously.

The waiter came by to top up their glasses, gave them a smooth white smile. 'Everything all right, ladies?'

'Perfect, thank you,' said Eileen. 'What's your name?'

'Marco,' said the waiter, straightening his waistcoat.

'The whore's pasta is excellent, Marco.'

'I'm glad you enjoy.' Marco looked a little uncomfortable but kept his smile in place. 'Anything else you ladies need? More wine?'

'No, thank you,' said Jill. 'We're fine for now.'

'Marco,' said Eileen, 'tell me, are you the son of the restaurant owner? Or the nephew or something? Family?'

'Me? No. I'm a student at the university. I'm in England for this year only. I'm from Firenze.'

'Really? How fascinating.' Eileen was satisfied.

'Excuse me,' said Marco, gesturing at another table who were waiting to order.

'Are you trying to tell me something?' asked Jill, when he had moved away.

'What?' Eileen's eyes were large, baffled.

'Eileen.' Jill reached across the table and gave Eileen's right hand a squeeze. 'I want to help you. But I can only help you if you let me. Why have you come to Manchester with no money and nowhere to go? What on earth were you thinking of?'

Eileen laid her cutlery down and sat very still for a moment, looking down at her plate. She seemed to be trying to decide whether to confide in Jill. When she spoke again, she kept her eyes down. 'I needed to get out of London. I'd got into a bad situation with someone.'

'What sort of bad situation?'

Eileen darted her an angry glare. 'I'm not a prostitute, if that's what you think, I was pissing around just now. Thing is, when you don't have a proper address and you don't have any money, you have to lean on other people a lot – put your faith in them. And sometimes people betray your trust. You know?'

Jill nodded. She didn't know, of course. She was trying to imagine, but this was a world she would never experience. She saw dark alleyways, shadowy figures, scenes that came straight out of the chamber of horrors.

'People have their own agendas,' Eileen was saying. 'They seem to be offering you a way out, but really they're pulling you in . . . Hey, Marco—' The waiter was passing again. 'I don't suppose you have a cigarette, do you?'

'It's very bad to smoke,' he replied, flirtatiously. Then he tapped the side of his nose and whispered, 'I have some behind the bar. I'll get you one.' He beetled off.

'Today I'd had enough,' said Eileen. 'I wandered over to Euston, thinking I'd just skip on a train and leave. I had it in mind to go to Scotland – you know, clean air and mountains and all that – but in the end I found a ticket on the floor. Just lying there – a ticket to Manchester. Seemed like fate to me.'

Was it fate? Jill wondered.

Marco returned with the cigarette. As Eileen held it between her lips he lit the end with a flourish.

'Thanks.' Eileen inhaled deeply.

'What I don't understand,' said Jill, 'is how you got into this situation in the first place. What about your home? Your parents?'

Eileen snorted. 'Oh yes, my lovely home,' she said in a sing-song voice, as though reciting a poem. 'I come from bungalow land, where it's all net curtains and garden gnomes, and everybody is nice to everybody else. Except that they're not.'

'Go on,' said Jill, leaning forward, trying to block out the comforting clatters and snippets of Italian language that surrounded them, trying to make the space between them empty of everything except Eileen's words.

'No,' said Eileen, blowing out smoke. 'I don't want to talk about that. It's private. I had to get away and I'm not going back.'

Now Jill's head was full of TV documentaries she'd watched about abused children, battered wives, alcoholics . . . She could almost see the abuse in Eileen's face, at the corners of her eyes, in her lips when she smiled and when she didn't smile. 'What you need,' she said firmly, 'is the chance to find your own independence – to stand on your own feet.'

Eileen was shaking her head, smiling sadly.

'Yes, you do. You need to get out of having to take handouts. You need a job, a place to live . . .'

'So tell me something I don't know!'

'Listen to me.' Jill spoke too loudly. People were twisting around in their seats to stare. 'I can give you the chance you need.'

'How?'

'My daughter has a flat in Didsbury. Just around the corner from here, in fact. She's away in France at the moment.' Jill dare not let herself think of what Andrea would say – or Marcus, come to that. 'You could stay there for a while – not too long

– a few weeks. Long enough for you to sort yourself out a bit, find a job.'

'But Jill—'

'No buts. It's all settled.'

Eileen was looking at her suspiciously, as though to say, And what's *your* agenda? 'But I can't—'

'Yes, you can. You can.'

5

Manchester

This isn't the first time I've been in Manchester. It was the first place I came to with Jason and Fran. I was their pupil, their apprentice – I was like one of those nuns – what do you call them? Novices, that's it. They were constantly teaching and preaching at me until I thought my head would burst with it all. How on earth was I ever going to remember all this stuff? In London, when they asked me to join them, I thought, why the hell not? There was nothing keeping me there – no job, no friends, no doting boyfriend coming round in the evening to warm my cold toes at night. Jason and Fran were the first people to show a real interest in me, to tell me that maybe I could be good at something . . . This was my opportunity to turn my life around, to make something of myself. So I said yes – and off we went to that little rented house in Stockport with the lilac walls and the chintzy curtains. Fran complained non-stop about the house, but I liked it. It was warm and cosy and friendly. It was home.

Why me? I still don't really know the answer to that question. Jason and Fran had been together for years – lovers, business partners . . . They were doing just fine – so why ask some random silly little girl to join up with them? Fran's explanation was that they'd come up with a great idea for a scam that required two girls. They couldn't work this one on their own. So they were keeping their eyes open, waiting for someone to come along – someone they'd instantly recognise as 'the right person'. And then they met me. But what made me so right? They couldn't answer that question to my satisfaction. I have some idea of what it was about. They sensed that I was hanging around waiting for something to happen, something out of the ordinary. I craved it, I needed it. And they knew I had no ties, nobody to ask questions, nobody to miss me. I don't actually think that's the complete picture – there was more to their decision than that – but it's as close as I can get to an understanding of it.

Trust was absolutely the most important thing. That's what they kept saying over and over, until I thought I would scream if I heard the word one more time. We had to know that we could totally rely on each other, whatever happened. We had to be as close and as sure of each other as three people could possibly be. I found that a bit tricky to begin with. I trusted Fran – she took care of me, listened to me – she was like the big sister I'd never had, taking me out clothes shopping, gossiping about men and sex. I looked up to her, adopted her tastes and views, tried to emulate the way she did her make-up.

It was Jason I was less sure of. He was slippery, somehow. When he said things, it was as though he meant something different – he seemed always to be laughing at me behind his words. And I'd catch him looking at me – not like a big brother, like – well, like a *man*. Looking at my legs, my tits. And we hadn't exactly got off to a good clean start, had we? ... But I must stick to the point. Anyway, how could you ever be sure of someone with ears as small as his?

I couldn't let either of them know that I didn't trust Jason. They might have kicked me out on my ear and I so desperately wanted to stay with Fran, to actually be a part of something. And as time went on I became used to Jason – I started to see that this was all just part of his style, his manner. He could no more help his lecherous sidelong glances or ironic comments than a pig can help having a curly tail. I grew to like him, and to admire his genius – oh yes, he certainly has genius. Jason is the ideas man, the one with the vision and the dreams. Fran is the realist.

But I had another problem with this important word, trust. I was to trust Jason and Fran with my life, and yet at the same time I was being taught that 'trust' is the first principle of the con. You have to really *work* your victims, coax them to trust you with their money. It's like when you encounter a dog that starts off by growling and eyeing you suspiciously but eventually, after being stroked and patted in abundance, rolls over to let you tickle its tummy – and thereby renders itself vulnerable.

I was nervous that first night as Fran and I drove away from the warm lights of the Stockport house and headed for Manchester city centre. Terrified, more like it. Fran was edgy too – she was chain smoking and tapping the steering wheel in an agitated manner as she drove. She was probably scared I would let her down, blow the scam.

'Just remember,' she kept saying. 'If you sense anything is wrong –

anything at all – we walk. We take no chances. And if you see me start to walk – you follow, no questions. OK?'

'OK,' I said. I had been to the toilet three times just before we left the house, but now I needed to go again. Badly. I crossed my legs and tried to pretend we were just two friends having an evening out, but all the time I could see Fran's fingers tap tapping on that steering wheel, and the nerve twitching in her cheek.

We parked the car in a side street near the bar. Sam's Bar, it was called – a dreadful cheesy place; cheap watery cocktails, high stools and wobbly tables. It was packed full of lone men in double-breasted suits eyeing up the talent, and girls with badly permed hair and white high-heeled shoes, giggling and flirting. I went straight to the toilet, leaving Fran at the bar.

I flushed and then stood at the washbasin for longer than necessary, trying to stop my hands from shaking, my jaw from quivering. I tried to hear Fran's voice in my head, her reassuring words:

'Don't worry. You can be the shy one if you like. You needn't talk much – just look coy and available. Leave the rest to me.'

Fran will do the talking, I told myself. *I don't really have to do anything*. Then I pushed the swing doors open and walked back into the bar.

At first it seemed that Fran had disappeared and I had a momentary panic. Then I spotted her sitting at a corner table on one of those high stools talking to a bulky pin-striped man in his forties with nasty yellow teeth, smoking a cigar. Fran was giggling like a schoolgirl, crossing and uncrossing her legs so that her skirt rode up her thighs. The man's bulging fish-eyes were roving up and down those long legs. Jesus, she didn't waste any time, did she!

'Over here, Jenny,' called Fran, beckoning to me.

I did my best to smile as I crossed the room, tripping on a step and almost falling. I could see Fran laugh and whisper to the man as I steadied myself, and then he laughed too.

'Jenny,' said Fran, as I arrived at the table. 'This is Bill. Bill, meet Jenny.'

'Delighted to meet you, Jenny.' He flashed his yellow teeth and reached out to give my hand an unwelcome squeeze. I caught sight of a gold wedding band.

'Likewise,' I muttered, feeling my smile turn to ice.

Fran reached for the jug that sat in the middle of the table and poured some pink cocktail into a glass for me. Ice cubes and lime slices splashed in. 'Long Beach Iced Tea,' she announced. 'Cheers.'

She should have been a theatre actress. It was like sitting with a total stranger – how could the Fran I knew be giggling like that, tossing her hair back and hanging on this lumpish man's every word? It was so alienating. I began almost to feel as though I, rather than Bill, was the victim of this scam. But somehow I kept my cool, giving him those shy glances, laughing at his awful jokes and sipping at my cocktail.

It must have been at least an hour before Bill got up to go to the loo, and my face was aching from the effort it took to keep smiling. The minute he was safely inside the gents, Fran's face started looking like Fran again. She reached into her tiny sequinned bag and brought forth a little plastic tube of white powder that reminded me slightly of the bottles of glitter I used to play with as a child. She pulled out the plastic stopper and poured the powder into Bill's glass of cocktail, mixing it in well with the plastic stirrer. Then she turned to me and asked, 'Are you all right?'

I nodded but my stomach was tight with fear. This was real. We were really doing this.

Bill emerged from the toilets, his beer belly sticking out in front of him as he waddled back to his stool. 'Hey, ladies,' he breathed, 'what say we blow this joint and go somewhere a little more exciting?'

'What's the rush, Billy?' Fran toyed provocatively with his tie. 'Let's finish these drinks first.'

Bill shrugged. 'Whatever you want, darling.'

A few minutes later I was squeezing into the back of the car with Bill while Fran slid into the driver's seat and started the engine. He moved up as close to me as he could and I could feel his putrid breath on my neck. His horrible hand was on my knee, and Fran was attempting to catch my eye in the driving mirror, warning me to stay calm.

'So where are we going, Julie?' asked Bill as we moved into the traffic. 'Where are you two little vixens taking me?'

'It's a surprise, Billy,' cooed Fran. 'But I think you'll find it worth the wait.'

Bill rubbed his hands together gleefully and then returned the right one to my knee.

We'd been driving for what felt like hours but was perhaps only forty-five minutes. He was becoming restless.

'How much longer, Julie?' he whined. 'Where the hell are we going?'

'It's not far now,' said Fran, lightly, taking a left at some lights.

I was getting panicky. Maybe Jason had been sold dud stuff – maybe we'd drugged Bill's drink with a packet of sugar. What would we do if he wouldn't fall asleep? I could feel my breathing getting fast and shallow. Bill had taken his hand off my knee now and seemed to be becoming more and more irritable. Bizarrely I realised I wanted his hand back on my leg – the withdrawal worried me. I watched the streetlights flashing across the skin of my arms, turning them a sickly green. I breathed in the air that Bill had just exhaled and tried not to heave.

And then, just as the fear was getting a real hold over me, Bill's eyes began to close. Soon he appeared to be in a state of deep sleep.

'He's gone off,' I called to Fran, and she checked in her mirror.

'OK,' she said. 'I'm going to pull over by this park.'

Fran moved quickly. She got out of the car and came around to the back. 'Don't look at me. Keep your eyes on the road,' she hissed. 'I need to know if anyone's coming.' But the street was deserted. God only knows where we were.

In spite of what she said, I kept glancing over as she reached across Bill, trying all the while to keep her face away from him, and delved into his jacket pocket.

'Right,' she said, as she brought out his fat leather wallet and tossed it onto the driver's seat. 'I need you to give me a hand.'

Together we heaved and struggled to get that fat blubbery man out of the car. Fran had her hands under his arms and was dragging him. I was trying to lift his legs and push. This must be how it would feel to move a dead body. But all the while I fretted that Bill would wake up. What would we have done if he *had*? Finally we got him out. We left him lying on the pavement at the entrance to the park like some drunken tramp and got back in the car.

I watched him through the back window as we drove away. 'Will he be all right?'

'Course he will,' said Fran. And then, in a commanding tone, 'Don't you go feeling sorry for him, Eileen. You mustn't *ever* feel sorry for them.' And she passed the wallet back to me. 'Look and see what we've got.'

It was a really great scam and we worked it five nights a week for a couple of months. All we had to do was turn up at a bar and choose our man. We looked for expensive suits, sleazy expressions and the all-important wedding ring. After all, how could a happily married man go to the police and say he got in a car with two pretty girls who drugged him and robbed him? It was beautiful in its simplicity. And we were raking in the money. My confidence grew.

What of Jason – what was he getting up to while Fran and I were working our con? Well, he was busy with his own little schemes, just like he always is, his dating scams. And although he didn't seem to be working as hard as we were, he made twice as much money as us in the couple of months we stayed in our Stockport house.

So what made us move on? There's always something – eventually. In this case, we found one night that we had a policeman in the back of our car. I've rarely seen Fran as grey and serious as she was when she pulled his ID out from his jacket pocket. I was already playing with the fifties in his wallet.

'Put those back!' she screamed at me.

'Why?'

'Do what I bloody say,' she shouted. God she can be scary when she wants to be!

She was tripping up and falling all over the place in her eagerness to get him out of the car and I had to tell her to slow down, take it easy.

After we'd been driving again for ten minutes or so, she began to breathe more freely.

'Fran, the guy had over three hundred quid in his wallet ...'

'Don't you ever defy me!' she snapped, and drove through a red light. Car horns rang out all around us.

So that was the end of that. In the morning we left and headed for Birmingham. I was worried that now the scam was over they wouldn't want me with them any more. But in the end there was no mention of them leaving me behind. It seemed I had got through my trial period.

We never stay in one place for very long. Even if nothing actually goes wrong, Fran gets antsy after a while. She works on the assumption that we must be making mistakes and leaving tracks even if we think we're not. The moment we get complacent is the moment we start to mess up. So my life now is like a join-the-dots puzzle – a cluster of towns and cities connected by train journeys. Sometimes our scams are carefully planned, sometimes they rely on chance meetings, odd happenings. Often I get this weird feeling that there's a process at work, some sort of picture emerging from these random dots and lines. Something is evolving.

'We can't stay here, you know. Not for more than a day or two, maximum. We'll have to find somewhere else.'

Eileen squinted up at Fran but couldn't take the direct sunlight that was streaming through the window behind her, and was forced to look back down at the parquet floor, at Andrea Foster's post, which was scattered around her feet along with Andrea Foster's CDs and Andrea Foster's Clinique make-up. Eileen was wearing one of Andrea Foster's Calvin Klein T-shirts and had a pair of Andrea Foster's woolly socks on her feet. She was drinking coffee from a yellow mug with an 'A' on it. She had made some for Fran in the twin mug with a 'C' on it. While going through Andrea Foster's underwear drawers, Eileen had found a bunch of letters in French, all from someone called Claude.

'Why? Don't you like it here?' Eileen liked it. She liked the minty green walls, the white blossom-covered tree outside the bay window, the crimson velvet curtains in the master bedroom where she'd just slept her best night's sleep in a long time, deep in the cushions of the giant futon, while Jason and Fran stayed at a hotel in town.

'That isn't the point.' Fran disappeared into the kitchen to refill her 'C' mug.

'Well, what *is* the point?' Eileen twisted around to direct her question to Jason, who was sitting in an armchair, immersed in the Lonely Hearts column of his newspaper.

'Eh?' He glanced up, but only briefly.

Eileen heaved a sigh and struggled to get to her feet and shake the pins and needles out of her legs. 'Look at this, Jason.' She fetched the beautiful classical guitar that she'd noticed sitting in a corner of the master bedroom gathering dust and presented it to him.

'Oh, wow!' He seized it eagerly and dropped the newspaper.

Fran stood in the doorway, sipping her coffee and watching as he tuned it up. 'This won't work, Eileen.'

'It could do with new strings but it's an excellent instrument.' Jason played a melancholy A-minor chord and then a triumphant G.

'Play us a tune.' Eileen settled back down on the floor and picked up the envelope she'd been opening – a bank statement that showed Miss A. Foster as being £1,766.87 in credit. She reached for the next, which offered Andrea Foster a gold card, 'Acceptance guaranteed'.

'It's too risky,' said Fran, as Jason broke into the opening chords of Simon and Garfunkel's 'Mrs Robinson'.

Eileen was annoyed. 'What makes it so much more risky than

anything else we do? It's because *I* found it, isn't it? You don't like it when either of us makes decisions. You're a control freak.'

'Yeah, sure,' said Fran, flippantly. 'Think for a minute, Eileen.'

Eileen *was* thinking. She was thinking about the pocket handkerchief lawn behind the house and how nice it would be in summer time, about the cute little roof terrace with the pot plants . . .

This flat was full of love. You could smell Andrea Foster in the bedroom even though she had been away in France for some weeks; a clean, fresh smell. She probably didn't wear perfume but had nevertheless scented her environment in the way that some women can. The kitchen smelled of home-baked biscuits, the lounge smelled of candle wax and wood. Romantic evenings in front of the fire?

The phone started ringing, prompting Jason to break off his song mid-chorus. It rang three times and an answer machine clicked on. Andrea didn't have a proper outgoing message, just a snippet of Tom Jones singing, 'What's new pussycat'.

'Hi, Eileen, it's Jill here . . .'

'You used your real name?' Jason was incredulous.

'. . . so anyway, I'll pop over a bit later. See how you're getting on. Hope you had a good sleep. Bye.'

'That,' said Fran, thumping her mug down on the table, 'is why we can't stay here. In a nutshell.'

Eileen wasn't ready to let this one go. 'Oh, *please*. Just for a while. I can handle Jill, she's easy. Anyway, I've already had the locksmith's over.' She could hear the needy child in her own voice. 'Oh, *go on*.'

Fran looked around her at the cool green walls, watched the playful shadows cast across the floor by the big blossom-covered tree. 'What do you think, Jason?'

But now Jason's mobile was ringing, and he was laying down the guitar and groping around for it in his jacket pocket, drawing out the phone and pressing the button to take the call. 'Samantha! What a nice surprise. Just a second.' He muffled the phone with his hand. 'Whatever,' he said and returned his attention to the caller.

'One week,' Fran said to Eileen. 'One week, then we move. Not a night more.'

* * *

Frances Pelt spent a couple of days making preparations; sorting through a variety of business cards she'd had printed up, reading through listings magazines and jotting down names and addresses of theatres, restaurants and cinemas in her little notebook. Her small, round, immaculate handwriting slanted sometimes to the left and sometimes to the right, but never changed direction on the same page. She took buses around Manchester and then wandered on foot, visiting the places she'd listed and making notes on the locations of doorways and fire-escapes, the cloakroom facilities and the bars.

Eileen was bugging her, trailing listlessly around the flat, indulging in some light credit card fraud and messing with Andrea Foster's post without any particular purpose or scheme, generally poking her nose in. Fran had told her she needed to work alone this time, but she didn't seem to get the message.

'Why don't you get yourself out and start looking for somewhere else for us to live?' suggested Fran, edgily.

'I'm too busy at the moment,' Eileen snapped back. 'I'm setting something up. You want to move – *you* go flat hunting.'

Fran shrugged. She didn't believe a word of it. 'Feel free to tell me what this "something" is . . . when you're ready.'

Fran avoided Jason – he was cluttering up her mind. She saw him at night, of course. To Eileen's displeasure they had taken over the master bedroom, and it had stopped smelling of Andrea Foster. Fran wasn't above dressing up for Jason, or giving him the occasional little bedroom surprise to remind him that he had a good deal with her. This didn't mean she was insecure; far from it. It was simply that Fran was a perfectionist in *every* area of her life. She never let him see inside her little 'box of tricks' as he called it, an old vanity case with a combination lock which she kept under the bed. She thought it a good thing to keep him guessing. Out of bed she was abrupt with him, almost monosyllabic. She knew this didn't bother him; he understood that she wanted to be alone with her thoughts. Anyway, he had plans of his own to make.

Fran started with The Castanet, a new theatre in the recently redeveloped Castlefield area, once a dark creaking mass of decrepit old warehouses, derelict buildings and rusting boats scattered along the Manchester Ship Canal, now buzzing with trendy split-level café bars, restaurants and street sculpture, which seemed to be breeding.

'The Castanet,' said *Top Entertainment: The Nation's Best,* 'is a shining example of what our dingy old theatres ought to evolve into. Its amphitheatre structure with round stage area at floor level, its intelligently tiered comfortable seating, its effective air conditioning and marvellous acoustics – not to mention its atmospheric Spanish bar with great wine list – make it a joy to visit. Manager Gregory Ingrams is doing a fine job.'

Fran liked the brashness of the bar – this was a place not afraid of being overstated. She was particularly amused by the giant pair of red castanets that hung from the ceiling on almost invisible wires and swayed somewhat disconcertingly in the breeze that blew in through the slatted windows just below the roof. She enjoyed the elaborate floor mosaic and the flamenco background music, though she did feel the management had gone overboard on the numerous – and pointless – lengths of coloured muslin suspended from everything you could suspend muslin from.

Wearing a short slip-dress in cream silk with matching jacket and strappy gold high-heeled sandals, Fran arrived ridiculously early for the play. She strolled beneath the castanets to sit on a high stool at the long zinc-topped bar, and ordered a gin-and-tonic from the prematurely balding goateed barman. He smiled sweetly as he took her money and keyed four digits into the semi-computerised till (8–5–6–3). The display flashed up, 'Hello, Toby.' Fran watched him hold the note up to the light before keying in the transaction and pressing the Enter button. The drawer slid soundlessly open and he stuffed in the twenty and counted out her change. The float in the till must have been at least £100.

Half an hour later the bar was teeming with people and the flamenco music was blaring out of the speakers at considerable volume. The goateed barman was rushed off his feet taking drinks orders for the interval and dispensing numbered tickets in garish luminous green. He had been joined behind the bar by a short shaven-headed girl with a nose ring and a tall man with slicked-back hair and an air of authority, who Fran took to be the manager.

The crowd were largely young, smart-looking professionals. They sipped their chilled Chardonnay, flicked through the programme for tonight's performance of *Who's Afraid of Virginia Woolf* and conversed in a manner they clearly took to be sophisticated, giggling with their young, vibrant mouths at each other's witty little in-jokes. Fran suddenly felt old and drab. She tried not to let their youthful vigour bother her.

Two minutes before the performance was due to start, in place of the habitual ringing of a bell, the castanets on the ceiling lurched and clacked together three times. Fran was so delighted at this silliness that she felt compelled to order herself another gin-and-tonic, a large one. The crowd began to file into the auditorium through two sets of doors.

Three TV screens above the bar showed the action on the stage, and Toby the goatee barman was half watching as he poured out glasses of wine for the interval, fetched bottled beer from the fridge and moved to the optics to fix the shorts. He arranged the drinks on metal trays with luminous green napkins and complimentary peanuts, and pinned a numbered ticket to each napkin. He would assemble three trays at a time before squeezing out from behind the bar and carrying them across the room to set on the tables and side counters. He was working hard; every so often he wiped the sweat from his brow.

It took him a long time to notice that Fran was still sitting at the bar on her stool, long legs crossed, deep in her notebook.

'Not watching the play, then?' he asked, needlessly.

Fran looked up and smiled brightly. 'No, not today.' She reached into her jacket and produced a business card that read:

Top Entertainment: The Nation's Best

Sally Bingham, features writer

'Top Entertainment, eh?' Toby was impressed, but puzzled. 'What I don't get, Ms Bingham, is why you're sitting here taking notes instead of sitting in there writing about the play.'

'Ah, well, you see I'm writing a different kind of feature tonight,' explained Fran. 'I'm working on an article about the real backbone of theatres.' She paused to wait for his reaction. He hadn't understood.

'I'm going to write,' she continued, 'about people like *you.*'

'Me?' He was blushing now, and still utterly baffled.

'Yes, you. I'm visiting six theatres this week. I'm talking to the bar staff, the cloakroom attendants, the box office assistants, the ice-cream sellers . . .' She slipped off her stool to walk down the bar towards him. 'I'm talking to the people whom nobody notices but who can make all the difference to the theatre-going experience. Without *professionals* like you, we're left to queue *endlessly* for our drinks, stuff our jackets under our seats, stand in pointless marauding hordes in the foyer . . . what kind of a mood does that put us in by the time the curtain goes up?' She smiled, coyly. 'I've been to many theatres in my time, and I can tell you . . . what's your name?'

'Toby.'

'I can tell you, Toby, that this is one of the most impressive theatre bars I have *ever* seen.' She paused for effect. 'Perhaps *the* most impressive.'

'Really?' Toby's neck was now as red as his face.

'Really. Are you the bar manager, Toby?'

'Me? No.'

'Aren't you?' – with a look of sheer amazement. 'My, but you certainly have managerial bearing.'

Poor Toby – even his ear-lobes were red now. 'You'll be wanting to speak to Melvyn,' he said, smiling shyly. 'Hang on a minute. I'll go and find him.'

With that, Toby plodded off through a doorway behind the bar, and disappeared.

In a matter of seconds, with just a quick glance about, Fran was behind the bar, keying 8–5–6–3 into the till. 'Hello, Toby,' lit up on the display, and Fran pressed at random the key for a bottle of Becks before hitting Enter. As the drawer slid open, she undid the clasp of her velvet handbag and held it at the ready. She pulled satisfying bunches of notes from the till and stuffed them straight in the bag. When she had all the notes, she went for the bags of one pound coins, and then scooped out handfuls of loose change. By the time she heard voices, she had bagged everything worth taking.

'Melvyn,' announced Toby, as he approached the bar, 'this is . . . um . . .'

'Sally Bingham.' Fran held out her hand to the slicked-back bar manager she'd clocked earlier. 'From Top Entertainment. Delighted to meet you, Mr . . .'

'Melvyn Simmons,' he lisped, shaking the hand. 'You can call me Melvyn.'

'And you—' Fran responded, graciously – 'can call me Sally.'

'A glass of champagne for the lady, Toby,' cooed Melvyn. 'And one for me, and . . . yes, why not, one for you too, Toby.'

'Thank you, Melvyn,' smiled Fran. 'Now, as Toby may have told you, I'm doing a feature on—'

'Yes, yes, he told me all about it, and we're most honoured.' Melvyn rubbed his hands together. 'Anything I can tell you, anything I can do, it's no trouble at all. What I don't understand, though, is why you didn't let us know you were coming. You didn't speak to Mr Ingrams, did you?'

'Ah, well,' said Fran, as a flute of champagne was placed in front of her, 'I'm rather like a restaurant critic, you see. I like to catch people on the hop. Warn people you're coming and out comes the red carpet, as it were. I'm not here for the red carpet treatment. I'm here to see you all at your normal business. And I like what I see.'

Melvyn smoothed his slicked back hair, and Fran caught a glimpse in his face of his past as a failing actor searching desperately for his big break. She opened her notebook at a fresh page.

'Right, Melvyn, tell me what it's like to manage a bar like this.'

Melvyn rubbed thoughtfully at his chin.

'It's dead busy,' chipped in Toby, and received a warning look from his boss.

'It is *rather* busy,' said Melvyn. 'Just as the Barcelona bars on which it is modelled are lively, bustling places. In fact, I'd say it takes rare skill to look after a theatre bar this big.' He nodded wisely, and Fran scribbled in the notebook. 'A theatre bar is not like your run of the mill café bar, oh no. It's the rushes, you see.'

'The rushes?' Fran looked up. 'Are you talking about hormones?'

'No, no, no. I mean the rush to the bar at the interval, and those huge surges at the start and end of the plays.' He leaned heavily on the bar, as though the strain were just too much.

'Gosh, that sounds very stressful,' soothed Fran.

'Stressful but rewarding,' said Melvyn, proudly. 'You should see how much cash we take in one evening here. You'd be staggered, I assure you. In fact—' His face lit up with an idea. 'I'll show you how much we've already taken tonight. You'll be quite amazed.' He wriggled off his stool and stepped behind the bar.

Fran swallowed her mouthful of champagne the wrong way and broke into a coughing fit. 'Not . . . necessary . . . no,' she forced out between coughs.

'Sometimes we can take as much as two thousand pounds in one evening,' continued Melvyn, ignoring the outburst, and keying in 9–6–3–4.

'Listen, Melvyn, we're getting a little off the point, here,' said Fran, recovering herself. 'My article isn't about money . . .'

'Hello, Melvyn,' said the display.

'. . . it's about care, service with a smile . . .'

Melvyn punched another key.

'. . . the silent spinal cord of a theatre.' Fran trailed off and closed her eyes as she saw Melvyn's finger move towards Enter.

She could hear the blood in her head.

'Fucking thing!'

Fran opened her eyes to see Melvyn hit the till with his fist. 'Toby, what's wrong with this fucker?'

'I don't know, Melvyn. It was all right earlier on.' Toby hovered uncertainly.

'Completely fucking jammed!' He hit it a second blow.

Fran slid off her stool, clutching her handbag to her chest. 'Listen, Melvyn, Toby, I'm afraid I have to be . . .'

'Oh, Sally, wait a minute, we'll have it open in a jiffy.' The slicked hair was working itself loose, hanging over his face in greasy strands.

'Sorry, guys.' Fran was backing towards the exit now. 'Tight schedule, you know how it goes. I have to be at the Royal Exchange before their interval, which is . . .' She glanced at her watch. 'Goodness, I have to be there in ten minutes. Thanks for the champagne.' She turned to scuttle. 'Great bar. I'll give it a rave,' she called over her shoulder. 'Love the giant clackers!'

Two weeks had gone by and they were still staying in Andrea Foster's flat. Jason liked it there – there was something about the place. He'd been spending time playing the guitar and thinking, watching Fran bustling in and out – too busy to do much about changing their accommodation. He watched Eileen drifting.

Now it was time to get to work. On a crisp, sunny evening he sat in Dukes 92, a large pub just across the canal from The Castanet, munching on some good gorgonzola and sipping a pint of Stella. His companion, one Patricia ('call-me-Patty') Hazeldon, preferred stilton. She licked her fat fingers tipped with purple nail varnish, and drank from her pint of Best, leaving a pink smear of lipstick on the rim. She didn't bother to wipe it off. Jason thought her a vulgar sort of woman.

'I'll give you a cut.' Patricia reached a plump arm across the table and ruffled Jason's hair. A heavy ring on her index finger bashed against his head as she did so. He winced.

'I don't think so.' He shrank from her hand, bashful.

'Oh, go on. I'd give you more than just a short back and sides, I can tell you.' Her mouth opened wide as she laughed the deep throaty laugh of a heavy smoker, revealing well-shaped but yellowing teeth.

'I bet you would.'

He hadn't been sure about this one. The message she left in response to his advert was too brash for his liking.

'Hi, I'm Patty and I'm looking for a guy who can give me a *really good time*. Are you up for it? I'm a big, blonde, gorgeous girl with a huge appetite, know what I'm saying? I like my men tall and moody. I don't care if they're blond or dark, just so long as they're not wishy-washy. I'm a hairdresser and I'm smart. I've just opened my second salon and I'm going to have a chain one day. Aim for the stars, that's my motto . . .'

He'd been about to delete the message when she started on about the salons. Too tempting to ignore.

'This is your first time, isn't it?' The lines around her heavily made-up eyes seemed to be showing kindness all of a sudden.

The full, mobile lips turned down at the corners with something approaching compassion.

'What makes you say that?' He came over defensive.

'Oh, sweetie, you're looking at an old hand.' She shook her head sadly. The carefully arranged curls and waves remained rigid and Jason imagined how they would crunch to the touch. 'I've had more of these kind of dates than you've had pieces of gorgonzola. I know a Lonely Hearts Virgin when I see one.'

'Is it that obvious?' Jason hung his head in mock embarrassment.

'It wouldn't be to most people,' she said, reassuringly. 'But you can't fool Patty. Patty knows these things.' She reached under the table and laid a hand on his knee. He tried not to flinch. 'Don't worry, Robbie. You just need someone with a little experience to show you the ropes, that's all.'

This was looking more and more like a CR by the minute. Jason would never manage to sustain a PW with this monster. He had a sudden and vivid mental image of how she would look naked, lying on her back with her sacks of flesh loose and flowing all over the bed, her massive lips parted in ecstasy and her blue eyes (was she wearing coloured lenses?) gazing up at him through false lashes as he pumped away above her, trying his best to pretend he was somewhere else.

Jason wiped a bead of sweat from his upper lip. No, this definitely had to be a CR. Shame, really.

'I know what you need,' said the monster, squeezing his knee with an iron grip.

'You do?'

'What you need,' she continued, 'is another drink.'

'Another drink, yes, you're right,' Jason stuttered, relieved. 'Same again, please.'

'Don't go away,' she called playfully over her shoulder. 'I'll be right back.'

He watched her teeter off to the bar on her stilettos, her arse wiggling from side to side in that tight mini-skirt that strained at the seams. He sat back in his chair and gazed around at the pub.

How long ago did he last sit in this pub? He tried to work it out. It was before he met Fran, so it must have been at least eight years ago. Then the pub had been only half its current size – they'd literally doubled the size of the building. It was always popular and famous for its cheeses, but at that time there was just a small bar and a glass-fronted cheese counter in the corner. Now there was a thriving restaurant serving panfried this and seared that with a whatsit coulis and a rocket salad on the side. The cheeses were still a feature of course. They were its gimmick, its focal point, the key to its success, thought Jason, as he bit into his gorgonzola.

Last time he was at Dukes 92, he was meeting an ex-gymnast who had lost her way and her confidence when she became too old to cut it on the international circuit. She was charming, lithe, vulnerable and rich. Prime PW material. What was her name . . . Nadia . . . Mikela? He convinced her he was starting a gym with special facilities for people with osteoporosis. She invested five thousand pounds in the end, or was it six thousand?

'Here you go, Robbie.' As Patty bent to place the pint of Stella in front of him, Jason found he was seeing more than he wanted to of her cleavage. 'Get your laughing tackle round that.'

'Thanks,' said Jason, and pulled his legs back under his chair so she couldn't squeeze his knee again.

'I must take a trip to the little girls' room,' said Patty. 'I'll be back in two shakes of a lamb's whatsit. While I'm gone, you have a think about where we should go for dinner.' She bent to whisper in his ear. 'Here's the deal. You choose dinner, and I'll decide what comes afterwards.' And she was off, clacking down the steps to the toilets, giving him a little wave as she went.

He waved back and smiled. Behind his smile he was cursing himself. He'd had 124 answers to the advert so far – 124 women to choose from and he'd kicked off with this total non-starter. Why hadn't he listened to his instincts? The real contenders for the PW were the needy ones, the desperate women looking for love who left gentle, nervous messages that nevertheless held deep undercurrents of pent-up frustration and unrealised dreams. But this gorgon, you couldn't make her fall for you even if you put your very heart and soul into it – she was playing the circuit, picking up her fun where she could. Those salons, those blessed salons. What a waste.

No, this was a CR – Cut and Run. Take what you can and

don't waste any more time over it. Patty had gone to the toilet without her handbag. It sat forlorn on her empty seat in all its leopardskin glory. How very unlike a woman of her sort not to take the handbag in with her so she could retouch her make-up. Perhaps it was tattooed onto her face.

Jason undid the clasp. As he reached into the bag, he found he was thinking of how it would be to feel inside her vagina. He did his best to banish the thought, but it continued to pester. He felt the shapes of the make-up bag, a filofax, some tampons, old tissues, a box of condoms. Yes, here it was – her purse. In the spirit of its owner it was good and fat. He drew it out and stuffed it into his inside jacket pocket.

This is not clever, he thought, as he drew a biro out of his pocket and wrote on the back of a napkin, *I'm sorry I had to leave. I'm not man enough for you.*

This is not elegant, he sighed, and replaced the biro in his pocket.

This is not stylish, he mused as he took a last couple of gulps from his pint and got to his feet.

This is cheap, he muttered as he squeezed between the busy tables and headed for the exit.

Ah well, this is what it is and that's that.

Jason had to wait half an hour for Samantha to arrive at Velvet. He'd called her on his mobile as he slouched sulkily in the back of the cab, hoping she'd help him to salvage this disappointing night and turn it to good purpose. Samantha, after all, was a definite PW – Play it for all it's Worth. He was more than happy to work her for as long as it took; she was high calibre and the payout, when it came, would be ample.

He was surprised nevertheless when she expressed herself free and in the mood to go out. He'd met her for lunch the previous week and she had done little more than toy with her food and tell him how guilty and annoyed with herself she was because she'd broken away from her studies for the sake of a plate of Greek salad and a chat with some guy she'd met on the train and didn't really know from Adam.

Tonight, however, she was bored, restless. And yes, she was

feeling lonely. She'd meet him for dinner at Velvet, a basement café bar on Canal Street, at the heart of the gay village.

Velvet was alive with gimmicks, from the fish tank built into the steps on the way in to the tiny TV screens in the toilets playing QVC endlessly. A waiter directed Jason to a corner table and settled him on a high-backed chair upholstered in yellow velvet. He ordered a Michelob, which was swiftly brought over, and sat quietly, sipping his beer and eavesdropping on the loud conversation of two *Coronation Street* bit-part actresses at the next table. The only other customers were a canoodling couple in a far corner and a pale spectacled girl reading a newspaper.

Samantha balked a little as she came down the stairs and stepped on the fish tank. She had the feeling her foot would go straight through the glass. She spotted Robbie in the corner, talking on his mobile. How she hated mobile phones. He ended the call abruptly when he saw her and his face, which had been serious, almost sombre, broke into a grin.

'Samantha, darling. You're looking . . .'

'Tired. Yes, I know.' She pulled back a red velvet chair and sat down.

'A little pale, perhaps.'

Why didn't men ever say what they meant? She knew she was looking awful. 'Can we have some wine?'

'Of course. White? Pinot Grigio?'

'Fine.' In fact *he* was looking rather wan, and more tousled than she'd seen him before.

He passed the menu over. 'I've already decided,' he said.

'What are you having?'

'The goat's cheese and then the duck with figs.'

'Sounds great,' she said, glancing at the list. 'I'll have the prosciutto and the penné carbonara.'

Samantha's carbonara was lumpy and unappealing, while Robbie's duck with figs looked delicate and pretty.

'So have you decided to like me?' asked Robbie, spearing a fig slice.

She had to think about that before answering. 'I've decided to allow you to amuse me. For a while, anyway.'

'Your life isn't very amusing on the whole, is it?' he said.

'Not really, no.' She'd been missing Greg all day. She tried to get him out of her head, but the harder she tried the worse it got. She could barely concentrate on her work. It had been six months now. When was it going to stop hurting?

'What's his name?' asked Robbie, through a mouth full of duck.

Samantha was startled. 'Am I so transparent?'

'I know about women,' said Robbie, with a wise nod.

'Yeah, right.' Egotistical bastard.

'So what's his name?'

'Greg. But let's not talk about him. He's a non-subject.'

'You've got a lot of non-subjects, haven't you, Samantha?'

She tried to read his expression – was he sympathising or mocking her? She noticed again how tiny his ears were, and had a sudden impulse to reach over the table and twist them really hard. She shook the feeling away. Was she drunk already?

'Non-subjects? Not really. I just don't like having my life dissected over dinner. You're supposed to be distracting me from all of that.' She forked a piece of limp pasta.

'Distraction. Yes, of course.' Robbie topped up both of their wine glasses and signalled to the waiter to bring a second bottle. 'And how exactly would madam like to be distracted? I'm already plying you with food and drink. I can offer sexual favours, but—'

She wrinkled her nose. She'd wondered how long it would take him to get around to that.

'No?'

'No.'

He looked hurt. 'Am I really so repulsive?'

She'd pushed him too far. His agenda was clear but she'd chosen to ignore it because it suited her to be taken out and given attention. Was that wrong of her? Was she toying with him unfairly?

'Don't be silly,' she said. 'You're a very attractive man. You know you are.'

'Do I?'

All that smooth talk, all that bravado. And now here he sat looking deflated. His eyes were big and sad. He was like a puppy left out in the rain. 'Stop playing little boy lost. It doesn't suit you.'

But it did suit him.

'Who's playing?' He shrugged and returned his attention to his meal.

She felt she had disappointed him. Why should that bother her? 'I'm sorry.'

The big eyes were on hers again. 'For what?'

She floundered. 'For trampling on your feelings.' That wasn't quite what she was sorry for but it was the best she could do.

He laughed. 'Lighten up, darling.'

They lingered over dessert, now the only two customers left. Robbie had lemon tart which he declared to be light and frothy, while Samantha's tiramisu was a vast improvement on the penné carbonara. Their conversation reverted to safer subjects; Samantha loved rugby, but Robbie thought it was a public school sport and inevitably preferred football. Samantha tried to tell him that he would feel differently if he was Welsh but Robbie wasn't having it. Robbie talked about art – it seemed he liked to keep up-to-date with what was going on, fancied himself as something of an aficionado. Samantha didn't have much to contribute to that. They spoke about books; he liked Updike, Mailer and James Ellroy. She tried to explain the gentle appeal of Carol Shields, but he didn't like the idea of books concerned with ordinary men and women and their mundane humdrum lives.

'Jesus, I spend too much time with those kind of people as it is. I don't have to *read* about them too!'

When the waiter came to clear the dishes away, Robbie ordered a Scotch for himself and a brandy for Samantha. He produced a cigar from his jacket pocket, and asked the waiter to light it. It was so big that it made him look like a child. She noticed those long fingernails again, and shuddered at the thought of them digging into her back.

'Do you know what gets to me more than anything else?' he said as he puffed away on the cigar.

'What's that?'

'Tight spaces.'

His pupils were dilated. She'd thought she was more drunk than him, but the cigar had apparently tipped the balance.

'What do you mean?'

He smiled, showing the gap between his front teeth. 'Sometimes I feel like I'm driving a massive articulated lorry.' He flung his arms out to convey something of great size. 'And I have to back it into this tiny little space.' He held the small space between thumb and forefinger. 'Worse still I'm actually trying to turn the fucking thing around. I'm moving it forward a couple of inches, back a few millimetres. I'm turning the steering wheel and trying again and again, forward and back, forward and back. I'm just not getting anywhere. The bloody lorry's too big, the space is too small. Understand?'

Samantha nodded. 'I think so. I guess everybody feels like that sometimes. I know I do.'

'Well I feel like that *all* of the time.' Robbie banged his fist on the table for emphasis. The cutlery jumped and tinkled.

Samantha twisted around to see if the waiters had noticed. They seemed to be busy cashing up and wiping glasses.

'I can really talk to you, Samantha.' His words were slightly slurred. 'You're a good listener. I bet you're a good doctor.'

'I don't know about that—'

'Don't knock it.' He reached across the table and touched her hand, gently; let his hand remain there, touching hers ever so lightly. She didn't withdraw, but watched him. 'You've got empathy. Proper empathy.'

'Yeah, yeah.' But still she didn't retract the hand.

'I've got to get out of those tight spaces,' said Robbie, undaunted. 'I want room to manoeuvre, room to stretch out.'

Samantha waited, knowing there was more to come.

'I'm working mainly with these two women at the moment.' Robbie finally withdrew his hand, to put out the cigar and return it to its plastic box. 'To put it simply, they have me making lots of little moves on their behalf. They like to play safe with their money.' He took a sip of his Scotch.

'And you want to do something else?'

'I want something bigger, more creative. I want a project I can really get my teeth into.'

'Like what?'

He shrugged. 'I don't know yet.'

'But they're holding you back, these women you're working

with? They're forcing you into the tight spaces you've been talking about.'

'I suppose so.'

Samantha played her brandy around the glass, held it up to let the light shine through it. 'I don't understand the ins and outs of this, Robbie, but it seems to me – as a layman – that you have to find your big project and go for it.'

'Do you think so?' His eyes were eager.

'Well, I don't know, really, do I? But you're sitting here telling me you're totally frustrated with these two women, whoever they are, and the way they do business.'

'That's right.'

'So do you really *need* them?'

'The women?' Robbie looked confused.

'Yes. Do you need them?'

'I don't know.' He was wincing now, rubbing at his head as though the thoughts were making it hurt. 'They're associates of mine. I've been working with one of them for a very long time. We have an understanding.'

Samantha was feeling powerful. It was as though her lack of knowledge of the flesh and blood of his world was making it easy for her to see the bones, to pick out the spine. 'It seems to me,' she concluded, 'that the first thing is for you to find your project. *Then* you see if these associates will come on board with you. It's no good considering some hypothetical situation. You need something concrete to put to them.'

Robbie smiled and drained his Scotch. 'Samantha Derby,' he said, 'you're a beautiful, intelligent woman and I want to make love to you.'

I don't understand how he can bear to do it. And I don't understand how Fran can bear for him to do it. But I suppose it isn't any of my business, is it? I mean I'm with them, but I'm not *with* them. It's a sort of sleazy thing that Jason does, isn't it – a sort of loathsome thing. If he ever went to prison he'd be given a really hard time there. It could be your mother that Jason is working on, your sister or your wife. Fran and I – we're more straightforward, above board. We tell stories and we steal – it's as simple as that. Jason forms relationships with his victims, he makes them fall in love with him. Fran and I leave people bitter and empty-walleted but Jason shreds his victims into confetti.

He's good at justifying himself.

'They choose their fate,' he says. 'I don't *force* them to give me their money. And maybe I've given them something in return. Some of these women have never been wined and dined before – they've never had a man tell them they're beautiful, take them away for weekends and send them flowers. They'll never forget the experience. It's theirs to hold on to for ever. They've had to pay for it, that's all.'

'And it doesn't come cheap, does it?' I say. And what I'm thinking is, does he really believe these women will hold on to those memories, nurse them on a cold winter night as they lie alone in bed? Of course they won't – because their wonderful lover was rotten at the core. They'll probably never trust a man again.

But he's right about one thing. They're suckers. If they're that stupid then they deserve all they get. Jason's teaching them a lesson about how the world works – and they won't make the same mistake again. There are much nastier people out there who want more from a woman than her money.

Drinking my morning mug of coffee, I watch Jason crawl dishevelled into the flat and head for the bedroom, where Fran is still sleeping. And I wonder, does she make him shower before she lets him touch her? Does she hate the knowledge that he has just spent the night with another woman or does she get a kick out of being the only one who *really* has him? I'd love to ask her but you can't ask Fran those sort of personal questions. She'd go all bristly and change the subject.

Actually there's something up with Jason at the moment. He's more distant than usual, more distracted. Generally Jason gets on a high when he's setting up his dating scams, but this time he's quiet, introverted, as though he's working something through at the back of his mind the whole time. Last night I dreamt that he announced he was leaving us. When I woke up I wondered if it could be true. Maybe he's bored, perhaps he thinks we're holding him back. After all, he can't give himself one hundred per cent to his scams, can he? Because at the end of the day he has to come home to Fran and me.

I told Fran about this over lunch and asked her if she'd noticed anything. She started laughing and pooh-poohed the whole idea.

'Jason would never leave me!' she announced.

At first I was reassured by her confidence, but then my worries took on a new shape. Maybe *I* am the problem. Could it be that Jason never wanted me on board in the first place and now he wants me out? If he gave Fran a 'me or her' ultimatum I wouldn't stand a chance! The more I think about this, the more worried I am. I couldn't bear to lose them – not now! What would I do?

But I'm starting to pull myself together. There is an answer to this situation – which, let's face it – may be all in my own mind anyway. The answer is that I must pull off some good scams all on my own and bring in serious money. If I show them I'm not just some pliable sidekick – prove I have real talent and aptitude, then Jason won't want to get rid of me. So that's what I'm going to do.

Mimi's was a plush, tacky night-club attached to the Metro Hotel. It was continually full of businessmen on short stay, off the marital leash. They would all roll up at the end of the evening, full of beer and curry and looking for a bit of skirt to make the perfect end to their night. The club was a sea of mirrors, brass, padded seating, glitter balls, cocktail menus and ugly men in suits who reminded Eileen of her father. She hated it. As she walked past the two bruiser bouncers on her way in, they made cheap comments about her legs and her tits loud enough for her to hear. She turned back to give them the finger but they just laughed and told her where they'd like her to stick it. She was wearing a pink strappy silk mini-dress from Karen Millen, with matching lipstick, thick mascara and high heels. She had smeared a little glitter cream just above her cheek-bones and Jason had fastened a silver chain around her left ankle as a finishing touch. They laughed at it together.

The chain moved slightly against her ankle, tickling in a not altogether unpleasant way, as she walked down a corridor with thick blue carpet on the ceiling and walls as well as the floor. The music – Hot Chocolate's 'I believe in Miracles' – grew louder as she turned a corner, past the cloakroom and two imitation palm-trees sprayed silver, and into the club itself.

'All right, darling, wanna leave your dress here?' called out the adolescent cloakroom attendant with a prominent Adam's apple and acne.

'Come back when your balls have dropped.' Eileen smiled brightly at him.

The flashing lights and mirrors around the dance floor created the illusion of hordes of people. In fact there were only eight people dancing; two couples smooching, three men shifting self-consciously from foot to foot while looking nervously over their shoulders, and one would-be disco king, striking poses and flinging his podgy arms and legs around in a rhythm entirely his own. Eileen counted seven women in the club, that was all. There must have been fifty or sixty men, mostly middle-aged, with ill-fitting suits, slip-on shoes and chunky gold rings.

The DJ put on Gloria Gaynor's 'I Will Survive' and the disco king went wild. Eileen watched the sweat flying off him. His polyester shirt sleeves were rolled up above his elbows and he had wet patches under his arms and on his back. His red face wore an expression of deep concentration and he puffed and blew like an all-in wrestler.

She made her way slowly around the edge of the dance floor. There was a waist-high barrier which she supposed was to stop flailing disco kings and queens from knocking drinks off the tables. Slung over the barrier was the disco king's jacket. Eileen stood watching him for a minute or so, checking that he was deep into his dance moves. When she was quite sure he was oblivious of her, she slipped a hand into the inside pocket.

'Hey, gorgeous, do your legs really go all the way up to there?'

Eileen started, made as though she had rescued the jacket from the floor, then pretended to be adjusting her dress. There was hot, sour breath on the back of her neck.

'Mm, is that Calvin Klein's Escape?'

She turned around to find a thin, grey man with a lopsided toupee standing too close to her and grinning.

She tried to smile back. 'Yes, that's right. How clever of you.'

He was pleased. 'I'm Des. And you're . . . ?'

'Lorraine,' she said, flatly.

'Lorraine. What a lovely name. I bet you're a Gemini, aren't you, Lorraine?'

'My, my, how on earth did you know?' Eileen made an effort to sound enthusiastic, but she could hear the strain in her own voice. How could Jason bear this kind of shit?

He tapped the side of his crooked nose. 'Trade secret. Can I buy you a drink?'

'Well, that would be nice. I'll have a vodka martini, please.'

'Great. Back in a tick. Don't move a muscle.'

He was off to the bar, taking his foul breath with him. Eileen turned back to the barrier. Shit! The jacket was gone and so was the disco king.

The Village People's 'YMCA' was booming in Eileen's ears and making her teeth vibrate. As she moved further away from the speakers, she tripped and twisted an ankle. Swearing under her breath, she stumbled across to a nearby table and slid herself onto the seat. She wished she was curled up on the couch in Andrea Foster's living room, watching TV and eating cornflakes.

Her ankle throbbed. She tried to ignore the pain. Then the sound of a cough made her realise there was someone else sitting at the table – a white-haired man so small and insignificant that he seemed to be a part of the seating.

'Do you have a cigarette?' she asked him.

'No. Leave me alone, please,' he said in a thin, high voice, keeping his gaze fixed on his half-empty pint glass.

'Keep your hair on, I was only after a fag,' said Eileen, reaching down to check on her ankle. It was swelling.

'I know what you're after, Jezebel. Kindly leave my table or I'll have the management on to you.' Flecks of spit flew out of his mouth as he spoke.

Eileen took a deep breath. 'Look, I don't want to bother you. I just need to sit here for a minute. I've hurt my ankle.'

'Bitch!' seethed the little man, and this time he did look her full in the face with pink rabbit eyes.

'For God's sake . . .' muttered Eileen, as the man picked up his pint glass, slid out from his seat and walked away.

Jesus, this place was full of freaks.

'One vodka martini,' announced toupee, as he placed the glass on the table in front of her. 'I couldn't find you for a minute there. Thought you'd left.' He sat down next to her and moved up close.

She tried to suppress the impulse to retch as his breath clouded warm and stale around her face.

'Black is black,' sang toupee, off-key and slightly slower than the music, *'I want my baby back.* Care to dance?'

'Well, I—' The ankle was swelling and pulsing. 'I just need to powder my nose. Back in a second.'

He had to get up to let her out. As she squeezed past him, she felt his hand on her bum.

The dance floor was thick with writhing, strutting bodies now. Eileen hobbled along by the barrier, leaning on it for support. Was her ankle broken? She could see disco king back on the floor, twirling and high-kicking. People were giving him a wide berth. And yes – there was his jacket, in just the same place as before. She dragged herself closer.

'Hey, you. Tart.' A stubby-headed bouncer with a broken nose and a bow tie laid a heavy hand on her shoulder.

'Take your hand off me,' Eileen snapped, haughtily.

He laughed, flashing a gold tooth. 'Bit of a posh tart, are we?' He leaned closer. 'We know your game, sweetheart. We're on to you.'

'I don't know what you're talking about.' She felt weak and tired.

'Yeah, sure.' He prodded her hard in the back so that she stumbled forward. Then he bent to whisper loudly in her ear. 'Now you can either leave quietly, or I'll have to throw you out.'

'I beg your—'

'This is a respectable establishment. We don't have whores in here.'

'I'm not a—' But what was the use?

Disco king was spinning out of control to Bonnie Tyler's 'I Need a Hero'. Toupee was twisting around in his seat, confused, disappointed. Eileen thought she caught a glimpse of rabbit eyes, smiling and nodding as she was frog-marched to the door.

Eileen was woken by the sound of someone banging on the front door. She reached out from under the warm duvet and groped about for her alarm clock. The green glowing numbers read 9.27.

'Eileen! Eileen, open the door. I need to talk to you!'

Shit, it was Jill Foster. That was all she needed after the disastrous night at Mimi's! If she hid under the duvet and ignored Jill, how long would it take her to give up and go away?

A key rattled. 'I don't believe this – she's changed the locks. You've changed the blasted locks, Eileen! Open the door. Are you in there? I'm sure you're in there!' She was becoming hysterical.

The bedroom door was thrust open and daylight flooded in. For a second Eileen thought Jill Foster had somehow got into the flat. But it was Fran.

'Get out of bed and talk to that bloody woman,' she whispered, pushing the door closed behind her.

Eileen rubbed sleep from her eyes. 'Oh, Fran, can't we leave it? She'll go away in a minute.'

Fran came closer. She had that look about her, a warning: don't mess with me. Eileen was reminded of her father.

'I can't have her making a racket like that,' said Fran, quietly but firmly. 'Get some clothes on and go talk to her.' She walked back to the door, and then hesitated, turned again. 'You'd better pull yourself together, Eileen.'

'What do you mean?' Eileen was startled. 'What are you trying to say?' But Fran was gone.

'If you don't let me in I'm going to get my husband down here. I mean it!'

Eileen's head was thumping as she scrambled out of bed and pulled on a pair of jeans. She'd really gone for it with Andrea's gin when she got in last night. Liquid consolation. Now she was wishing she'd gone straight to bed with a cup of cocoa.

'Jill, I'm sorry it took me so long to get to the door. I'm afraid I was still asleep.'

Jill was red-faced and flustered. She pushed past Eileen into the flat, heading straight for the master bedroom.

'What—' Eileen began.

'You've got people here, haven't you?' snapped Jill. 'Mrs Travis from downstairs says she's seen people going in and out. Lots of them.'

Where was Fran? 'Jill, come and sit down. I'll make us some coffee.'

Jill emerged from the bedroom, holding Fran's satin wrap. 'Who does this belong to?'

'Me.'

'And these?' She had a pair of men's boxer shorts.

'Me,' Eileen repeated rather weakly. 'I like sleeping in them.'

Jill gave a little huff and crossed to the bathroom. 'What about this?' she said, producing Jason's twin-blade razor.

'It's mine. I shave my legs.' Eileen tried to grab her by the arm but Jill shook her off. 'Look, Jill, come and sit down. I can explain everything.' Her head was still throbbing. She wondered if Andrea had any paracetamol in her bathroom cupboard.

'All right,' said Jill, curtly. 'I'd like to hear it.'

The minty green of the living room walls cast a cool calming glow over Jill Foster. Eileen could sense a slight relaxing of the tension, could almost see her breathing slowing down.

'Would you like a cup of coffee?'

'No, thanks. I'd like an explanation.'

Eileen had hoped she'd want the coffee. It would have given her a few minutes to work out what to say.

She took a deep breath. 'I had the locks changed because I lost a purse that had my keys in it. And I was stupid enough to have left a piece of paper in the purse with the address written on it.'

'Oh, Eileen—' began Jill.

'I know it's really dim of me,' said Eileen. 'I wrote the address down when I'd only just arrived, and I forgot to get rid of the piece of paper when I didn't need it any more. So I had to get the locks changed. It would have been too much of a risk to leave it.'

Jill rubbed her brow in a gesture of tiredness. 'Why didn't you tell me?'

'I felt really stupid,' said Eileen, knowing this sounded convincing. 'And I thought you'd be angry that I could be so careless with Andrea's keys.'

'Well, you'd better get a set cut for me,' said Jill. 'Goodness, what is Andrea going to say when I tell her? So, what about all the people Mrs Travis has seen? Who's been staying here?'

'Nobody,' said Eileen, giving what she felt to be a wide open innocent look. 'That Mrs Travis must have nothing better to do than nose into other people's business. I've had a couple of friends from the bar round, that's all.'

'What bar?'

'Oh, I got a job in a bar. There were some nice people there. I've made some friends – friends who don't seem to want anything from me beyond friendship. Not like in London. Everyone there seems to want you for something. Everyone has—'

'Their own agenda, yes, I know,' said Jill, wearily. But she was softening. Eileen could see the kindness seeping back into her face like ink into blotting paper. 'So you have a job?'

'Not any more,' said Eileen, sadly. 'It was all going really well, and then the boss came on to me.'

'He did *what*?'

'It was awful,' said Eileen, and her voice cracked. She tried to force out a tear. She was good at making herself cry. 'He made me stay back to clear up and he let all the others go home. Then he got me in a corner and—'

And out came the tears, lots of them. Eileen let out some great painful sobs. In a second, Jill was on the sofa next to her, putting an arm around her.

'How far did it go, love? He didn't—'

'No. I kicked him in the balls and got away.'

'Good for you.' Jill gave her shoulders a squeeze. 'Are you all right?'

'Yes. I've had worse happen to me before.' Eileen got up to get a piece of kitchen towel to blow her nose on. 'But it did bring back a lot of bad memories.'

Jill's face was now the picture of sympathy and concern. 'Have you told the police, Eileen?'

'No!' Eileen tried to sound frightened.

'Well, maybe you should. He might try it again on somebody else. What's the bar called? Where is it?'

'No, no, I can't tell the police. They'd never take my word over his. There's no witnesses, no evidence, nothing. I can't face it. You can't tell anyone about this, not *anyone*. Promise me.'

Jill sighed. 'OK, if that's what you want. I promise. Look, Eileen, you don't have to face things alone, you know. I'm here.'

'I know,' said Eileen, bowing her head. 'And I'm sorry I didn't return your calls. I just couldn't face anyone. Not even you. I was really low.'

Jill shook her head slowly. 'Honestly, Eileen, you can't blame me for assuming the worst. My husband, Marcus, he was so angry when he heard I'd let you stay in the flat. He thinks I'm a soft touch, that I let people walk all over me.'

'I know. I'm so sorry for all the trouble I've caused you. I'll leave . . . I'll pack my stuff and be out by tomorrow morning.'

'Don't be silly. You've nowhere to go.'

The sun was shining strongly into the room, rippling through the leaves of the trees outside, casting playful shadows on Andrea Foster's coffee table and parquet floor, illuminating Jill Foster's gentle face. For a moment, Eileen felt embarrassed about her behaviour towards this kind, vulnerable woman. She felt the shame deep in her gut, solid like a lead weight.

'Now, Eileen, you have to pull yourself together.' That sounded strangely familiar . . . 'You're going to go out this afternoon and start looking for another job. Get a local paper, see if there's any shop or office work. That should be a little less hazardous than bar work. Go down to the job centre. Be *active* about it.'

'Yes, I'll do that. Today.'

'And keep in touch. Call me. Let me know what happens . . . Whose are those?' Jill was pointing at Jason's trainers which sat in the corner of the room.

'Those? They were always here. I think they must belong to Andrea's boyfriend. How is Andrea?'

'Oh, she's well, very well in fact. She's getting engaged to Claude.'

'Really? How wonderful. You must be thrilled.' Eileen could just imagine the perfect Andrea Foster in her perfect white wedding dress.

But clearly Jill was far from thrilled. 'Well, yes. She's happy and that's the main thing. But she's still so young . . . I worry about her.'

When Jill Foster had finally gone, Eileen went delving in the bathroom cupboard and found an almost full bottle of paracetamol. She swallowed two tablets and was gulping some water when Fran came in from the roof terrace.

'Well handled,' said Fran. 'But that's enough now. We have to find somewhere else to live. Take a shower, get dressed and go see some letting agents.'

* * *

Later that same day Jason sat in the bar of the Cornerhouse arts centre, waiting. He glanced at his watch – almost eight o'clock. His date was an hour late. He was tired of this, so tired. Was he experiencing his own version of City boy's burn-out? He could feel the life energy flooding out of him. He felt as though he'd been driving a very long way down a busy motorway in the pouring rain, and with every swipe and judder of the windscreen wipers his eyelids grew heavier and heavier.

The Cornerhouse bar clientele were young and arty – lots of hennaed hair, nose studs and round spectacles. A slouchy young man on a bar stool was slurping cappuccino and reading from a battered edition of Ibsen plays. Three butch women at the next table were discussing an Iranian film they'd just seen in one of the Cornerhouse's three film theatres. A cluster of bright young things across the room were complaining about the work they had ahead of them in the run up to their final exams. They were dolled up in hot pants, mini-skirts and bustiers, no doubt making this their first port of call on a big night out.

For the first half hour Jason had enjoyed watching them, but then he felt that familiar bitterness at the back of his throat. He should have had his chance to be one of them; to go to university, live the life of the mind, dye his hair purple and fritter his time away trying to outwit his sidekicks in arthouse bars. This had all been denied him – and because of what? Some stupid accident of nature, nothing more.

His thoughts turned to Samantha – the heat of her hands when she massaged his stiff shoulder. The lightness of those same fingers as she stroked down the length of his back. That wonderful combination of strength and gentleness that was present in her every touch, that distinguished her lovemaking as something out of the ordinary. Her delectable sadness. The smell of her . . .

Ten past eight. He'd been stood up. Wearily Jason slapped his empty glass down on the bar and headed out.

The foyer was bustling with people arriving for the next showing of the Iranian film. He was jostled by a group of students eager to get to the bar and down a pint before the film started, and he almost tripped over a free-standing sign advertising the exhibition which had just opened in the gallery.

He swore and steadied the sandwich-board as it toppled. He was about to move on when its image caught his attention.

It was a photograph of a heart – not a real one; a story book heart in the traditional emblematic shape, big and red and glossy – but this heart appeared to be melting, dripping. It was slowly being reduced to pulp. There was something in the image that disturbed Jason, and he found he rather liked the feeling of being disturbed ever so slightly.

Owen Meredith – Liquefaction, the sign proclaimed, and an arrow pointed up the stairs. Owen Meredith . . . the name was familiar.

'We're just closing,' said a young man with a Welsh accent and a prominent Adam's apple, barring the way into the gallery.

'Oh.' Jason was more disappointed than he would have expected. 'Can't I just take a quick look?'

The attendant looked at his wrist as though to double check the time, but he wasn't wearing a watch. 'Damn,' he said, and his Adam's apple bobbed up and down. 'It's at the repairers,' he explained. 'Battery's flat, I think. Got the time on you?'

'Quarter past eight.'

The attendant sighed. 'We close at eight. Why don't you come back tomorrow?'

Jason was becoming irritable. 'I want to see the exhibition *now,* not tomorrow,' he said, turning away. 'Tomorrow I'll have lost interest. Just forget it.'

'Sir!' called the attendant as Jason descended the stairs. 'Come back, sir.'

Jason paused. 'Yes?'

'I'll let you in. But you'll have to be quick. You can have ten minutes, that's all.'

The first work to draw Jason's attention was an enormous glass container, roughly the shape of a human body – perhaps eight feet high and four feet wide across the shoulders. It was filled with bright yellow liquid that bubbled fiercely, and in the midst of the liquid was a red heart, with a soft appearance to it – it might have been made of rubber or something similar. The body was lit internally by something in its metal base, and a flex led from the base to a power point on the wall. The heart bobbed around, buffeted hither and thither by the bubbles.

Jason stood staring at it for several minutes, before remembering that he only had ten minutes to get round the whole exhibition.

The heart sculpture that appeared on the poster was suspended from the ceiling by almost invisible wires. It was made of wax, or something that resembled wax, and was also extremely large. Jason supposed that the blobs and globules dripping down its sides were set hard, but the artist had succeeded in creating the illusion that the gigantic heart was actually liquefying as it hung there. Jason longed to reach out and touch it, but he was sure the attendant must be watching him. He was oddly moved by the red monster.

'What do you think of the lovers?' came the attendant's voice from the doorway, startling Jason.

'The lovers?' Jason wheeled around, and there in front of him was a sculpture even more huge and imposing. A gnarled, twisting tree-like male figure was wrapping its branch-arms around a delicate, spidery female, which in turn threaded its flimsy limbs around the trunk-body so that the two were entwined. They were made of what appeared to be a combination of wax and plastic in shades of orange, brown and gold, and they too were liquefying – merging with each other as they melted, becoming one awesomely hideous entity.

'The lovers . . . well, they're . . . amazing.' Jason's mouth was dry. He became aware of the presence of someone standing very close behind him, too close, and he whipped around fast to find himself staring straight into the eyes of the attendant. The eyes were black and unfathomable.

'Owen Meredith?' Jason tried the name, slowly.

'That's right,' said the man, without looking away. 'That's me. This is my work.'

'I suppose I've always been fascinated by melting forms,' said Owen Meredith, drawing deeply on his cigarette. 'I've been developing my ideas for three or four years now; trying to melt all sorts of different substances; glass, metals, plastics . . . Liquefaction is a sort of culmination. I regard most of my art as a progression, leading towards it.' He placed his pint glass down on the table, which rocked and wobbled, slopping Jason's lager everywhere. Jason swore quietly as beer dribbled onto his linen trousers, and hunted for his handkerchief to wipe the table. Why did pubs never have beer mats any more?

The Canal Boat was a dark, smoky pub; dull brass and battered oak fittings, upholstery that was faded and ripped in places. Its narrow bar was crammed with middle-aged men and women with permed hair and eyebrows that had been plucked bare and then drawn back with kohl pencil. There was a powerful smell of ancient alcohol that had spilled and soaked into the floor boards time and again over many years. Jason found the place seedy and rancid, but it was Owen's favourite drinking hole: 'They pull the best pint in town . . .'

They were on to their third round, and Owen's dark eyes seemed blacker with each pint.

'I think your work is extraordinary,' said Jason, for once entirely sincere. 'I can't remember when I was last so moved by an exhibition. And I consider it a great privilege to have this chance to meet you and talk to you.'

'Good God, mate, calm down!' Owen was laughing. 'I'm not exactly Mr Exclusive, you know.' The laughter transformed his face; gave it life and vitality. In repose it looked grim and austere.

'But you will be,' said Jason, with conviction.

Owen shrugged, stared into his pint. 'I don't know, Robbie. I used to believe that, but I'm not sure I do any more. It's all I can do just to keep on working.'

Jason was studying Owen as they talked. He was tense and seemed unable to sit still. There was always some part of him on the move; he would tap tap tap on the floor with his left foot and then drum his fingers on his right knee. He would cross his legs and swing his right foot until he kicked the table by mistake (spilling Jason's beer again), and then uncross them. When he wasn't speaking he would bite his lower lip until it appeared sore and chapped. He had a silver ring on the second finger of his left hand, and he continually twisted it while they talked. Jason expected that he would relax as he consumed more alcohol, but if anything he grew more and more manic.

Jason was still trying to remember why the name Owen Meredith was familiar to him.

'The trouble is, Robbie, that I haven't been able to break out of the provinces. I'm well known in Wales, Cardiff in particular, and I'm starting to make a reputation for myself in Manchester and also a few other cities where I've exhibited: Birmingham, Bradford, Leeds, Bristol . . . But I can't seem to crack London. And you need to crack London if you're ever going to be anybody.'

Owen was getting worked up. His Adam's apple bobbed up and down with increasing frenzy, and he twisted his ring so much that his finger went white.

'So, have you never exhibited in London?'

'Well, yes, in a small way. But nobody came. At least, nobody who really counts; dealers, critics, serious buyers. I often wonder if it would have been different if I'd studied in London. I went to Birmingham, you see. I have this friend who was at the Slade; his stuff is on show at the Lisson Gallery at the moment. And Charles Saatchi has bought just about everything he's ever produced. Saatchi sends his people over to Mike's studio and they start grabbing things . . . sketches, maquettes, the lot. And paying silly money for it. I think he'll be up for the Turner prize next year.' He sighed and drained his pint. 'Shall we have another?'

Two hours later, Jason and Owen were seated at a corner table in a Wilmslow Road curry house, The Indian Cottage.

Owen's eyes were filled with tears as he looked at Jason over his balti chicken. 'The art is all about Annie; me and her and what happened to us,' he said. 'That's why it moved you. You didn't know it but you sensed it. People talk about broken hearts – that's all very well, but what I have suffered is worse than that. Annie *melted* my heart, reduced me to pulp. It's been over a year now since she left, and I just can't seem to put myself back into any kind of shape.' He wiped his eyes with the back of his hand and took a mouthful of curry. 'It's a dangerous thing, you know – to let someone become that powerful. Are you in a relationship, Robbie?'

Jason tasted the muttar paneer and tore off a piece of paratha. 'Kind of. I have a very long standing arrangement with a woman. I suppose you could call it a relationship. But it isn't exclusive. I see other people.'

'Does she?' asked Owen.

'No. At least I don't think so.' Did Fran see other men? Jason wasn't entirely sure. 'I don't think she's interested in sleeping with other people. She's not a very sexually oriented person.'

'Oh dear.'

'Don't get me wrong – we have great sex, she and I – but that's enough for her. That's as much as she needs.'

'Whereas you need more.' Owen was smiling.

'I like to have more. I enjoy women, and I don't see anything wrong in that. I like the diversity. But I always return to her.'

Jason thought of how Fran had looked that morning when he came back from Samantha's. It was early, 5.00 a.m., and he stepped lightly, trying not to make any noise that would wake her. She was lying on her side, the top half of her uncovered. Her arms were tucked up under the pillow. Her face was so peaceful, soft in sleep. You'd never catch Fran looking so tranquil when she was awake; there was always so much going on in her head, so much calculation behind her eyes. But sleeping there, she was like an innocent young girl. The lines of her thin body were elegant, beautiful. Jason sat down on the floor beside the bed, close up to her, and he stayed there for almost an hour, just listening to her breathing. During that hour he didn't think of any other woman. Only Fran.

'Seems to me,' said Owen, reaching for more rice, 'that you're having your cake and eating it too.'

'Nothing wrong with that, is there?' said Jason. 'I don't like having too many limits in my life. Society works to restrict you, to pen you in. I believe one should find where one's limits are, and then move beyond them.'

'Well my limits seem to be pretty firmly in place,' said Owen. 'I can't get out of the bloody provinces. Not without my father's help, anyway.'

'Your father?' Dim memories were stirring in Jason's mind.

'Tony Meredith. You know. The helicopter-parts manufacturer.' Owen spoke the name with contempt.

And now Jason knew where he'd heard of Owen Meredith before.

Multi-millionaire Tony Meredith talks exclusively to the *Mail*

> about the son who disowned him . . . All the money in the world can't buy the love of his son . . . Come back Owen, pleads Tony Meredith . . . I will always love you, my son . . .

'My father would pull strings if I wanted,' said Owen. 'He'd probably buy me the bloody Tate gallery if he thought I'd come back like the prodigal and be his son again.' He rubbed wearily at his forehead. 'But, Christ, Robbie, what kind of an idiot is he? Does he really think the best way to make up with me is to sell his story to the bloody *Daily Mail*? Jesus, the man actually managed to cash in on our falling out!'

'What on earth did he do to you?' asked Jason.

But Owen didn't seem to have heard. 'He still writes to me, you know, tries to send me money. I'm not having any of his dirty money, I can tell you. I just write "Return to Sender" on all the envelopes.'

'But what did he do?'

'Oh, you don't want to know.' Owen signalled to the waiter to bring him another beer. 'And I don't want to tell you. I don't talk about it.'

A plan was forming in Jason's mind. And it was beautiful. It was the answer to everything that was going wrong, and going nowhere.

'You know what, Owen,' said Jason, wishing he wasn't quite so drunk. 'I can help you. I can get you to the next stage.'

'What?' Owen was startled, and suddenly suspicious.

Jason reached into his inside pocket and produced a business card, which he passed across to Owen.

'Creative Consultant,' read Owen. 'What the bloody hell is that, then?'

'That,' said Jason, 'is *my* art.'

At night when I sleep, they're all there – every one of them parading through my head – the fat middle-aged married men we drugged and robbed, the kindly rich women whose heart-strings I have pulled, the sleazy guys with their desperate faces who want to dance with me in the clubs, and now that nasty little rabbit-eyes man who had me down for a whore. Every bloody night I dream about them – or about some of them anyway. They've stamped their mark on my consciousness. Don't get me wrong – it isn't guilt. If anything, as time goes by I feel more and more that I'm the one who's hard done by. After all, I have to suffer their company on a nightly basis. No, these dreams are more to do with fear – fear that they're going to *get* me, or that someone else will. I don't dream about prison, but prison is there somewhere in the background. What are the odds that I'll get caught one day – that all three of us will? If I was a betting girl, I wouldn't want to stake my money on us never getting banged up.

I tried to tell Fran about it once. She said I *should* be afraid. She said fear of prison – or worse – is what keeps you on your toes. It's when you stop being frightened and become casual about it that you get caught. I know she's worried that Jason is more and more blasé. I've noticed the worry in her for some time. It sits behind her eyes and peeps out.

Yesterday two policemen came round looking for one Robert Wilson in connection with a theft. One of them was a big fat bloke with a wart on his nose – or was it a mole? Whichever it was, I couldn't take my eyes off it the whole time they were speaking to me. The other was ginger-haired and freckled, not much older than me. Perhaps even younger. They kept trying to peer past into the flat as they spoke to me, but I stood my ground at the front door, barring the way in.

'No, I've never heard of Robert Wilson ... Me? I'm a guest here. You can ask Jill Foster, who owns the flat ... A man, here? That couple downstairs, they've nothing better to do than spy on people ... Yes, it was my boyfriend, Ian ... Well, ex-boyfriend actually – no, he won't be coming back ... I'm in rather a hurry. I have a job interview ... I'm sorry I can't help further – do call again if there's anything more I can do ...'

I told Fran about it when she got home. She said very little but I could see she was angry. That little Fear man that hides behind her eyes was jumping up and down and waving his arms about. Her lips were tight and tense. She said they'd be back. It was Jason she was angry with, but as he wasn't home she took it out on me.

'Didn't I tell you to get down to the estate agents and go look at some flats? Didn't I tell you we have to move?'

When Jason got back he was as casual as could be.

'Yes, some dumb hairdresser, I nicked her purse ... You know how it is, they're usually too embarrassed to go to the police – or if they do, they say they've been mugged ... most women don't like to let on they've been using Lonely Hearts, especially women of the kind of social standing that I see ... I should have known *she* wouldn't give a shit about embarrassment, she was *so* vulgar! . . . Not a dignified bone in her body . . . Don't worry, Fran, the police won't waste time on it, we'll be fine . . .'

He waltzed off and Fran started nagging me again about flats. I had the feeling we'd be moving soon enough – getting out of Manchester altogether. I'd seen Fran in that mood before.

'That . . . is *my* art,' said Robbie Warren, tapping the side of his nose as though he was sharing some great secret.

Owen smirked. 'Your art! *Creative Consultant* . . . Sounds like bullshit to me.'

'And so it is,' said Robbie. 'The art of professional bullshitting.'

'Tell me more.' Owen liked this man. He was interested to hear what an arts enterpreneur might have to say. Owen himself was afraid of the world of business – he liked to feel he had made a choice not to dirty his hands in commerce, but he knew deep down that there were other more personal reasons for him to shy away from it.

'Creative Consultant is a great job title,' said Robbie, pushing his half-empty plate away to concentrate exclusively on what he was saying. 'It enables me to be whatever I want. I'm an agent, a manager, a PR guru, an advertising executive . . . you name it, I can be it – all under this wonderful umbrella title. Basically I follow my instincts and channel my energies into whatever project excites me at any given time.'

'What sort of projects?'

Robbie smiled, showing his chipped tooth. 'I've been working in Manchester because I was called upon to be involved in the group that's redesigning the Arndale Centre.'

'Really?' Owen was impressed.

'Yup. But that work came to an end today. Before that I was on a team looking at the problems of the Royal Opera House.' He wrinkled his nose in disdain. 'I pulled out of that. Too many arseholes – we were going nowhere and taking valuable time over getting there.'

'So what are you going to do next?'

'Well, that's the golden question,' said Robbie, laying his napkin on the table. Owen couldn't help noticing how small his ears were – a baby's ears on a man's head.

'I've half accepted a commission to go to work for a German publisher in Munich for six months, investigating on-line potential. On the other hand I have an offer from the Council of Europe, who want my input on multi-language theatre. But between you and me, my heart's not in it. I want my own project, something I can really get my teeth into. I'm sick to death of corporations, arts council executives and all those other jerks I have to spend my time with. It's so hard to get anything done when you've got to work with committees and forums.'

Owen was puzzled. 'So where do I come into this?'

'You,' said the irrepressible Mr Warren, 'have been going about this business in entirely the wrong way.'

Owen felt himself becoming irritated. What the hell did this man know about his life?

'No offence intended,' said Robbie Warren.

'None taken,' said Owen, but without conviction. 'What have I been doing that's so wrong, then?'

'You don't open a locked door by bashing against it with your fists, if you'll pardon the cliché,' said Robbie. 'Sometimes you need to look in unexpected places for the key.'

'So where should I be looking?'

Robbie beckoned the waiter. 'I think we're done,' he said, although Owen was still munching on his paratha. 'Two coffees, please.' The waiter glanced over at Owen, who smiled his acquiescence and laid down the remains of the bread. The waiter began to clear the table and Owen reached into his shirt pocket for his cigarettes.

'You won't make it big in London by showing your work in shitty little galleries in Peckham and Balham that nobody visits. You need a more commercial approach.'

'What do you mean?'

'Allow me.' Robbie produced a lighter from his pocket and lit Owen's cigarette.

Owen coughed hard on the first drag. His chest was in a bad state. His asthma, which he'd grown out of at sixteen, seemed to be coming back.

'You need to do something more than just show your work to get yourself noticed,' continued Robbie. 'Take Damien Hirst for example.'

'I'd rather not.'

'Bear with me for a minute.' Mr Warren had mischief in his eyes. 'What does an artist like Damien Hirst do to make himself a household name?'

'He slices up pregnant cows, amongst other things,' said Owen, with disdain. 'That's not for me, thanks very much.'

'Yes, but it's not just the nature of his art that gets him noticed,' said Robbie, still smiling smugly. 'He designs pop videos, restaurants . . . Look at Quo Vadis . . . look at the Pharmacy, the amount of attention it got when it opened – a merging of art and business – a novelty, a trendy place that gives Hirst money, notoriety, credibility.'

Owen had seen the problem with Robbie's reasoning. 'Hirst got involved in all that stuff when he'd already become famous. Everyone already knew about the shark, the sheep . . .'

'Yes, but who's to say you can't do it the other way around – use commercial success to push the art?'

'I just don't think—'

'Think of it, Owen—' And Robbie grabbed Owen's wrist across the table, held it too tightly. His eyes looked almost crazed. 'A restaurant, designed by you, owned by you, full of your work – serving the best food in town – it would advertise your art, fund you, bring you to a wider audience . . . link your name with chic . . . make you into Mr Exclusive, as you put it earlier.'

I'm superstitious. I know it's daft but I can't help it. It isn't the kind of superstition where you're afraid to walk under ladders or put up an umbrella in the house. It's more to do with things I tell myself. It's a childish habit I can't seem to grow out of. If I'm walking down the street towards a paper shop and a bus is following up the road behind me, I might say to myself: *I have to get to the paper shop before the bus passes me or I'll never have a baby.* And although rationally I know it makes no sense, I have to do it. I'll be walking briskly one minute, then as I hear the bus pulling away from the stop and charging up behind me I'll break into a run. As I'm nearing the shop I'll see the bus reflected in its windows and I'll almost knock over some poor old lady in my haste to get to the door. I'll just about make it inside before the bus goes lumbering by.

It could be anything. *If the old man sitting opposite coughs again during the next thirty seconds, I'm not going to get the chance to have sex again for at least a year.* Or maybe, *If I don't hear Jason mention the word 'art' before lunchtime, they're going to sling me out on my ear within the next month.* As soon as I've heard the voice inside me make one of those declarations, there's no escaping it – I believe it and I have to obey it. The trick is to try to mediate what the voice dictates, to weigh up the consequences before allowing myself to hear what it is saying to me. I always give myself a fighting chance.

It started when I was a kid as these sort of things tend to do – a typical only-child game, like having imaginary friends. I'd be sitting in my room doing my homework and I'd think to myself, *If Mum doesn't call me down for my tea within the next five minutes, Dad will come home pissed and hit her.* Sadly I was generally on to a loser when Mum and Dad came into the picture.

That awful night when I went to Mimi's night-club, I knew I wasn't going to manage to steal anything. When I walked down that blue carpeted corridor I thought, *If the cloakroom attendant shouts something at me before I get into the club, tonight will be a failure*. And sure enough, the wanker did shout at me and I got mistaken for a prostitute and slung out. If only I hadn't had that superstitious thought, then maybe I would have been fine. But I can't seem to help it. It's at those moments when I'm telling myself not to think like that, that a prediction pops into my head.

This morning was one of those delicious mornings in early May when you suddenly feel it is summer, and Jason suggested a picnic on Platt Fields. Platt Fields is the kind of city park that can look like the face of a haggard old woman when the weather is foul, but today it was more like a young bride with its pink and white blossom-covered trees, the rich green of the grass and the warm, clear sunshine. You know how certain scenes and pictures are frozen for ever in your memory in all their vivid detail? Well, walking across Platt Fields this morning was one of those scenes for me: groups of boys playing frisbee, families with teetering toddlers on reins and large dogs lolloping off the leash. Girls, anxious to take advantage of the first really sunny day of the year, lying on the grass in the briefest of shorts and bikini tops, while lone men wearing shabby clothes and disconnected expressions stood among the trees watching.

Around the pond were tragic weeping willows, while on the water couples in pedal boats laughed and splashed, disturbing the overweight ducks. We picked our way past marauding ice-cream sellers, giving a wide berth to a bunch of elderly women practising Tai Chi, to a quiet patch of grass bathed in sunlight, surrounded by trees.

As we popped olives into our mouths, munched our baguettes, gorged on early strawberries and swilled the whole lot down with a bottle of Dom Perignon, chilled to perfection, Jason began to unveil his plan. His face grew animated as he talked. His eyes had about them a glitter of madness, his mouth continually slipping into a manic grin. I had never seen him like this.

It was exciting. Jason thought he had found a way out of the petty con, a way for us to make big money – bigger than we'd ever dreamed possible, and get out. The more I heard, the more I wanted to believe we could pull it off, but I could see that Fran was not buying this scam. She had stopped drinking and was picking at her nails, refusing to look Jason in the eye. I trust Fran's judgement above all – I have ever since I've known her – and yet I silently wished that Jason would be able to convince her that his idea was viable. As he talked and she continued to frown, plucking blades of grass and splitting them into tiny hair-like strands, I let my gaze wander up to the branches of the big oak tree nearby. There was a magpie sitting up there watching us.

Jason talked on, weaving his colourful story with greater enthusiasm, as though the energy of his story-telling alone would be enough to convince Fran: a Welsh artist who had disowned his multi-millionaire father ... a restaurant that would never exist ... a secret investor ...

I was staring up at that magpie and it was staring back at me. And suddenly the voice inside me piped up clearly, as it always does at such moments: *If that magpie isn't joined by a friend in the next five minutes, this scam will end in disaster.*

Owen reached for his beer and sat quiet for a moment, just looking at Robbie Warren, whoever he was. He tried to get his mind around all of this. Slowly he shook his head. 'I don't know.'

'What don't you know? What more is there?'

'Look, Robbie, I see what you're getting at, but this just isn't *me*. Restaurants . . . Christ, I don't give a damn about them. I'd just as soon have a chicken balti in this place as go to Damien Hirst's Pharmacy. In fact, I'd *rather* have a chicken balti in this place.'

'Don't worry that this isn't your kind of thing. It doesn't need to be,' said Robbie. His face was red and sweaty, a mere thin lid on a head bursting with pent-up energy. 'You design it, you own it, you make money out of it, but you don't have to run it day to day.'

'And who would do that, then?'

Robbie looked at him as though he was stupid. 'Me, of course. Well, at first, anyway – until we got it off the ground. Then we'd hire someone to take over.'

Owen looked down at the bright red curry stains on the table. One of them looked like an elephant, another like a dog. He imagined them moving towards each other, touching, melting into one big stain. 'You're a fucking loon,' he said, after a moment.

'No, I'm not,' said Robbie. 'I'm the man who's going to save your career.'

The waiter arrived with the coffee. Robbie was now gesticulating so wildly that he almost knocked the cafetière flying.

'And what would be in it for you?'

Robbie laughed. 'Oh, plenty. Fifteen per cent of the takings – for the life of the restaurant. Plus a salary while I'm working for you full-time. I'd have to work out what that should be.'

Owen was beginning to find this funny. Just how far would this man go in his wild fantasy of art and business? 'And what exactly would your role be, Mr Warren?'

'I'd get you the finance. I'd do the PR, the advertising, I'd oversee the whole operation, work with you on the concept, hire the chef, run the place when it opens . . . I'd only draw the line at cooking and waiting table.'

Owen giggled nervously and stubbed out his cigarette. 'Sorry, Robbie. I just can't see myself swanning around in some Chelsea bistro with my name over the door.'

Robbie paused, the smile slipped. 'Oh, no, Owen. We wouldn't do it in London. We'd do it in your home town: Cardiff.'

'But I thought—'

'No, no, Owen.' He wagged an admonishing finger. 'You're bashing on that locked door again. These places are two a penny in London. We do it in Cardiff – there can't be many really first-class, modern restaurants in a town like that. The ground rent is cheap, and you have a name there – people will come.'

'So how would that help me with London?'

'Word would spread, Owen. I would be the one spreading it. Believe me, this is the answer. Trust me.'

Owen let his laughter seep out like smoke. 'It's madness.'

Fran thought it was madness. Jason said she was the second person to say that. I was busy watching that magpie, counting the minutes. Four minutes in it was still alone on the branch, apparently friendless. Just before the five minutes were up, a pigeon settled on the tree beside it. Could I bend the rules? A friend, I'd said. Did a magpie's 'friend' necessarily have to be another magpie?

Jason turned those glittering eyes on me. 'You're very quiet, little Lena. What do *you* think?'

'I'm not sure,' I said. What else could I say? I hadn't even worked out whether pigeons were allowed in the game, let alone whether we should decamp to Cardiff and embark on the biggest scam we'd ever undertaken.

Jason was losing patience with both of us. 'Where's your imagination, girls? Where's your vision?'

The pigeon flew off. I tried to focus on the conversation. 'It's exciting,' I said. 'And it could be fun.'

'Oh, please!' Fran reached for her cigarettes.

I forced myself to be practical. I couldn't bear Fran's disdain. 'I think it's workable except for one crucial point,' I said after a moment.

Jason looked interested. 'And what would that point be?'

'I don't see how we can get away with the money. They won't let us.'

'She's right,' said Fran. 'That's where the whole thing falls down.'

'What's the matter with the two of you?' said Jason. 'We're not going to hang around, are we? We'll just take off. We'll fly away.' He fluttered his hands like a bird, and again my mind was filled with the magpie and the pigeon. The magpie was still up in the tree, watching me. A gentle breeze was ruffling its feathers.

'Don't be so fucking naive,' said Fran. 'He'll come after us.'

And then it flew into my mind. The answer to this problem. The key to the success of this scam. Finally I had a chance to really prove myself.

I opened my mouth to tell them, and I watched Fran's face begin to change, soften. But even as I was speaking, my attention was wandering. Could a pigeon be considered to be the friend of a magpie or was I cheating at my own game?

5

The Train

Jason, Fran and Eileen always travelled by train and never travelled together.

'You must be constantly alert to the opportunities that may arise at any time, and be in a position to capitalise on them,' Fran told Eileen in the early days of their acquaintance. 'The unattended bag, the gang of lecherous youths on holiday, the short-sighted old lady in mink, the drunken businessman . . . Take hold of the situation, assume your role, slide in for the kill. Think of yourself as being like a doctor on call – if your bleeper goes off you must move straight into action with consummate professionalism.'

Eileen reflected that if they were doctors then Fran was the chief surgeon, slicing and dissecting, tweezing and stitching with the greatest precision. Jason on the other hand, was some mad experimental quack, blending killer viruses with harmless stomach bacteria to develop some revolutionary vaccine. She herself was a mere auxiliary nurse.

Sometimes, as with their journey to Manchester, the events on the train would actually give shape to their stay in the city. At other times, like today, the very air seemed thin and flat, empty of opportunity.

'Tickets please.' The red-faced inspector lurched down the aisle as the train rocked from side to side. He came to Eileen first and she meekly produced her train card, which he clipped with a friendly wink. Moving on to the snogging couple further down the carriage, the inspector had to clear his throat loudly to get their attention. With some reluctance they separated like a pair of suction plungers being pulled apart. Giggling, they searched in each other's clothing for their tickets.

'I dunno. Young people these days, no sense of decency,' muttered the inspector, but not unkindly, as he staggered away. And Eileen felt jealousy bite at the inside of her stomach; bite hard and begin to chew. She'd never had a boyfriend to snog with on trains. She'd never been in a relationship so sublimely ordinary, so wholesome.

* * *

Of all the regular characters who bought breakfast at the Silver Square Sandwich Bar, Soho, the man with the small ears was the most fascinating. The majority of the customers worked in the offices based on the square – there were people from film companies, advertising agencies and radio stations; media types with their sunglasses and their mobiles and their loud, abrasive laughter, coming in every day for their croissants and their focaccia; 'No butter please,' with a meaningful pat on an entirely flat stomach. Then there were the taxi-drivers, the builders and the motorbike couriers who would sit in for their fry-ups, lingering over cups of tea and watching the smart set stream in and out.

The man with the small ears somehow didn't fit in. He had in common with the media types a look of confidence, but he was less obvious than them. He had an air of mystery about him, some secret life hidden behind those big, friendly eyes. If Eileen saw him in the queue she would make a point of trying to be the one to serve him, even if that meant shoving short-sighted old Sophia roughly out of the way and ignoring her as she tried to protest, her false teeth slipping and her trembling hands flying up in an expression of outrage. Nobody paid attention to Sophia's half-coherent mumblings – she was really only there on tolerance because she was the owner's aunt.

'Your usual, sir?' Eileen asked one morning, blushing as always at the very fact of speaking to him. His usual at breakfast time was a poppy seed bagel with smoked salmon and cream cheese, and a large cappuccino to go.

'Yes, thank you, Eileen,' he replied with a look that Eileen felt was directly flirtatious. 'And don't forget the black pepper.'

'How did you know my name?' asked Eileen as she sliced the

bagel in two and put both halves into the industrial sandwich toaster.

He tweaked at his tiny right ear-lobe to indicate that he only had to listen, and as he did so blowsy Maria, the owner, called out from the other end of the counter, 'Eileen! Pass me a baguette, would you, darling?'

'OK,' muttered Eileen. 'Stupid question. What's *your* name, anyway?'

'Richard,' said Small Ears, and gave her a friendly smile that revealed a chipped tooth. 'What time do you get off?'

Old Sophia was listening, edging closer along the counter, her stiff petticoats rustling, her large bottom sticking indignantly out. Eileen did her best to ignore her.

'Five-thirty,' she said. And then, stupidly, 'Why?'

'Shall I pick you up here or do you want to go home and change?' asked Richard.

Sophia caught her breath. Eileen knew this was because Maria didn't like the staff to fraternise with the regulars. Across the counter you could be the customer's best and only friend: *You like your marmite nice and thick, don't you, darling? . . . You're in early today, is it busy in the office? You work ever so hard, don't you? . . . Nice weekend, wasn't it? We had the sun for once, didn't we, eh? Oo, darling, you look a bit peaky, everything all right?* . . . But step out from behind that counter with a customer and Maria would be down on you like a ton of bricks.

'Sophia, I think I smell your ciabatta burning,' said Eileen, and the old woman swore in Italian and went bustling over to the sandwich toaster.

Small Ears was clearly amused. He bent forward to whisper in a loud stagey manner, 'So, where am I picking you up? Here or at home?'

Eileen hesitated. She was living at the YWCA, and certainly didn't want Richard to know that. But she couldn't have him coming *here* to meet her – as it was she could see Sophia anxiously tapping Maria on the shoulder. Thankfully Maria was busy with a customer and shook her off.

'I'll meet you in the pub on the corner at quarter to six,' said Eileen, and felt a flutter of excitement in her chest.

* * *

Eileen had never known anyone like Richard before. Over a pint at the Black Bull he talked about his contempt for the media types who frequented the Silver Square Sandwich Bar.

'They're clawing their way up some dodgy old ladder, trampling each other in the process like so many rats,' he said, 'and they don't even know why they're climbing or what's at the top. They've never questioned anything in their lives.'

Eileen could have told him that she thought this was a generalisation. She could have asked him how it was that he knew so much about these people – but then she thought about all those plastic looking women in their designer clothes who treated her as though she didn't have a brain, and she found she didn't want to contradict him.

Over a bottle of wine in Fantasma bar, he started again. 'Society is constructed to keep people like us down,' he said, and Eileen was surprised that he considered her as being in the same category as himself.

'People like us?'

'Yes. We don't possess those few bizarre character traits that mark the difference between succeeding and failing in this restrictive country.'

Eileen felt insulted. What could he possibly know about her and her character traits? And why did he see himself as being so unsuited for success? He certainly had a smooth tongue, and she would have thought that kind of verbal confidence was an invaluable tool in the quest for worldly achievement. But before she was able to say anything he was off again.

'There are other ways to be successful, Eileen, other things you can be if you are willing to work outside the normal social structure.'

'Like what?'

'The trick is,' he said as they strolled down Brewer Street, past the strip clubs, the tawdry girls in doorways and the fat men with cigars and bow ties standing behind them, 'the trick is to work out where your limits are – and then to go beyond them. Just pretend they aren't there and break straight through.'

Eileen wondered if Richard was a pimp.

Walking down Old Compton Street, Richard asked Eileen how long she'd been in London.

'Oh, you know, a year or so. I'm trying to save money to go to college.' This was what she always said when asked, and it was a better reply than the truth, which was that she really didn't know what to do about the shapeless greyness of her life.

'I see,' he said, and she knew he didn't believe her.

'How about you?' she asked.

'Me?' He seemed surprised at the question. 'I move around. I don't like to get stuck in one place for too long; keep on my toes. I'm leaving London in a couple of weeks.'

Eileen experienced a sudden heaviness, like something dropping inside her. Why did Richard have to go and leave just when things were getting interesting?

'Well,' he said, as they came out on Charing Cross Road. 'I'd better be off home.'

'Oh, right.' Eileen had assumed he was taking her to dinner somewhere. Disappointment crept over her.

'I'll see you tomorrow,' he said brightly. And added, 'In the sandwich bar.'

Eileen could tell from his forced smile that he had guessed what she was thinking, and felt embarrassed.

He leant over and gave her a quick peck on the cheek.

He didn't turn up at the sandwich bar the next day, nor the next. Eileen couldn't understand it – what could she have said or done that was so bad as to drive him away entirely? But it was vain of her to even presume to think she could have that much effect on him. No, the answer had to be that he'd already left London, earlier than planned. The more she thought about it, the more she was certain this must be the explanation.

But knowing what had happened didn't really help. Everything was grey, and Eileen couldn't imagine how she hadn't noticed its dullness before. The worst thing was the hope that he would still appear. Eileen tried to banish it, but still she jolted and fluttered every time someone walked into the shop.

If Sophia burns the toast within the next ten minutes, Richard will come back and take me out again, she said to herself, feeling certain that Sophia had forgotten about the two pieces of bread in the toaster. But Sophia was surprisingly on the ball and rescued the toast just in time.

After a few days even the hope was gone.

'I'm watching you, my girl,' sneered Sophia one busy lunch time, as Eileen struggled to reach into the cold counter to retrieve some change that had fallen in the chicken tikka.

'A customer once complained he took a mouthful of his sandwich and bit on a two pence piece,' said Maria to the old man across the counter. 'I asked him for it back but he wouldn't give it to me. Bloody cheek, I say.' She burst out laughing, adding: 'Next time he came in, I overcharged him by two pence to make up for it.' The customer began laughing too, and Eileen triumphantly dropped a tikka-smeared five pence piece into the till. The old man thought Maria was joking. He didn't know the half of it.

'Don't think you can pull the wool over *my* eyes,' whispered Sophia, squinting myopically at Eileen and wagging a wizened finger.

'What are you talking about, you stupid old bag?' muttered Eileen. And more loudly, 'Next, please.'

As Eileen left work at the end of the day and headed off for Piccadilly Circus tube station, someone tapped on her shoulder, making her jump. Startled, she wheeled around. It was Richard.

'Here we are,' he said fifteen minutes later, as they turned into a narrow street just off Charing Cross Road. 'This is home. For the moment, anyway.' He fumbled in a pocket for his keys and opened a heavy blue door at the side of a musical instruments shop. Inside, a narrow hall with tatty bare boards led to a flight of steep stairs. Eileen hesitated.

'Something wrong?' asked Richard.

'No, nothing,' she said, hastily, and stepped inside.

The flat was on the first floor, directly over the music shop. It was painted white throughout and was sparsely furnished. Eileen's shoes were loud on the polished wood floor. She wandered into the living room, which was empty except for a black leather couch, an enormous TV, a glass-topped coffee table and a classical guitar propped up in the corner. She sat down on the couch, and the leather creaked satisfyingly.

'What do you think?' asked Richard, appearing in the doorway behind her.

'You haven't got much stuff, have you?'

'I move around a lot,' said Richard. 'Want to see the rest of the flat?'

'Sure.'

He led the way, showing her the kitchen; stained red wood units and lots of glass – immaculate; not so much as a crumb on the shining surfaces. The bathroom was gleaming white with a sunken bath and a deep-pile green carpet. It was showy, cold and impersonal; hard to believe anyone really lived here.

'This is the bedroom,' said Richard, opening the door to a sunny room with a sloping ceiling. The bed must have been emperor-size; it dominated the room. The bedhead of curling wrought iron reminded Eileen of the front gate at her parents' house; she used to swing on it when she was a little girl, pretending it was her horse, while her mother pulled weeds out of the flowerbeds, pruned the roses and complained about the poor soil . . . no, mustn't think about that.

At the foot of the bed was an expensive looking Turkish rug, and on the rug were a pair of shoes, women's shoes; high heels and a dolly look to them, the kind of shoes Betty Boop would wear . . . An old pine dressing table stood against one wall, and spread out on it was a selection of women's cosmetics; lipstick, nail varnish, hair spray and cleansing lotion. In one corner sat an old vanity case, with a silk scarf draped loosely over it. Hanging from the back of the door was a kimono style wrap. The disappointment was overwhelming.

'Something wrong?' asked Richard, coming into the room with two glasses of white wine.

'No, nothing,' Eileen said, too quickly.

Richard's smile taunted her. 'Really?'

'Yes. I think I'll go now.' She stood up and smoothed her skirt. He was blocking the doorway.

'I'd like to go, please.'

'So soon?' And still he stood in her way.

She could feel panic rising, and thought of trying to push past him. Would he let her leave?

'I know exactly what you're thinking,' said Richard. 'I promise you there's no woman here.'

Just how stupid did he think she was? 'So who does all this

stuff belong to? Don't tell me you're a transvestite in your spare time!'

He laughed, and held out one of the glasses of wine. 'Relax. Have a drink.'

But she didn't take the glass. 'Richard, what is going on here?'

He sighed, and set both glasses down on the dressing table. Then he walked over to the bed and sat down. 'I think we both know what's going on, don't we, Eileen?'

And now that flutter in her stomach again. Eileen was annoyed with her stomach. It had no business fluttering so infuriatingly at such a moment, when she was busy being outraged and indignant.

'Don't we, Eileen?' The smile had gone. His face, without it, was dark, intense – intent on something – on her.

'What *is* going on, Richard? Who does this stuff belong to?' Her voice, big and angry while inside her, emerged small and thin in the musky air.

'It belongs to a friend of mine who owns the flat,' he said, sadly. 'She's away for six months and she said I could stay here while I'm in London. We're old friends, that's all.'

While they fucked, Eileen kept bashing her head against the iron bedhead – it didn't hurt too much, but it did distract her somewhat from the business at hand. He kept kissing her deeply, and her jaw clicked as it always did at such moments. He didn't seem to notice but it made her feel self-conscious and tense. She liked his body – it was lean and smooth, perhaps a little thin but she liked thin men. She liked his touch, too; he had strong hands and long, sensitive fingers. A bit of a pencil dick, but at least he knew what to do with it. While they fucked, he put his face into her hair and smelled it. She heard him say something, and thought it might be, 'You're beautiful.' When he said it a second time, she heard the words more clearly: 'You're cute.' This was less pleasing.

Afterwards they lay side by side, sipping wine.

'Are you really leaving next week?'

'Day after tomorrow.' He turned his puppy eyes on her. 'What will you do?'

'What do you mean?'

He shrugged. 'Well, you're not going to stay working at that shitty little sandwich shop forever, are you?'

There was a distant noise – it sounded like the front door being closed.

'Richard, what was that?'

'Shh.' He lay absolutely still; rigid.

'Richard, what's—'

'Are you in the bedroom?' came a woman's sharp voice. And there she was – standing in the doorway, all straight lines and strong colours. And she was looking right at Eileen.

She stood for a moment, just looking, saying nothing, as Eileen, suddenly aware of her nakedness, covered her breasts with the duvet.

The woman turned to Richard. 'I'm going to sit in the kitchen for five minutes and I'm closing the door. While I'm in there, I want you to get your little slut out of here. Understood?'

'Richard,' said Eileen as she fastened her bra – but he was sitting on the edge of the bed facing the wall, ignoring her. 'I should have known,' she muttered to herself, pulling her tights over her legs. And she had known, really. It was just that she had decided not to know. 'I'm so bloody stupid.' Still his back was turned to her.

Stepping out onto the pavement, she looked back over her shoulder. The woman was standing at the lounge window, arms folded, watching her leave. Eileen could see her outline but couldn't make out her features, her expression. She was just a shape. An impulse of devilry prompted Eileen to give her a little wave as she walked away.

The world was more colourless than ever when Eileen woke the next morning. She tried to chivvy herself along as she walked to the tube, preaching to herself about the importance of finding a direction, something to aim for – she must stop drifting. No wonder the prospect of a romance with a stranger had made such a difference to her; her life was entirely empty. If your life has meaning, you don't need other people – they are simply an added bonus when they happen to come along. And when you're happy, people flock to you because they sense that you don't need them.

Rounding the corner of Silver Square, Eileen could see the sandwich bar was already busy. Sophia was red-faced, puffing and struggling with the cappuccino machine, Maria was throwing bread into the toaster and barking orders, and little Mayer the Polish girl was spreading cream cheese on a bagel. Sophia scowled at Eileen as she closed the door behind her and edged through the queue to the back room.

She was reaching to hang her jacket on one of the hooks when she heard someone come into the room behind her.

'I wouldn't bother taking that off if I were you,' said Maria.

'What?' Eileen spun around, puzzled.

Maria was looking fierce, more fierce than Eileen had ever seen her. 'Don't come the innocent with me, miss. I've treated you well enough, haven't I? I paid you the going rate, didn't I?'

'What's the matter, Maria? Have I done something wrong?'

Maria snorted her contempt and took a step closer, hands on her hips. '*Have I done something wrong?*' she sneered. 'Go on, get out of my shop. I never want to see you here again.'

Eileen was amazed. She stood, trying to make sense of this. Then she began to understand. 'It's Sophia, isn't it? She's got it in for me, I don't know why.'

Maria was stony-faced. 'That's right, try and blame Sophia, *my aunt*.'

But Eileen was undaunted. 'What's she been saying about me? Is it Richard? Is this about him?'

'Richard?'

'I only went out with him twice. Two dates, that's all. And I won't be seeing him any more, I promise.'

Maria shook her head and her chins wobbled. 'I have no idea who Richard is or what you're talking about.' But she was more calm now. She was beginning to look almost sorry for Eileen, like a great St Bernard.

Sophia was calling her from the shop, and Maria shouted something back in Italian. 'Darling, if you have some kind of problem, if you needed money, you should have come to me. I would have tried to help.'

Eileen was feeling weak. She wanted to sit down but there was no chair in the room. Just coats, boxes and rubbish bins. 'I don't have a problem. I'm happy here.' She tried a weak smile.

Now the thunder cloud was moving back over Maria's face. 'Then why do you take from me?'

'But I didn't—'

'No, no, I don't want to hear any more of this.' Maria moved behind Eileen, grabbed her by the shoulders and gave her a shove in the direction of the door. 'I need to have staff I can trust. There's no room here for thieves. Come on, get out.'

Eileen lay very still on her bed in the YWCA, staring up at the ceiling. The room was hot and stuffy but she couldn't find the motivation to go and open the window. She knew she should be out looking for another job, asking around at cafés, shops and bars, but she didn't have the energy for that – not today. She'd start tomorrow . . . starting again; how terribly tiring the idea was.

Out in the corridor, Denise and Jackie were arguing about teabags. Denise had pinched some of Jackie's, apparently, but felt justified in doing so because last week Jackie had stolen her baked beans. Their voices were escalating, rising to the level of a banshee screech.

'Slag!'

'Bitch!'

'Fucking whore, I'll 'ave you.'

'Oh yeah, you and who else.'

Eileen kept her own food in a cupboard in her bedroom. She had learned not to trust the lockers in the communal kitchen.

Living in the YWCA was not really so bad. It was clean and the facilities were good, far nicer than you'd get in your average crummy London bedsit. The only real problem was the noise. When she first moved in, she had barely been able to sleep at night for the screaming and shouting. Joanne in the room next door was the worst; she was supposedly off the smack, but had taken to wailing to herself all through the night. Eileen had thumped on the wall a few times but it didn't seem to make any difference – the poor cow probably didn't even know she was doing it. Eileen felt sorry for her, and had that slightly uneasy feeling of, *There but for the grace of God* . . . Now she had become more successful at blocking the noise out of her head. She visualised sun-drenched meadows; herself lying under a shady tree, the leaves rustling ever so slightly in a gentle breeze. A picnic would be spread out on the grass in front of her with all of her favourite foods, and sometimes she would be accompanied by a dark man whose face she couldn't quite make out – although she could feel the warmth of his smile.

The loud buzz of the intercom interrupted Eileen's reverie, and with an effort she dragged herself off the bed and across the room. Perhaps it would be Maria, humble and apologetic, ready to plead with Eileen to take her job back – well, if it *was* Maria, she could stick her bloody job!

Eileen picked up the receiver. 'Who's there?'

'I'm . . . well, I'm the woman from yesterday . . . you know . . . Richard's flat? Can I come in?'

What the . . . 'How did you find me?'

'I asked at the sandwich shop. I'd like to talk to you.'

The voice was well-modulated, gentle. Not like yesterday when it spoke haughtily to Richard. What had it called Eileen? *Little slut*, that was it.

'Why? Why do you want to talk to me?'

There was a sound that might have been a sigh. 'I'm sorry about yesterday.'

'Why should *you* be sorry? You found me in bed with your – what is he – boyfriend, husband, fiancé?'

'But it wasn't your fault.' The voice was insistent, intense. 'You didn't know – he's told me. It's *his* fault, not yours. Would you let me in, Eileen? Please, I just want to talk to you.'

Richard's woman wandered around the room, touching things – spraying a little perfume on her wrist, opening a carved wood box only to find it was empty, flicking through a magazine that lay on the bedside table. Eileen sat on the edge of the bed, watching and waiting, half expecting this woman to start going through her underwear drawers.

Suddenly the woman started and blushed, as though she had been caught doing something she shouldn't. 'Sorry, how rude of me. I'm incurably nosy, I'm afraid.' She extended a hand. 'I'm Fran.'

Eileen slowly reached out and shook the hand, gestured to Fran to sit down on the dressing-table stool. She thought about that hand touching Richard, touching his face, his chest.

'I'm sorry about your job,' said Fran, and her sharp face adopted what passed for a sympathetic expression.

Eileen shrugged, attempting nonchalance, trying not to be intimidated by the immaculately arched eyebrows and the close cut charcoal-grey suit. 'Who cares? It's just a shitty little sandwich shop. I wasn't planning on staying there forever.'

Fran folded her hands serenely on her lap. She looked like a Holbein painting. 'I want to apologise – for Richard, really.'

'Why doesn't *he* come and apologise?'

Fran gave a helpless smile. 'Because he's a man. He should have been straight with you – told you the situation . . .'

'Which is?'

'We live and work together. We're partners . . . of a kind. We have an open relationship. We're both at liberty to do what we want, be with whoever we want. But he shouldn't have brought you back to the flat; that's where he broke the rules. That's why I was angry. I'd been away and he wasn't expecting me back so soon . . . Could I possibly have a cup of tea?' She put a hand to her throat, as though to indicate how parched she was.

'Richard *should* have been straight with me,' said Eileen, ignoring the request for tea. *Let her go thirsty.* 'Did he send you here?'

Fran laughed. 'He doesn't send *me* anywhere.' And Eileen could believe that.

Joanne in the room next door began her wailing. It was like listening to a dog howling at the moon. It was the sound of despair.

Fran visibly shivered. 'What in God's name is that?'

'Just the girl next door,' said Eileen. 'She's come off heroin and she's having a bad time.'

'It bloody sounds like it,' said Fran. 'Look, why don't you let me take you out for a drink? I'd like that.'

'I don't understand why you're doing this,' said Eileen. 'It isn't necessary.'

Fran got up and smoothed down her tight skirt. 'Just humour me, will you?' she said. 'Unless you have something better to do . . .'

Joanne let out another cry, and this one sounded like the laugh of a hyena.

'OK,' said Eileen, perking up. 'I'll come. Would you take me to the Atlantic? . . . I'd like to go for cocktails.'

Eileen hadn't been inside the Atlantic, but she'd heard about it from Maria. Maria said that in the early evening you'd find it crowded with all the media types who piled into the Silver Square Sandwich Bar at lunchtime with their mobile phones and their designer sunglasses. She said they liked to go there to flash their money around and to be seen with the right people. She also said if you went into the toilets you'd see all the scrawny advertising women coming out of the cubicles in twos, wiping their noses on the backs of their wrists, their pupils widely dilated.

The heavily made-up girl on the door gave Eileen a disparaging look as they walked in the main entrance, and seemed to be about to say something – but then she glanced across at Fran and converted the look into a smile and a 'Good evening. Just having drinks, are you?'

Something was troubling Eileen as they descended a flight of steps into the foyer. She stopped at the bottom. 'How did you know where I live?'

'As I said before, they told me at the sandwich bar,' said Fran, impatient to get into the bar.

Eileen put a hand on her arm. 'I don't believe you,' she said. She knew that Maria was too concerned to keep the staff and customers apart for this to be likely – and she certainly didn't consider it possible that Maria would send a potential customer to see someone she'd *sacked* that morning.

Fran sighed and looked Eileen straight in the eye. 'All right. Richard looked in your bag and saw it on a bank statement.'

'Of all the—' began Eileen.

'I know, I know,' said Fran. 'I'm sorry, but that's how it is.' And she strode off before Eileen could say anything else.

The bar was dark and cavernous, purple walls and gold leaf on the ceiling, marble pillars and drapery. It was like walking into an old and extravagant cinema, or perhaps into the film itself – Bogart might be about to sidle up to the bar, or Monroe to pose on a stool with a martini and a cigarette in a long holder. Eileen felt glamorous just being there until she looked down at her battered old corduroy skirt and realised how she must appear. Fran seemed entirely at home. She steered Eileen towards a couple of easy chairs in a corner.

'How do you fancy a champagne cocktail?' she asked. 'They do a great one here with peach. Wait here – I'm going to put my card behind the bar.'

She moved with a wiggling walk. Eileen watched her bending forward, putting her head close to that of the young, blond barman. She saw him laugh and reach for two glasses.

How dare Richard search through her bag! What could he have been looking for? It wasn't as though she had any money. But then Eileen remembered how she had, on more than one occasion, searched through the jacket pockets of a prospective lover, to see if he was carrying condoms. Her sense of outrage began to subside.

Fran was still laughing with the barman as he trickled champagne very slowly into a glass, stirring with a long spoon to mix it evenly with the vibrant peach pulp. The result was like molten gold.

As Eileen raised the glass to her lips, she felt as though she was about to drink from a magic elixir. She let the moment linger before allowing herself to taste. The bubbles tickled her lower lip. Then she took a first small sip. The warm, sunny sweetness of the peach washed over her tongue, undercut by the sharp fizzing edginess of the champagne, which tingled at the back of her throat as she swallowed. She looked up and her eyes met Fran's. Fran was watching her quietly, with satisfaction.

'I've never had champagne before.'

'Well, you should make a point of having it as often as possible from now on,' said Fran. 'Your mouth was made for it.'

They moved from the peach concoction to another champagne cocktail filled with raspberries. Eileen rolled a raspberry around on her tongue and then sucked on it until it burst into fiery alcoholic juice, while Fran talked about the pleasures of moving from place to place, recreating oneself in as many different roles as the imagination would allow. The way she described it made it sound almost as though she assumed whole new identities as she moved along, becoming someone new with each day. Eileen finished her raspberry cocktail and switched to strawberry; sweet and syrupy, the essence of summer – reminding her of long days spent picking soft fruit as a child in Kent.

No matter how many questions she asked, Eileen couldn't get a grip on what exactly Fran did. It wasn't that Fran didn't answer the questions – she somehow twisted them sideways, came at them from an angle, pounced on them from behind rather as a politician might, but with considerable charm. The more Eileen drank, the more difficult it was to pin Fran down. She was elusive, out of reach, and in Eileen's mind she evolved into a butterfly, whose many colours kept changing in the light.

When they had exhausted all of the champagne cocktails on the menu, Fran announced that they should simply continue by sharing a bottle of champagne in its neat form: 'The lightest and giddiest of all drinks, absolutely guaranteed to lift your heavy soul.'

The bar was full of people now, laughing and squawking. The music was loud; the bass throbbing through the floor and vibrating in the upholstery of the chairs. Waitresses kept appearing and placing tiny paper napkins beneath Fran's and Eileen's glasses like coasters to protect the table. After a few minutes the napkins would go skidding off, forgotten, and again the waitresses would appear with fresh ones. At the next table, a large woman with the biggest reddest mouth Eileen had ever seen was laughing uproariously at a joke told by the slender, androgynous person she sat with. Eileen peered hard at the androgynous person – male or female, who could tell? She couldn't see that there were breasts under that tight black T-shirt, but neither could she make out the shape of an Adam's apple at the graceful neck. Big Mouth laughed again and Eileen stared dizzily into the back of her throat, feeling she was about to be sucked in, along with the tables and chairs, the blond barman and the smart Japanese waitresses, the champagne bottles and the tiny paper napkins.

She noticed the golden hairs on Fran's right arm as it reached over to top up her glass again. Baby hair, soft and downy, perhaps the only soft thing about her. Fran wore a large silver ring with a blue stone on her middle finger – was it a sapphire?

Eileen realised she was talking about her childhood; she could hear her own voice, distant and thin, as though it were someone else's. Talking about her childhood was something she never did; even thoughts about it were too painful to be endured.

And yet that *was* her voice chuntering on, these *were* her memories parading around the table like a bunch of circus acts marching around the ring at the end of a show.

She can see her father, bleary-eyed, slavering slightly like a dog, white shirt crumpled and yellow at the collar, soaked with sweat under the arms. Face shiny and bloated, heavily lined around an ugly letter-box mouth, head balding, with grey shaggy hair in unruly tufts like an old tennis ball, belly hanging slackly over the beltless top of his old brown trousers. Drunk and shouting, fists clenched.

Mother is here too, worn and faded like an old armchair, bad perm frazzling the roots of her brittle brown hair, shoulders rounded and drooping. Voice still soft and musical even after all this time, but face dried out and thin like old parchment that might crack if you fold it, eyes mournful and hopeless.

He lurches forward, lunges with his fist and she backs away, cowering. He stumbles into action, begins to chase her around the table, just as he chased her around the Broadstairs bungalow all those nights during all of those years. Eileen watches, helpless, forbidden by her mother to interfere, as her mother martyrs herself. *Stay out of it, love. He'll only start on you and that is something I just couldn't bear to see.*

The watching is the awful thing – you have to watch because you cannot hide from it – if you go to your room there are still the noises. It would surely be better in the end to be hit than to watch this hideous pantomime night after night.

'You're ashamed of what you do to her. I know you are.'

I don't know what you're talking about.

'And you're afraid too. Afraid to admit what you are.'

I don't have to listen to this.

'Can't you at least be honest? Hit her in the face for once

instead of in the ribs, the back, the belly. Make some marks that you'll have to look at over the breakfast table. See if you can live with yourself then.'

I couldn't leave him, darling. What would I do?

'Anything. Anything at all.'

Where would I go?

'Anywhere. I don't know. I'd help you. I'd go with you.'

Oh, stop being silly, Lena. What do you think would happen to your father if I went?

Maybe all the alcohol would start to build up inside him, turning him into a big red beer balloon until finally he burst into a ball of flames.

What are you two whispering about? You're always whispering in corners, you two.

Hemmed in with mother and father as he chases her around the bungalow. Out there, behind the back garden, there is nothing – only field after field of cabbages and beyond the cabbages only the great rolling sea.

'I flunked my exams,' said Eileen. 'I'll never know if that was because of what was going on, or whether I'm just plain thick.'

'And is that when you left?' Fran lit a cigarette.

'Oh, no, I stayed there for ages until I felt I would suffocate with it all. I didn't want to leave her alone with him, you see. I was afraid of what he might do.'

'So what was it that finally made you go?'

'Can't you guess?' Eileen drained her glass and reached for the bottle. It was empty.

'One day he hit you,' said Fran. 'And she expected you to pretend, like she did.'

'Got it in one.'

The small Japanese waitress brought a second bottle of champagne to the table, filled the two glasses and put it in an ice bucket. Eileen was now so drunk that when Fran asked her if she had ever considered going on the game, she burst into helpless giggles.

Getting control over herself again, she said, 'You know, I wondered the other day whether Richard was a pimp.'

'He's no pimp,' said Fran, with contempt. Then, more kindly, 'Listen, Eileen, whatever you do, don't go on the game. All right?'

Eileen was startled by her sudden seriousness. 'Why, what do you know about it?'

Fran stared down into her glass. 'Just don't do it. The money's good, but there are other ways to make money.'

Eileen was about to ask another question when Fran looked up, and said more brightly: 'You know, you and . . . Richard . . . have quite a bit in common.'

'Oh yeah? Me and the sleaze ball?'

'He's no sleaze ball. He's running from his past too.'

'Did he have a dad that hit him?'

Fran shook her head and lit another cigarette. 'His father was an accountant with pots of money who always felt he'd taken the wrong path. He wanted his son to be an academic; a writer, a professor . . . he was obsessed.'

'So what went wrong?'

'The son did badly at school,' said Fran. 'He worked so hard, he did all he could, but he failed . . . in spite of all the fancy schooling his father paid for, he failed every exam he ever sat. His father was disappointed. He began to ignore him; it was easier to pretend he didn't have a son than to accept that his son was so far from being the perfect golden boy.'

'And how did Richard deal with this?'

'Oh, he found he had other talents. He wasn't academic but he was smart. He knew how to make money, and he began at school by buying chocolate and sweets in bulk and selling them to his classmates at inflated prices. When he got older, he teamed up with some local boys, nicking bikes, giving them a respray or changing a few parts here and there, selling them on.'

Fran paused to tap ash into the pristine ashtray on the table. Her face seemed closer than before. It appeared to be growing, becoming more vivid. Eileen shook her head to try to rid herself of the illusion, but still Fran's face was getting bigger, her eyes locked on to Eileen's.

'Then his father got wise to what was going on. There was a massive row and Daddy threatened to get the police involved.

Called his son worthless, called him a brainless idiot, a cretin. So, like you, he ran and he didn't go back.'

Eileen's eyelids were becoming heavy. Images blurred, crossed. Now there were three Frans in front of her, and three champagne bottles. She reached for her glass again.

'And you know what?' Fran paused for effect. 'A couple of years on he made a discovery. All those second-rate private schools that his father had poured money into had missed something that any decent state school would have picked up on just like that—' And she clicked her fingers with a little snap that made Eileen jump and chased away the heaviness from her eyes. 'The boy wasn't stupid, not a bit of it. He was dyslexic, quite severely so.'

Eileen remembered what Richard had said about success and failure, about the way success is measured, and how people needed to be of a certain character in order to achieve it. She recalled how odd she'd found his implication that he and she were both misfits in some way.

'Richard said something to me . . .' she began.

'Jason,' said Fran. 'His name's Jason.'

Eileen struggled to make sense of this. 'Why did he tell me his name was Richard?'

'Because he doesn't trust people. It comes with the territory.'

The champagne bottle was empty at some stage, and there was definitely Scotch later on and something else with a strong taste of aniseed. Eileen remained dimly aware that Fran was nowhere near as drunk as her, even though she matched her glass for glass. Fran kept talking – on and on, telling her stories, giving her advice – or so it seemed. Eileen could remember very little of what was said after the story about Jason's dyslexia. At some point there seemed to be mile upon mile of purple carpet and never-ending stairs – and then there was the night air, cool and fresh, and the little glass screen separating them from the taxi-driver. And finally there was the inside of the flat that Richard – no, Jason – had taken her to.

Afterwards Eileen recalled that at some point during that first evening, Fran had talked to her about the con. *When you think of a con artist, you think of a seedy man in a raincoat trying to tell an old lady that she needs a new roof on her house, or a spiv with greased-back hair cheating at poker . . . There's more to it than that. We* are Artists. *We create, transform and triumph as surely as any painter or sculptor. We practise the art of the con.*

* * *

The train arrived at Shrewsbury, and mercifully the snogging couple got off. Eileen watched them walking down the platform hand in hand until the train began to move again and left them behind. An old man wearing a macintosh tied at the waist with string came staggering down the carriage and with a groan that actually seemed to emit from his ancient aching limbs rather than his mouth, he eased himself into one of the seats vacated by the young lovers. Eileen was glad he hadn't come any closer – she was sure he would smell sour and unwashed. He searched furtively through the pockets of his mac, at last bringing forth a boiled sweet in cellophane, which he unwrapped noisily and popped into his mouth.

A hand landed on Eileen's shoulder, and she twisted around with a start to see Fran standing there. What was she doing here?

'You made me jump, sneaking up on me like that.'

'Sorry.' Fran slipped into the seat opposite.

'What do you want, anyway?'

Fran's face wore what passed for an expression of kindness. It looked unnatural, as though she were wearing someone else's clothes that didn't fit properly. 'I wanted to see if you were all right. I'm concerned about you.' Fran reached out and took hold of her hand. 'Look, I just wanted to say that nobody expects you to do anything you don't feel comfortable with. OK?'

Eileen nodded. 'I'm fine.'

Fran carried on, regardless. 'If you change your mind and decide to back out, it won't matter. We'll understand.'

'I'm not going to change my mind.'

Fran's grip tightened. 'Well, anyway . . . I just wanted you to know.'

Eileen withdrew her hand from Fran's, stared out of the window at green fields and electricity pylons. She was beginning to see what was happening here. 'It's you that doesn't want to go ahead with this. And you're trying to use me as your get-out.'

'That's crap.' Fran laughed but her eyes didn't laugh along with her mouth.

'No, it isn't.' Eileen noticed the way Fran was fidgeting around in her seat. 'I'm with Jason on this one. I think this scam is what we need.'

'Eileen, honey,' tried Fran, picking absentmindedly at something grey that had dried and stuck to her seat, '*I* wouldn't want to do what you're going to do. That's all. Not for Jason, not for anyone.'

'*He* does it all the time.'

Fran got to her feet, holding on to the top of the seat to steady herself. 'Yes, he does. But that doesn't mean *you* have to.'

She teetered off down the aisle, keeping her balance with some difficulty while the train rocked and lurched. As she reached the door she turned back to give Eileen a smile. Perhaps, after all, she was genuinely sincere about this.

Eileen was left alone – alone, that is, except for the vile old man just down the carriage, who was delving in his horrible pockets again, searching, no doubt, for another boiled sweet.

There was no need for Fran to be concerned. It had been entirely her own idea – not Jason's. And after all, wasn't it about time she came up with an idea? Perhaps it was taking a leaf out of Jason's book, but no real harm had ever come to him, had it?

The old man gave an odd moan. Ugh! He wasn't just delving in his pocket. He was masturbating under cover of his mac, and he was staring at Eileen as he did so.

'Shame on you!' she yelled, more loudly than she'd actually intended, surprised at the strength of her anger. 'Shame on you!' she shouted again, when he showed no sign of stopping. She slipped off her right shoe and threw it hard at his head.

The train slid on, down into the valleys of South Wales.

5

Cardiff

I was overwhelmed by the fruity, cloying stench of hops as we got into a taxi outside Cardiff Central Station. So often my first impression of a place comes via my nose. Smells have a way of cutting through everything else.

'The Brains brewery is just over there,' said the taxi-driver, as though he had read my mind. 'When the wind blows a certain way you can smell the hops all across town.' He took in a deep breath and made the kind of sound you make when you're really savouring something. My mind was filled with a picture of an enormous vat full of molten brains stewing in their own foul juices, being stirred by a red-faced man with a giant ladle.

It was a damp grey day and people were scurrying down the murky street. There was no sense of the swagger of the West End here.

'It doesn't feel like a capital city,' I whispered to Fran, quietly so that the taxi-driver wouldn't hear. 'It's more like a small town.'

'Don't you believe it,' said Jason, out loud. 'This city is on the up, big time. There couldn't be a better moment for our little project.'

'We got the Welsh Assembly coming soon,' chipped in the taxi-driver. 'Then we'll show 'em.'

'If this city was a woman,' mused Jason, 'it would be a delicate pubescent girl – still in bud as it were, just ready to flower. London, on the other hand, is an overweight middle-aged tart with swollen ankles and a face full of broken blood-vessels.'

Fran rolled her eyes and stared out of the window.

Jason was off on one. 'And like a blushing teenage girl bashful about her swelling breasts, this city is painfully self-conscious. You'll never see another place so conscious of itself. We've arrived at exactly the right time. You mark my words.'

'Just ignore him,' Fran advised the taxi-driver. 'He's full of shit.'

We drove past a huge building-site dominated by a half-completed structure, a mess of steel and scaffolding.

'That's going to be the new Millenium Stadium,' explained the taxi-driver. 'To replace the one they've torn down ... The Rugby National Stadium,' he added on catching sight of my baffled face in his mirror.

'What was wrong with the old Arms Park?' Fran was peering out as we stopped at traffic lights.

'Absolutely bloody nothing, if you ask me,' said the driver, scratching his moustache. 'It's a colossal waste of money. They're turning the city centre around to make it face Cardiff Bay, the docks. And that means turning the stadium around too. It's all going to be tree-lined boulevards and what-have-you. Like Barcelona. La Rambas or whatever the bloody hell it's called.'

'Told you.' Jason gave a knowing nod. 'Self-conscious.'

'It's bloody crazy, that's what it is,' huffed the cabby. 'They're so desperate to get this place finished in time for the 1999 World Cup the council have given permission for the building work to go on twenty-four hours a bloody day. Non-bloody-stop it is – and this a residential area – with them houses not a hundred yards away! Scuse my French, ladies.'

It was prettier out of the city centre. We drove down a wide street with elegant Victorian terraces and trees in blossom.

'This is Cathedral Road,' pronounced the taxi-driver, as though that should mean something to us. 'Bit trendy round here. House prices are booming.' He sniffed and pulled over next to a hotel. 'Here you go, kids.'

Fran and Jason didn't waste any time. When we'd dumped the bags we headed straight off to an estate agents down the road with a sign in the window that said they did rentals. Fran told the crumpled agent we needed a one-bedroomed furnished flat that was ready to move into straight away. After we'd viewed only one place Jason announced we would take it. He said we wanted it that very day. The man started shaking his head and creasing up his brow, talking about bank references and contracts. With a disdainful look, Jason produced his wad and counted out three months' rent plus one month as deposit. The man promptly shut up and delved in his drawer for keys.

* * *

This flat is mine, all mine. That's how it feels. I've never had a place to myself before. I feel like a little girl in a Wendy House. I've been here three days now and I don't think I've ever been so happy. I've cleaned the flat all through, right down to scrubbing the insides of the kitchen cupboards and drawers and washing the windows. It's on the ground floor – a garden flat as they called it in the estate agents, in a converted Victorian house in a leafy cul-de-sac (again that is the agent's description) just off Cathedral Road in 'trendy' Pontcanna. I've got a cute living room with bay window and original fire-place, a kitchen with pine units and quarry tiles on the floor and an airy bedroom with white walls, a brass-knobbed single bed and French windows leading through to the garden.

And the garden is the best bit of all. I can have breakfast at the picnic table on my own private patio. There's a lawn and flowers and a shed full of gardening tools. This morning I hung my washing out on the line for the first time and chatted over the fence to Mrs Evans, the woman who lives next door. She's married to a retired vicar and she says I must call her Tabitha. She bakes her own bread. I told her I need to find a job and she says Energy, the health-food shop down the road, has a sign in their window to say they're looking for a part-time assistant with retail experience. A health-food shop – I think I might fancy that! I can just see myself delving into sacks of seeds and oats, sniffing at bottles of essential oils, munching on oat cakes and talking to women in tie-dye with hennaed hair about meditation and organic vegetables. You never know, perhaps some of the wholesome-ness might rub off on me.

I'm going to miss Jason and Fran, though. My time with them has been the only time in my life I haven't felt lonely. They're renting a house on the other side of town, and I'm not to contact them more than is absolutely necessary until it's all over. They would prefer that I don't phone them at all unless I really have 'something to say' – and we all know what that means. Fran says she'll get hold of me when she needs to. It's important that Owen Meredith – or anyone else for that matter – doesn't find out I am linked to them. Nevertheless I think they're going way over the top with this. It's typical Fran-type paranoia.

Soon enough I will be taking up my role in the scam. For now I'm having fun – wandering into town over parkland alongside the River Taff, buying shisha embroidery cushions, linen throws, bed sheets from Habitat and a green bicycle with a basket from a shop called G. Williams, learning how to make pea soup, and today going out to get myself the kind of job a nice simple girl would have – a girl who is not too clever but not altogether dumb – perhaps a little innocent, the kind of girl who is sent a monthly envelope of top-up money by her well-to-do parents who are hoping she will change her mind and go back into education, a spoilt but sweet-natured middle-class girl who is used to taking certain things for granted but is perhaps more concerned than many with 'the realm of the spiritual'.

I told myself last night that if I opened my curtains in the morning and saw a clear sky over my garden, then this scam would be a success. When morning came the sky was a stunning vivid blue – so I guess everything is going to be OK. Perhaps now I will be able to forget about that blessed magpie.

Owen Meredith hated Tuesdays. Especially the evenings when he taught a life-drawing class at Meirion Hall, a teaching centre for sketching, photography and pottery; a ramshackle old house full of dust, rotten wood, ancient electric heaters that gave out the smell of burning hair, and orange plastic chairs that wobbled on the grey lino floor.

Freda Lawrence had taken the classes for him while he was away in Manchester, and he was hoping she might want to carry on with them. But when he got back and played the messages on his answer machine, the very first was Freda's tired, drab voice:

'Owen, my dear. I do hope you get back and hear this message before the twelfth of June. You didn't leave me a number in Manchester, otherwise I would have called you. You see, I'm going off to Cork with Tamarind for a month, and I'm leaving on the twelfth. You did *say* you'd be back . . . Sorry, darling, but I need to give this relationship one last try. I know what you'll say but it isn't poor Tamarind's fault that her mood has been so sour lately. It's the candida albicans. But she's been on a yeast-free diet for three weeks now and . . .'

Owen wiped the message, unable to bear another word about Tamarind and her moods. Today was the nineteenth so last week there would have been nobody to teach the class. The regulars would arrive tonight in a foul temper, cursing the success that took him away from them while he cursed the lack of success that had brought him back. The model would be sulky and uncooperative from having lost last week's money – if she turned up at all.

He had been alarmed to find his house so untouched, though it shouldn't have been a surprise as he hadn't asked anyone to call in, not even to water the plants. His favourite blue mug sat dirty on the kitchen table next to a copy of the *Guardian* from two months ago. A small plate lying on top of the paper was still covered in the crumbs from that last hurried breakfast. The unexciting post from that day – an array of bills and junk mail, lay unopened alongside.

In the bedroom he picked up the shirt, jeans and dirty underwear that he'd balled up and thrown into the corner of the room, and put them into the washing basket. His bed was unmade, the pillow still carrying the indentation of his head. It was like entering a house for the first time after its owner has died.

He paused by the phone. If he were to press redial he knew which number would come up. The night before he left he had called Annie, knowing she wouldn't actually pick up – Annie screened all her calls. He just wanted to hear the sound of her voice on the answer machine.

The house plants were all dead.

But things will be different soon, he told himself as he locked the front door and headed off down the too-familiar street. *Because Robbie Warren is going to change my life.*

'So you're back, then,' said Hilda, the Meirion Hall evening receptionist, without taking the cigarette from her drooping painted lips.

'Evidently.' Owen leaned into the little hatch to reach his register. God forbid that Hilda would actually be so helpful as to pass it to him!

'Pauline thought we might have seen the last of you,' continued Hilda, whilst writing something into her crossword. 'But I knew you'd be back.' She smiled cruelly and broke into a coughing fit. Vicious old hag.

Owen climbed the creaking stairs, nursing the thought that there were only three weeks left in this term. And then – finito. For ever.

Reg and Marjorie Stern, keen as ever, had already arrived when he entered the studio. They had set up their easels and were pulling pristine boxes of expensive unused pastels and charcoal pencils from a large canvas bag. 'Ah Owen, you've returned,' said Marjorie, taking off her glasses and letting them hang on the chain around her neck, primping her perm. 'Do you know, we didn't have a teacher at all last week!'

'You'll be proud of us, though,' said Reg, stroking his moustache. 'We made our own fun.'

Owen, in order not to let them see him laugh, crossed to the window and struggled to try to open it. It was jammed shut.

'I think someone's painted the outside,' explained Reg. 'And they painted it shut. Last week it was so hot in here you could have fried an egg on the floor.'

'Owen, sweetheart!' It was fat Philomena, third year from the art college; bit of a leading light and boy did she know it. Perhaps she could be persuaded to take over the teaching next term . . . She rushed over to give him a smacker of a kiss on the lips. Owen heard the tiny sounds of hairpins breaking free from her elaborate hair arrangement and dropping to the floor. 'Thank Christ you're back. I was on the verge of abandoning this class for good. I've had all I can take of Freda Lawrence making free with my pastels and breathing all over me!'

Well, at least they were glad to see him. He supposed he should feel cheered by the welcome.

Within minutes, all eleven of the class had arrived and the studio was heating up like an oven. No sign of Tara, the life model, though. Owen took the register to play for time, and chatted a little of the exhibition.

He was just about to ask Philomena if she'd mind modelling when the door was slowly opened.

'Tara – about time . . .' he began, and then saw that it wasn't Tara. It was Annie! He felt his heart leap – but no – it wasn't Annie either. It was someone who was younger than Annie, and smaller. Big eyes, a low-cut cotton sun dress and a ridiculous straw hat.

He cleared his throat. 'Yes?'

'Am I too late for the life class?' She smiled prettily and took the hat off, tossing back thick dark tresses of hair.

He swallowed and recovered himself. 'That depends.'

'On what?' she asked, playing with the wide ribbon on the hat.

'On whether the life model turns up. It doesn't look like there's going to *be* a class at this rate.'

'Oh.' The girl gazed around the room. Reg and Marg were busy selecting pencils from their vast array. Lucy and Helen the A-level students were giggling together in the corner, Derek the gothic stood quietly – he looked as though he was praying. Philomena beamed.

The girl seemed to be about to say something else when Tara the life model arrived. She stumbled blearily into the room and headed straight for the screen in the corner without so much as a hello for Owen.

'So can I join the class?' asked the girl.

'What?' Owen knew she had spoken but hadn't heard a single word. She really did look remarkably like Annie – the way Annie had looked when they first met, before she changed and became hardened.

'Can I join the class?'

'Er, yes of course.' He stood about awkwardly. How old and wan he must look to her.

Philomena came to the rescue. 'Have you done any life drawing before, love?'

The girl shook her head.

'No matter. We all have to start somewhere,' said Philomena. 'Come over here, there's a spare easel next to me.'

Owen laughed. 'Who exactly is running this group?' In fact he was glad of her help.

Tara appeared from around the screen, as bruised and stoned looking as ever, scratching her left buttock and yawning as she slumped down on the pile of cushions arranged in the middle of the room.

Owen, standing behind the newcomer, saw her dress rise up at the back as she bent over to sort out her pencils, and caught a glimpse of smooth brown thighs. He looked away quickly. To his embarrassment he was getting an erection.

It only took a few minutes for Tara to fall deeply asleep. She lay on her side, head resting on a cushion, snoring. It was the same every week. Owen remembered wistfully the days when Karen Lacey used to model for the group. Her ample flesh belied an innate grace and poise. Karen would begin with a series of lightning poses, throwing herself into all manner of shapes and positions, moving every two minutes. After that she would settle herself into a pose that was somehow completely different every time. Tara, on the other hand, had only two positions in her repertoire – or one and a half, really. The first week she came, he had asked her if she would do some lightning poses, and she looked at him with such contempt that he wondered if she had misunderstood and thought he was trying to proposition her.

'Excuse me, Mr Meredith.' It was the new girl. She was beckoning him over. He crossed the room – still she motioned for him to come closer. She wanted to whisper to him. He was aware of her perfume as he bent his head close to hers; Calvin Klein or something – fresh and clear. Her skin looked soft and brown. He tried not to think about how close he stood to her.

'Have you noticed that the model is asleep?' she whispered, genuine concern on her face.

'Don't worry about it,' he whispered back. 'She does it all the time.'

She didn't seem at all satisfied with this. 'Shouldn't we wake her up?'

He imagined the way Tara would snarl like a wild animal if disturbed. 'No. Leave her be. We'll wake her up for the break.'

'But she's snoring.'

And so she was. Her in-breaths were deep and rumbling, climaxing in an odd clicking sound. She breathed out with a tortured whistle down her nostrils.

'Don't worry about it.' He resisted an urge to pat her on the head as you might a small child. 'Let me see your drawing. What was your name?'

'Meg,' said the stranger, with a dimply smile. She moved to one side to let him look at her easel.

Eager and determined though she was, the new girl couldn't draw. She had begun to sketch a very tiny figure in the centre of her paper. She had got bogged down in detail, trying to get a hand right, and there were marks on the paper that showed much rubbing out.

'Well, Meg,' said Owen, sucking in his lower lip. 'Let's just get another piece of paper and start again, shall we?'

'But . . . Oh no, is it that awful?'

He tried to sound as kind as possible as he removed her drawing and laid it down on the floor. 'Not at all. But you've got to start by loosening up. You've a whole huge piece of paper here. *Use* it – be bold. And no rubbing out. Make some big, strong lines . . . get the general shape and proportions first, don't let yourself get lost in detail. See the left arm there? Well, from this angle it looks much shorter than the right, so forget the idea that it's the same length – draw what you actually *see*. Do you understand?'

She nodded, silently. He could see she was afraid.

'Come on, then.' He took her by the shoulders – they were so slender, so narrow – and pushed her gently back in front of the easel. 'Have another try.'

He watched as, with a slightly shaking hand, she drew a line that was the curve of Tara's back, and tried to make the shape of a leg. It was clumsy, but better. 'That's right. Good. Now, keep that up. I'll come and check on you again later.'

'Mr Meredith,' she said quietly as he was about to walk over to look at Philomena's work, 'is the model a drug addict?'

He looked back at Tara. She *was* thinner than she'd been before he went away. Her breasts were saggy, like half empty plastic bags, and he could make out the shapes of her ribs. Her pubic hair seemed somehow more bedraggled and pathetic. There were great dark circles around her eyes. If he took hold of one of her arms and examined its under side, would he find little puncture marks?

'Possibly,' he said to Meg. 'But that's her business, not ours.'

In the break Owen found himself snared by Marjorie and Reg. He was backed into a corner, and try how he might he couldn't get away from them.

'. . . We were thinking of going on one of those weekend Flighton courses, you know the ones.' Marjorie's words drove on relentlessly, like a pneumatic drill. 'I'd be interested to know what you think of them, actually. You go and stay in a thatched cottage in Dorset with about eight other people—'

'I know. I taught on one last year.' He was crushing his empty paper cup.

'—And there are two tutors. They're usually well known, or semi-well known, anyway, and you all cook together in the cottage and have a sort of sharing experience—'

'Yes, I taught on one.'

Her mouth was moving so rapidly, it was as though she were on film and someone had pressed the fast forward button. 'Of course, it's not only the communal experience. You do lots of drawing and painting . . .'

Across the room he could see Meg giving up her chair to let Tara sit down. Tara was clutching her head as though she were in pain. Meg crouched down on the floor beside her, looking concerned. She was listening intently, nodding frequently as Tara talked. Owen had never known Tara to speak more than about five words in one go so this was truly amazing.

'Good enough to eat, isn't she?' said Philomena, coming up behind him.

At that moment Tara tried to stand up, tottered and fell.

She lay on the floor, one arm outstretched, the other slack at her side, mouth slightly open revealing a ball of grey chewing gum, eyes closed. One breast poked out of the grubby white wrap, more obscene now than when she was completely naked. Owen fought an urge to go and poke it back inside the gown.

For a few seconds everyone stood staring. It was like a painting. Then Meg was at her side feeling for a pulse, checking to see if she was breathing, putting her fingers into Tara's mouth to remove the chewing gum, gently slapping at her cheeks to try to wake her. Philomena called for someone to bring a chair so they could raise her legs and get the blood to her head. The others stood about uselessly, watching. Derek the gothic looked as though he was about to pass out too.

'Is she all right?' asked Owen.

'I don't know,' said Meg. 'She's breathing . . . I think we should get her to hospital.'

Owen moved closer, crouched down beside them, took hold of Tara's hand and, just as he'd imagined earlier, took a look at the inside of her arm. Pale skin, so white that it was almost green. Wide scars, lots of them; slashes. And yes, puncture marks.

* * *

Tony Meredith lived in a large, low, modern house with an incongruous tower that he'd had his builders construct.

I've always wanted a tower, like in stories. I look at my tower and I can just imagine Rapunzel trapped up there in the little round room, letting down her hair out of the window.

His wife had hated the idea, so he had the courtesy to wait until after she died to have it built. Now it was his favourite part of the house. And the little round lounge at the top became his preferred room for receiving visitors.

Fran and Jason held hands in the back of the taxi as it wound its way out of Cardiff, up a steep hill and down narrow, winding, tree-lined lanes into the village of Dinas Powys.

They got out and paid at the heavy iron gates to the house, and Jason spoke into the intercom. 'Robert Warren and Marsha Freeman to see Mr Meredith.' There was a buzzing sound and the gates slowly opened.

Sprinklers played over the smooth green lawns. The flower-beds were filled with rose bushes and geraniums, neat and orderly, while here and there was a bush, sheared meticulously into the shape of a peacock or some ridiculous geometrical figure. 'A man of taste, our Meredith,' muttered Fran.

The long drive wound past a tennis court, where a blonde teenage girl was practising her serve, watched by an elderly woman with a visor and a large bottom.

'That's Meredith's daughter, Sîan,' said Jason. 'She wants to be a professional. Her coach was a US number one years ago – I forget the name.'

Beyond the shimmering blue chlorinated surface of a large swimming pool sat the house; white walls and dark windows, an absurd tower tacked on to one side.

'It's like a great big phallus,' said Fran, amused.

'Oh, don't be so bloody Freudian.' Jason strode ahead to the front door.

'Mr Warren, Ms Freeman. Welcome,' said Tony Meredith, as the heavy, suited employee who'd answered the front door showed them into the round lounge, and then retreated. 'Drink?'

Meredith was smaller than either of them had expected, only about five feet five. He was wearing immaculate stiff-looking jeans and a checked shirt that was open at the neck revealing wispy chest hair, and which strained over his beer belly. His smile was wide and friendly, but mean button eyes peeped out from under the thick grey hair.

Fran thought there was something of the leprechaun about him. 'Just a glass of water for me, please,' she said.

Meredith looked at Fran with contempt. 'And you, Mr Warren?'

'I'll have a Scotch, please.'

'Scotch in the afternoon – my kind of man,' laughed Meredith, and moved to the cabinet at the side of the room, where he began plinking ice into glasses and reaching for bottles.

The room was dark; the air stuffy. A large fly buzzed noisily around their heads, settling for a moment on Meredith's neck, only just escaping as he tried to swat it. Fran felt slightly claustrophobic and wondered if this was something to do with the fact that the room had no corners. It was hard to work out where things began and ended. Corners helped you to know where you were.

The walls were covered in chocolate-brown felt, and they seemed to be absorbing everything; light, sound, movement. Fran found the overall effect oppressive – it was as though the room was draining her of energy.

Standing next to one of the small windows was the waist-high carved wooden figure of a naked oriental woman. Fran didn't like it much.

'That's one of Owen's,' said Meredith proudly, Scotch bottle in hand. 'I don't have many but I'm kinda fond of that one.'

'It's wonderful,' said Fran. 'Very . . . organic.'

'So,' Meredith handed the drinks over and waved at them to sit down. 'Let's get straight to the point, shall we? You're going to make my son rich and famous using my money.'

They sat down on the low couch, which was the kind you sink right into. Fran realised she would have to struggle to get up again, and Meredith would watch them, amused, from his leather swivel chair. As it was they had to look up at him as he talked to them. It was probably a deliberate set-up, enabling this tiny man to have the advantage of height for once.

'I would prefer to say,' said Jason in his smoothest tones,

'that we are going to enable *you* to make your son rich and famous.'

'Ah, I see.' Meredith smiled, reclining slightly on his chair. 'So *you're* the ones doing *me* the favour, is that it?'

Jason shrugged, grinning his charming gappy grin. Fran felt uneasy.

'And what makes you think I can't help my son by myself?'

Jason leaned forward, giving what Fran recognised as his compassionate look. 'Forgive me, Mr Meredith, but we do know a little of your relationship with your son.'

'You don't know a bloody thing!' snapped Meredith suddenly, and the smile disappeared from Jason's face. He swallowed.

Fran thought she'd better intervene. 'We don't presume to understand what has happened to cause the rift between you and your son,' she began hoarsely. 'But we do know that Owen refuses to accept your offers of help.' She cleared her throat. 'Owen has already decided to work with us on this. We need to get funding, and you were the obvious person to come to. But if you're not interested, I'm sure . . .'

'All right, all right, that's enough.' Meredith closed his eyes, as though he were tired. 'What is it you two say you are? A *creative consultancy*?' He spoke the words with heavy emphasis.

'That's right,' said Jason. 'We've worked on a variety of projects; the reconstruction of the Arndale Manch—'

'Spare me the details, please!' Meredith held up his hands as though to blot Jason out of his field of vision. He turned to Fran. 'Bit of a wanker, your business partner.'

Fran looked at him levelly, aware that Jason was squirming next to her. 'He'll do a fine job for your boy.'

Tony Meredith sipped his Scotch and gave a little chuckle. Then abruptly, he got up and reached for a pile of CDs next to a stereo system. 'Do you like Tom Jones?'

Jason rolled his eyes at Fran, who was trying not to laugh.

'I wish I could sing like that man,' said Meredith, and pressed Play; 'It's Not Unusual' at high volume. Meredith turned it still higher and stood jigging to the music.

'Mr Meredith—' tried Jason, but now Meredith was shaking and grooving his way around the room, singing along with Tom.

'Go on, have a dance!' he shouted above the music. 'It's good for you.'

Fran shook her head, with a smile, while Jason stared down into his Scotch. The track seemed to go on for ever – Meredith was whirling and kicking his way around the room while they sat uncomfortably – oddly embarrassed – it was as if they had been forced to watch Meredith go to the toilet.

Mercifully when the song was over Meredith switched the CD off. Breathless he slumped into his chair and drained his Scotch glass. 'You're a couple of stiffs, you two,' he said. 'You could do with relaxing a little.'

For once Jason seemed to be lost for words. Fran delved into her briefcase. 'We've taken the liberty of preparing some figures. Perhaps you'd have a look.' She reached out to hand him the bound proposal but he waved it away.

'No, no, Ms . . .'

'Freeman,' Fran supplied.

His breathlessness had turned into wheezing. He drew an inhaler from a pocket and took a puff. '. . . Ms Freeman. No, I don't want to see your figures, thank you very much.'

'But, Mr Meredith—' began Jason.

Meredith took a second puff from his inhaler. 'Asthma,' he explained. 'Terrible curse, it is. Had it all my life. As a boy I used to dream I was drowning; someone pushing my head under the water and holding it there. I'd wake up to find I was in the middle of an attack.'

'Please, Mr Meredith,' whined Jason. 'If you'd just—'

'Now, listen.' Meredith's voice was suddenly serious. 'I've no wish to find out any more information from you two shysters – oh, yes, I know exactly what you are. You think I don't know bullshitters when I see them?'

Fran put her hand on Jason's arm to warn him not to speak. She could feel the desperation like static electricity crackling off him. 'I'm sorry if you feel we've wasted your time, Mr Meredith,' she said.

'Creative consultants, my arse!' scoffed Meredith. 'You're a couple of chancers out to make a quick buck.'

'But—' Jason began, and Fran dug him hard in the ribs with her elbow.

'I have no intention of becoming your dupe,' said Meredith, folding his arms.

'If you'd be so good as to call us a taxi,' Fran tried to muster up some dignity, 'we'll be glad to leave you in peace.'

Meredith laughed – a big, wheezing, floor-shaker of a laugh that Fran could feel reverberating in the pit of her stomach.

'Oh, no,' he said. 'You're not leaving yet. Not until I've explained the situation.'

They waited, uneasily.

'You see,' said Meredith, 'you actually have a good idea here. And you're quite right; I very much want to help my son and I don't have a way of doing it. You tell me Owen's sold on this. If he really does want to work with you then I'm stuck with the pair of you. For better or for worse.'

Again Fran had to grab hard at Jason's arm to warm him not to speak out.

'Now here's the situation. I'm not going to be your dupe – I'm going to be your boss. This is my show now.' His mean little eyes were alive, burning. 'I have a building down in the docks; a warehouse. I've emptied it, and you can have it for the restaurant. It's in a great position, right near Atlantic Wharf. The docks redevelopment has made it really trendy down there. I was planning to sell it but now . . .'

He reached into a drawer in the walnut sideboard, and drew out a sealed A4 envelope. 'The details are all in here. You can go down there tomorrow. Keith, the guy who showed you in, will take you and show you around. Then it's all yours, or rather – all Owen's.'

'Mr Meredith!' gasped Jason. 'This is amazing.'

'I'm also going to give you one and a half million pounds in three instalments,' continued Meredith. 'You'll have the first payment next week, the second at the beginning of next month, and the third the following month. You will use this money to kit out the restaurant and get it going.'

'One and a half million!' repeated Fran, slowly.

'You'll give any leftover money to Owen.' Meredith poured himself another Scotch and reached over to top up Jason's glass. 'You'll have to think of some pretext for giving it to him. And when the restaurant opens I want both of you out.

You understand? You'll have your ten per cent or fifteen per cent, or whatever you planned to charge. But you'll get out of Owen's life and mine.' He paused and his face took on a grim expression. 'And don't go thinking you can pull one over on me because I'll be watching you.' He looked slowly from Jason to Fran and back again. 'Now, I take it we have a deal? Let's celebrate!'

And he was back at the CD player again, cueing up 'The Green Green Grass of Home'.

'This song has me in tears every time.' He wiped one away.

Owen Meredith is one of those appalling men whose seduction technique is their vulnerability and supposed sensitivity; the kind who makes women want to wrap him up and keep him warm. The art would draw them in in the first place. They'd think, *Here's a man with depth, a man not afraid to be in touch with his feminine side. He needs a good woman who will respect his art and understand him ...*

Then they'd see how thin and fragile he is, and the maternal instincts would switch on – they'd want to take him out clothes shopping and fatten him up with roast dinners.

It must have been like that for Annie, his great love – the woman he can't stop talking about. After a while her nurturing instincts must have exhausted themselves. You can only feed someone's ego at the expense of your own for so long – in the end she would have been overcome by the urge to stamp on him. She probably enjoyed it.

It was late and I was stifling the yawns as I made cocoa for him in my kitchen, trying not to think about the fact that I had to be up early in the morning to go to work at the health-food shop. I made a cup for myself too – I'm not mad for the stuff but Meg is the kind of girl who'd drink it by the gallon. She'd probably dip a chocolate biscuit in it too so I searched about in the cupboard for the packet of McVitie's Homewheat while 'the sensitive artist' sat at my kitchen table torturing himself over poor Tara the life model. He felt guilty for not having taken enough notice of her, for not having seen she was ill. He felt responsible.

Truth is I felt guilty too. But my guilt arose from the fact that I'd taken advantage of her collapse to get closer to Owen. I volunteered to go with them to Accident and Emergency for entirely selfish reasons, and throughout the four hours we sat in the waiting area I was pondering how to get him back to my flat and fretting that maybe I'd adopted the wrong tactic. We only left the hospital when we'd been assured she would be all right. Turns out she's a diabetic – hence the needle marks – and hasn't been looking after herself properly. Diabetes doesn't explain the scars of course; I suspect our Tara indulges in the odd bout of self-harm, but that's irrelevant. Poor cow.

She tried to say something to me in the coffee break, just before she collapsed. She whispered something that I didn't quite catch. And she looked at me with those big needy eyes of hers. It was an awful moment – it made my stomach turn over. I think it was a sort of recognition. Not that she knows me from Adam – no, I mean that she saw something in me. Wait up – what am I thinking? Jesus, Eileen, pull yourself together, girl!

So anyway, I boiled the milk and spooned in the cocoa powder, while Owen crapped on about Tara – '... I should have realised she was ill ... I hardly see her as a person, just a model ... maybe there's something I could have done ...' And I had to fight back the urge to tell him that it is a kind of vanity to see himself as being implicated in Tara's life; to believe he could have made a difference. I bet she's only barely aware that he exists.

We carried the cocoa through to the living room and he sat down on the couch. I took the beanbag. Christ, I've never seen a man fidget so much! Owen could twitch for England, I swear. All that nervous energy – it made me exhausted just looking at him. Predictably, once he'd finally finished talking about Tara the conversation began to revolve around him. He asked the occasional question but was satisfied with the briefest of answers. Meg is the kind of sympathetic attentive girl who would be fascinated to learn about him, so I let him chunter on.

He talked of Annie, of course, of how she melted his heart. The whole time he spoke his eyes were full of tears, making them look like two black glassy beads set deep in his face. I found myself marvelling over the idea that someone can become that important in your life. I have never been in love. I don't know what it feels like. Fran and Jason are closer to me than anyone else has ever been, but that's not the same, is it?

When he started to whinge on about the trials and tribulations of life as an artist I lost my patience entirely and had to really struggle not to yell at him. After some inner wrestling I decided that even Meg might find this a bit much, and so I said – very gently – 'At least you have a vocation, Owen. Some of us can only drift.'

He was embarrassed, and rightly so.

'I'm sorry, Meg,' he said, seeming to get a grip. 'God knows what you must think of me – crapping on like this. But it's so rare that you meet someone you can really talk to ...'

I suppose I should have been glad that I was making such good progress, but his words sent me into a bit of a panic. I offered him another cup of cocoa so I could be alone in the kitchen for a few minutes and sort myself out.

You know how sometimes you stand looking at yourself in a mirror or a window and you stare so hard that your eyes bore into the back of your head and your face sort of melts away until all that's left is the skull? You get completely freaked out and have to look away – afraid of your own face. Know the one? Well, that was me in the kitchen waiting for the milk to boil. And when I couldn't look at myself in that window any longer I started thinking about Owen, visualising him sitting on my couch fidgeting and fretting, all elbows and knees and those eyes so dark you could barely distinguish the pupil from the iris. And I thought, Can I really do this?

When I got back to the lounge with the cups of cocoa, Owen had fallen asleep. His head had lolled back and his mouth was slightly open. His breathing was deep and smooth. He looked softer asleep, younger. I fetched a blanket and spread it over him.

Through a veil of sleep Eileen became aware of the pattering of the rain on the window. The sound was reassuring; it made her feel warm and safe in her bed. But no – that wasn't the rain. It was a tapping on her bedroom door. Owen! She'd left him sleeping on the couch, covered with a blanket, a cushion propped behind his head. Blindly, she reached out to switch the lamp on and rubbed her eyes.

Now his voice. 'Meg, are you awake?'

'I am now,' she yawned, and peered sleepily at her alarm clock. It was just after four.

'Can I come in?'

Oh, God. This could be it! She'd never imagined it could happen so soon. She'd barely had a chance to prepare herself. She felt her heart thud with fear, and remembered Fran's words on the train: *Nobody expects you to do anything you don't feel comfortable with*. She struggled to order her thoughts. If only she wasn't so tired . . .

'Meg?'

'What do you want?'

'Oh, I'm sorry. I'll just go. It's been really kind of you to—'

'Come in, Owen.' She could hear the nervousness in her voice.

Slowly, the door opened. He came into the room and stood awkwardly, shifting from foot to foot and twisting his hands around each other. Tufts of his hair were sticking out and standing on end where he'd been sleeping on it.

If you change your mind and decide to back out, it won't matter.

'I'm sorry I woke you up.'

'It's OK. What do you want?'

'Oh God, I'm sorry.' And he stared down at his feet.

He was so much more scared than she was – the realisation calmed her. 'Owen, what's wrong? Do you want to talk?' She patted the bed. 'Come and sit down.'

He perched on the edge of the bed, almost but not quite sitting on her feet. He looked shame-faced, like a penitent schoolboy.

She waited for him to explain himself.

'I don't know what I'm doing here,' he said, at length. 'I woke up in your living room. You'd put a blanket over me.' He sounded choked, as though on the verge of tears. 'I thought I'd better go home, but then . . .'

'Yes?'

'I just knocked. I wanted to speak to you, but God knows what I wanted to say.' He sat silent for a moment, playing with his fingers. 'I wanted some warmth,' he said, at last. 'That's all. You're a warm sort of person, Meg. Don't you need some warmth . . . sometimes?'

'Sure. Doesn't everyone?' She was looking at his face, at the effort this was taking. His continued unease was making her feel more confident. Maybe she should make it easy for him.

'Night is lonely,' he said. 'Often I get up and work. Stupid thing is, I used to work in the nights when I was with Annie – to get away from her, to be on my own. Now I do it for company – the art keeps me company.'

'I know what you mean,' said Eileen softly, and drew back the duvet.

He looked away, embarrassed, and she worried that she'd done the wrong thing, pushed him before he was ready. He glanced up, and seemed reassured to see she wasn't naked. She was sure he was blushing, though it was impossible to tell in the weak orange light. Was she blushing too?

'I'm not trying to sleep with you,' he stammered.

'I know.' Then what the hell *was* he doing?

'At least, I suppose I *am* trying to sleep with you, but *sleep* – not . . . you know, anything *else*.'

So that was it – one of *those* things. He didn't have the guts to admit what he really wanted. 'Sure. I'd like that.' She moved over to make room for him.

Still fully clothed in his jeans and T-shirt, he moved forward and extended his stiff body onto the bed. Was he shaking? It was only a single bed, so they had to lie very close. She was surprised when he curled onto his side, facing away from her. 'Thank you,' he said.

For what? She had an idea. 'Do you like to lie in spoons?'

'Yes, of course, but—'

She reached out to switch off the lamp, and then curled herself around him, pushing her knees up under his, her breasts up against his back. It wasn't so difficult. Carefully, slowly so as not to alarm him, she put her arm around his waist. He flinched slightly and then relaxed. It was as though his whole body gave a sigh. She let her arm lie there. Nothing more.

'Did you lie like this with Annie?' she whispered.

'No. She couldn't sleep like that. She always had to roll away at some point.'

I wouldn't want to do what you're going to do. That's all. Not for Jason, not for anyone.

'I like to sleep like this,' she said.

'Me too.'

She waited, expecting him to pull her hand down onto his penis, but he didn't. She couldn't quite believe that he could lie there so close to her, touching her, and do nothing more. The anticipation was terrible. *Come on,* she thought. *Come on, let's get it over with.* Still nothing. Maybe he didn't fancy her. This lack of action was excruciating – she wanted the job done. The fear was returning. She thought about how it would feel if his hands began to move over her body. She was trembling now, her breath tense and shallow. Perhaps she should make a move on him? But that might blow everything. That infuriating vulnerability of his! Little boy lost.

As the minutes passed, she began to realise that nothing was going to happen. First she was annoyed, and then the relief swept over her. She began to relax, even to enjoy his warmth, his nearness. The curtains were slightly open, and soft moonlight was glowing through the crack, comforting, soothing. She fell asleep still holding him.

'Hi, darling. I hope you don't mind me calling so late.'

'Samantha . . . No, of course not, babe. How are you?'

'I'm missing you *so* badly. I'm lying here all alone, thinking about you.'

'Yeah? Me too.'

'I can't sleep. I'm on call tonight and I'm too edgy to relax. My bleeper could go off any minute.'

'Poor honey. I don't know how you do it.'

'Nor do I, sometimes . . . Robbie, when am I going to see you?'

'I don't know. Soon. You know how it is. I can't get away yet. There's too much going on with this project.'

'Not even for a weekend?'

'Well . . .'

'I could come down to Cardiff, if you like.'

'I don't know if that's a good—'

'I have to *see* you, Robbie. I'm free this weekend.'

'It's difficult, Samantha.'

'Oh, *hang* difficult! You should be here . . . with *me*. You said you would be. This was supposed to be *easy*. No games, no stress. You *promised*, Robbie. You said you'd be my friend.'

'And now I'm your lover.'

'Yes!'

'Love is more complicated, Samantha. You of all people should know that.'

'I know it isn't love that's taken you away from me. It's business.'

'And you know how important this project is to me.'

'How important am *I* to you, Robbie?'

'OK, look, I'll try and get up to Manchester at the weekend . . .'

'Yes!'

'It's not definite, Samantha, but I'll do my best.'

'I understand.'

'What are you wearing?'

'I'm naked.'

'Naked . . . mm, that's nice. What are you doing?'

'I'm touching myself.'

'Where?'

'*You* know.'

'Say it.'

'I'm touching my clit, touching my cunt.'

'Are you wet?'

'Oh, so wet, babe. Are you hard?'

'You bet.'

'What is it? Is that a voice I can hear?'

'No, it's just the TV. Look, the battery's going on my phone. I'd better say goodbye.'

'Oh, darling, I love you. Please come this weekend. You will, won't you?'

'I love you too. I'll try. Bye.'

'Bye, Robbie.'

'Oo, yeah, babe. *Say* it. Are you wet? I love you too,' mimicked Fran as she came into the bedroom in her kimono wrap, towelling her hair. 'Bloody gigolo!'

'Give me a break, will you.' Jason laid his mobile down on the bedside table and stretched back against the pillows.

Fran sat down at the dressing table and started running a brush through her hair. 'Did I hear you promise her you'd go to Manchester this weekend?'

Jason stared out of the window at the rain. 'I told her I'd try.'

'You don't have time for this any more, Jason. We've too much to do. Drop it.'

'I know. I'm going to. It's just—'

'What?' She swizzled around on her stool.

What, indeed. Why was he so reluctant to let this one go? 'Look, she's a nice girl, OK? I want to find a way of letting her down gently.'

Fran raised her eyebrows. 'Bothered for her finer feelings, are you, darling?'

How could he get Fran off this subject? 'You don't know this girl. She's different. She's nice. I don't want to hurt her more than I have to.'

Fran picked up the brush again and worked it through her hair with strong, even strokes. Jason could hear it scraping against her scalp. 'What is the matter with you, Jason? You've been through enough *nice* girls, God knows how many. You're not even working this one for the money any more. We've got business to do. She's a total waste of time.'

Jason nodded. The less said about the money the better. 'Don't worry,' he said. 'I'll sort it.'

'Good.' Satisfied, she laid down the brush and reached for her bottle of cleansing lotion.

Fran was acting clingy, not at all normal for her. Maybe it was the house that did it – the fitted wardrobes, pine kitchen, waste disposal unit, three piece suite, sloping drive, garage . . . a modern suburban family house in one of those streets where people wash their cars on Sunday afternoons. If they stayed too long in this place there was a danger that she might evolve into a suburban wife who bothers what the neighbours think, reads the leaflets that drop through the letter box about neighbourhood watch and car boot sales and the cat missing from number 13, gets involved in charity committees . . . Jason shuddered.

'After all,' Fran was saying, 'we have Tony Meredith to cope with. I knew he was going to be trouble.'

'Leave that to Eileen,' said Jason, brightening. 'She'll have that under control in no time.'

'Will she?' Fran reached for her moisturiser. 'You're pretty confident.'

'Yes, I am.' And he realised he was. 'Eileen knows this is her chance to prove she can cut it. She won't let us down. Come to bed, babes, we've got a long day ahead tomorrow.'

Fran smiled and screwed the lid onto the jar of moisturiser. She slipped the gown off her shoulders and walked across to the bed, standing a while to let Jason admire her before pulling back the duvet and getting in.

'You will sort out that other little thing, won't you, honey?' she whispered in his ear as she reached to turn off the lamp.

Have you ever been worried for your soul? I believe in the soul as some sort of essence of the self that hides inside you and makes you the person you are. I wish I could believe in heaven and hell too but they seem a little too convenient to me – conceived to keep the simple-minded on the straight and narrow just as we might tell a child that it won't get any ice-cream unless it shuts up and eats its dinner. But I do believe in the soul.

There's an ache in me today – it hurts when I speak and when I move, even when I breathe. I've tried to pinpoint it but I can't quite. One moment it seems to be in my chest somewhere under the diaphragm, the next it's hiding in my stomach, jabbing at my womb or pulsing in my eyelashes. I don't think it's real at all in the physical–medical sense. I think it's my soul registering its protest at what I'm doing.

I've been a thief, a swindler, a cheat and more. But I've never been a whore, and that feels to me like a worse thing to be. Now I'm going to become one. And more awful than that, I'm not even plying an honest trade like the girls on the street. I'm going to prostitute myself to the con.

How naive I've been, playing house in my cute little flat, putting the job to the back of my mind, assuming somehow that it would all just 'happen' and then I'd be off with my share of the money for a break in the sun and a life of luxury. WRONG.

Last night I lay in my bed curled around a man I do not find remotely attractive – actually *hoping* that he would make a move on me, bracing myself for it like you do when the dentist approaches with his whining drill. Starting to tell myself, *This won't be so terrible. He doesn't have bad breath or BO, it isn't as though he's repulsive. Think of the money* – and then being horrified that I could actually think like that. And finally the absurd relief when it didn't happen. A temporary reprieve for my nagging twisting soul.

And maybe I've blown it. I coaxed Owen into my bed before he was ready. He was out of bed by six, fumbling about for his socks with shaky hands, stammering that he had to get home to work. He wouldn't even stay for a cup of coffee. He's ashamed of himself, that much is clear. He thinks he's taken advantage of me by getting into my bed. He's embarrassed. I can understand his thinking. In a way it's worse than if we had fucked. Using somebody for sex is normal – it's accepted that we all have physical needs and desires that need to be satiated. But to use someone for warmth and comfort? – to get into bed with someone you've only just met for a mere cuddle? That's plain weird.

All morning I've been dragging myself listlessly around the shop, trying to resist the urge to phone Fran and Jason, and only half listening to Eddie the owner talking mournfully and incessantly about his partner Julian (currently out walking their snappy little Scottie dog) who he thinks is giving him the run-around again. (I think he's right about Julian, but I can't say that to him.) I'm putting on my best sympathetic expression for Eddie and uttering the occasional caring word, but deep in my gut my soul is jabbing and needling me and inside my head the questions are buzzing around. *Should I wait to see if he contacts me again? How long should I leave it? Should I seek him out? ... How can I rescue this situation?*

The day was bright blue and clear. It was one of those summer mornings when there's something in the air that lifts you, makes you feel alive. That was how Jason felt, full of the thrill of living, ready to face this challenge. He sat in the back of Keith's Saab peering out at Cardiff, while in front Fran was lighting her first cigarette of the day, coughing as she always did in the mornings. Keith opened a window.

They were heading out of town, through industrial estates, under bridges.

'Look at that bloke.' Keith pointed and Jason saw a man at the side of the road pushing a huge silver ball.

'Jesus!'

Keith cracked up, laughing. 'Gets 'em every time,' he said. It was just a statue.

'This place is full of sculpture,' said Keith. 'It's all supposed to represent stuff, you know. The past and the present of the docks. A bunch of arty bullshit if you ask me.'

He was more chatty than Jason would have expected.

'I grew up round here,' he said. 'Down in Tiger Bay.'

'Why's it called Tiger Bay?' Fran asked, blowing smoke out.

'People don't call it that so much now.' Keith turned a corner. 'At one time it was a real melting pot round here. Multi-cultural, know what I mean? Blacks, whites, Hispanics, Indians, the works. And they all blended somehow. We didn't used to have no trouble. Not like these days. Outsiders thought it was as rough as fuck down here. Full of whores and murderers. But we looked after our own, see?'

Crazy structures were coming into view. Concept buildings that resembled ships; sharp angles and roofs shaped like waves.

'There was a song they used to sing down the old drinking halls and pubs,' Keith continued. 'A song called Tiger Bay.'

In between the mad structures were large expanses of waste ground. Then clusters of old buildings made from brown and grey weather-beaten stone – the old pay offices from the glory days of the docks. Many of them derelict.

'This place used to be full to bursting with people. Not empty like it is now,' said Keith. 'My old dad can't bear to come down here no more. He can't stand the silence. Time was you'd be deafened of a morning by the sound of boots on stone – all the men tramping down to the docks from town looking for casual work – whole bloody armies of them, there was.'

They swung around onto Atlantic Wharf. Another of the ship-buildings loomed large among Barcelona-esque mosaics, curls and spirals. A small white church sat at the head of the bay, forlorn and out of place.

'That's the Norwegian Church,' Keith announced as though that explained everything. 'They moved it here.'

'Who did?' asked Jason.

'Cardiff Bay Development Corporation. They're redoing the whole place – building a barrage so they can have a big yachting marina. That upset the local greens – birds on the mudflats, that kind of thing. There's a new multi-plex over there, and a Harry Ramsden's. Great chips.'

'Funny, I didn't realise Cardiff was on the coast,' mused Fran.

Keith darted her a fierce look. 'This was the biggest and busiest dock in Europe at one time.'

He pulled over and parked on a patch of waste ground. The wind was blowing strongly across the bay as they got out of the car, taking them by surprise – it was so calm in town.

'There's another story about Tiger Bay,' said Keith, locking the car. 'Portuguese seamen used to say that the water was so rough as they sailed along the Severn Estuary and into Cardiff docks that it was like sailing into a bay of tigers.'

Fran raised an eyebrow.

'Well, what do you reckon?' Keith turned and gestured. 'This is it.'

It was a lumbering Victorian giant of a building, sad with age and disuse, moss growing out of the walls, windows boarded up, broken slates littering the ground around it. But it held a hint of faded grandeur – there was energy in the vibrant red brickwork.

Jason was taken aback by the sheer size of it. Why hadn't Meredith sold this place off years ago? The land alone must be worth a packet. 'It's fantastic. Let's go inside.' He looked at Fran to see what she thought, but she was busy pulling chewing gum off the sole of her shoe. Gulls were swooping and calling above and Keith swore as the keys jingled and slipped between his big fingers.

'Here, let me,' said Fran, and he was only too glad to allow her to gently remove the keys from his grasp. The first key she tried shifted stiffly in the padlock and then clunked as Fran turned it the whole way.

'That's fate,' said Jason, looking admiringly at her. She smiled at him – with her eyes as well as her mouth, and he knew everything would be all right.

I was too busy to notice the bell over the shop door ring – too busy counting packets of carob-coated biscuits, wrestling with my internal dilemmas and trying to listen to Eddie who was spooning vile horehound tea into a glass jar and saying,

'I should have upped and run the first time I saw Julian's toes. How can you trust a man with webbed feet? Half man half duck, that's what he is.'

Imagine my surprise when I looked up and saw Owen standing in front of me. Imagine *his* surprise – I hadn't told him I worked at Energy. He'd only come in for a jar of bouillon powder and a box of vegetarian schnitzel. Poor sod, he blushed bright red and started stammering and looking at his feet. Eddie was perceptive enough to see he should make a tactical withdrawal to the store room.

I decided to adopt the 'pretend it never happened' tactic, and began chatting to him in as normal a way as possible, making no reference to our little snuggle-session in my bed. But then, suddenly, Owen seemed to recover himself. With a deep gulp that sent his prominent Adam's apple bobbing up and down, he reached out and took my hands in his.

'Meg,' he whispered. 'You've no idea what last night meant to me.'

He was right – I had no idea.

'You're such a nice person,' he continued. 'So open and giving. So different from ...'

I put a finger up to his lips to hush him up and stop him from saying her name. He smiled and let go my hands, fiddled with his box of schnitzel.

'I have to go somewhere tonight,' he said, looking up again. 'It's a really important business thing. I have to meet up with some people down in the docks, make a visit to this place ...' He trailed off.

I could feel the excitement building inside me. It gripped my nagging soul in a strangle-hold and squeezed. I waited for him to continue.

'Thing is, these two people want me to go into business with them. It could be exciting; it might even be the thing that *makes* me, but I have some doubts – I'm a lousy judge of character.'

'Why are you telling me this?'

He took a deep breath. 'I don't think it's just coincidence that I've run into you today, Meg. I think it's a sign. I want you to come with me tonight. I want you to tell me whether you think I can trust these people.'

I felt weak. I gripped the edge of the counter. 'Owen, why me? If this thing is so important, you should decide for yourself. I'm no psychic.'

'You've got good instincts. You noticed something was wrong with Tara last night, something I couldn't see for myself. Please, Meg. Please do this for me.'

'Well ... OK then.'

Poor sucker.

Owen picked me up from work in his knackered Volvo stacked high with junk; pieces of metal and plastic, sheets of perspex, blow-torches and tins of house paint. He was nervous – so was I. On the way he told me about Robbie Warren, the 'brilliant spiv' who'd walked into his exhibition in Manchester and who was promising to make him famous through this crazy scheme for a restaurant full of his art. He told me about Marsha Freeman, Robbie's partner in business 'and in other things too, I suspect', the clever cold woman whose role was clearly to make sure Robbie kept his feet on the ground, but who was ostensibly the 'finance expert'. She had apparently already got together a consortium of investors to put up the money.

'The thing I can't work out,' said Owen, keeping his eyes on the road, 'is why they want to do this for *me*. There must be thousands of artists out there more bankable than I am. And yet I get the sense that I'm the first person they've approached. It makes me uneasy.'

He talked fast, the words falling over each other in their eagerness to escape from his mouth. He seemed to leap from thought to disparate thought without realising that there was no continuity in what he was saying. It was hard to keep up – like listening to a verbal version of the junk in the back of his car. It was touchingly honest, though. I'd never met anyone so direct.

And then we were driving into Cardiff Bay, and I was struck first by the sadness of the old buildings, an endangered species scattered along the redeveloped landscape like dying flowers whose heads are about to be snipped off and thrown away.

'What's wrong?' asked Owen.

'Nothing. I'm just thinking.'

We pulled over next to a nearly new blue Mercedes. Jason had been shopping. The sight of the car cheered me.

The building was so *red*. Walking into that dark doorway was like entering a huge cavernous mouth. Inside I could smell rotting vegetable matter and pigeon-shit. The birds themselves flapped about uselessly among the eaves of a much perforated roof. The smell of decay seemed to emanate from a stack of ageing crates. The whole place was derelict, the beams creaking and groaning in the wind. It was so rackety, I wondered if we should be wearing hard hats. Was that a rat scurrying across the floor as we came in?

'Darling!' Fran walked in behind us, picking her way over the rubble in her stilettos, narrowly avoiding a deep puddle and air-kissing Owen on both cheeks.

I glimpsed her quickly concealed delight at seeing me here with him. She asked to be introduced.

'This is my friend, Meg. I asked her to come along. Hope you don't mind. This is Marsha.'

'Isn't it just fabulous!' Jason bounded in and grabbed Owen by the shoulders. 'Guess what this place used to be. Go on, guess!'

Owen was puzzled. 'Didn't you say it was a warehouse?'

'*Before* it was a warehouse,' said Jason, impatiently.

I gazed around at the broken chairs, the heap of old blankets – tramps? – at the curious raised platform at one end. Was that the remains of a staircase leading up to what must once have been a sort of balcony ...

'*Come* on. Guess!'

'A fire station,' I said to appease him. 'A workhouse ... A hospital ...'

Owen had bent down and was throwing pieces of wood aside, clearing a space, *rubbing* at the floor.

'What do you think, Owen?' asked Fran.

Owen was smiling when he looked up. His cheeks were smeared with dirt. 'This is a proper sprung floor,' he said. 'It's an old dance hall, isn't it?'

And now I could see it – the band playing on the stage at the far end, the couples whirling around and strutting their stuff. The brightly coloured dresses, the laughter ...

Owen stood up and brushed himself down. 'This place is going to be perfect, just perfect.' He pointed up to the broken old balcony. 'I want to put a massive sculpture up there – a woman with her arms outstretched – a freedom statue towering over the restaurant, looking down on everyone.' He turned to me. 'This is right, isn't it, Meg? This is going to work.'

'Yes, Owen.'

We toasted the restaurant with champagne in a nearby wine bar. Jason was overflowing with ideas. He was an entirely different person from the languid moper who sat around in Andrea Foster's Didsbury flat strumming guitar and staring into space.

'... We're going to call the restaurant "The Melt", which refers both to Owen's art and also to the history of the area – a multi-racial *melting* pot. We could serve food from a whole range of cultures – maybe even vary it for each evening – Italian night, Creole night, Jamaican night – have a different chef for each day of the week. Then we could have Melting night – all the food has a *melting* theme to it: dishes of chilli with thick sour cream running over it, hunks of meat oozing with molten cheese, ice cream covered in thick chocolate sauce ...'

Owen was joining in too, animated and energised: 'We could restore some of the dance hall feel to the place. I could create some dancing figures that would hark back to the old days. Maybe we could get jazz bands in to play on the stage ...'

Listening to them talk, it made me feel sad that this restaurant was destined never to exist.

I caught up with Fran in the toilets. She looked happier than I'd seen her in a long time. She told me about their visit to Tony Meredith, and about the money. She hugged me tight and we laughed until my mind was spinning with champagne and dancing couples and whirling pound signs.

After we'd emptied a third bottle of champagne, Owen drove me over to his house for dinner, 'to say thank you'. It was a friendly house not far from my flat, painted out in bright yellow and blue. I wondered if Annie had chosen the colours. I sat at the big pine table in his kitchen and watched him chopping onions, garlic and mushrooms and throwing them in a big pot with some minced beef. There were two mugs on a shelf, one with an 'O' on it, the other with an 'A'.

'I'm not much of a cook,' Owen said apologetically, 'but I do make a mean spaghetti bolognese.'

It smelled good, bubbling away on the stove. I thought back to the bolognese my father used to make – when he was sober enough to cook. Those had been the best times; my mother interfering playfully and Dad shooing her off with a wooden spoon. She would laugh at his absurd appearance in her frilly apron and he would chase her around the kitchen pretending to be a monster. Funny to think what a thin line separates games and reality.

'So did your mother teach you to cook?' I asked.

'Nah.' He opened a bottle of red wine and slopped some into the pot. 'Taught myself. You either learn how or get stuck with a life of take-away.' He fetched two glasses from a cupboard and filled them, passing one over. 'My mum didn't think her little boy should have to do *women's* work.' He turned back to his cooking, taking jars of dried oregano, basil and bay leaves from a shelf.

This was interesting. 'Quite a traditional family, then?'

He gave a kind of snort. 'My mum was doing all she could to give me and my sister some kind of normality. Would you pass the black pepper?'

I handed the large wooden peppermill over. 'So what was so unusual about your family?'

He looked surprised. 'You don't know about my father?'

'Should I?'

He took a sip of his wine. 'Tony Meredith – consummate game-player and professional bastard.'

I tried not to get too excited. 'Why ... what does he do?'

He grabbed his wooden spoon and stirred energetically. 'What *doesn't* he do? In the name of profit, advancement, wealth?'

I was hoping he'd say more, but he changed the subject. I let it go – not wanting to push too hard at this early stage.

He talked about the restaurant, about what it could do for him – how tonight, for the first time, he had begun to believe in it as something that was really going to happen.

While he was dishing up, I noticed a beeswax candle on a shelf in the corner and brought it down. 'Shall we?'

He hesitated, and I realised this must be a candle that he and Annie had lit many times before for romantic meals. But then he pulled himself together and delved in a drawer for matches.

The food was good – wholesome and *real*. I was surprised at my own hunger. I tried to remember through my sozzled state to be Meg. I told Owen that this was really special – that I'd never had a man cook dinner for me before. He seemed amazed at this, and started asking me questions about myself.

'I move around a lot. Can't seem to settle. Truth is I don't really know what to do with my life. I always have it in mind that one day I will arrive somewhere and suddenly everything will make sense; I'll know what to do – I'll be home.'

Owen had taken a large mouthful. He took a minute to chew and swallow. 'I don't think you'll ever feel at home anywhere without working at it,' he said. 'What are you running from?'

Good question.

'Meg.' Owen laid down his cutlery and looked at me intently. 'How would you feel about posing for me?'

'What?'

'The statue for the restaurant – it's about freedom, and it's also about good fortune, a bit like a contemporary version of a ship's figurehead.'

I felt hot, flushy. Owen's cooking?

'I want to base the statue on you, Meg.'

The attic-studio was full of dust. Chalk dust, charcoal dust, pastel dust, the dust from dried crumbling paint. And life dust too. Wire maquettes stood about on tables, chatted to each other on the window sill, danced on shelves, crowded and queued on top of the old filing cabinet, and lay crumpled and mangled in the waste basket like dead bodies stacked up for transportation after a battle. The room was full of surfaces that hid under clutter. Tables covered in old rags, battered tubes of paint, pencils, sketchpads, plates of biscuit crumbs and glasses of murky water with the paint brushes still standing in them, left to rust. Shelves of books of art history, sculpture, biographies of renowned artists and artists nobody has ever heard of, books on psychoanalysis by Freud and Jung, books on geology and natural history. And bizarrely a couple of dog-eared Jilly Coopers – Annie's?

Eileen walked across the paint-spattered floorboards – were they white under all the splatters and splodges or was the white merely another of the colours that had been spilled or thrown across the room?

'When you're famous you could pull up your floorboards and sell them off individually.' She heard the slur in her voice from all that champagne and cheap Chianti. 'You'd make a packet.' She smelled white spirit, paint fumes and stale air beneath it all. 'Can we open a window?'

Owen was clipping large sheets of paper to an easel and searching around for intact charcoal sticks. 'Sure. Go ahead.'

She heaved at the old sash window and it shifted grudgingly with a whine. Her hands were smeared with dirt and she wiped them on her jeans. 'Where are the sculptures?'

'I hire a studio in town. This place is too small for that.'

'Oh.'

'You can undress behind the screen.' Without looking up, he indicated a murky yellow hinged screen in the corner – a wooden frame with shiny stained material stretched across it.

Eileen obediently went behind it. What was the point in such modesty when she was about to show him everything she had anyway? Weird.

'You like Keith Jarrett?' he called out.

'Yeah, sure.' Who?

She heard the click of a tape machine, and the room was filled with intricate, babbling jazz-piano.

She fumbled with the zip of her jeans. Her stomach felt fat and bloated. Why, oh why had she eaten so much? Oh, God.

'Do you have any more wine?'

'Sorry, no. We finished the last bottle,' came his voice.

Damn!

As she stepped out from behind the screen, Eileen caught sight of her naked reflection in a piece of jagged broken mirror leaning against a wall. She didn't look so bad.

'What do you want me to do?' Goosepimples were breaking out on her arms. She rubbed them briskly.

'You could just stand over there.' Owen gestured at a well-lit corner with an old wooden rocking-chair and a dead plant.

He was professional, officious even. Didn't he care that she was *naked*? Did it have no effect on him at all? As she crossed the room to stand in the corner, one hand on hip, she began to worry that this was a miscalculation. He was seeing her body as a work-tool, not as a body. What could she do about this?

'Do you think you could manage some lightning poses?' asked Owen, charcoal stick at the ready. 'Is something wrong?'

'No, I'm fine.'

'I do appreciate this, Meg,' he said, with a look of gratitude. 'I know it's a bit of an imposition but well, you know, seize the day and all that.'

'Yes.' Her voice was flat.

She stood with one foot on the rocking-chair, she sat cross-legged, she bent like a weeping willow, she got down on one knee as though she was about to propose, she even stood on one leg briefly. And all the time she was thinking about how different he was from the shy boy of the previous night who stood awkwardly in her bedroom and lay stiffly on her bed. Tonight he was the artist and she the model. How typically male of him to be able to compartmentalise his life in this way.

'You're a natural,' he said. 'You could pose for my class. The money's not good but . . .' He trailed off. Perhaps he had remembered Tara lying on the floor with her robe gaping open.

The longer poses were more difficult. Even the simplest seated position was hard to sustain. Eileen felt as though her back had frozen up. Her arms and legs ached terribly and she had an itch at the base of her neck. But she was determined to conquer this.

'Let's take a break,' said Owen.

'No. I'm just getting into this.' Without stopping even to take a look at his sketch, Eileen got down on the floor on her hands and knees, turning side on to Owen and twisting her head to look at him.

'It'll be tough to hold that,' he said.

'Get on with it.' She arched her back, knowing he would like the curve, the way her breasts hung down. In the background Keith Jarrett played on, softly, gently. Owen bit hard on his lower lip as he clipped another sheet of paper to his easel.

By the time he'd finished the sketch, Eileen wasn't even feeling the aches and pains any more. 'Let's do another.'

'No, that's enough,' said Owen. 'You must be knackered. It's getting late.'

Eileen was disappointed. She had achieved nothing. But then she rallied. The moon was full and glowing through the dirty window pane, and she felt as though she were drawing energy from it.

Owen looked up from his work and saw she was standing tall, arms outstretched, head thrown back. It was the pose for the restaurant statue. It was perfect.

'Hold that. Don't move a muscle!' He scrabbled about for a clean sheet of paper.

She thought she could hear lust in his voice. He bit his lip so hard he drew blood, and began to sketch frenziedly.

'I want you,' she said quietly, almost without thinking. But he was so wrapped up in his work that he made no response.

'I want you,' she said again, more loudly, after another few minutes had passed.

'I know. I heard you the first time.' He didn't look up.

She was baffled. Surely he fancied her? He'd been practically drooling over her all evening. Was it because of this damned posing? Had she effectively neutered herself in his eyes? 'I don't understand,' she said eventually.

'What's there to understand?'

This was exasperating. 'Don't you want *me*?' Her voice seemed to echo around the white-washed walls, float in the jam jars on the murky water, creak in the wooden rocking chair. She could hear her words in the scraping of his charcoal on the paper.

He sighed. 'It's not a question of whether or not I want

you. It's . . .' He trailed off, but he may as well have said the name, *Annie*.

She could feel her anger building. His bloody ex was not here now. She was not going to let this go. It *had* to happen.

He was done. He threw his charcoal down and moved to a sink across the room, his back to her. He ran cold water over his hands.

Slowly, she let her arms fall to her sides and went to take a peep at the sketch while trying to think of what to do. It was a good likeness. There was a kind of grace to it. If only she could get him to see her as a woman again instead of a series of lines, angles and curves.

She sat down in the chair and began to rock gently. 'Last year I went on holiday to Portugal. I found this secluded little bay. You had to scramble down a cliff face to get to it – I thought I was going to fall . . . It was beautiful down there – golden sands, blue sea.' She glanced back at him – he was still facing away from her, drying his hands on a grubby towel.

'There were only a few people down there. They were naked – all of them. I'd never been naked in public before. It was really weird, exposing those parts of yourself that are always covered and being entirely unselfconscious about it. Just lying there in the sun along with everybody else – pretending it was normal. It was like all the taboos were gone, melting away.'

He was leaning on the sink now, his back still turned to her.

'It was erotic, feeling the breeze play over my body . . . Afterwards, I realised the taboos weren't gone at all – it was just that the boundaries on that beach were different. You could be naked, but God forbid that you were *sexual*. In that bay we were all pretending that we had no sexuality – we may as well have been fully dressed.'

Still he refused to look around.

'You know, one of my favourite fantasies now is about the breaking of that taboo.' She got to her feet and took a step towards him. 'I'm back on that beach, naked, but instead of just lying there in the sun, I walk across to where a man is relaxing in the shade, watching me.' She took another step. Her heart was beating in her mouth. 'And as I get closer I see he's hard for me. I reach out—'

And suddenly he turned to look at her, and in his face she saw the shy boy of last night, and the hunger. She took his face in her hands and kissed him full on the mouth. He pulled away, stood staring at her like a frightened child. She kissed him again and put her arms around his neck, pressed her body against his, and felt him begin to relax. When he broke free again it was to speak.

'You kiss with one eye open and one eye closed,' he said. 'It's as though part of you is enjoying yourself and the other part is watching, checking on things.'

'Sorry,' she said.

'No. It's nice.' He touched her breasts, and bent to kiss them. Then he worked his way down to her cunt, reaching his arms around her waist to pull her closer to him. She cradled his head in her hands, holding him there.

'I'll be getting off now, Mr Warren, if that's OK.'

'What?' Jason jolted out of his day-dream to see Emily the secretary smiling and dimpling at him around the office door.

'I just said I'll be off now, if that's all right with you.'

He looked down at his watch – 6.45. Jesus! 'Emily, I'm so sorry. I completely lost track of time. What must you be thinking of me! In future, remember that your day finishes at 5.30. There's no need for you to stay a minute longer, is that clear?'

'Oh yes, Mr Warren. I don't mind though. Honestly.' She blushed. Such a sweet girl in that cute little dress.

'Excellent first day, Emily.'

'Thank you, Mr Warren. See you tomorrow.'

Alone again, Jason reflected that the first week in their new Cardiff Bay offices had been a roaring success. He opened his wallet and fingered the notes inside. Six crisp smooth fifties, new and pristine, shiny; five twenties, a little smaller but equally satisfying, a slight sheen illuminating the queen's face; five tens – a humble note but nevertheless the most versatile of all.

How Jason loved money – not just its buying power but the money itself. When he held a paper note in his hands he felt he was holding something artfully designed, carefully crafted, and what a history . . . As a child he had been fascinated with the metallic strips buried inside them, and had even teased the strips out of one pound notes only to become saddened that he had destroyed them. When he reached his teenage it was the watermark that held his attention – that magic picture hidden in the design, visible only when you held it up to the light. Now, in his thirties, it made him melancholy to handle grubby, torn, crumpled old tens and twenties, to be aware of their slow disintegration. When notes became old, they lost their marvellous texture, their showiness. It was hard to accept that they still had value. But *these* notes . . . he gave a little sigh . . . These were perhaps the nicest notes he had ever held in his two hands, straight from the coffers of Tony Meredith, part of that wondrous first half million which had come through this very day.

He supposed he'd better get going if he wasn't to be late meeting Fran. She'd been out of the office all day but they were having a celebratory dinner at Bernelli's in town. And he had a bit of a surprise for her.

'I thought the veal was rather average.' Jason slurped from his wine glass. 'How was the wild boar sausage?'

'Boring,' said Fran, smiling. 'When am I going to learn that bangers and mash is just bangers and mash when all's said and done? Shall we have some more wine?'

'I should say so.' He gestured to the waiter and then reached across the table to stroke her hand.

She found him pretty when drunk. He didn't go red and sweaty like many men. He just smiled a lot and his pupils dilated rather sweetly.

'I do love you, you know, Jason.'

'Franny babes. I never doubted it for a moment.'

The waiter brought the wine and uncorked it. 'Would sir like to order any dessert or coffee?' They were the only customers left in the whole place.

'Not yet,' said Jason. 'Maybe in a bit.'

The waiter retreated with a resigned look.

Jason leaned forward. 'I've been thinking—'

'Be careful!'

'Cheeky bitch!' He slapped her hand playfully. 'I've been thinking about what we'll do. You know . . . when it's all over . . . after the third half million comes through.'

'Oh yes?' They were probably too drunk to be having this conversation.

'And I've worked it all out.' He almost elbowed the bottle of wine over as he started searching about in his inside jacket pockets. His wallet fell on the floor and when he bent down to pick it up he hit his head on the table. Fran felt the urge to laugh but suppressed it, not wanting to hurt his feelings.

The smile slipped from her face when he finally produced a small box.

'No, Jason.' It was one of those instantly sobering moments.

'But you haven't even looked at it.'

'I don't need to. I know what it is.' She pushed it away.

'Please look. I took ages over choosing it.'

Now she did laugh, but it was a laugh without humour. 'Your vanity is astounding. You're not even bothered about whether I say yes or no. You just want me to admire the bloody ring!'

'That's not true.' Were those really tears in his eyes? 'You're like a goddess to me, Fran. I couldn't stand to lose you.'

The anger ebbed away. 'You silly boy. You're not going to lose me.'

'Then why won't you marry me, you cow?' He banged his fist on the table and the cutlery jumped and tinkled. He was shouting, slurring. 'Do you think you're too good for me? Are you turned off at the idea of some thick fucking dyslexic fathering your kids?'

Fran smiled at the anxious head waiter in an attempt to reassure him.

'And now you're embarrassed of me too. Stuck up bitch!'

'Shut up, Jason, for God's sake.' To appease him, Fran reached for the box and opened it. It was a large ruby surrounded by tiny diamonds. Large enough to be called vulgar.

'What do you think of it?'

'I think I need a fag.' She groped about in her bag for the pack of Marlboro and the lighter.

'It was the first thing I wanted to do when the money came through.' His eyes were desperate. 'It was the only thing I could think about.'

Fran drew deeply on her cigarette, trying not to let her face show how tempted she was. 'Jason. Honey . . . It wouldn't work. You know that. You *must* know that.'

'I know no such thing!'

She took his hand again, gently. 'Listen to me, sweetie. We've got a good thing going, you and me—'

'And it could be even better.'

She squeezed the hand. 'Let me finish. We've got a good thing going, and it works – just the way it is. You get to sleep with other women because it's part of the job.'

'But I don't *want* to sleep with other women.'

'Jason, I know you. You aren't cut out for marriage. You'd be miserable as hell playing the monogamous husband.'

'No, I wouldn't.' His voice was rising again and she hushed him gently, raising a finger to her lips.

'You'd never manage it, sweetie. You'd be off with the first tart who flashed her tits at you.' The next bit was difficult to say but she had to say it. The tears were fighting their way through and it took all the effort she had to push them back. 'The way things are, I can stand it. Because it's part of the job, you see? I can tell myself it isn't real. It's as though you're not really sleeping with those women. You're just acting. Understand? If I married you and we settled down and tried to play husband and wife, everything would be different. Do you see?'

Slowly she closed the box and pushed it back across the table.

Jason seemed calmer now. He sighed and put the ring back in his pocket. 'But, Fran, everything *is* different. I'm not doing any more dating scams. It's all over. When we leave Cardiff with the money, we'll be making a new start. I just want to be with you, that's all. There's only ever been you.'

Fran couldn't meet his gaze any longer without crying. She looked down at the ashtray. 'What about Eileen? What's going to happen to her when we leave Cardiff?'

Jason shrugged. 'I don't know. She probably has her own plans. She can't stay with us indefinitely, can she? Three's a tricky number. She surely doesn't think we're sticking with her for ever?'

Fran ground her cigarette into the ashtray. 'You reckon?'

* * *

Eileen was tortured awake by the bright sunlight that seemed to have got inside her eyelids. When she peeled them open everything began hurting – her head, her throat, the insides of her nostrils, and for a moment she couldn't work out where she was. The Venetian blind, the alarm clock, the dead plant, the hard futon on which she lay – nothing was familiar. Then she heard a voice talking in another room – Owen's voice. On the phone. She heard him say the name 'Robbie'. She heard him giggle.

'Please God, no,' she groaned and pulled the pillow over her face, trying to muffle the world. There was no real excuse for this memory blur – she hadn't been particularly drunk . . . or had she?

She thought about the way Owen had knelt down before her, giving her head. He had pushed her down on the hard boards of the studio floor and fucked her there and then. Jesus – had they used a condom? Yes, she remembered now. He fetched one from a drawer – fancy keeping condoms in your studio . . . maybe he wasn't such a nice boy!

The sex had actually been *great* – urgent. His tears fell on her face as he drove into her, and she let them run down her cheeks and onto her neck. Had anyone ever wanted her so much? She came hard. Later, in the bedroom, she came again as she fucked him, leaning forward to let her breasts brush against his chest – he liked that. He was a good lover. But she was more turned on by herself than by him – he was merely a means to an end – he enabled her to feel empowered. She might as well have been screwing her own reflection.

She shuddered at the memory. It was an ugly thing that she should have enjoyed playing the prostitute. She was disgusted with herself.

When she lifted the pillow, the talking had stopped. All was silent. Had Owen gone out? She was so thirsty. Clutching her head, she eased herself up on the pillows and spotted a half-full bottle of Evian by the side of the bed. She grabbed it and pulled it to her mouth, gulping. The water was unpleasantly warm but at least it was wet. She drank too fast and felt a sudden pain somewhere between her ribs and her stomach.

A soft cooing sound startled her. There was a pigeon on the

sill outside the open window and for a moment she thought it was going to fly into the room. Frightened, she let out a strangled yelp and it flapped off. As her anxious breathing slowed she began to feel foolish – fancy being afraid of a stupid pigeon! *They're flying rats,* came her mother's voice in her head. That pronouncement had terrified her as a child and caused her to have repeated nightmares in which rats really could fly and bombarded her with their sharp teeth and their nasty tails. She shook the memory away and slumped back on the pillows, exhausted.

What am I going to do now?

'Morning.' Owen was standing in the doorway, carrying a tray. On it were two glasses of orange juice, two plates of smoked salmon and scrambled egg on toast, a cafetière and two cups. The coffee smelled good.

'Oh, my!' she croaked, unable to say anything else.

He cleared space on the bedside table and put the tray down. 'You were sleeping so deeply I didn't want to wake you. You looked so peaceful.'

'How long have you been up?' asked Eileen, confused.

'Oh, a few hours. I've been doing some work. I wake early as a rule.' He busied himself pouring coffee and she sat up again, trying to prepare her stomach for the onslaught of food.

'This is really sweet of you,' she said.

'It's the least I can do.' He looked down at the tray, spooned sugar into his cup of coffee and stirred it for longer than was necessary. There was a new softness about his eyes. He was smiling shyly. 'Last night was . . .'

'Don't.' She reached out, put a hand over his mouth.

Immediately his expression turned to one of confusion.

'I just want to hold it in my head for a while,' she explained, somewhat feebly. 'Let's not talk about it yet.'

'OK. Whatever you want.' He passed her a plate of food, and perching on the edge of the bed took the other for himself. Then, hesitantly, glancing up at her, he added, 'It wasn't a one-off, though, was it? *Please* tell me it wasn't a one-off.'

'It wasn't a one-off,' she said in a heavy voice.

Cheered, he tucked into his breakfast.

And it was true. It couldn't be a one-off. There would be more of these nights, of these mornings. She had asked herself what she should do, but she already knew the answer: she had to stick around, get under his skin, be the person he thought about as he woke each day and as he fell asleep each night. She had to be the person he would confide in about why he hated his father so much.

I'm not just a whore. I'm a gatherer of dirt.

'Robbie's fixed up for some architects to come over to the site this afternoon,' he was saying.

'Aha.'

'You know, Meg.' He laid his plate down on the floor. 'I've always been an atheist, but at a time like this it's hard not to believe in fate.'

Gently he took her plate away from her, and moved closer, reached out a hand to touch her face.

'Christ, is it really quarter to twelve!' she exclaimed, catching sight of the alarm clock.

'Er, yes.'

'I have to go!' She pushed him away and jumped out of bed. 'Oh, God, where did I leave my clothes?'

'In the studio.' He was crestfallen. 'Do you really have to go now?'

'I have to be at Energy in fifteen minutes!' she snapped. 'Eddie's going to kill me.'

'I'll drive you—' he began.

'No, it's OK. But I need to get going.' She slipped out of the room and began to climb the steep stairs up to the studio.

'Meg? When will I see you again?' came his plaintive voice from below.

'In hell,' she muttered under her breath.

Owen was already at the site when Fran and Jason arrived. He was wandering slowly around the outside of the building, gazing up at the walls, at the flaking, rotten wood of the window frames, at clumps of moss and weeds growing out of the brickwork. He had a small sketchpad in his hands and was scribbling on it. He appeared to be creating a kind of visual diary, documenting the state of the building before its transformation. When Fran called out a hello to him, he didn't even acknowledge her – so lost was he in contemplation. He reached out his right hand and held it against the brickwork, moving it very gently, almost as though he was stroking a dog. Fran found this gesture slightly creepy – it made her think of the hulking red building as some sleeping animal, about to wake up. She remembered Keith's story of the Portuguese seamen sailing into a Bay of Tigers.

Getting up this morning and groping around in the kitchen with a dismal hangover, she'd begun to fret about the events of the previous night. She hadn't wanted to hurt Jason, but what else could she have done? She hoped he would understand that she wasn't rejecting *him* – it was the idea of him floundering about in a conventional marriage like a fish ripped off the hook and tossed aside to bleed and suffocate – while she, the reluctant fisherman, pondered whether to throw him back in. She made him a full cooked breakfast to show him she cared, taking the scrambled eggs off the heat at exactly the right moment – just the way he liked them. When he appeared in the kitchen, buttoning his shirt cuffs and putting on his tie, he seemed neither to notice the special effort she'd taken with breakfast, nor to show any hint of having been wounded by her. Instead he wolfed his food, gulped down his coffee and talked about the architects and what he hoped to achieve – or rather fail to achieve – that day.

'The trick is, Fran, to make sure we move as slowly as possible. We don't want to go spending all the money on the building, now, do we? We need to be infuriatingly indecisive, obsessively bureaucratic. We'll dot our "i"s, cross our "t"s and then dot them and cross them all over again as many times as we can get away with. The difficulty is going to be keeping Owen on the leash walking at heel . . .'

'Put him on a choke chain.' Fran sipped her black coffee and lit her first much needed cigarette of the day, unsure whether she should be glad that Jason was so chirpy or worried that he was smiling on the surface but bleeding heavily somewhere deep inside.

Now she lagged behind as Jason strode up to Owen, slapping him on the back, still flippantly cheerful. She let them walk ahead into the building, Jason twittering brightly, complimenting Owen on his sketches, confiding new ideas and plans for the restaurant. Hearing him talk, you wouldn't for one moment imagine that

The Melt was never actually going to open. Her thoughts were interrupted by the sound of a car pulling up outside.

'Ah. The architects.' Jason looked at his watch. 'Nicely on time.'

Outside the sky had turned dark and stormy where just a few minutes before they had been standing in brilliant sunshine. A silver Jaguar XJS had ground to a halt next to a pile of battered old crates. The air was filled with the smell of exhaust. After a few seconds the driver's door opened, and a short man with an enormous beer belly and sideburns squeezed out. Without looking at the three of them, he paused to smooth the strands of hair that were brushed ineffectually over his bald patch, coughed a deep cough that rumbled on into a wheeze after the cough itself was over and staggered around to the passenger door.

The shadows that played over the car made it impossible to see inside. The passenger was a woman – Fran could just make out the shape of elaborately set hair but nothing further.

'Thank you, Ted,' came a throaty Welsh accent, as the door creaked open. The balding man offered an arm for the passenger to steady herself on as she got out of the car, but it was waved away by a veiny hand tipped with vibrant pink nails.

Fran glanced across at Jason, who was looking bewildered but trying to conceal his confusion with a smile.

The woman was short, though a couple of inches taller than her driver, and perhaps a few years older than him, late fifties to early sixties. The intricately arranged hair was a rich, chemically assisted auburn, while the skin of her face was thin and stretched. Fran thought that if she got close enough she would see the tell-tale bunching of the skin near the eyes that indicates many surgical nips and tucks. The heavily made-up eyes were a piercing green.

'I'm looking for a Mr Warren.' That voice again. It sounded as though it had scraped its way around the murky grey dust of a million pub ashtrays.

Jason cleared his throat. 'I don't suppose you're from Stubbs and Palmer, are you?'

'No,' said the woman, tugging at the bottom of her smart cream jacket, edged in navy blue, which was riding up slightly at the back. 'I'm Sadie March. March, like the month – comes in like a lion, goes out like a lamb or so they say.' She pronounced the name as though it should mean something to Jason. 'And this is my husband, Ted.' The short man nodded.

'Robert Warren.' Jason was edgy. He didn't extend the usual hand of greeting. 'And this is my business partner, Marsha Freeman. What can we do for you?'

Fran looked around for Owen, who had melted away when it became apparent that these people were not the architects. She spotted him at the far side of the building, where he had resumed his sketching. Well, he could just stay over there out of the way, while she tried to work out what was going on here.

'Ah, Mr Warren, delighted to meet you. I've been hearing so much about you. This is the site for the restaurant, I suppose?' The woman gestured at the building. Without waiting for a reply to her question, she walked straight past Jason and Fran towards the warehouse, followed by her wheezing husband. 'We'd love to have a look around if that's all right,' she called back over her shoulder.

Fran mouthed silently to Jason, *Who are these people?* But Jason simply shrugged. Helplessly they followed Sadie and Ted March into the building, leaving Owen outside with his sketching.

'Sad, really, isn't it?' said the woman. 'To see such a wonderful place reduced to a state of dereliction and decay.' She paused, seeming to wipe an invisible tear from the parchment skin of her cheek.

'On Saturday nights this place used to be the life and soul of the Bay,' said the man. 'You wouldn't believe it . . . they'd have great bands on and they'd all be packing in in their best togs. But the *fights* that broke out . . . Gee, it doesn't bear thinking about.'

'Still, it's going to be a terrific restaurant, isn't it?' said the woman, ignoring him. 'Perhaps you could have one of those salad bars over there – you know the kind of thing – where you can take as much as you can fit on one plate.'

Jason had been looking vaguely worried, but now Fran could see his concern change to irritation. Salad bars indeed! They had caught him out of his stride but now he had recovered himself. He stepped forward, hands on hips, confrontational. 'Look, Mr and Mrs . . .'

'March,' the woman helpfully supplied, as she whispered something to her husband. 'Like the month.'

'Mr and Mrs March,' Jason began again. 'Would you mind telling me exactly why you're here?'

Sadie March's hand flew to her wrinkled throat in a gesture of humility. 'Oh, goodness, how dreadfully rude of me. I knew we should have fixed an appointment. Didn't I say so, Ted?'

'You did, Sadie,' barked the man on cue.

'I knew it, Mr Warren. But your secretary . . . Emma, is it?'

'Emily,' said Fran, with a polite but utterly brittle smile.

'That's right . . . Emily.' There was a fleck of lipstick on one of Sadie March's front teeth – a red so vivid it was almost orange. 'Well, she was ever so helpful. She said if we came straight down to the site we'd catch up with you here . . . And so here we are!' She gave them a beaming smile and then strode away down to the far end of the building. Were those teeth false?

'Here we are,' echoed Ted, parrot-like, and staggered after her.

Fran and Jason caught up with the Marches over by the old stage, Fran – increasingly uneasy – making a mental note to have a stern word with Emily.

'You know,' said Sadie March to Jason, 'you could make a deal with Brain's brewery, I'm sure you could. They do most of the places around here. What sort of food are you going to serve – pizzas? Burgers?'

'Mrs March,' tried Fran, hitting a moment of intense frustration. 'What are you doing here? What is your interest in our business?'

Sadie March wheeled round, startled. 'Oh, didn't you know, dear? It's my niece I'm here for. We've come to take a look at her investment.'

What?

While Fran was still struggling to make sense of this, Jason had snapped into action. He began escorting the Marches around the building, pointing out the old balcony and explaining Owen's intention to put a statue up there, telling them that the restaurant was to be called The Melt and was to serve food from a range of cultural traditions reflecting the melting-pot community of Tiger Bay.

All Fran could do was to stand there, thinking, wondering. The only thing she knew for certain was that Jason had not been straight with her. Her head was filled with the sound of Sadie March's rasping voice: 'So will I get special discounts as investor's relative? . . . Who's going to be your chef? I've got this cousin, you see, and he went to catering college . . . You could have special lunch buffets on a Sunday, that would pull in lots of people . . .' Ted tended to repeat the last five or six words of each pronouncement. Fran wanted to punch him hard in the mouth.

Then suddenly all was made clear. The name was casually dropped among Mrs March's general tittle-tattle, somewhere among the bottled beers, the bar codes, the Australian wine and the cocktail waitresses.

'. . . You see, Mr Warren, we just had to come and take a look because our Samantha is like the daughter we never had. I *had* to know she's putting her money into something worthwhile, for my own peace of mind. She's a lovely girl, Samantha.'

Fran felt the strength seeping out of her. 'Samantha?' She had spoken so quietly that no one heard her. 'Samantha . . . Derby?' she repeated, louder.

Mrs March flashed her a brilliant smile. 'Yes, of course. *Lovely* girl, my niece. She's a doctor, you know,' she added, proudly.

Jason was suddenly very busy pulling a loose board away from one of the windows. Fran was clenching her fists, digging her nails so hard into the palm of her hand that she almost drew blood.

At that moment the door swung open and Owen appeared.

'Ah, Owen,' called Jason. 'Come and meet Mr and Mrs March. This is our young artist, Owen Meredith. Do you know his work?'

'The architects are here,' said Owen.

An enormous ruby surrounded by tiny diamonds . . . She wanted to ram that fucking joke of a ring down his bastard lying throat.

I phoned Eddie, told him I was sick and hid in my flat, watching TV in my dressing gown and calling out for take-away pizza. I wasn't stupid enough to believe this was any kind of solution – I was buying myself some time to think. Though in fact I didn't think very much at all. On the second day a cheque for £1000 arrived from Jason and Fran, along with a note that said, *A little something to tide you over. Lots more where that came from. F.*

I knew they must have the first half million, so I had my own private celebration, dancing around the flat to an old Malcolm McLaren record, 'Waltz Darling', which always makes me feel elated. But I was too lonely to celebrate for long. I wanted to call them but I knew they'd ask me how things were going, and I wasn't ready to answer that question. So instead I ventured out to the Chop Suey House on Cathedral Road and picked up half a crispy aromatic duck and some plum sauce and pancakes. As I walked back up Teilo Street I spotted Owen outside my house ringing the front door bell and bending down to peer through the letter box. He hadn't seen me. I panicked and slipped down the alleyway that led through to Dogo Street to wait a few minutes for him to give up and go away.

He phoned later and I let the machine take the call. He said he'd been thinking about me and he'd like to see me. He'd been in to Energy and was told I was off sick. He hoped it was nothing too awful. He didn't mention that he'd tried to call round. The message was full of effort. He stammered, paused awkwardly and grappled for something to say that wouldn't scare me off. In the end he settled for repeating that he'd like to see me again soon and left his number. The very sound of his voice made me feel heavy and leaden. What the fuck was I going to do?

I slept until mid-morning of the third day and was woken from some nasty dream – a dream I couldn't quite remember but which left me rigid in my bed, my teeth gritted and my hands clenched into fists – by the ringing phone. Again I let the machine pick up, but a moment later I was scrambling out of bed and tripping on the steps down to the kitchen in my eagerness to grab the call. It was Fran. She wanted to meet up that day. She wouldn't say what it was about but it was clear from her voice that something was very wrong.

We chose The Black Pig because we'd be unlikely to run into Owen in there – or indeed anyone else either of us knew. It was a dingy old pub that stood grubby and defiant amid the genteel teashops and twee giftshops of Llandaff. Two Japanese tourists were snapping pictures of the cathedral as I came up the hill and two old ladies with bouffant hair and blazers were nattering outside the post office. The birds in the trees were the only other life around. The tranquillity was shattered suddenly as the heavy wooden doors of The Black Pig were opened and a shabby drunk was ejected onto the street by a burly moustached barmaid who shouted at him to forget the idea of coming back unless he wanted 'some more'. The old soak shambled away swearing and the barmaid wiped her hands on her jeans and retreated into the pub. The two ladies in blazers whispered behind their hands and tried not to look at the drunk as he staggered past.

We had picked a really choice venue for our meeting!

It was dark and gloomy inside after the bright sunlight of the street. The carpet, which had long since lost its colour and pattern, was sticky beneath my feet. A group of seven or eight men of indeterminate age, with brylcreemed grey hair and drab colourless clothes were sipping pints and talking rugby. Two teenagers in shell suits were playing on the Trivia machine and three thirty-something crusties with vest-tops that revealed a mass of sprouting armpit hair were drinking bottles of Newcastle Brown. Their mangy dog-on-a-string slept at their feet.

It took me a minute to spot Fran through the haze of dense smoke that shrouded the room. She was sitting in a corner drinking whiskey. I waved but she just nodded her acknowledgement without smiling. As I paid the barmaid and carried my pint over, I noticed how pale her face was. She was smoking – the hand that held the cigarette looked shaky. I was afraid; afraid that Meredith had rumbled us, that the scam was off. And where was Jason?

'Bloody awful dump, this,' she said as I pulled up a stool.

'Yeah. What's up?'

She sipped from her whiskey. 'How are things going with Owen?'

'Oh, OK.' Insecurity gnawed at my stomach.

'Would you care to enlarge on that, Eileen?'

'Well, you know.'

'No, I don't. Tell me. Have you made any progress at all or have you just been playing house in your nice flat?'

The cow! My insecurity turned to indignation. 'He's been drawing me. I've slept with him. OK?'

'And?'

'You want to know what we did?'

'Don't act thick.' She rubbed her forehead wearily.

'It happened a few nights ago.'

'And have you seen him since?'

A nerve in my left eyelid began to twitch and pulse. I wondered if Fran could see it.

'Well?'

I took a gulp of lager. 'I've been ill.'

'Jesus, Eileen, what the fuck is wrong with you?'

She'd raised her voice and the men with the brylcreemed hair turned to stare at us. Fran looked down into her glass and waited for them to return to their conversation.

I groped about in my mind for something to say that would please her. 'It's OK, Fran. I've given him a few days' breathing space. He's so fucked up about his ex – I wouldn't want to scare him off, now, would I?'

She seemed to make a conscious effort to calm herself down. Her shoulders visibly relaxed. 'No, of course not. Just don't leave it too long. Has he said anything?'

Had he? I struggled to think. 'He mentioned Meredith for the first time the night we shagged. He said Meredith has done all sorts in the name of money and success.'

'Go on.'

'Well, that's all. Like I say, I haven't wanted to push him too much so early on.'

She drained her glass. 'I guess that's a start. But don't forget, we're relying on you. We need to have some dirt on Meredith by the time the third lot of money comes through. He's a nasty piece of work, Eileen. I wouldn't rate our chances of getting out of here if we don't have something on him.'

'Don't worry, I'll get something.' My voice sounded much more certain than I really felt. 'Owen didn't cut his father out of his life for nothing. I think he stumbled on a secret – something really mucky. I'll get it out of him, Fran. Soon.'

'You'd better.' Fran went to the bar to get another whiskey. She bought me a second pint. As she walked back to the table carrying the drinks one of the old guys made a comment and she turned and gave him the finger, sending the whole table into raucous laughter. She wasn't smiling.

'Fran, what's going on? Is it Jason?'

She nodded, lit up another cigarette. 'You're not going to believe this.'

She told me that yesterday a Mr and Mrs March had turned up at the site to take a look at their niece's investment. Their niece? Samantha Derby, Jason's Manchester date-con. Unable to simply walk away from a half-completed scam, he'd convinced her to invest £10,000 in the restaurant. As though we needed that money with everything we were going to get out of Meredith! Jason didn't know Samantha had any connection with Cardiff but it turns out Mummy grew up here and Auntie Sadie and Uncle Ted have lived here all their lives.

Fran was fuming. 'Here I am trying to cover our damn backs, make everything water-tight – and you having to *sleep* with Owen just so we can get something on Meredith – and all the time Jason's playing around, getting an extra few thousand here and there, just for the hell of it. It's like he doesn't even see the danger. God, you wouldn't *believe* he could be so stupid.'

I'd had another thought. 'So what's he done with this money then? Was he intending to share it with us?'

Fran smiled wryly. 'Good question. He says he was waiting for the right moment to tell me – but God knows whether that moment would ever have arrived.'

'Do you think there could be more "investors"?' I was starting to understand why Fran was in such a state.

Fran just shrugged. 'He says not. But do we believe him?'

My mouth was dry. I gulped from my pint. 'You've always told me that trust is the most important thing of all. We *have* to be able to trust him.'

'Yes. I know.' She reached over and stroked my cheek. She looked sad. 'Don't worry too much, honey. He's promised to give the money back and that ought to get rid of the Marches and their ridiculous suggestions about salad bars and breweries. He loves me, you know. He's a typical weak man but he needs me more than he needs anyone or anything else. I think that gives us some security. And I'm keeping a close eye on him . . . We can't afford to have any more unexpected visitors at the site.'

I took hold of her hand. It was small and cold. 'And don't you worry about Tony Meredith. I'll get a result.' And I meant it.

Owen peered through the letter box into Meg's hallway. The door to the kitchen was open and evening sunlight was streaming through. For a moment he thought he could smell onions frying inside, but then he realised it was coming from the house next door. He let the flap go and tried the bell again. Was it working? It was disconcerting to press the button but not to hear the responding ring. He bent down again, almost cricking his neck in the process. Perhaps he should call out to her.

'Meg? Meg, are you there?'

A curtain twitched next door and he glimpsed a face. He straightened, feeling as though he'd been caught doing something he shouldn't. As though he'd been about to break in or something. He stood about awkwardly on the path. Maybe she'd just nipped out. Maybe if he waited for a while she'd be back, carrying a pint of milk or preferably a bottle of wine. She'd smile with surprise and pleasure when she saw him, invite him in, perhaps cook him a meal, ask him to stay the night . . .

Oh, God, the longing. The longing! For the last two days he'd been able to think of nothing and nobody but her. The colour of her skin, its softness, her tiny feet, the curve at the small of her back, the insides of her elbows . . . all of it. And her passion – most of all her passion. He had been attracted to her from the start but he hadn't suspected she could be so intense, so overwhelming . . . But in the morning she was different. So cold, as though it had meant nothing to her. It seemed she could hardly wait to get away.

He'd known he shouldn't phone her. He sensed she needed space and told himself he should leave it as long as he possibly could. So many times over these two days he'd had to stop himself from picking up the phone. But now he couldn't bear to leave it any longer. Was that so wrong of him? The pessimistic voice that lived somewhere in his gut told him he was going to lose her no matter what he did. In which case better to get it over with now than to keep on hoping.

Out of the corner of his eye, he saw a figure darting off the street into the alleyway. Was it . . . no, he was surely being paranoid.

Why the hell should anyone want to sleep with you?

That's what Annie said when he tried to reassure her that he wasn't having an affair with Madeleine Jones. He'd misinterpreted Annie's darkening moods, the sulky restlessness, the endless questions about where he was going and when he'd be back. He'd thought she suspected something. Madeleine had been posing for him at the studio in town and sometimes they would stop off for a drink afterwards.

You've got about as much sex appeal as a coat hanger, Annie had pronounced. And then, *Go and hang around somewhere else.*

Ha ha.

Turned out she was the one having the affair. A week later she was gone.

What he had never been able to understand was why she had been so bitter towards him, why she had felt the need to fling this verbal abuse at him, hurling it at him relentlessly before leaving, so that he felt as though she had stoned him within inches of his life.

You're better off without her, his friends said. *We never liked her, that one. Always thought she was better than everyone else. The cow. Forget her.*

But he couldn't forget her. And now, turning away from Meg's door, giving up, her jeering voice jabbed at the inside of his head until he gritted his teeth and growled aloud with the pain of it.

Fuck Annie. Fuck the bitch. Fuck all those witches that toyed around with guys like him, picking them off the peg, wearing them around for a while, turning them inside out and back to front, then tearing – ripping them to shreds before dumping them on the scrap heap.

Fuck 'em all. He'd let the past disable him for too long. He had to shake it off. He wanted Meg. If she wanted him too – fine. If she didn't – well that was fine too. Just fine. He'd wait for her to call him. The ball was in her court now. As for him – he was going home to cook some dinner for himself.

Purposefully he strode down the path. By the time he was half way down the street he was whistling happily. By the time he passed the Conway pub he was in the mood to stop off for a quick pint, to sit outside and watch the sun go down.

By the time he got home, sozzled, he was longing to phone her. Giving in to temptation in his beered-up state even though he knew it was the wrong thing to do. Getting her answer machine. Blathering. Wondering if she was sitting by the phone screening her calls.

Hi, Owen, it's Meg. I'm sorry I've been slow returning your calls. I've had some lousy virus and I've been laid up in bed. I'm afraid I have been avoiding you but just for a few days while I got my head together. This sort of thing doesn't happen to me every day ... I guess I've been scared. Are you free tonight? Can I see you?

He called me back within the hour and said he was really happy to hear from me. He wanted to take me out on a proper date that night. There was some jazz band he knew playing at a bar in town. He thought it would be fun. I started feeling weird again, and hit the gin bottle to steady my nerves – it was one thing seducing him, but quite another to try to turn that one night stand into a relationship. However, the meeting with Fran had acted as a good hard slap in the face, and I knew I had to get my act together and pull this off. I had one or two more shots of gin while I waited for Owen to pick me up.

We arrived at the bar in good time and got seats at the front near the stage. Owen was nervous and kept jogging the wobbly table by accident – I had to keep hold of my gin-and-tonic for fear he would knock it over. It seemed Owen was a popular guy, more so than I'd have thought. People kept coming over to say hello to him, asking him when he was next exhibiting in Cardiff. One man bought us both a drink, but when Owen asked him to join us he refused, giving a conspiratorial wink. I felt as though everyone was looking at me, judging me. I downed my drink and headed off to the bar to get us both another.

The band were loud so we couldn't talk much, which was just as well – I was getting pretty pissed. The music was too twiddley-widdley for my taste but Owen clearly liked it. The dissonant screeching and warbling of the saxophone got right inside my skull, and combined with the heavy smoky atmosphere and the dim blue lighting to make my head throb like crazy. Every so often I would catch Owen looking at me, admiring me – seeming hardly to believe I was really there with him, and I would try to smile through my headache.

My drunkenness was advancing slowly but steadily until the moment came – as it has a tendency to do – when it reached the edge of the precipice and tipped over. I bolted for the toilets.

Irritatingly I couldn't actually be sick, but just bent over a toilet bowl sweating and dry-retching for a few minutes before the disaster began to abate and normality came creeping back. I washed my face in cold water before realising there were no hand towels and stood before the mirror for a long time, my face dripping, staring into my dilated pupils and thinking, *Eileen, you are one first class twat.*

Eventually, feeling better, I returned to the bar, and switched to mineral water.

* * *

We took a taxi back to Owen's house. Stepping into his living room, I felt like a murderer drawn back to the scene of the crime. He made two mugs of milky tea. I hankered after something stronger but perhaps it was just as well he didn't have any booze in the house. I settled down on the moth-eaten couch with my mug and he put on a CD of the band we'd just heard. Yet more of that endless twiddling-widdling! I started to dwell on the prospect of the night to come and became gloomy, but my spirits lifted when he reached into a ceramic pot on the mantelpiece and brought out a small lump of dope, some rizlas and some cigarettes.

He built a good joint; tight and strong. I'm lousy at rolling: my spliffs always turn out slack. The roach falls out after the first puff or two and bits of tobacco come out in your mouth. Owen's joint was just what the doctor ordered. I felt my body begin to relax, a delicious mellowness came over me and my worries about having to sleep with him again drifted away in a cloud of spicy smoke. We sat together in a comfortable silence, passing the spliff back and forth. Occasionally I could hear giggling somewhere in the distance, and then realised it was me.

I looked over at Owen and noticed that in spite of the effects of the joint he was as nervous and twitchy as ever – his left leg jigging up and down feverishly.

'Don't you ever manage to just chill out and stop fidgeting?'

'I wish I could. My mind just zips along – images, colours, pointless ideas ... I can't stop them coming. And I can't sleep either.'

'Jesus.' Poor sod. I took another drag and experienced a pleasurable rush that made me smile gormlessly even though I was trying to look sympathetic. 'Have you seen a doctor?'

He laughed. 'You should see the inside of my medicine cupboard! I've tried everything; sleeping pills, anti-depressants, meditation, yoga, acupuncture.' Suddenly his face was sheepish. 'The other night – that first night at your flat ... when you held me ... I slept better than I have for months. I haven't slept so well since before—'

'I know, I know.' Not that again. 'Since before Annie left you.'

'Actually, I was going to say that I haven't slept so well since before my mother died.'

Oops. Clanger. He looked all doleful and sad now. We needed a mood change – enough of this bloody twiddly music. I shlumped down on the floor by the stack of CDs and started rifling through. Not a bad selection.

There was music here that I'd forgotten all about. I could feel a nostalgia trip coming on.

Owen was talking somewhere in the background. '*He* sleeps like a baby. Not one tiny shred of guilt to trouble his conscience. He doesn't have one is all. A conscience, I mean. And my mother dead.'

Oh, wow! Here was that old Sade album, *Diamond Life* – years ago in Kent when I was barely more than a kid that dusky velvet voice had enticed and charmed me into the arms of a man who was supposed to be teaching me to play the violin. I surrendered my virginity on the floor of his teaching room among the spindly metal music stands, singing along to 'Smooth Operator', his cock deep inside me while downstairs his wife baked Victoria sponge and Bath buns. The affair was short-lived, ending when I discovered he'd given me crabs. After that the violin sat in its case in the corner of the room gathering dust.

I still love that Sade album in spite of the rather soiled memory, and I put it on for old times' sake.

'Oh, it doesn't matter,' came Owen's voice from far away, while I drifted off with 'Your Love is King', and the soothing effects of the spliff.

Somehow we were having sex. I don't remember going upstairs to the bedroom or taking my clothes off but suddenly there I was wrapping my legs around his back and sticking my tongue in his mouth as though it were the most natural thing in the world. He whispered that I made him relax like nothing and nobody else. He played my body every bit as well as that randy old bastard of a teacher had played his violin and it turned into the best shag I'd ever had.

It was only afterwards, lying beside him and stroking his back as he fell asleep, that I realised I'd fucked up really badly in my stoned state. What had Owen been saying when I went cruising off down memory lane at high speed? Something about his mother? That night it was Owen who slept and me who lay awake, my mind racing.

'What's this?'

'A cheque.'

'Well, I know that!'

'Take it. Put it in your bag.'

Samantha let the cheque flutter out on a gust of wind and Jason was forced to scramble for it, grabbing it just before it could be carried over the cliff edge.

'What the hell is the matter with you!' But he had known it would be like this.

She was holding a hand up to stop her hair from blowing in her face. He had imagined how her eyes would look filled to the brim with tears, and now – yes – here came the tears, making her eyes resemble the glassy marbles he collected as a child.

'You want to know what's the matter with *me*!' She turned away to look out over the choppy sea. 'God, Robbie, you make me so angry!'

The waves were lashing fiercely against the rocks down below them. It had seemed like such a good idea to bring her here for the weekend, with forecasts of temperatures in the thirties. She'd wanted to come to Cardiff, but he'd said, no, let's go to West Wales. He said he wanted to get to a nice bit of coast while they still had the weather to enjoy it. But now, here they were, arguing in the freezing wind under an iron-grey sky that might just break at any second.

'I don't understand why you're so upset,' he said, limply, wearily. 'I'm giving you your money back, that's all.'

'But *why*?'

'I don't need it any more. I've found another investor.' He made his voice as calm and flat as possible. The more cold and rational he could manage to sound, the more emotional she would become – she would accelerate rapidly like a sports car, edging closer and closer to breaking point, and just as she was about to topple into total hysteria she would suddenly become distanced from herself, would hear her voice remotely, as though from outside her own head, and would realise how ridiculous she was sounding. And then she would calm down and accept what he was telling her. Jason knew this would happen – had made it happen hundreds of times before with other women.

'You're dumping me, aren't you?'

'What?'

Dump her, Jason.

'You heard!'

'Samantha.' He reached out to put an arm around her, but she shrugged him off.

'Don't touch me. Just tell me the truth. You're dumping me. Admit it.'

Get rid of her.

The sobs were growing bigger, in harmony with the waves down below. She was hugging herself, shivering uncontrollably. He thought perhaps he should offer her his coat, but didn't.

'This whole weekend,' she continued, her voice shaking, almost inaudible. 'This whole weekend you've been pretending, lying. When we made love this morning I thought to myself, I've never been so happy. I've *finally* got over Greg and I'm in love with someone who really cares about me. God, what did I know! How can you do that? How can you act one way when all the time you're feeling something completely different!'

'You've got it all wrong.' Jason maintained the dull tone. 'It's because I care about you that I'm giving you the money back.'

She snorted her disgust.

'I don't want you to take unnecessary risks. What do you think would happen to us if I lost your money? Eh?'

'This is bullshit. You want to get rid of me!'

Get rid of her.

She was accelerating, flapping. They all did.

'You think I take women to expensive hotels when I want to get rid of them? See sense, Samantha. I could have just put the cheque in the post.'

She was gripping the iron railings. Her knuckles were white with pressure. Her hair was wet with tears. Jason didn't want to look at her; he was troubled by images of her body in the half-light, her mouth when she bent forward to kiss him, her long elegant hands . . . So he looked at the gulls that were calling and swooping. For a moment he imagined one of the squawking gulls had Fran's head.

She tried to say something else but couldn't get the words out.

Gently, he put his hands over one of hers and began to prise her fingers away from the railings. She let him do it.

She was a tall woman but today she seemed so small and frail. He stood holding her cold hand in both of his, listening to the gulls, the wind and the sea, looking into her blotchy face. She refused to look back at him, keeping her eyes down, letting her hand rest in his while she cried. Slowly he reached into his pocket to draw out the cheque, still holding on to her with the other hand. He placed it in her palm and wrapped her fingers closed around it.

'Take it,' he said. 'Trust me, it's for the best.'

She wasn't shaking so much now. Her breathing was calmer. He sensed she had reached the peak and was on her way down. Patiently he waited, feeling the first drops of rain fall cold on his head. More rain. Any minute now they would be caught in a deluge. He let go of her hands.

'Oh God, I'm sorry,' came her voice, meek, apologetic, little. 'I should never have doubted you.'

'Silly girl.' He reached out to stroke her soft, wet cheek.

Samantha's fingers tightened on the cheque, making it crackle. She looked up at him with the face of a stubborn little child and a smile crept over her, fierce, almost demonic. Keeping her gaze fixed on him and smiling all the while, she ripped the cheque clean in half.

'Samantha!'

Again she tore it, and again and again, shredding it up into confetti and finally hurling the pieces out on the air as hard as she could.

'I believe in you, Robbie. And I want us to be in this together.'

'For God's sake, what are you—'

'Do you love me, Robbie?' She dropped to her knees on the ground.

'Please get up, Sammy.' Embarrassed, he glanced around to see if anyone was watching them, but they were alone on the cliff top. 'Sammy!'

She was fumbling with his flies. He made a feeble motion to brush her away, but at the same time felt a flutter of excitement.

'Tell me you love me.' She was unzipping him. He knew he should stop her but couldn't gather the will to do it.

This wasn't supposed to happen. They weren't meant to do this.

He could hear Fran's voice: *Put a stop to this, Jason. End it this weekend. Take her away somewhere quiet, give her the money back and break it off. I don't want to hear the name Samantha Derby ever again.*

Her mouth was like heaven.

'I might go to India next year.' Sîan lounged back against the cushions, stroking her smooth tanned calves, her feet pulled up on the couch; pretty purple-tipped toes matching her fingernails, her Nike trainers placed on the floor in front of her. 'You know – just hang out for a while, get a bit spiritual . . . Or maybe South America. Salsa and all that. I suppose I'd have to take Spanish lessons . . .' She wrinkled her tiny nose at the prospect and jiggled the ice cubes in her empty glass.

'Would you like another?' asked Eileen, taking the hint.

'*Bien sûr.*'

Eileen fixed her another gin-and-tonic and called out to Owen in the kitchen. 'Everything all right, honey? Do you need any help?'

'I'm fine, thanks,' came Owen's frazzled voice. 'You just work on keeping my sister happy. She's got a low boredom threshold and a short attention span, haven't you, Sîanie?'

'Shut up, bro,' Sîan drawled. 'What does *he* know,' she said to Eileen, adopting a sisters-together attitude – a sort of 'Owen is our common ground and we will find a way to bond by uniting in ridiculing him' approach to the evening.

Eileen smiled tensely and tried not to be intimidated.

'What's for eats?' called Sîan. 'I'm supposed to be off dairy at the moment, I forget to tell you.' She patted her stomach as though there was something there to be patted.

Owen stuck his head around the door. 'Well, we're starting off with brie in batter, then veal escalopes in cream, followed by *crème brûlée*.'

'Fuck off, fish-face. What are we having *really*?'

'A sort of chicken thing.' He retreated into the kitchen.

'Did you hear that, Meg?' Sîan ran a hand through her shiny bobbed hair and fiddled with a heart-shaped stud earring. 'My brother is cooking a chicken *thing*. Oh, what delights!'

Owen had warned Eileen about his sister; *seventeen going on thirty-seven; the world loves me and I'm forced to tolerate it*. 'You'll like her, though. Everyone does. She's smart. She's talented.' They were close, but certain subjects were not to be discussed. Owen was on a mission to save Sîan from the influence of their father, to salvage what was left of her personality before it was mutilated beyond redemption.

'So, how did you two meet?' But before Eileen could reply, Sîan had moved on. 'I'm *so* glad you're together,' she whispered conspiratorially. 'It's about time he got that Annie out of his system.' She wagged a warning finger. 'You'd better treat my brother good, Meg, or you'll have me to answer to.'

She always called him 'bro' or 'my brother', never just 'Owen'. Eileen supposed she was asserting her importance, a sort of unconscious proprietorial gesture. How different her own life might have been if she'd had a brother – a 'bro' who may have grown up to be bigger and stronger than Dad, who could have put a stop to the violence. Or a sister – a 'sis' to confide in, to share the strain of day-to-day life with their tempestuous father and cowering mother. She swallowed her jealousy with difficulty.

'Well, that settles it. I'm going to have to be nice to him now. There's no way on earth I'd want to get into a scrap with you, Sîan!'

This seemed to satisfy Sîan, who wriggled her toes and preened like a sleek well-bred cat.

Owen ladled the 'chicken thing' onto plates; breasts and thighs in a sludgy red liquid that he accidentally splashed on Sîan's baby-pink T-shirt, and then sponged clumsily with a grubby towel. Sîan snatched the cloth away and dabbed at the stains herself but they wouldn't shift. 'What the hell is this sauce, molten grease?'

'Wine, tomato, stock . . .' Owen explained, but Sîan had lost interest and was reaching for the bottle of Chianti that Eileen had just opened.

Eileen watched her pick her way through the meal, neatly slicing away the chicken skin and piling it up at the side of her plate, picking up green beans with her fingers and slipping them whole into her mouth, ignoring the roast potatoes altogether. Observing Sıân swallow huge gulps of red wine, Eileen thought she looked as though she'd like to swallow the whole world and wasn't expecting it to put up much of a fight. Had *she* been like that at seventeen? She supposed not. You'd need a lot of attention and indulgence to become so self-assured and unselfconscious; you'd need a great deal of money lavished on you.

Owen had the same parents, had been given the same upbringing as Sîan. Why then was he so nervous, so insecure? Eileen watched him forking a piece of chicken, chewing and swallowing; the rather too-prominent Adam's apple bobbing up and down – and she felt a rush of affection for him. Somewhere in the genetic make-up of these siblings, the brother had inherited all the fear, the suspicion, the awareness – the long dark night of the soul, while the sister could see only light and sunshine, a wonderfully shallow dazzle. And perhaps that was all she would ever see.

'I think I'll have my nose pierced, what do you reckon?' chattered Sîan, who'd now abandoned the meal only half-eaten. 'Or perhaps my belly button. Josie Hawkins has one of her nipples pierced but I couldn't abide that. I'm sure it would chafe terribly against my tennis shirt, don't you think so?'

'I think Dad would go ballistic,' commented Owen. And there it was, the name not to be spoken. The word 'Dad' seemed too friendly, too familiar for Owen. His face registered shock and surprise that such a word could have emitted from his mouth. 'Dad' had floated out over the table, casting a shadow over the three diners.

'I'll get the black pepper.' Owen stumbled off to the kitchen.

Sîan turned to Eileen, and her eyes were suddenly sad and worried. 'Daddy isn't a bad person, Meg,' she said, almost under her breath. 'He really isn't. Owen has it all distorted and twisted.'

Eileen saw the opportunity. 'But why? Why does Owen hate him so much?'

'Oh, it's because of Mum. But Owen's wrong!'

'Wrong about what?' Owen came back into the room with the pepper grinder.

Sîan looked as though she had been caught stealing. 'Nothing,' she said, unconvincingly. 'Tell me about this restaurant thing. I'm dying to know more.'

While Eileen cleared away the dessert dishes and the empty Häagen Dazs pot, Owen skinned up a joint. He rolled it tightly, manoeuvring it precisely between his long sculptor's fingers. He talked of the figure he planned to create, the statue with the outstretched arms to hang over the restaurant, of the way he planned to construct it around a wire frame, of the plastics he would use and how he would melt them down to just the right malleable state. Sîan seemed to be only half listening. She had become languid and sullen, as though she herself was disintegrating, sinking into a mushy little heap.

Eileen spooned coffee into a cafetière and poured water onto the grains. Listening to the sound of Owen's voice chuntering on, she felt an odd contentment. Odd because this kind of ordinary happiness was something she felt so seldom. Tonight she felt more like Meg than Eileen: just a normal nice girl making coffee for her new boyfriend and his sister.

Owen had already lit the joint when Eileen came back into the room and set the coffee on the table. He reached across Sîan to pass it to her.

'Hey, what about me!'

Owen laughed. 'Since when have you been smoking draw, Sîanie?'

'Oh, for years and years.'

Eileen drew guiltily on the joint, and plunged the cafetière.

'Bollocks!'

Sîan was indignant. 'OK, I'm exaggerating about it being years, but I have smoked loads of times, at parties and stuff.'

'What about your tennis?' teased Owen. 'I don't suppose there's many Wimbledon champions who indulge in the old weed. What would your coach say?'

'Oh, screw the tennis and screw you!' Sîan looked as though she might cry. She gulped at the dregs of wine left in her glass and poured herself some more.

'Sîanie?' Owen was concerned, big brotherly. 'What's wrong?'

Sîan's shoulders seemed to slump. Her head drooped. 'I'm not good enough. I'm never going to cut it on the international circuit.'

'Hey, what's all this?' He reached over to hold her hand, but she pulled it away. 'Of course you're good enough. All that time you spend practising, all the tournaments you win . . .'

Sîan flashed him an irritated look. 'Think about it, Owen. I'm seventeen years old. That might not make me old enough to vote, but it's old enough to be the fucking Wimbledon champion! Do you see me winning grand slams? Do you see me even *qualifying*?'

Perhaps Sîan did understand about the darkness after all . . .

'But, Sîan—'

'No!' Sîan shook her head determinedly. 'Were you even listening to me earlier on when I was talking about going away? I've got to get out of here, get away from all this pressure . . . from Daddy. Bless him, he doesn't mean to give me a hard time – he wants the world for his little girl, that's all. But I've got to go away and get my head straight so I can work out what to do next. I'm going to finish school and get my A-levels, no matter how lousy the grades. And then I'm going to take off.'

Eileen glanced at Owen to check whether she should pass the joint to Sîan. Owen gave a sort of half shrug. Eileen handed it across.

'Thanks.' Sîan took a deep drag, and then burst into a round of coughs and splutters.

'I thought you said you'd smoked before.' Owen's voice was suspicious.

'Course I have.' She took another puff.

'Take it easy,' said Owen.

Eileen was oddly touched by Sîan's openness. She wanted to say something to her, to make a gesture. 'I never knew what I wanted to do with my life,' she tried. 'I still don't. But it must be harder for you. It must be really tough to want something so badly and find you can't have it.'

'Oh, God!' Sîan was suddenly on her feet, shoving the joint at Eileen and bolting for the door, her hand over her mouth. They could hear her running up the stairs. The bathroom door slammed.

'I knew she was lying,' said Owen. 'That'll learn her.'

'Could we have the fire on?'

'It's summer!'

'But it would be so cosy. Romantic.'

'Forget it. We'd boil,' said Owen.

It was late now. Three o'clock or thenabouts. They lay, spent, under the spare duvet on the living-room floor while Sîan snored drunkenly in the bed upstairs. Eileen could smell Owen's scent on her body. She liked it.

'It used to run in phases,' she said. 'He'd go for months without laying a finger on her, and then, just when the thought came into your head that he'd finally found a way to stop doing it – just when Mum had stopped jumping like some scared rabbit every time someone banged a door or called out her name – he'd start again. And it would go on and on; he'd come in drunk every night and beat her up so she'd cry and scream and you couldn't blot out the sounds – on and on, night after night, until you started to get used to it – you adjusted your idea of normality the way your eyes adapt to the darkness and start to see through it. And you'd come to take the beatings for granted . . . you'd become de-sensitised. And then he'd stop. It was the stopping that was the worst part of it. It made it harder to take when he started again.'

She lounged back against the cushions and he kissed her shoulder lightly and stroked her head. She had planned to tell him about her parents in order to draw him out to talk about his father, but when she began speaking she found it was more than that; she actually wanted to share her past with him.

'How have you turned out so normal after what you've been through?' asked Owen. 'How have you learned to trust people?'

Eileen shrugged. What the hell was normal? 'I have two very close friends. They sort of appeared in my life when I was at a low ebb. And they lifted me out of it. I suppose they gave me love. They made me feel I was worth something. They're pretty damaged themselves, it has to be said. But we have the damage in common. I think maybe it was the damage that drew us together.'

'Where are they now?'

Eileen smiled, enjoying her secret knowledge. 'Oh, they move around a lot. They're worse than me for not staying in one place for any length of time. They'll turn up at some point.' She pulled herself back to business. 'Tell me about *your* parents.'

'Oh, God, I need another drink for that.' He pushed the duvet back and walked naked across the room to fetch another bottle of wine from the kitchen. Eileen looked at his long legs, the thin body and slightly stoopy shoulders. Not what you'd call a stunning physique but at least he wasn't flabby. If only he'd stand up straight he'd look *so* much better. The carpet had made a meshed imprint on his buttocks.

'Was it really that bad?' she asked as he came back with a bottle of red and started to twist in the corkscrew.

'That bastard killed my mother,' he said simply, and the cork came out with a pop.

The 'nice girl Meg' persona disappeared in a split second, leaving Eileen the con-artist lying on the floor under the duvet rigid with excitement. She'd waited weeks for this, sitting through films holding his hand, listening to more twiddley-widdley jazz than she'd thought could possibly exist, posing in his studio day after day, blushing and dimpling and flattering his ego, letting him fuck her at night, and this evening being nice to his sister. Her heart was thudding with excitement. She made herself count to ten before she spoke again. She tried to control her voice, to soften it, to be concerned, slightly shocked – Meg-like. 'Are you saying that your father murdered your mother?'

He poured two glasses of wine and passed one over. She tried to stop her hand shaking as she took it from him. He drank from his.

'Owen?'

His silence was almost insufferable.

'My mother was a lovely woman,' he said at last. 'The best. I tell myself it's different for Sîan. She was so young, she barely knew Mum when she died. But still, it's hard to see how she can bear to be under the same roof as him.'

Eileen struggled to control her impatience. 'Sîan's still a child. She needs her dad, no matter what he's done. What has he done, Owen?' She tried to make out the expression on his face in the poor light that shone from the corner lamp. It was unfathomable.

'He thinks he's a king,' said Owen. 'He's turned the house into a castle, or tried to. He's built a turret on it. Can you imagine anything so stupid?'

Eileen breathed deeply. Why was he being so infuriatingly

evasive? 'What happened to your mother, Owen? What has made you hate him so much?'

And still he was circling around the real issue: 'He struts about puffing out his chest like a cockerel . . . crowing, making noise, ordering people around, shitting on people whenever he needs to. He's a monster – what's more he's ridiculous. He's a bloody joke with his cowboy boots and his Tom Jones records. I don't know how anyone in business can possibly take him seriously!' He laughed a hard humourless laugh, and took a mouthful of wine. 'The worst thing is knowing that at some level, deep down, I must be like him . . . He's my father – he's all woven up in my genes. I sometimes look in the mirror and see him looking back at me.' He gave an involuntary shiver.

'And you loved your mother,' tried Eileen. 'She deserved better.'

He sighed. 'I remember my mother growing thin. She was tired – exhausted . . . she would feel faint. She'd be wiping the sweat from her face and you'd ask her if she was all right. I'm fine, love, she'd say. Just one of my headaches. She was feverish sometimes, you'd see it in her eyes when he came stomping in asking why dinner was late.' And Owen rubbed at his eyes. Was he wiping tears away? 'I kept trying to tell him, she's ill. Can't you see she's ill? She needs to see a doctor. But he insisted there was nothing wrong with her – said it was the menopause, that all women got like that. I was too young to know better. He was my father – he knew everything – I believed him. Eventually she realised for herself that something was wrong with her. I heard them talking – she was saying she thought she ought to see a doctor – that she "wasn't quite right" – *wasn't quite right*! There's nothing wrong with you, woman! That's what he'd say. Bloody women, bloody hypochondriacs. Me – I've not been ill a day in my life. I can hear him now.

'But it wasn't the menopause, Meg. It was leukaemia. And by the time she saw a doctor, it was too late.' He drained his glass. 'He killed her, Meg. As surely as if he'd taken hold of her neck and squeezed the life out of her. He killed her.'

The night was quiet, so quiet you could hear the boiler in the kitchen, the clock in the hall, footsteps in the street.

'Hey, Meg. Are you all right? God, I'm sorry if I've upset you. I shouldn't have gone on and on like that. Meg?'

He reached out and took her in his arms, held her against his chest. She listened to the beating of his heart, feeling absolutely empty. Hollow. She'd thought her idea was such a good one. *What could this wealthy, powerful man have done to drive his son away? Why does a son cut himself off so completely from his father that no amount of time, money and declarations of love will bring him back? How much muck would a man like Tony Meredith leave in his tracks all hot and steaming and fresh – ready for a guileful little girl to come poking about in with her rake? The way to uncover the father's secret is to get close to the son,* really *close . . .* All that waiting, all that time spent pretending to be somebody she wasn't. It had never once occurred to her that Tony and Owen Meredith could have fallen out over something purely personal. She'd immediately assumed that there were dark deeds and dodgy business at the heart of it, and she'd convinced Jason and Fran that this must be the case.

She'd hoped for murder and all she got was a sad tale of common-place domestic neglect. Owen's story was useless.

Jason switched off his torch and stood still, waiting for his eyes to make sense of the darkness. After a moment, he could see the messy scaffolding, seemingly haphazard and unstable, like a pile of matchsticks balanced precariously against the walls. It had been erected only that morning by big men with thick necks, tattoos and builders' banter. They would be back tomorrow to place more matchsticks on the stack and pass judgement on the state of the roof.

Earlier in town Jason had been smiling at strangers on the street; drunken men, secretarial women, beggars and landlords and people carrying baskets of individually wrapped rose buds – and he had been thinking, *None of you would ever guess in a million years that I have a cheque in my pocket for half a million pounds. Oh yes.*

And the thought made him bountiful. He dropped a pound in the beggar's cup and bought a rose from a tiny Japanese girl which he then deposited in a bin around the corner.

He didn't know what had made him get back in his car and

drive to the site. He supposed he shouldn't be driving after the number of drinks he'd had, but somehow he felt so calm and clear-headed that he couldn't accept the idea that his senses would be impaired. He supposed he shouldn't be going *anywhere* with the second cheque still in his pocket – but after all, who'd ever guess in a million years what he was carrying? He'd been safe thus far, standing at the bar in some greasy hole of a place, drinking Scotch, chatting up the barmaid without really meaning to, out of habit. He congratulated himself at having thought of phoning Fran to tell her he would be late. He congratulated himself further at his presence of mind in not telling her that he hadn't made it to the bank with the cheque quite yet.

Jason stumbled over the debris on the ground and tilted his head back to look at the stars through the holes in the roof. There was something quite magical about this place. He thought about how it could be – if things were different . . .

The phone ringing . . . again. A frenetic waiter barking that, no, there wasn't a table tonight, no, nor tomorrow, no, nor next week. When would there be a table for dinner? Let's see . . . we could do a table for three at nine o'clock on June 14th, but it's only available for two hours . . . yes, sir, we are well aware that it is only March 3rd – we're terribly sorry to disappoint sir . . .

'Melting Night'. People laughing, chatting, bitching as they fork up that molten camembert, stick a sneaky finger into the dollop of sour cream dripping down over their veal escalope, as they watch that hot raspberry sauce oozing over the basil and pepper ice cream . . . Vampy women eyeing up the waiters in their immaculate white jackets, lumpish men hoping the waitresses would have to bend a little lower, reach a little further to pour the first dribble from a bottle of Georges Duboeuf Fleurie . . . would sir like to taste?

Oh, the dresses; the velvet and the silk, the Paul Smith suit, the Ralph Lauren tie, the Rolex at the hairy wrist. Is the lady's coat the mink or the fox fur? The green fake fur number? My, it's so fun, so 'street'. Dress code? No, of course not. Come in your undies if you like – but no M&S, we beg of you, no BHS, no C&A.

Yes, of course we take VISA, Mastercard, American Express,

Diners' Club, Switch, Delta . . . US dollar traveller's cheque? No problem, madam. Euros? But of course.

It was rather a shame that the restaurant would never come into existence. A damn shame, actually.

Meredith had called that morning, insisting Jason came to collect the cheque in person, alone, and Fran had taken this as a bad omen.

'Why doesn't he want me to come too? What do you think he wants? Maybe he knows something about us.'

'I think he knows *everything* about us,' Jason had replied. 'Or senses it. But he's stupid enough to think he can control us.'

'Then what does he want? Do you think he's found out we haven't given any money to Owen?'

'How could he have found out? The only person who could have told him is Owen, and Owen isn't speaking to him. This is the fatal flaw in Tony Meredith's plan – he has no way of discovering what's happened to his money.'

Fran was not convinced. And as Keith led Jason up to the lounge in Meredith's turret, Jason wasn't convinced either.

But Meredith was friendly, talkative.

'In some ways you've become a sort of foster father to my son. It makes me want to know you better.'

'Wait up – a foster father? He's only a few years younger than me!'

'In real time perhaps so – but in *experience* – my God, you must be old enough to be his grandfather . . . And it's experience that counts.'

'You think I'm a man of the world then?'

Meredith laughed and his tiny pinprick eyes seemed to disappear into a deep crevice somewhere at the back of his head. When he stopped laughing the eyes came back, as cold as ever.

Meredith showed Jason around his tower. As well as the lounge there was a bedroom with a single bed and en suite bathroom, an office and a tiny kitchenette. It was like some sort of bunker. Jason could just imagine Meredith holing himself up in there, moving markers around on maps, making his war plans, conducting his secret business, deciding who to destroy next . . .

A hard slap on the back made him jump.

'So young Robert, what say you to another Scotch and a spot of music? We won't have Tom today. Even *I* listen to something different now and again . . . what say you to a bit of Bonnie Tyler, eh? "Total Eclipse of the Heart", now there's a song and a half!'

And Jason was stuck there for hours, making his way through an excellent bottle of single malt, while his host gyrated and twirled around him. After a time the whiskey began to muddy the endless music, rendering it hazy and dreamy in quality. He began almost to enjoy himself. And when Meredith finally slumped down on the couch, exhausted, Jason began to tell him a story – the story of The Melt, Owen Meredith's restaurant, and how it would be.

Jason knew he should go home and get some sleep, but he didn't feel like going, not just yet. This night was special, this place was special. He'd sit himself down on the edge of the stage and stay there for a while. Just to think a little, just to mull things over. He dug his hands deep into his pockets. The engagement ring was still there in its box. What was he to do about these bloody women of his . . .

Two blue lines. Parallel. That's all they were. They meant nothing, represented nothing. No portent of doom, no sign of great wonders, no life-altering event.

This was what Fran told herself as she leaned heavily on the bathroom sink and caught sight of her drawn, worried face in the mirrored door of the medicine cabinet. This was what she tried to make herself believe in order to buy a moment or two of sanity before she had to face the music. I'm too old for this, she thought. Or too young. I don't have the right instincts, I can't do it. This doesn't fit in with *anything*. She wrapped up the testing kit in a brown paper bag before throwing it in the bin, so Jason wouldn't notice it.

While she splashed cold water onto her face, Fran considered what a complicated business testing used to be. She remembered how, as a teenager, she had poured liquids from one test tube to another, stuck litmus paper into pink solutions, tried to ascertain whether that colour was the red you were so afraid of, or merely innocent pink. And of course, you had to test your first wee of the day, so when you woke up bursting and rushed to the toilet without thinking, you had blown it for another twenty-four hours. Twenty-four hours of worry and uncertainty – am I really feeling sick and what kind of sick is it that I'm feeling? Am I feeling sick because I'm thinking about the idea of feeling sick?

There was nothing uncertain in those two blue lines.

And that was the doorbell. Ignore it? Where the hell did Jason get to last night?

'Good morning, Ms Freeman.'

Fran stared blankly at the short man standing on the step. The sun was directly behind him, making it difficult to see his face as anything beyond a dark blur. 'Good morning?' she said brightly, trying to work out who this was. Did she know him?

The man cleared his throat, and smoothed several long strands of hair ineffectually across his large bald patch. 'Here on your own, are you?' he asked, glancing past her into the house.

Fran didn't like this. Perhaps she should call out to a fictitious group of people serving breakfast in the kitchen. Perhaps she should slam the door in his face. Instead she said nothing, and waited. She was sure she ought to know who this was.

He took a large white handkerchief from his pocket and blew his nose loudly. 'Would you mind coming with me, Marsha? May I call you Marsha?'

Fran was gripping the door frame with her right hand. She gripped it so hard that one of her nails folded unpleasantly back on itself. She flinched away from the door frame, teeth on edge. 'What's this all about?' She was still reluctant to ask him who he was because she really *should* know.

'I think I'll leave that for the boss to explain,' said the man, shuffling his feet. 'Do you want to get a jacket, Marsha?'

Fran was panicky. She couldn't work out the proportion of the panic that was due to her pregnancy or how much it was concerned with the unexpected visitor. 'Is it Tony Meredith?' she blurted.

'What?'

'Your boss. Do you work for Tony Meredith?'

'Tony Meredith?' he parroted, thrusting his hands deep in the pockets of his battered old suit.

But Fran had another thought. 'Are you a policeman? . . . I'd like to see your ID please.'

The man scratched at a sideburn and turned slowly to point down at a silver Jaguar XJS parked in the street. There were two large male shapes in the back. 'Come on, Marsha. We don't want to keep the boys waiting, now, do we?'

'No,' said Fran, recognising the car. 'No, we don't.'

She sat in the passenger seat, feeling 'the boys'' eyes on her, roaming all over the back of her neck. She didn't want to turn to look at them, preferred not to see their broken noses or stupid eyes, whatever features they might happen to have in common with others of their trade. She groped about in her bag for her packet of cigarettes. But perhaps she shouldn't smoke – not now that . . . ? Oh God, how ridiculous.

'Marsha, would you mind?' asked the driver, bending to press the tuning buttons on the car radio with his fat fingers, while turning the car right onto the main road, out of Lisvane and into Llanishen, past stately Victorian houses with verandas and brass door knockers.

'What? Oh.' Fran removed the cigarette unlit from her lips and returned it to the packet.

'No, no,' said the man, immediately, as he changed gear. 'Not the fags. The seat belt. It's the law, you know.'

Elton John was singing 'Candle in the Wind', the Diana version. The speakers were poor quality and his voice was thin and tinny.

Fran breathed slowly out. 'Sorry.' She reached back for the belt and it was handed to her by a hand with a signet ring and a long scar running from the base of the index finger right down under the shirt sleeve. There was an elaborate gold cufflink – Fran had always hated those. She did her best not to touch the hand as she took the belt from it. 'Thanks,' she said.

'You're welcome,' came a disembodied voice with a heavy Cardiff accent as the hand retreated to the back of the car.

'Red Dragon Radio,' sang the jingle, and the Manic Street Preachers began to jangle and rasp.

Fran fastened the belt and placed her cigarette back in her mouth, fumbled in her bag for a lighter. Another hand, this one coated in fine ginger hairs with fingers like lumps of dough appeared under her face, clicking a silver lighter aflame and holding it to the end of the cigarette. 'Thanks.'

'You're welcome,' came a second voice, slightly lower pitched than the first.

The car swung past Roath Park. The lake was alive with rowing boats and pedalos, and the weeping willows were stirring gently on the breeze. But the lake wasn't so blue, the grass not so wonderfully green as it had been a few weeks before. The summer was fraying around the edges, slowly unravelling and disintegrating. Soon the days would start to feel like strands of thread connecting nothing to nothing.

'Where are we going?' Fran tried to make her voice sound normal, tapping her cigarette over the ashtray.

'Round to the house,' said the driver, keeping his eyes on the road.

'And that'll be where, exactly?' She hoped her frustration didn't show.

'Grangetown,' said the man. 'Do you know it?'

Fran shook her head.

'Great place. Terrific sense of community, even these days when most people don't know the name of the family next door, let alone the names of the people at the end of the street.'

'Some of us prefer anonymity,' said Fran quietly.

'Why's that then?' asked the man, with a wheezing chuckle. 'Got something to hide, have you?'

The car slunk by the Welsh office and past the university into the town centre. The castle appeared briefly on their right – brown and cheerful in the sunlight, flags fluttering brightly. Then it was down St Mary Street, stopping at a red light. The street was busy, and Fran gazed out at some women looking longingly at wedding dresses in a department store display. She watched a mother with a pushchair containing a small blond child of indeterminate gender trying to get past the hordes of people at the fish stall near the entrance to the indoor market. The crowd had spilled out onto the street where they blocked the pavement, and nobody made way for the frazzled woman to get by. Nobody so much as gave an inch. Fran shivered and leaned back against the head rest, closing her eyes for a moment until the car began to move again and they left the woman far behind.

Where did Jason get to last night?

'Nearly there,' said the man, as they passed the station and the crumbling old water tower painted all over with giant daffodils. They crossed over the river, which was rank and muddy on this side of town, and turned left under a dark railway bridge, emerging onto a road drained of all colour. Nothing but grey. They took a few turns and the streets began to look eerily identical – road after road of squat terraced houses. The legend above a shop painted in a murky yellow that was somehow grey like everything else read 'Flower Trends'. A couple of streets further the man pulled over and parked behind a knackered old transit van.

'Here we are,' said the man. 'Home sweet home.'

It was a terraced house much like all the others except for the stained glass flower that graced the front door. Its windows were newer than those of the neighbouring houses, its tiny front yard (you could hardly call it a garden) was smarter, and a second glance at the intricate iron gate revealed the letters 'S' and 'T' intertwined at the centre of the design.

The boys hulked out of the car ahead of Fran, and now she had no choice but to look at them – one dark, one ginger, big square heads, chunky gold jewellery, ill-fitting suits that looked cheap but probably cost considerably more than Fran's, and ill-fitting grins. They shuffled up the front path in their loafers, dwarfing their father with their enormous shoulders.

The narrow hallway smelled of cats, and the heavy flock regency-striped walls seemed to push in on Fran so that she had to fight the nausea. A huge barometer dominated one wall, and over the stairs hung a sampler fussily embroidered with the words, *God is as near as He is far away.*

'Ted? Is that you?' shouted a familiar voice.

'Yes, love,' called the man, and pushed a door open.

Sadie March – March like the month – was wearing a lurid pink pant suit with lipstick to match. She was ironing white shirts –

several were neatly folded in a pile on a chair next to her while the plastic washing basket on the floor was almost full of shirts still to be done.

'Hi, Mum.' The ginger boy bent to kiss her on one cheek.

'All right, Mum?' The dark boy kissed the other.

Alvin Stardust was being interviewed by Richard Madeley on the television, and Ted picked up the remote to switch it off.

'I was watching that!' snapped Sadie, but then seemed to change her mind, and flapped an acquiescent hand before resuming her ironing with a cloud of steam.

The boys shifted uneasily in the doorway. They seemed too big for the room.

'Skidaddle, kids,' said Sadie. 'We can't have you standing around here wearing out the carpet, now, can we? Sit down, Ms Freeman, do sit down. Would you like some tea?'

'Yes, please,' said Fran. The cream leather couch was wrapped in plastic sheeting, which crackled as she sat. 'Milk no sugar.'

'I'll have one too, Ted, and some biscuits.' Sadie dispatched him with another vague flap of a hand. 'Now,' she said, closing the door behind him, 'I think we should have a little talk, woman to woman.' She bent to switch off the iron at the plug.

Fran was taking in the details of the room – one wall was dominated by a mantelpiece of fake unfaced stone. The walls were white, with some kind of plastic textured wall covering, and the carpet was brown, deep-pile and old-looking. But what struck you immediately was that every surface was covered in knick-knacks; porcelain milkmaids and crinoline women, wooden elephants, glass poodles, miniature china cottages, ceramic ashtrays, alabaster eggs, straw dollies, golfing trophies, silver Priapuses – a veritable swarm of ornamentation. Was Sadie March afraid of empty spaces? And the walls too were far from bare; a cuckoo clock, a set of horse brasses, a copy of a Canaletto Venice in a heavy gilt frame, a black and white photo of the family dressed in circus costume; the boys in red noses and silly wigs smiling stiffly, Ted proudly sporting the ringmaster's top hat and Sadie herself at the centre, with a beauty spot, a spangly low-cut top and a tiara, the circus darling, queen of the flying trapeze.

An enormous orange cat dozed on the window ledge.

'Nice cat,' said Fran absently.

'Isn't he lovely, my little Happy, my boy,' cooed Sadie, and to Fran's alarm her hostess scooped up the cat and shoved it right at her so suddenly that she almost dropped it.

A glass eye looked up at her. The cat was stuffed. Fran almost retched. She passed it back to Sadie as rapidly as she could without revealing her revulsion.

'He got knocked down by a car last summer,' said Sadie, and her eyes filled with tears. She cradled the cat in her arms for a moment or two, stroking it, whispering, 'My boy, Mummy's precious,' before finally setting it back on the window sill.

'Now then.' She moved the folded shirts onto the floor so she could sit on the wooden dining chair, drawing it closer to Fran. 'Forgive me for prying, but there's something I'm curious about – about you and Mr Warren – you and Robert.'

Fran could feel the tension gathering in her jaw – focusing itself there. When she tried to speak, her mouth creaked its way open, achingly. 'What's this all about, Mrs March? If you want to speak to me I'm at the office every day. You only have to call my secretary to fix an appointment. You don't need to have your husband and sons drag me out of my house before I've even eaten breakfast and bundle me into your Jag.'

'What I'm curious about,' continued Sadie, unfazed, 'is the *nature* of your relationship with Robert. You work together, you live together – I assume you share a bed . . .'

'I don't think that's any of your business, Mrs March.'

Sadie picked at a molar with a long pink-painted nail. 'So you *do* share a bed,' she said, and gave a helpless little shrug. 'I find it all rather difficult to understand.'

'What's to understand?' Fran's jaw was almost rigid with pent-up tension.

'You don't strike me as a stupid woman—' said Sadie.

'Gee, thanks.'

'You surely realise that Robert – to put it bluntly – sleeps around.'

Ted appeared with a tray and set it down on the glass-topped coffee table. He passed a mug of tea to Fran and one to Sadie. Sadie's mug was yellow with a blue 'S' on it. He had made a cup for himself too – his mug bore a 'T'. There was a plate of custard creams and chocolate digestives. He began to ease himself down into one of the armchairs, but on catching sight of Sadie's face changed his mind and stood up again.

'Shut the door behind you, please, Ted,' said Sadie as he retreated. 'Now,' she turned back to Fran. 'Where was I?'

'You were in the middle of slating my relationship.' Fran's jaw was so tight now she could barely move it. She sipped at her tea and burnt her tongue.

'Oh come on, Marsha.' Sadie gave another of those dismissive flaps of the hand. 'We both know he's been sleeping with my niece. I'm just wondering how many *other* girls he's bedding and then conning out of their savings. Do you sleep easy, Marsha, lying next to him, listening to his breathing? Doesn't it bother you to think of him touching those other women, perhaps thinking about them even when he's home in your bed? We're all so innocent in our sleep, aren't we?' She crunched on a custard cream.

Fran set down her mug and got to her feet. 'I don't have to listen to this.'

'Ah, but you do.' Her smile was strangely sympathetic, even while she threatened. Were the boys standing outside in the hall, guarding the front door in their clown outfits?

Fran sat down again. The plastic sheeting was sticking to her legs. 'Listen, Mrs March—'

'Call me Sadie.'

'Whatever – Sadie – Robbie isn't seeing Samantha any more. He broke it off with her a couple of weeks ago. And he gave her back her money. She's out of this now.'

Slowly Sadie shook her head, made a couple of little tutting noises.

'What's the matter? That's what you want, isn't it? That's why you brought me here – to tell me you wanted your Samantha out of this. To sort it out "woman to woman" as you put it? Well she's out, Sadie. She's out.'

'Wrong.' The sympathetic smile was gone and Fran felt a tremor of fear rumble right through her, down through her stomach to settle in her womb. Instinctively, she placed a hand there as though to protect it.

'He's still seeing her, Marsha. And he still has her money.'

'No he can't be. I promise you.'

'He *is*. Take it from me.'

And Fran knew it was true. She took a deep breath and tried to get her thoughts straight. There was a photo on the mantelpiece in an oval frame, a snapshot of a pretty girl with large eyes and blonde hair. So that was what Sadie's precious niece looked like. 'Do you mind if I have a cigarette?'

Sadie slid an ashtray across the table, and Fran reached into her bag for her packet of Marlboro.

'Now,' Sadie said when the cigarette was lit, 'it's like this, Marsha. I love that girl as much as my own sons, and I won't see her frisked over by you or your partner or anyone else on this planet. I'm only going to ask one thing of you. I'm going to overlook the fact that you're operating on my patch – and yes, you are, my dear, although you didn't know it. You damn well should have known it, but let's set that aside. I'm going to overlook whatever it is that you're doing to Tony Meredith and his son. The less I know about that, the happier I'll be. No – the only thing that really bothers me is the happiness and well-being of my niece, Samantha.'

'I understand.' Fran tapped ash from the end of her cigarette, noticing how much her hand was trembling, realising Sadie March would notice too.

'You will give Samantha her money back and you will keep your shit-head of a partner away from her.' Slowly, deliberately, without taking her eyes off Fran's, Sadie extended a hand and removed Fran's cigarette from her mouth, stubbing it out in the ashtray. 'Now,' she said, 'I've things to do.' She gestured at the basket of ironing. 'Ted will drive you home.'

Waking up on Owen's living-room floor this morning was not a good experience. I had one of those hangovers where your head pulses too much to allow you to sleep on, but being awake is unbearable. I ached all down one side from lying in one position for too long, and my eyelids scraped excruciatingly across my eyes as if they were lined with sand. My sole consolation was that when Sîan emerged from the bedroom she looked even worse than I felt.

Owen whistled and hummed to himself as he washed up and made coffee for us. I think he was happy because he felt we'd reached a new, deeper stage of our relationship. Funny how people can believe they are closer to you because they have told you a secret. You don't even have to reciprocate – you only have to listen. This common phenomenon is continually exploited by low-life like me. The more we tell our loved ones, the closer we feel to them – the closer we feel the more we want to tell them and so it goes on and on – and just at that special moment when we have disclosed everything and we are feeling blissfully happy in our state of ultimate sharing – at the moment when we think we are at our strongest, united in perfect harmony with our partners – well, that is when we are at our most vulnerable to the more unscrupulous characters that operate within our sentimental society. It's only afterwards, nursing that vicious wound or that empty wallet that we realise it was all one-way traffic – we gave everything we had to give and what did we get back? Usually a sharp kick somewhere painful.

Call me cynical, call me emotionally stunted – decide that I'm the unlucky one because if you can't ever really give of yourself you ultimately lose out. But just wait until someone suckers you and see if you still feel like that. Chances are that next time around you'll be the one doing the kicking.

However, my new – and possibly insurmountable – trouble is that Owen has not rendered himself and his father as vulnerable as I had hoped; maybe he doesn't know anything about Meredith that we can use. I really should have thought about this before. Why the hell would Tony Meredith have told Owen a secret so bad that it might turn son against father? And how could a man like that be careless enough to allow Owen to discover something by chance?

I can feel myself begin to despair. Despair is creeping over me like my hangover. What the hell am I going to do?

While Sîan and I sat clutching our mugs of coffee and wincing at Owen's exuberance, the phone rang. It was Jason, ringing to invite Owen and me to a celebratory champagne breakfast at the house in Lisvane. The story was that they'd secured another substantial investment. Reading between the lines I realised we must have got the second instalment from Tony Meredith. My spirits lifted and so did my hangover. There had to be an answer to my predicament. It would come to me all in good time.

Jason was carrying chairs onto the front lawn when we arrived, placing them under the shade of the apple trees. The roses were in bloom; red, white and all kinds of pinks and yellows. Owen went to give him a hand, leaving me to wander over the grass. In this sunlight, everything and everyone was golden. A man across the road, polishing his car, stood up to admire his handiwork and waved at me. The sun does that to people, doesn't it? Makes them to want to talk to total strangers for no particular reason. I waved back and called out, 'Lovely day.'

'Better make the most of it,' he shouted. 'There won't be many more days like this.'

Jason and Owen appeared through the French windows, one at each end of the kitchen table. They staggered and grappled with it and I went to help. Laughing and joking with them as we dragged it across the lawn, I could almost believe this was real, that we were two normal couples meeting for breakfast on a gorgeous summer morning. No ulterior motives, no deception, no con. Funny stuff, sun.

Owen caught hold of my hand while Jason went back into the house. He was grinning like a schoolboy. I knew what he was going to say even before he said it.

'I love you, Meg.'

I wasn't sure what to do with my face. I didn't seem to have any control over it. I had no idea whether I was smiling or grimacing, but judging by the way his expression changed I think I must have been doing the latter:

'I'm sorry. Pretend I never said it. The last thing I want is to scare you off. Me and my big gob!'

I was touched, I don't know why. Maybe because Owen is a nice guy, maybe because no man has ever told me he loved me before. I suppose everyone wants to think they are capable of inspiring those kind of feelings in someone else.

He was prattling on, trying to un-say it: 'I don't want to put any pressure on you, Meg. I don't expect you to feel the same way – not yet anyway – though obviously I hope you'll feel like that one day. Oh God, I'm doing it again! I'm sorry, I'll just shut up.'

I managed a smile. 'It's OK, Owen. I'm glad.'

Jason reappeared with a glass bowl of fruit salad.

'Mangoes – fruit of the gods,' he announced. 'Blackberries – fruit of the wicked ...'

It was then that we all noticed Fran down in the street climbing out of an old silver Jaguar XJS. I hadn't even registered that she wasn't here. I suppose I'd assumed she was in the house or something. She was bending to speak to whoever was in the driver's seat, then she slammed the passenger door. She didn't wave as it pulled away.

Jason called out to her. 'Marsha! You're just in time for bubbly.'

'Not for me, thanks.' Fran was trudging wearily up the drive.

'What? No champers for my honey? I don't believe it!' Jason threw up his hands in mock horror. 'Where've you been, babes?'

'Where were *you* last night?' Fran snapped back.

I was surprised to hear her speak like that in front of Owen. She stood with her hands on her hips. The way she looked at Jason he could have been a piece of dirt.

'I went to the site. It was sort of magic there. I just sat there thinking. I didn't want to move.'

'You mean to say you spent the whole night in that place!'

'Yeah, I did ... Honestly.'

She pulled up a chair and sat down. '*Honestly,*' she mimicked. 'As though you even know what the word means!'

'Why don't I go and get the champagne and some glasses,' suggested Owen, tactfully. 'Come on, Meg. Give me a hand.'

He set off into the house, but I hung back. 'What's going on, Fran?'

'Ask him!'

'Oh, give me a break,' said Jason. 'Everything was fine when I left last night. Where have you been? Who was that in the car?'

'That was your girlfriend's Uncle Ted.' She gave him a look of pure hatred.

The breeze picked up strength and started shaking the branches of the apple tree. A few stray leaves blew down onto the table.

'Fran ...' Jason was frightened now. You could see it in his eyes. 'I tried to give her the money back. She ripped up the cheque ...'

I could barely believe what I was hearing.

Fran found a cigarette and gripped it between her teeth as she searched for her lighter. 'I'll have you know, Jason darling, that I've just been put in that Jag by Ted March and his sons, taken to some shithole in Grangetown and given a little lecture by Sadie fucking March. It was very enlightening.'

'Meg!' shouted Owen, from the kitchen.

'Just coming, sweetie.'

'Franny, Franny,' Jason wheedled, pathetically. 'That girl means nothing to me, I swear to you.' He leaned forward and grabbed her by the shoulders, forcing her to look at him. 'I'll sort it out, OK? I'll make her take the money back even if I have to ram the cheque down her throat! OK?'

'You told me Sadie March was a nobody,' Fran said, quietly.

'And so she is.'

Fran removed his hands from her shoulders. 'Jason, Sadie March is a fucking gangster!'

'You're exaggerating,' said Jason. 'Don't forget, I've met the woman too . . .'

'Don't you *dare* tell me I'm exaggerating.' Fran lit the cigarette and brandished it like a weapon. 'Not after what I've been through this morning.'

'Oh *please*.' Jason began to laugh, but nervously.

'Sort it out, Jason,' said Fran, getting to her feet. 'Today. And as for you.' She turned to me. 'Snap out of your little dream world and get your job done. If that boy can't give us anything to use on Meredith, you'll have to find it somewhere else.'

And she turned around and stormed into the house.

We sat, the three of us, drinking champagne and pretending that everything was OK. The fizz had gone out of the morning. I was shivering uncontrollably – whether from anger or fear I didn't really know. Whenever I looked up at Jason he was trying to smile, to be nonchalant.

Owen couldn't keep up the act for long. 'Robbie, mate, what the hell have you done?'

'Do you remember when we went for that curry on the night we first met?' Jason's mouth was full of strawberries, making it look even redder than usual.

'Of course.'

'Well do you remember I told you about my relationship . . . my long-standing but *open* relationship?' Jason nodded towards the house.

'So, you've been playing around,' said Owen. I watched his foot tapping agitatedly.

'I suppose.'

Owen shook his head. 'I don't understand you, Robbie. Marsha's a great woman. You're a fool to risk losing her.'

Jason shrugged. 'What can I say? I'm a man. We do things like that.'

'I don't,' said Owen. And I knew it was true. This man would never play around – his feelings were too intense to be shared between women. He needed to focus them on one object alone.

'Get off my case, Owen.' He was doing his best to make light of it. 'You're giving me the jitters. Let's have some more champers.' He reached for the bottle.

'What about Marsha?' asked Owen.

'Oh, she'll be OK.'

'No, she won't,' I said. I had just noticed something – there was a magpie sitting in the apple tree. Alone.

5

The Heart

Tony Meredith is an eccentric eater – so like a true dictator he imposed his eccentricities on everyone else around the table. He believes that talking while eating upsets the digestion. Consequently the whole table was silent. He also thinks you shouldn't drink while you are eating, so all four of us munched our way through medium-rare sirloin steak, baby new potatoes and salad without so much as a sip of water let alone a glass of wine. I was absolutely parched, but bore it in silence. As a child going to tea with friends whose parents refused to give you a glass of squash with your meal, I would sulk and strop and not be invited back. Tonight I struggled not to return to my childish persona.

The most fascinating oddity was the way Meredith chewed. He took tiny mouthfuls of food and worked at them thoroughly, industriously, rotating his jaw slowly, smoothly in a clockwise direction. He gave careful attention to each mouthful as he crunched and mulched and crushed, and finally – *finally* – swallowed. I have a tendency to gobble and did my best to slow down under his penetrating glare. Three quarters of an hour after we started the meal he was still slicing, forking and chomping his cold steak, while I stared down at my empty plate, craving a drink.

As if she'd read my mind, Sîan got up and announced she was fetching a bottle of wine. 'Daddy's potty about eating,' she said, examining the wine rack. 'He pays absurd attention to *how* food should be eaten – but none at all to *what* one should eat.'

'Sîanie!' growled Meredith, but without menace. I had the sense that Tony's Little Girl could get away with saying things that nobody else could. She kissed him on the top of the head before going to the sideboard for a corkscrew.

The heavily made-up blonde woman at the end of the table giggled nervously. Her name, apparently, was Louisa. She was Meredith's 'current' and Sîan loathed her.

So simple, so obvious, so why hadn't I thought of it before? If Owen didn't have any dirt on Meredith, I would have to get it somewhere else. Where? From the horse's mouth, of course. And how to get to him? Through Sîan. Sweet, spoilt, needy little Sîan who so badly wanted her brother and her father to make their peace. I wish I could lay claim to having hit on this myself, but in fact the idea came from her. She had phoned me at the health-food shop a few days after that awful champagne breakfast:

I've told Daddy all about you, Meg, and he wants to meet you. Yes, I know Owen would go mad if he knew, but you wouldn't go telling him, would you? He's wrong about Daddy, Meg, plain wrong. It's so unfair. But I don't expect you to take it from me. I'm asking you to come to the house for one weekend and make up your own mind. Meg – you might just be able to reunite a father and son here. One weekend, that's all I'm asking.

I made the right amount of protest. How could she expect me to do this terribly disloyal thing? Did Sîan really want me to lie to Owen about something so important? I'd never lied to him and I didn't want to start doing it now ... a secret like that could kill my relationship stone dead if it ever came out ... or even if it didn't. I let her plead and wheedle for a good long time before finally, reluctantly, agreeing.

I told Owen I was going to visit friends up North. He was upset that I didn't want him to come with me, but didn't seem suspicious.

After dinner we relaxed in a lounge decorated tackily in a sort of fake country-cottage style; rose printed curtains and matching comfy suite, wooden beams, a large open hearth, vases of dried flowers and bowls of fruit; horse brasses ... Meredith poured out Scotch for himself, port for Sîan and brandy for me and Louisa.

He nursed a fat unlit cigar, rolling it between his fingers, smelling it, playing with it. 'How is Owen?'

'Oh, he's well. He's so excited about the restaurant. He really believes it's going to raise his career to another level. He's expecting so much from it that it almost makes me nervous.'

Meredith smiled, nodded. 'You needn't be worried, Meg. Between you and me I'm delighted about this restaurant. Owen's talented, don't get me wrong, but I'll be relieved to see the boy getting into business. He's never going to make decent money from the art world, let's face it, and if he makes a success of this maybe it'll give him some stability. He might start thinking it's time to settle down and have a family.'

I could feel myself blushing.

'You're a nice girl, Meg. Owen could do much worse.'

'Daddy!'

'Ah, stop telling me off, Sîanie. One of the privileges of being in your dotage is that you get to say whatever you like, and you get away with it.'

Louisa giggled over her brandy glass. Everyone ignored her.

'I somehow don't see you as a man in his dotage, Mr Meredith,' I said.

Meredith smiled. 'Call me Tony.'

I hadn't expected to like Tony Meredith, but I found I did. I knew I was seeing him at his most pleasant and courteous, that there was another side to the man lurking in the corners of the wide mouth, a coldness glinting in those tiny eyes. But tonight he was a loving father, desperate for news of his lost boy, hugely grateful to me for agreeing to come to meet him.

He puffed leisurely on another cigar. The room was quiet except for the occasional crackle of burning tobacco. I'd been anticipating the moment when he would jump to his feet, put on a Tom Jones CD and insist we all danced. But it was past midnight now and still no Tom. This was a muted, reflective Tony Meredith. I suppose he was thinking about his boy, and maybe also about his dead wife.

At some point he stood up and handed me one of two photos in silver frames that stood at either end of the mantelpiece.

It was a black and white picture of a mother and child sitting on grass. The woman was big boned, all elbows and jaw. Her shirt sleeves were rolled up, workmanlike. An expression of determination seemed to sit just behind the camera smile. The little boy was two, maybe three years old. Dark hair and darker eyes – cute, cheeky; grazed knees and battered sandals; he clutched a sandwich in one hand, a daisy in the other.

'I'd know Owen anywhere. He looks exactly like he does now. But his mother isn't how I imagined her.'

'Actually, it isn't Owen and his mother.' Meredith returned to his seat.

'What?'

'It's me and my mother.' He was smiling, happy at having caught me out.

It was obvious now he'd said it. The photo was far too old to be Owen and his mother. The fashions were wrong and the hair styles. The ancient grainy quality of the image itself should have given it away. I felt foolish.

'Now look at this one.' He passed me the second photograph. This too was of a mother and son. The woman was more attractive but with a slightly unearthly fragility; red hair, large kind eyes but wrists too thin and pale to the point of transparency. The little boy looked strikingly similar to the child in the first picture; the black hair and eyes, the grazed knees, the way he smiled.

'What do you think?' asked Meredith.

I looked closer at the picture, at the position in which the mother and son sat together on the grass. 'I think what everyone must think. That you and Owen are astonishingly alike.'

Meredith seemed to be preening, revelling in my pronouncement. I knew this was the comment he'd been after.

Dare I challenge him? Yes. Tonight he was a pussy cat. 'But it's a set-up, isn't it? You wanted to create an identical picture so that everyone would be amazed by the resemblance. You've even got both boys holding a sandwich and a daisy. Overkill, I'd say. You've tried just a little bit too hard.' I handed the photo back to him.

'But you do think we look alike?' He was anxious.

'Of course.'

This was enough for him. Satisfied, he sat back and puffed on the cigar. After a few minutes of contented smoky silence he turned to Sîan. 'Isn't it a bit late for you, Sîanie? Hadn't you better be getting to bed?'

Sîan's face became sulky. 'I'm not some kid, Dad.'

'But you've got training in the morning. It's only three weeks till the Florin tournament, don't forget.'

'How can I bloody forget it! You go on at me all the bloody time!'

'Watch your language, missy.'

Sîan drained her port glass and got to her feet, flushed and tearful. 'Oh, what's the use.' Her voice cracked and she struggled to control it. 'See you in the morning, Meg.'

'Nightie-night, tennis star,' smirked Louisa, as Sîan pulled the door closed behind her.

Meredith looked at me, embarrassed, and shrugged. 'Kids, eh? What can you do with them? Another drink?'

Half an hour later I laid down my empty brandy glass. Meredith was still waxing on about his children.

Louisa, who had been slumped on the couch for some time let out a sudden whistling snore, jolting Meredith out of his reverie. Irritated, he moved behind her and tapped his cigar so that ash dropped down into her blonde hair. 'Ridicule my daughter, will you?' he whispered into her ear. She didn't so much as stir.

'The point is,' said Meredith, regaining his composure and sitting down again, 'it's futile for Owen to go around pretending I don't exist. You've only got to look at those photos to see how much of me that boy has in him.'

I found myself thinking of Dad. I have his build, his hair, his skin ... what else have I inherited from him?

'I think I need to hit the hay,' I said.

'Sure.' He stubbed out the cigar. 'I guess I'd better get Sleeping Beauty here to bed too.'

I headed for the door. 'Meg,' Meredith called out.

'Yes?'

He was meek, almost humble. 'I've done some bad things in my time, but I'm not a bad man. There's a difference.'

It was almost as though he wanted me to lay my hands on his head and bless him. I looked into the tiny eyes, which seemed sadder than before, oddly translucent. It could have been Jason or Fran saying those words. It could have been me. I felt morose but I managed to smile. 'It's that difference that lets us sleep at night, isn't it.'

Meredith looked confused.

'Good night, Tony.'

On the other side of town Jason was playing with menus again. What were the possibilities in toffee? Were there ever circumstances that would lead one to consider toffee as sophisticated cuisine? Could one, for example, use it with savoury food rather than sweet? There was a Brazilian recipe for chicken in chocolate, but was there any equivalent for toffee? Would it be unusual or simply revolting?

His whiskey glass was empty.

'Drink?' he asked Fran, who was curled up on the couch scribbling maniacally in one of her notebooks. The scribbling was almost a compulsion with her.

Fran shook her head, no, without looking up.

'Are you ill?'

This time she did look up. 'No. I just don't want a drink.'

'Exactly,' said Jason. 'I think you must be ill.' He reached out to feel her forehead in case she was feverish, but she batted his hand away. He sat down on the couch next to her and she drew her feet up, shrinking back from him.

'Frannie,' he wheedled.

'What?' Her voice was hard, cold.

'Nothing.' He felt his shoulders slump in despair. He stood up to pour his Scotch and then moved around behind her, peering over her shoulder to try to get a look at the notebook.

She slammed it shut and got to her feet.

'Where are you going?'

'To bed.'

'But it's early.'

'So?'

God, she was infuriating. He swallowed his Scotch in one gulp. 'Shall I come too?' he tried.

'No.'

'Why not, for God's sake?' He could hear the desperation in his voice. How he hated not to be in control. 'When are you going to let me back into the bedroom?'

'You know what you have to do, Jason.'

Of course he knew it. She'd virtually tattooed it across his forehead.

'It's not as simple as you think.'

'Evidently.'

He followed her into the hall and watched her climbing the stairs. 'She's in love with me, Fran. She won't accept the money. She's obsessed!'

Fran gave him a withering look over her shoulder. 'I'm tired, Jason.'

'I know. Look, it's in hand.' She wasn't the only one who was tired. His mind was drifting back to the toffee. Only now there was a vat full of the stuff and he was trying to swim even as it sucked him down.

'Show me a bank statement, Jason,' said Fran. 'I want to see that money debited from your account in black and white. Then you can come back in the bedroom. OK?' She turned and walked away across the landing, leaving him alone with his Scotch glass and his ideas, gloomy and frustrated.

Fran undressed carefully, sliding her trousers onto a hanger, folding her jumper. She sat at the dressing table to cleanse her face. God, she was dying for a drink. It didn't have to be a *drink* drink – any kind of liquid in a glass would do. Anything that might quench this raging thirst. But she'd been told at the clinic that she shouldn't eat or drink anything for twelve hours before the procedure in case of complications. *Complications*. She set the alarm clock and eased herself down between smooth cold sheets. She switched off the lamp. Lying alone in the dark, listening to Jason thumping about downstairs, she allowed herself to feel the fear. She nursed it.

'There's a chill in the air this morning,' said Sîan, as she and Eileen got up from the table where they'd been eating breakfast alone. 'Can't you just feel the end of summer coming? It makes me want to cry.' She topped up Eileen's coffee cup. 'Come on. I want to show you my room.'

Sîan led the way through a door and up a twisting back staircase. She was wearing a very short tennis skirt, and whenever Eileen looked up she was treated to a view of pure white sports knickers and smooth brown thighs. Embarrassed, she kept her eyes down, looking at the stairs.

'Would you show me around your Dad's tower?'

'Oh no, I can't do that. Daddy doesn't like people going in there. Not even me.'

Eileen felt despondence creeping over her. She'd come here without a plan, assuming an opportunity would arise. She'd imagined herself creeping around the house at night, going through secret files in his office by torchlight. But now she was here the notion seemed ridiculous. She had no idea if there were alarm systems or security men, and she couldn't imagine Meredith would be careless enough to leave important files lying around in unlocked cabinets. Come to that, did she even have enough knowledge to recognise an incriminating document if it smacked her in the face? No, it was all absurd. What a waste.

'My mother hated this house,' Sîan was saying. 'She thought it was tacky. My mother had good taste,' she added.

She opened the door to her bedroom. 'I've only just finished decorating it. I did it myself. What do you reckon?'

There was an all-pervasive smell of pot pourri – to blot out the smell of emulsion, no doubt. The window looked out over the front driveway and the tennis court. The walls were pale green to about halfway up and bright yellow above.

'Getting the line straight where the colour changes was the trickiest thing.' Sîan wrinkled her nose. 'Oh, and sanding the floor, of course. That was a nightmare. Daddy had to ask Keith to help me. He was worried I'd do my back in or something.'

The floor had been varnished in a warm golden tone. The ceiling was a rather odd combination of pale blue and dappled white. Sîan caught Eileen staring up at it.

'It's supposed to be the sky, with clouds in it,' she said. 'But I don't think it's quite worked. I might just paint blue all over it.'

'Oh, I think it looks great as it is,' Eileen lied.

It was very Spartan for a teenager's room; just a futon bed, a pine wardrobe, dressing table and desk with computer. Some school books lay on the desk along with the pot pourri and a mobile phone that was charging. A pair of Grommit slippers lurked under the dressing table. A small alarm clock and a book on tennis technique sat on the floor next to the bed, but otherwise the room was devoid of anything personal.

'It's very tidy.'

'I'm kind of into empty spaces,' explained Sîan.

'What's through here?' Eileen reached for the handle of a door in the far wall.

'No, don't!'

But Eileen was already opening the door.

Heaped up inside what should have been a walk-in dressing room was all the flotsam of childhood that she would have expected to find in Sîan's bedroom: teddy bears, cuddly crocodiles and rabbits, games of Monopoly, Scrabble and Risk, stacks of children's books, an old battered doll's house, plastic skittles and a glass jar filled with marbles . . .

'It's hard to get rid of shit like that.' Eileen experienced an odd pang.

'No, it isn't. I just haven't got around to sorting it out yet.' Sîan was annoyed that her cool had been blown. 'Come and have a look at my computer.' She eased herself between Eileen and the store room, slamming the door shut. 'Dad gave it to me last week.' She guided Eileen over to the desk. 'It used to be his but he's upgraded. It still works well. I can do all my A-level stuff on it. I've got some great games too.'

Sîan sat down at the desk and flicked the switch at the power point. Then she turned on the monitor and the computer. 'It's got Windows and Word and all that. Look.'

Eileen slowly dragged the dressing-table stool up close. 'This was your Dad's, you said?'

'Yes.' She booted it up. White numbers flashed and flickered against the blank screen. It beeped. 'Actually I think it's a bit stingy of him not to have bought me a brand new one. He spends the *Earth* on my tennis coach. Do you know much about computers?'

Colour displays flashed in quick succession across the screen. Eileen saw the word 'Windows' appear briefly before finally the screen settled on a pale blue display with small pictures dotted here and there, labelled 'Word', 'File Manager', 'Control Panel', 'Games'. There were other pictures too, but Eileen didn't get a chance to look at them before Sîan made a couple of clicks with the mouse and sent the screen into 'Word'.

'A little.' Weren't these things supposed to be 'user friendly'? That was a phrase Eileen had heard countless times. Any fool could use them – why, some of the stupidest people she had ever known worked with computers. How difficult could it be to operate them?

'I've got Sim City,' said Sîan. 'Want a go? It's excellent.'

Eileen was staring at the screen, at the weird little icons lined up at the top; pairs of scissors, pictures of open files, paint brushes, arrows – was all this supposed to mean something to her?

'Oh, shit!' Sîan jumped up, looking flustered.

'What?'

'It's gone eleven. I'm supposed to be down on the tennis court now for my practice. Maggie's going to kill me.'

She rushed to the window. A small figure in a tracksuit was standing on the court, hands on hips. Sîan knocked on the window and waved frantically. The figure tapped at an invisible watch on her wrist.

'Look, sorry, Meg. I won't be long. I'll tell her I've got a friend staying – just an hour or so.'

'Don't worry,' Eileen smiled. 'I'll be fine.'

Sîan was sitting on the edge of the futon now, lacing up her tennis shoes. 'Have a go at Sim City. It's fab. You'll be all right on your own for a bit, won't you?'

'Yeah, sure.'

'Great. Well, see you later then.' And with a flash of white tennis knicker and a rustle of stiff cotton, Sîan was gone.

Eileen sat staring at the screen. Could this really be happening? She'd imagined herself ransacking cupboards, delving through piles of paper and ledgers. But now, here were the files, the papers, the secrets, all held safe somewhere inside this machine – ready and waiting to dish themselves up to her at the merest push of a button. If she only knew which button to push . . . Suddenly the Word display vanished and was replaced by clouds of coloured stars exploding against a black background. Alarmed, she pressed a random key and Word was back.

Fran. Fran knew about computers, Fran would know what she had to do. She'd call her. Eileen didn't have her mobile phone with her but Sîan's phone sat waiting, sheathed in its charger. She grabbed it and checked the display. 'Charged'. She pressed the numbers, waited for the ringing sound, dimly aware of the regular 'pop' 'pop' of Sîan and her coach punching the tennis ball back and forth down on the court.

There was a click, and then Fran's voice. 'This is Marsha Freeman. I'm not available to talk to you now, but please leave your message and I'll call you back.'

'Fran!' Eileen blurted, panicking. 'Call me. I need to speak to you urgently. Call me the *minute* you can.' She switched the phone off. But – oh, God – how was Fran supposed to call her? What was the number of Sîan's phone?

Jason. He didn't know as much about computers as Fran, but he knew a damn sight more than *her*. Maybe he'd know enough to be able to help. She dialled quickly.

'Hi, this is Robbie. Talk after the beep and I'll get back to you.' This was useless.

There was nobody at the office, but what the hell did she

expect on a Saturday morning? The phone just rang and rang and rang. She tried the house in Lisvane. 'This is Robbie and Marsha—' She hung up.

I need some instructions – something to tell me what to do. I need a manual. Eileen began opening the desk drawers. Pencils, biros, rubbers shaped like sweets and lipsticks, a stapler, some disks. Sîan was serving the ball now, over and over, grunting and groaning like the professionals every time she hit it.

She stared at the screen, at the words lined up along the top, her eyes lighting on the word 'Help'. Trouble was she didn't know how to access it. Slowly, falteringly, she found the keys to type the word 'Help' on the screen, knowing all the while how ridiculous she was. She pressed Enter. Predictably nothing happened. She cursed her own lack of skills. *A survivor, am I? Someone who knows how to scam her way into a life?* Fifteen minutes had already passed while she sat there floundering.

Then Sîan's phone gave a sudden trill, making her jump. It trilled again. Should she answer it? Well after all, why not? She picked up the phone, held it in her hand letting it ring on. What if it was Owen? Hesitantly she pressed the OK button to take the call. 'Hello,' she said, putting on a voice more high pitched than her own.

'Hello?' came a woman's voice.

'Fran!' The relief was monumental. 'Fran – how did you get this number?'

'My phone stored it. Eileen, where are you? What's going on?' Fran's voice was faint, thin. She sounded tired.

'I'm at Tony Meredith's house. Listen, I'm sitting at this computer and—'

'You're at *Tony Meredith*'s house?'

'Please, Fran, listen to me. I don't have much time. I'm on my own and I'm sitting at Sîan's computer.'

'Eileen—'

'It was Meredith's computer until a week or two ago. There must be stuff on it, documents . . . I need to know how to get at them. Help me.'

There was a pause at the other end of the line. Fran was thinking, trying to take this in. 'He would have deleted everything when he gave the computer to Sîan.'

Eileen sagged. 'You mean, that's it? There's nothing there? Maybe we should check. Tell me how to look and see.' Coloured stars were exploding across the screen once more.

'Shut up, Eileen, I'm thinking.' There was another pause. It seemed endless.

'Fran?'

'Right. How long have we got?'

Eileen looked at her watch. 'Forty minutes, maybe longer. Sîan said she'd be about an hour. She's outside practising her ground strokes.'

'OK. Meredith isn't stupid – he *will* have deleted everything. But hopefully we'll be able to recover the deleted files. Unless he's done something more thorough than just deleting them.'

Eileen felt her pulse quickening. 'What do you mean, something more thorough?'

'It's too complicated to explain. Look, what sort of machine is it, Eileen? What's it running?'

'It's an Admin Cure,' said Eileen, reading the label on the keyboard.

'No, no!' Fran's voice was irritable, impatient.

'I don't understand, Fran. That's what it says it is.'

There was a deep, exasperated sigh. It made Eileen want to cry.

'All right.' The voice was calm again, but forcibly so. 'Can you tell me anything about what software the computer is running?'

Eileen hit a key again to bring back the Word screen. 'I'm in Microsoft Word.' Her voice was small and childlike. 'And there's Windows as well.'

'OK.' Fran was struggling to be kind. 'Move the mouse up to the top left of the screen and click the left button over the word "File". Then click Exit.'

She did as she was told, mechanically, like a pair of robotic arms being controlled by the brain at the end of the phone line. Fran was barking orders too fast. It reminded her of days in the kitchen at the Silver Square Sandwich Bar, juggling plates of bacon and bowls of soup while Maria and Sophia shouted for set breakfast, chips, baked potato with beans and cheese. If only she knew how to type. Her fingers scudded clumsily about. She had to search for each letter before she could type it.

They had left Windows now. The screen was black. A little line that Fran called the cursor flashed rhythmically beside something called the 'C' prompt.

'We need to know what version of DOS this is,' said Fran, making no sense at all to Eileen. 'Type v e r enter.' Eileen stumbled along.

'It says MS-DOS Version 6.22,' she reported.

'Good. We're in business. Now type Tree enter.'

Great long lists of words appeared, branching off into other lists of words, which themselves divided into further twig-like words.

'Loads of stuff has come up, Fran.'

'Thank God,' said Fran. 'That probably means he hasn't done more than simply delete the files. Read me the first column.'

Sîan's coach was shouting at her. 'What's the matter with you, Sîan? That was total crap. Try it again. You did it perfectly yesterday. Concentrate!'

'DOS, Word,' read Eileen. 'Windows, Applications . . .' She read on and on down the list. This was going to take a long time – longer, surely than the time they actually had. '. . . Sharp—'

'Wait – stop. Write that last one down.'

Eileen grabbed a biro and scribbled the word 'Sharp' on a piece of scrap paper.

'Carry on.'

'Westland,' read Eileen.

'And that one too. Write it down.'

Eileen checked her watch as she scribbled down more and yet more of these hieroglyphics. They had less than half an hour left. At length, she reached the end of the column.

Fran's voice drove on, relentless. 'Type c d c colon back-slash Sharp.' 'Type undelete.' 'Type Y.' Sometimes when Eileen pressed Enter the machine replied 'Error' and then Fran would tell her to try again, to listen more carefully, to type *exactly* what she had said. At other times the computer would give them a message, a sign of some sort, and Fran's voice would sound pleased. Occasionally she would say, 'Good. Now we're getting somewhere.' Eileen punched at the keys until her fingers ached, while outside the tennis ball was punched back and forth, back and forth.

Then, without any warning the line went dead. Fran was gone.

'Fran?' Eileen redialled, her fingers slipping on the tiny phone buttons. She waited for Fran to answer. There was a familiar click.

'This is Marsha Freeman. I'm not available to talk to you now, but please leave your message and I'll call you back.'

'Fran, where are you? Fran!'

'Sîan?' A voice Eileen didn't know. A woman. Outside the room, just outside the door. 'Sîan?' And now a knock.

Eileen sat very still, her pulse beating at the inside of her head. Maybe if she waited and was completely silent, the woman would go away.

The door handle was turning now. Oh, for a lock!

The door was opening, an arm coming in, tipped with immaculate pink nails. Blonde curls, thick mascara, sunken cheeks. 'Meg. It's you. What are you doing in here?'

'Morning, Louisa.' Eileen tried to tell herself that this could be worse. She could surely handle Louisa. 'Did you sleep well?'

'Like a top.' She came right in, munching on a green apple, teetering on stilettos.

'You'll mark Sîan's floor with those shoes.' Eileen leaned back on the chair.

Louisa shrugged.

'She worked hard on that floor, you know. Or Keith did, anyway.'

Louisa sat down on the bed. 'What are you doing?' She peered past Eileen at the screen.

Eileen quelled her instinct to try to cover the screen with her hands. After all, the chances of Louisa being able to understand anything of what she was doing must surely be zero. 'Sîan asked me to sort out some problems with her computer.'

'Oh, yes?' Louisa looked interested. 'I know a bit about computers. I used to temp. You come across that many systems you have to be a bit versatile.' She nodded wisely.

Eileen tried to sit in such a position that her back obscured the screen. 'You must have had quite some experiences,' she wittered, nervously.

'You wouldn't believe the heaps of old junk they have in some of these offices,' drawled Louisa, her mouth full of apple. 'I got an electric shock off one once – a bad one – I could have sued. Anyway, what's the problem?'

'It's all right, I've nearly finished,' said Eileen, quickly.

Louisa threw her apple core and it landed on the floor some six inches short of the waste basket. She let it lie there. 'So she's got *you* running around after her along with the rest of us, then.' She picked a tooth with a long fingernail. 'She's a spoilt little whatsit, that one. Doesn't know she's bloody born if you ask me.'

'You shouldn't be so quick to judge.' Eileen felt suddenly defensive of Sîan. 'She's been through a lot.'

'Yeah?' Louisa raised her immaculately plucked eyebrows. 'Like what? Nasty case of tennis elbow? Swollen ankle?'

Eileen wanted to put her hand over that painted face, give the make-up a good smearing, maybe apply some pressure . . . 'Sîan lost her mother when she was only a kid.' She was struggling to control her temper, but mightily relieved that Louisa's attention was no longer focused on the computer. 'And now she's scared of losing her brother.'

'That so?' Louisa's smile was half malicious, half vacant.

Sîan's phone trilled out and Louisa got there first. Eileen sat helpless, frozen, as Louisa answered in her best temping voice: 'Hello . . . Who? Eileen? . . . Sorry, I think you have the wrong number, this phone belongs to Miss Sîan Meredith. Goodbye.' She laid the phone down on the desk, announcing, 'Some woman. Wrong number.'

Eileen looked at her watch. The hour would be up in fifteen minutes. She tried to make her facial muscles relax, to stop the panic from showing. 'I don't think Tony would be too pleased to hear you talk about his daughter like that.'

Louisa cocked her head to one side like a dog. 'Well I'm not going to say it to *Tony*, am I? And neither are you.' She folded her arms and waited, pathetically aggressive.

Eileen was desperate to be rid of her. She forced a fake softness into her voice. 'Louisa, I'm not your enemy. I'm not here to try to drop you in the shit with Tony.'

Those eyebrows rose up again, defiant, disbelieving.

'Actually you don't need anyone else to drop you in the shit. You'll get there all by yourself.'

Voices down on the drive. Raised voices. Tony Meredith was shouting, bellowing for all he was worth. You could make out the occasional word rising out of the rant. 'Fucking scum! . . . Loser . . . Wanker . . .'

Eileen and Louisa were both at the window, jostling for position. Meredith paced back and forth on the gravel drive, pausing only to yell more streaming vitriol at the man Eileen now knew as Keith and the two other men who stood with him, men she hadn't seen before. Keith seemed to be protesting, though his words weren't audible.

'Not another fucking word!' yelled Meredith, thrusting his chest out, hands on hips. 'Get the fuck out of here and do your fucking job!'

Keith seemed to have given up his protest. The men strode off together, crunching over the gravel, heading for a blue Toyota parked a way down the drive.

'Dad!' shouted Sîan, from the tennis court. 'Daddy, what's going on?'

'Nothing, love. Nothing you need worry about.' Meredith, still swearing to himself, walked back into the house.

Eileen and Louisa glanced at each other, both searching the other's face for clues. 'I'd better go to him,' said Louisa, quietly, and scuttled off out of the room, the door swinging closed behind her.

Eileen waited, listening to the sounds of her footsteps as she made off down the corridor. She was on the stairs now, running. Eileen reached for the phone.

Fran wiped away the tears with the back of her hand, but they kept on coming. Why couldn't she stop crying? She pressed OK to take the call.

'Eileen, thank God.'

The girl in the bed to her left was sleeping, but the woman with glasses in the bed on her right was giving her evil looks. Fran got down as low as she could in her bed and drew the covers almost over her head to try to muffle the sounds.

'I'm sorry about before. Meredith's girlfriend came in,' said Eileen's voice at the other end of the line. 'Anyway, what happened to you?'

The bed smelled unpleasant. Medical. Or was the smell coming from her body? Fran tried to stop the shivering that was moving steadily down her back. 'I got interrupted. Now, have we recovered all of the files on the list?'

'Yes. Meredith's got some kind of shit going on, Fran. He was out on the drive just now bawling at Keith.'

The shivering wouldn't go away and neither would the tears. 'OK, Eileen, we'll talk about it later. We have to copy the files onto a zip disk.'

'A what?'

Fran sighed. 'The big disks you said were in the drawers, remember? The ones that look like CD boxes?'

'Oh, yeah. Are you all right, Fran? You sound strange.'

'I'm just a bit tired.' Boy, was she tired. What she wanted to do more than anything else in the world right now was sleep. She wanted everything and everyone to go away. 'Listen, we don't have time to chat. Put a zip disk in the slot in the big white box. Then type copy c colon back-slash Sharp star dot star back-slash s.'

'Hold on, hold on. Say that again?'

'What is your problem, lady?' snapped the woman with the glasses. 'Some of us around here want to get some rest!'

'I'm sorry,' said Fran, weakly. 'I won't be long. It's a really important call.'

'Fran?' came Eileen's voice.

'Yeah? Well my health is important,' said the woman. 'My peace of mind is important.' Her lip began to tremble. 'My baby was important.' She dissolved in huge sobs.

'Fran, what's going on?'

'Copy c colon back-slash Sharp star dot star back-slash s,' repeated Fran, grimly, without faltering. 'Just type it, Eileen.'

Jason was biting into the first of his bag of lychees as he arrived at the office. Atlantic Wharf was alive with families taking walks, visiting Techniquest and going for chips at Harry Ramsden's. It was quite a contrast to Bute Street, a mere half minute's drive away. He'd looked out on the dismal run-down housing estate and the few moth-eaten whores wandering along the pavements as he drove down to the docks, and found it impossible to imagine Bute Street transformed into Cardiff Bay Development Corporations's tree-lined Barcelona-style boulevard. What would they do with all the people who lived in these nasty little flats? That would be a scam and a half and no mistake!

The security man at reception was asleep with his head on the desk.

'Morning, Arthur.' Arthur didn't stir. Jason walked right up to him and shouted in his ear, 'Morning Arthur!'

Arthur made a snuffling noise and eased his head off the desk some three or four inches. He struggled to open his eyes.

'Ah, Mr Warren. Good day to you, sir.'

'Nice to see a man so dedicated to his job in these cynical times.' Jason smiled brightly at him and headed for the lifts.

As he pressed the button for floor 7 the mobile phone in his breast pocket started to trill. He reached inside his jacket and flicked it off. He was expecting a call from Samantha but didn't feel able to sustain a conversation with her. Not just now.

As the lift doors opened, Jason could hear the phone on Emily's desk ringing. Who would call the office on a Saturday? Samantha? No, she didn't have that number. Owen perhaps, or the builders? He quickened his pace and broke into a run down the corridor, but the paper bag he clutched somehow broke free of his grasp and the lychees scattered across the floor. Damn! He stopped in his tracks and crouched down to gather them up. The bag had split so he was forced to shovel the lychees into his pockets. The phone stopped ringing.

Jason opened the blinds and took a minute to admire the view over Atlantic Wharf before turning to his desk. He enjoyed going into the office at weekends. He could envisage the whole building; all those offices, all those corridors and floors – all empty, silent, resting. This idea worked some kind of psychological wonder in his mind; made him feel at peace with himself. Of course, in all likelihood he wasn't alone in the building – there would be others here, ferreting away, trying to catch up or get ahead. But Jason preferred not to think about them – they spoiled the illusion. No, this whole great place was empty apart from the sleeping security man. Here, today, he would have the physical and mental space to resolve that little bit of business that was getting so worryingly out of hand.

Sitting down, he emptied the lychees out of his pockets and placed them in a row across the front of the desk. Then he moved his computer keyboard up on top of the monitor to get it out of the way. He took from a drawer his favourite Parker pen, the one with the nib that slid across paper like a skier down a mountain, and reached for a piece of best quality cartridge paper.

He began by writing the Lisvane address and the date at the top right, but suddenly felt foolish; it was far too formal, cold and unfeeling. He scrunched up the page and took a second sheet of paper.

Writing letters was never simple for Jason. Words that slid so easily from his tongue in speech were left to splutter and choke their way forth when he wrote. He had to take it slowly, to keep reading and re-reading what he wrote so he could be sure the spelling was correct, the grammar passable, all of the letters the right way around. Under normal circumstances he would do all he could to avoid having to write letters. But somehow it was right that this message should take the form of a letter. A situation so fraught with emotion, difficulty and dilemma should be settled through a process equally taxing and strenuous. He owed it to Samantha to make this effort. He owed her his pain.

Fran did her best to ignore the nasty aching in her womb. It was becoming sharper, evolving into something that jabbed and tore. Thoughts kept flickering through her mind about the *complications* the leaflets warned about.

'What now, Fran?'

The word *haemorrhage* appeared in Fran's head and she struggled to send it away.

'Fran? Are you still there?'

She tried to focus on Eileen's voice. 'Oh . . . yes. Well, I think we've finished.'

'Have we?'

The leaflets warned of pain – pain that might go on for a week or two. And prolonged heavy bleeding. How did you know when your pain was normal and when it was not?

'You said you weren't going to be long,' barked the woman with glasses. 'But you've been on the phone for ages. I'm calling the nurse.'

'Two minutes more,' said Fran. 'Just two minutes.'

'What?' said Eileen, at the other end of the line.

Fran took a deep breath. 'We undeleted all the files, then we copied them on to the zip disk, then we deleted them from the hard disk again. I think that means we've finished, Eileen.'

She was wearing a cream silk night-dress that she was fond of. They'd said you should bring your own night-dress with you. When she got home she would throw it away.

Dear Samantha,

I'm in love with you. That is the truth, the honest truth, and I've been holding on to the feeling, to the experience. Another truth is that I've never met anyone like you before – nobody has been so warm, so soft and so open with me.

But while this is all true, I must confess that I have lied to you. I'm not by nature an honest person – I lie to survive, lying is intrinsic to me – it is how I make my way in the world. I'm sorry to say that the very strength of our relationship poses a great threat to me; to the person I am. You're a doctor, of course, and perhaps in time you could cure me of this disease of congenital dishonesty, but if I stopped lying what would I do instead?

I'm sure you'd like some specifics. Well, I must tell you that I am involved in a relationship with another woman. It is not a conventional relationship and neither is it in general a monogamous one, but this woman has been the corner-stone of my life for some years and has in many ways made me the person I am. I have slept with countless others over time – I have used them and I have discarded them. My partner has never so much as batted an eyelid at my behaviour – indeed she has encouraged me – until I met you, Samantha. She is perceptive enough to see that what we have is different, and she has told me I must give you up.

You'll find a cheque with this letter. I beg you not to tear it up. The truth – have I ever told so many truths at one time? – is that if you leave your money with me you will lose it. You gave me that money as a sign of your faith in our relationship, but now you will understand that your faith was misplaced. Pay the cheque into your bank straight away – the cheque is valid now but in a few weeks' time it will become a worthless piece of paper. Don't try to call me – I'm changing my number.

I know you have a huge capacity to forgive and to sympathise – but don't pity me, whatever you do. I'm sorry to be losing you, but I'm about to begin a new and exciting phase of my life. Better to hate me, though I know that's not a part of your usual emotional make-up. Hate me for a while and then forget me and move on. I am moving on already, even as I sit here writing this letter. Thank you, Samantha, for what you have shown me about love.

Robbie

'I'm sorry I left you on your own for so long.' Sîan turned to close the door behind her.

Eileen looked up from the history text book she was reading as she lounged on the futon. 'Oh, hi. How was the coaching session?'

With an odd little snort and a huff, Sîan sat down on the dressing-table stool and unlaced her tennis shoes.

Eileen felt a flicker of irritation but then realised something was wrong. 'Sîan?'

Sîan pulled off the shoes and socks. 'I just fired Maggie,' she said, and her voice shook slightly. She got up and opened her wardrobe, searched about among the clicking hangers.

'You've done what?' Eileen closed the book and set it down on the floor.

'Daddy's going to go absolutely ballistic,' said Sîan, with a giggle that was edged with hysteria.

'Jesus, Sîan. What happened?'

Sîan held up two blouses; one in pale pink, synthetic with a slight sheen from Karen Millen; the other white cotton from Jigsaw. 'Which do you think would go better with jeans?'

Eileen pointed at the white cotton.

Sîan wrinkled her nose. 'I knew you'd choose that one. I think I like the pink.'

'Sîan!' Eileen let her exasperation show through.

'It's all so pointless. What was I supposed to do?' She returned the white blouse to the wardrobe. She pulled off her tennis shirt and put on the pink over her Sloggi sports bra. 'She was going on and on and *on* at me. She's like a fucking army sergeant, I'm sick to death of it!'

'But why fire her? Surely it would have been better to talk to your father first, to tell him how you're feeling.'

'Ha!' Sîan buttoned up the blouse and reached back into the wardrobe for her jeans. 'You think I haven't tried? He treats me like a child, Meg. Pats me on the head, slips me fifty quid to go get myself something nice. But it's not his money I want!' She balled up the tennis shirt and threw it down hard in anger.

'And what *do* you want?'

'I want him to *listen* to me for once!' Her face was flushed, her eyes glittered. 'I want to stop playing tennis! That's all.'

Eileen got up from the bed, walked over to Sîan and hugged her. Sîan's body felt tiny, insubstantial. She began to cry and Eileen kept holding her tightly. 'Would you like me to be there when you talk to him? A bit of moral support?'

Sîan shook her head, no, against Eileen's chest. 'He's going to have to listen to me now,' she sobbed.

Jason was re-reading the letter when they came in. Keith and two men. He hadn't seen the other men before. They didn't knock on the door; they just burst in.

'Keith, hi. This is . . . a surprise. What can I do for you?' He slipped the letter into a drawer.

'We've got a message for you,' said Keith, awkwardly.

'From Tony?'

Keith nodded. He seemed reluctant to meet Jason's eyes. This was unsettling. It was unlike Keith to be so evasive.

One of the men took a lychee and began to peel it. The other was wandering around the room. He opened Fran's desk diary, flicked through a few pages.

'Excuse me, would you leave that alone, please.' Jason was on his feet, crossing the room towards the man at Fran's desk.

He knew what was about to happen, and he was tensing, stiffening his stomach muscles against the fist a moment before the impact. Then he was falling backwards, struggling to breathe, trying to get his balance.

'Tony doesn't like being taken for a fool.' Keith's voice was devoid of expression.

Jason was coughing, gasping, trying to straighten, to look up into the face of the man who'd hit him; the man with the lychee.

'Keith,' spluttered Jason. 'What's going on?'

The second blow was to the right side of his face, and he went straight down, collapsed like a deck chair, folded up on the floor, his ears ringing, his head filled with an intense heat. Perhaps he was about to explode.

'You know,' he slurred at the impregnable face above him, 'nobody's ever hit me as hard as that. That's quite a punch.' He made to sit up.

'You reckon?' said the man who'd been going through Fran's diary. 'What about this, then?' He kicked Jason hard in the stomach, in just the place where he'd already been punched.

Jason groaned and retched, curling into the foetal position. 'No, that was a kick,' he grimaced. 'I said before that was the hardest anyone's *hit* me.'

'Prat.' The man kicked him again in the same place.

Jason pointed feebly at his stomach. 'X marks the spot.'

'This is a warning,' came Keith's voice. 'It's just a taste of what will happen if you do a runner with Mr Meredith's money.'

'Keith . . . hey, we're friends, aren't we? You and I?' Jason tried to chuckle but couldn't. And the next boot to make contact with his stomach was Keith's.

'I've . . . done . . . nothing . . .' But Jason could get no further – one of the men was standing on his left hand, crunching his fingers. Then he moved around to the right hand.

The kicking began with the stomach, but then he was being kicked in the back too. When he tried to roll over, they got him in the sides. Five, six, seven kicks . . . eleven, twelve . . . he lost count. At some point he had the impression that Keith had stopped and was telling the others to stop too, but it was hard to be sure . . . It was all so confusing. And the shoes continued to

drive in on him . . . such unpleasant shoes, so tacky, so nouveau. He wouldn't be caught dead wearing shoes like that . . .

I'd done it. I'd done my job and I'd done it well! By the time the bus had wound its way through Llanishen to arrive in Lisvane, I was delirious with excitement. I ran all the way from the bus stop to the house, finally standing panting at the front door, impatient for Jason or Fran to answer. I couldn't *wait* to sit down at the computer with them and uncover the secrets held in the zip disk. I rang the bell.

Imagine my disappointment when nobody answered! Their car was missing from the drive. How dare they be out when it was supposed to be my moment of glory! Jason had the excuse of not knowing what was going on but I'd have thought Fran would have come straight home after our tense computer tuition session on the phone. I rang the bell again and again, hoping that Jason might be asleep in bed recovering from a long night. I lifted the flap of the letter box and peered in, seeing nothing but the hall table, the coat hooks and the stairs. There were no sounds, no movements. *Nada.*

I hung around for a few more minutes, hoping to hear the sound of the car rounding the corner and slowing into the drive, or Jason's whistle as he strolled back from the shops with a bag of fruit and a newspaper. But no, nothing. I hoped to God that Jason hadn't sneaked off to spend the weekend with Samantha Derby . . . Given recent events, this seemed sickeningly likely. It also explained why Fran had been so weird on the phone. Shit.

I eventually gave up and posted the zip disk through the letter box. In all likelihood they would get back soon, and would discover Tony Meredith's secrets without me. How typical that I would end up being left out yet again! I was doomed to be on the bloody outside for ever and ever . . . I caught the bus home – if home it really was.

There were no messages on my answer machine. Nothing to break the monotony of this lousy anti-climax. I felt like the kid who wakes up thinking it is Christmas only to discover there are still three weeks to go. I lay on my bed sulking, allowing my mind to wander. I thought about Sîan; wondered whether Meredith had given her the roasting she was expecting. Poor little brat – I was becoming fond of her. I thought about Owen – what would he be doing today? Maybe he'd be at the studio in town, working on the statue. Or at home trying out one of the recipes from the curry cook book I'd lent him last week. Thoughts of Owen's cooking made me hungry and I went to search in the fridge for food, finding only half a tin of tuna and a courgette. Great.

I slumped on the couch in front of the telly and zapped between channels, trying not to let myself call Owen – after all I was supposed to be 'up North', wasn't I? But Owen would be so genuinely happy to hear my voice on the phone ... No, I ought to wait here for news from Fran and Jason.

Cilla Black was cackling away on the TV screen, while a man with no shoulders and too much gel in his hair did a pathetic little tap dance. I hit the remote and Noel Edmunds appeared, pretending he didn't know who was ringing the bell of his fake front door. He gasped in surprise and delight as two actors from EastEnders were revealed standing on the doorstep and the audience cheered and whooped. Well whoopy-doo. On BBC2 a python was digesting something large that seemed still to be struggling as it was slowly forced down the snake's gullet.

Fuck it. I gave in to temptation and called Owen.

He'd been in the garden, cutting back brambles and pulling out weeds. When I arrived he was piling up the dead branches for a bonfire. The garden, which was usually wild and unruly now looked like the head of a scraggy young boy who's just been clippered at the hairdresser's – harsh and bare, wounded. Owen explained that he was no good with gardens; it was all he could manage to keep everything cut back sufficiently so that you could still sit out there every now and again. I thought it could be really pretty if somebody actually put some thought and effort into it. I told him what I'd do if it were my garden; I'd mend and paint the old shed and plant rose bushes in front of it. I'd have honeysuckle and clematis all along the fence. I'd grow pansies, tulips, daffodils ... I'd have a little strawberry patch at the back and maybe a herb garden with oregano, mint, chives and rosemary. I'd grow basil if I could, but basil's tricky.

When I turned to look at him, he had a weird expression on his face – sort of sentimental, dewy-eyed. My stomach plunged and I had a horrible intuition that he was about to ask me to move in with him. Worse still, I had caught *myself* fantasising about the life we could have together. I muttered something about making coffee and scurried back into the house.

By the time I came out with the cups he had poured some petrol over the pile of branches and lit the fire. We sat on the step sipping our coffee and watched it burn.

Owen lay propped up on one elbow watching Meg sleep. She

was lying on her back with one arm at her side, the other curled around her head, palm upturned. Her fingers twitched now and again, and there were slight eye movements. What was she dreaming about tonight? Her breathing was deep and relaxed. At the peak of each in-breath a tiny clicking sound was emitted from somewhere at the back of her mouth. She'd hate to think he was lying here listening to those noises – she'd consider them ugly, something to be embarrassed about. She was more self-conscious than she'd like to admit. Actually he found those little clicks endearing. They were a part of the hidden Meg, the Meg she thought he didn't know about.

He would never let on that he knew things about her. That would be sure to drive her away. No, he was biding his time, waiting for her to tell him of her own accord. She was becoming more and more relaxed and at ease with him – how long would it take for her to trust him with the real deep-down secrets? And she *could* trust him, whatever those secrets were. He wouldn't push her.

On the surface Meg was cheerful, even-tempered, placid. She was pleasant and friendly – the kind of person who says good morning to strangers in the street and always puts her litter in the bin. You couldn't fail to like her, but if you didn't know her well you might feel that she lacked something; ambition, fire . . . you might choose the word innocuous as the one which characterised her best. But Owen liked to think he had always sensed some deeper contradictory impulse in this girl, and that was what drew him to her. There was a restlessness in Meg, a passion that belied her outward manner. At first, he merely glimpsed hints of it but when she seduced him in his studio, the 'other Meg' hit him head on. He never knew when her alter-ego would make itself known and it became a fascination for him. Usually, of course, it was in bed that he had the chance to experience it – those moments during sex when you can't mediate your behaviour or reactions. Sometimes it would sneak out of otherwise harmless conversations in the form of a prickly raw comment. Owen would sometimes provoke her deliberately, wanting to see her get angry, wanting to see the 'other Meg' break through when she lost her temper.

But it was when she slept that he was most aware of the

alter-ego. The nightmares came and grabbed her almost every night. She would thrash about in the bed, cry out inaudible words and make unspeakable guttural sounds. When he held her, tried to soothe her, to wake her up, her eyes would come open but she would still be asleep, oblivious to him. He would stroke her head to calm her and she would lie in his arms like a child being held by its parent, sinking gradually back to normal restful sleep.

The first few times he was more than a little frightened. He wanted to talk to her about it, to find out what lay behind it.

What are your nightmares, Meg? he'd ask. *Is it the same dream every time?* She'd look at him then as though he were a monster or at the very least a particularly frightening and austere Jungian analyst trying to diagnose and dissect. Even an innocent question like, *So, did you sleep well last night?* seemed to give rise to such extreme nerves and evasiveness that in the end he decided it was better to say nothing and let her have her peace. He wondered if she had these nightmares when she slept on her own. He didn't like the thought of her thrashing around in her bed with nobody to take care of her.

He began to listen more carefully to the words she spoke, muttered and shouted in her sleep. Much of it was incomprehensible, but now and again he could catch the sense of something. There was one name in particular that came up over and over; Jason Fran.

Owen supposed Jason Fran must be an ex-lover. Meg spoke very little of her past. She had told him about her unhappy childhood, her alcoholic violent father and cowering abused mother. But the space between the day she finally ran away from home and the day she appeared in his life was just that; empty space. She talked only in the vaguest terms of moving from place to place, never settling, never finding a niche, and the only people she mentioned were the two friends of hers to whom she apparently 'owed everything'. He supposed it was these two friends that she had gone to visit this weekend, 'up North' (—how vague could the girl be?), but he also had a nagging worry about this mystery man, this Jason Fran – was he a figure from the distant past, or was he still a part of her life now?

Owen couldn't have been more happy when she'd called him earlier that evening, having come back a night early. When he asked her why she was already home, she simply said, *I've missed you. I want to see you,* and what could he do but believe her?

Wherever it was that she'd been, and whoever it was she'd been with – she'd come back to him safe. It had been magical spending this evening in the garden with her. And now here she was in his bed, where she belonged. He reached out and stroked her forehead gently. 'My love,' he said. 'My Eileen.'

Oh yes, Owen knew Meg wasn't this girl's real name, had rumbled that little secret some weeks ago. *Eileen* was the name she'd written with a finger on the misted-over window of his studio. As soon as she'd written it she seemed to realise what she'd done, and immediately rubbed it out with the palm of her hand – but not before he'd seen it. He hadn't thought much about this at the time, but then a day or two later, browsing through a curry recipe book she'd lent him, he noticed the name *Eileen* written inside the cover. Getting up one morning to find himself alone in the house, he found a note on the kitchen table – 'Gone to buy breakfast, back in half an hour, love *E*.' While on the phone to Eddie from the health-food shop, she'd doodled distractedly on the message pad. After she'd gone to work he delved in the waste basket and found the scrunched-up scrap of paper. On it was written that one name over and over, *Eileen Eileen Eileen Eileen,* as though she missed it, needed to say it to herself because nobody else was able to say it to her.

'My love,' he whispered to her now, idly playing with a strand of her hair. 'My Eileen. I'll keep you safe. I'll wait for you.'

Eileen got back to the flat at ten the next morning, feeling guilty for not having hung around the previous evening to wait for word from the others. The light on her answer machine was flashing. What she heard when she played back the message filled her with fear and horror.

Lost and panicking in the white glossy labyrinthine corridors of the hospital, she retreated into a lift and randomly pressed the button for floor 2, Llewelyn Ward. The doors opened to reveal an old woman with a shrivelled face, a pink knitted bed jacket and slippers, pushing a saline drip on a stand. She stared at Eileen without seeming to see her as she tottered into the lift. At the sight of her Eileen felt the fear rising, and struggled to retain control of her legs and feet as she walked out into the ward. Passing along a corridor she caught glimpses of its inhabitants: a young girl with a large skull-like head balanced on a tiny stalk neck slept with her mouth wide open, cheeks hollow, closed eyes set so deep in their sockets that you could hardly see them. A forty-something woman with a frazzled perm sat up eating grapes slowly, mechanically, plopping them into her mouth and seeming to swallow them whole. An old dear was swinging her legs out of bed and reaching for her walking frame. Her night-dress rode up at the back revealing a large wrinkled arse and Eileen shuddered. Finally she found the desk.

Two nurses broke their conversation to smile with friendly professionalism. The older one spoke. 'Can I help you, love?'

Eileen tried to make words with her useless mouth. 'I'm looking for Jason Shoe. He's a patient but I don't know which ward.'

'Just a second.' The nurse keyed his name into her computer. She looked puzzled. 'I'm sorry, love. I can't seem to find him here. Is Shoe spelled s-h-o-e?'

'All right, Mrs Peterson, I'm coming,' called the younger nurse, getting up. 'She's at it again,' she said to her colleague and pinned her smile firmly in place as she slipped out from behind the desk.

'Oh. Sorry,' Eileen blurted. 'I've got it wrong. It's Robert Warren that I'm looking for. Robert Warren.'

The nurse gave her an icy look, and seemed about to make some pithy comment. But then she sighed and apparently decided that if she asked a question she might get herself involved in something she didn't have time for. She typed in the name. 'Fourth floor,' she said, looking Eileen up and down. 'Owain Ward. Turn left out of the lift and ask at the desk.'

Eileen spotted Fran straight away. She was talking to a man and a woman. He had short hair, a brown leather jacket and new looking jeans with creases ironed into them. She wore a smart, beige trouser suit and sensible shoes. Police. Fran was looking pinched and old – *so* old. Eileen drew back and pretended to be studying some public information posters on a notice-board. After a couple of minutes the policewoman handed over a card and Fran smiled bravely and nodded her thanks to them as they walked past Eileen into the lift. Eileen waited for the doors to close before rushing over.

'You shouldn't have come,' said Fran.

'I had to.'

'They'll have asked the nurses to tell them who comes in to see him.'

'Why would they care?'

Fran gave her a look.

'I *had* to come, Fran. I have to see him. Where is he?'

'Just don't tell Owen, whatever you do. We can't have him hanging around here bumping into the police . . . You *haven't* told him, have you?'

'Of course not. What do you take me for?'

Fran softened, led her over to a couple of plastic chairs where they sat down. 'He's told them he doesn't want to press charges. I'm not sure that was such a smart move – it'll make them more suspicious of us. They'll be back, I know it. They won't just leave it at that.'

Eileen was becoming frantic. 'Where is he, Fran? I want to see him.'

Fran took her hand and squeezed it. 'He's had an operation. They've removed his spleen.'

'Oh God!' Eileen felt dizzy and sick.

'He's going to be all right. But he took quite a beating. They kicked him, you see.' Her eyes were angry. 'They kicked him over and over until they ruptured his spleen.'

'He could have . . .'

'Yes. He could. The security guard found him lying on the floor in the office. If he'd been there much longer . . .'

'I want to see him. Now.'

Fran led the way, past young boys with tragic faces, chirpy old guys and bland men in dressing gowns with expressions of alienation.

'Who did it?'

'Three men. Keith and two others. It was a warning, apparently. The security guard was asleep so they walked right in.'

Eileen remembered what she had seen through Sîan's window; Meredith so angry, Keith and the two men getting in the Toyota. If only she'd realised . . . If only she'd gone over to the office . . . The guilt started to bite, gnawing away like a snail at a lettuce leaf.

He looked like a wax model of himself; pasty and grey, his hair colourless and greasy, his mouth in contrast redder than ever. One side of his face was purple and swollen like an aubergine, the eye closed up. He was wired to all manner of alarming devices, drips and computerised syringes. His body under the covers could have been that of a corpse under its shroud. His feet were a pathetic little bump in the blankets that made Eileen want to weep.

'Hi.' His voice was strange. It seemed to struggle its way out of his mouth.

'Hi, Jason.' Eileen was forcing herself to smile; the effort was almost unbearable.

'Sit.' He patted the bed and she perched on it. He tried to signal to Fran to sit too, but she had wandered over to the window and was gazing out.

Eileen didn't know what to say. 'I should have brought you some grapes or something.'

'Don't worry. Nil by mouth.' Jason pointed to a sign at the end of his bed.

There was something peaceful about him, oddly spiritual. Eileen was reminded of priests and monks. As if he knew what she was thinking, Jason laid his hands over his chest in a tranquil, prayerful manner.

She couldn't bear to keep looking at him, and gazed around at the other inhabitants of the room. A large man with a toupee in the bed opposite was making horribly liquid noises in his throat. A teenager further down was being visited by a noisy family who crowded around his bed, talking over him. A refined looking gentleman in silk pyjamas had fallen asleep over his book, his glasses had slipped down his nose.

'Well, talk to me then!' Jason's voice was sharp, startling Eileen back to attention. 'What's the point of you being here if you won't talk to me?' He tried to lift his head off the pillow but the effort was too much. 'And you!' he snapped at Fran, who slowly turned and dragged herself over to sit down on a chair beside the bed.

'Sorry,' said Fran. 'I'm tired.'

'*You're* tired!'

Eileen tried to think of something to say. 'Are you in much pain?'

'Ah, now there's the clever thing.' Jason opened his right hand to show her a simple push-button device wired up to one of the machines by the bed. 'When I press this it gives me morphine. It's great.'

'Oh.' Eileen nodded. 'That's good.'

'The nurses are a bunch of slappers.'

'Oh, please!' Fran rubbed at her aching forehead.

'They are!' Jason insisted, looking annoyed. 'They'll give you anything you want if you flirt with them.' He lowered his voice to a stagy whisper. 'They're all on the look-out for rich doddery doting old men. They're on the make, the lot of them.'

'We should talk about what we're going to do,' said Eileen, looking from one tired face to the other.

Jason waved a limp dismissive hand. 'Not today, for God's sake.' He took a deep breath and seemed to be trying to gather energy. 'I can't take it, not yet. My wounds are still weeping. They cut me, you know, from just below my belly – right the way up.' He traced a long line. 'Almost up to my chest. Your spleen is here—' he pointed to his side – 'but they have to slice you up the front and kind of prise their way around the ribs to get to it. Fun, eh?'

Eileen was overwhelmed by the horror of it. They sat talking about nothing in that rigid stilted way you use when communicating with a distant relative. And all the while they talked, the notion was growing in Eileen that it could as easily be *her* lying there in the bed, *she* who was kicked half to death, *she* who was cut all the way up and put on a morphine drip. Thank God! Of course she couldn't help but be glad that in reality it hadn't happened to her – and then the gladness brought back the munching, chomping guilt.

Eventually Fran started groping around on the floor for her handbag.

'What are you doing?' asked Jason.

'I'm going home.' Fran got to her feet. 'I need some sleep.'

'I'll come too.' Eileen was alarmed at the prospect of being left alone with the sepulchral Jason.

'What about me?' Suddenly he looked smaller, his head tiny against the big white hospital pillow.

'You'll be all right,' said Fran. 'You've got all those slapper nurses to keep you company.'

As they wandered out Eileen looked back over her shoulder at Jason. He seemed so alone, so lost.

While they walked through the hospital car park together, Eileen tried to speak to Fran about the zip disk.

'I put it through the letter box. There was no one home. Maybe I should come back with you now. We could go through the documents together.'

Fran held up a hand to stop her. 'I can't do this, Eileen. I was here all last night drinking bad coffee and trying to speak to doctors while Jason was under the knife. I'm knackered.' She looked scathing, contemptuous. 'You've no idea what I've been going through. Neither of you have. You both expect me to be there all the time, to bail you out of whatever shit you've got yourselves into. Well, I've got my own shit too.'

'What? What are you talking about?'

They arrived at the car and Fran delved in her handbag for keys.

'Nothing. It's private.' She unlocked the driver's door.

'What am I supposed to do now?' Eileen asked, aware how pathetic her voice sounded.

'Oh, sorry. I'd offer you a lift but I'm just too exhausted to drive right across town and back.'

'That's not what I meant.'

Fran shrugged. 'Christ, Eileen, do whatever you like. I'll see you here tomorrow. One o'clock.' She got into the car and seemed surprised that Eileen was still standing there, gaping at her. 'You'll be OK,' she said, softening. 'And so will I, and so will Jason. Go home.'

Eileen went straight to Owen's house. It felt more like home than anywhere else right now, and she couldn't bear to be alone. She told him she'd run into Marsha, who said Robbie had gone away for a few days to end his messy love affair. It wasn't so hard to tell the lie. She began to feel better sheltering from the truth with Owen. Retreating into her Meg persona she found she could almost believe her own fabrication. But when she closed her eyes all she could see was Jason's swollen purple face.

I am crouching under the kitchen table with the dog. It keeps licking my face and I want it to stop but I can't move my arms to push it away from me. Why won't my arms move? The clock on the wall has a white face and orange numbers. The hands are black. The second hand is straining to move forward but it keeps sticking – perhaps the battery has died. The dog licks my face again and its tongue is like a piece of hot wet rubber. I wish it would leave me alone. Now the clock has no hands at all. Where did they go? Mum is cooking something, stirring frantically at the pot. There is a lot of steam. She has her new apron on and she uses it to wipe her face. Now she is moving back to the table to chop vegetables. She seems to be crying but maybe it's just the onions. If only this blessed dog would leave me alone!

I ask her what she's cooking but she doesn't hear me. It seems my voice isn't working either. Dad is sitting at the table on one of the hard kitchen chairs. I'm looking at his legs in the old brown trousers. I don't know why I didn't notice him before. He is loading tobacco into his pipe. I can't see his hands do it because they're up on top of the table, but I hear those noises that I know so well. He strikes a match and starts that strange puffing blowing steam engine thing he does to light the pipe. I smell it. I smell the booze too.

Mum hates it when he smokes his pipe in the kitchen. Even before she speaks I know she is about to tell him to go in the other room. The dog is still licking my face. Its breath smells bad.

She's done it now. She's told him. He's growling a bit like the dog does. He's saying things with his drunk voice. Why won't my arms work? Actually, they don't seem to be there at all. Where have they gone? Did the dog eat them?

When he gets up and hits her she falls. The fist makes a dull thunk against her face. If she had any sense she'd stay down on the floor, but she doesn't have any sense. She's getting up again.

I can see her face as she gets up – it's Fran's face! Why has Mum got Fran's face? Dad lunges at her again – and, yes, it isn't Dad at all – it's Jason!

I ask them what's going on but of course they don't hear me. I try to stand up but my legs have disappeared along with my arms. I'm nothing more than an outsize tennis ball. I daren't look at the dog in case it turns into Owen.

Now things are getting really confusing. Mum and Dad are grappling with each other. He seems to be trying to throttle her but then – no – it's her throttling him. I can't separate them out from each other any more. I can't see who is who. One of them is grabbing the chopping knife – but which one? Jason Fran Jason Fran Jason Fran Jason Fran

'You're looking better today.'

'Jason, it's *me* that's supposed to say that to *you*!'

'But you are.'

And Eileen did feel better today. It was Owen – he had a way of soothing her. It was an automatic and unquestioning thing with him. He had no idea what she was going through but he looked after her anyway.

'Well, you're looking better too.'

Jason smiled. His skin had lost that nasty sick sheen, his eyes were brighter. And he was propped up on a pile of pillows, not flat on his back. The bruising on his face was a more vehement purple than the previous day, but the swelling had gone down a little.

'I hurt more today. But it's a healing pain, or so they tell me. It's absolute *agony* when I cough or laugh.'

'Where's Fran?'

'Gone to the coffee machine. She'll be sneaking a quick fag somewhere too, I'll bet.'

He still had that tranquillity about him, that priestly quality. Perhaps it would remain after he recovered, a long term personality change.

'The doctor came round this morning. He said I might be able to have some water tomorrow!'

The man in the bed opposite was coughing deep fluid coughs and gasping for breath.

'Do you think we should call the nurse?' asked Eileen.

'Oh no, he does that all the time. Kept me awake half the night, actually. This place is so noisy.'

'Maybe we could get you a private room. I'll speak to Fran.'

Jason tried to shrug. 'It won't work – I don't have private

health insurance. I'll be out soon, anyway. Maybe ten days, the doctor said.'

Ten days! The idea of ten days in this place seemed like an age to Eileen.

'You know, when they took me down for the operation, I thought I saw her – she was wearing a mask, of course, but I really thought it was her. She's a doctor, after all.' He looked suddenly distant, wistful.

'Who? What are you talking about, Jason?'

'Samantha. I know it's mad – I know it couldn't really have been her, but at the time . . . I thought she was there looking after me.'

'Hi, you two.' It was Fran, with her coffee, looking fresh, revitalised, a veil drawn over the dark mood of yesterday. 'Let's make this a little more intimate, shall we?' She drew the curtain around Jason's bed, swooshing it over the rail, and dragged a chair up close.

'Eileen, you're a bloody miracle-worker!' She grabbed one of Eileen's hands and gave it a squeeze.

'What's she done?' asked Jason.

'She's done her job. Just like you said she would.' She turned to Eileen. 'I'm sorry I gave you such a hard time, honey.'

'The zip disk . . .' Eileen felt her excitement rising.

Fran nodded. 'Our Mr Meredith has been a very naughty boy.'

'What's he done?' asked Jason, confused.

'He's only been selling helicopter parts to a "group" in Afghanistan.' She could barely control the volume of her voice. Jason tried to hush her.

'Not just ordinary parts,' she continued more quietly. 'They're special brackets – made for guns – you fit them into your helicopter to convert it into a helicopter gun-ship!'

'Jesus.' Jason looked dewy-eyed, almost sad. 'What have we got on him?'

'We've got his side of the correspondence with a Mr Muttar from the "group". There's plenty of it. We've got Meredith by the balls, Jason!'

Still Jason seemed melancholy. 'Shame we didn't have him by the balls two days ago.'

The guilt took a big bite out of Eileen.

Fran was relentless in her new-found positivity. They listened to her plans, which fell over each other in their eagerness to spring forth from her mouth.

'In ten days you'll be out of hospital. On that day – that *very day,* mind – we'll empty the account, post a copy of the Muttar letters to Meredith, and leave.'

'Fran, I may not even be out of this place in ten days.'

'Your doctor did say ten days, didn't he?'

'I *might* just be well enough in ten days to go home to bed and be waited on hand and foot. I certainly won't be up to skipping the country!'

'God, you're *so* defeatist.'

'I'm being real.'

'All right. We'll go as soon as you're well enough. And you've got to *try* to get well. Then it'll be off on a plane to somewhere exotic and tropical.'

'But I can't go to tropical countries. Not any more.'

'Why ever not?'

'Because I don't have a spleen. I'll be more vulnerable to infections. One mild dose of some tropical virus and I'd be out like a light! I'll have to watch my health carefully from now on.'

Fran was clearly irritated by the obstacles he was creating. 'OK, we'll go to the States. Or Scandinavia, the Greek islands, Monte-bloody-Carlo – who the hell cares? Just leave it all to me.'

'What about the third instalment?' asked Jason, weakly.

'I hardly think we can count on more money from Meredith after what's just happened to you.'

'It was a warning, that's all. Meredith told the guys to give me a bit of a going over – enough to scare me, but it just got out of control. They went a bit too far.'

'A *bit too far.*' Eileen's mind boggled at the way he could belittle what had happened to him.

'Are we really going to walk away from the last half million?' His eyes were wide, perplexed.

At that moment a nurse drew the curtain open a few inches and stepped inside.

'How are we then, Mr Warren?' Her huge smiling mouth had

too many teeth in it. Her strong capable hands were too large for her wrists. 'Would you like your pillows plumped?'

The nurse had to call a colleague to hold Jason up while she reached behind him to plump the pillows. Jason hung limp in her arms like a rag doll.

This time, Fran did offer Eileen a lift home. She drove fast, more aggressively than she normally did, cursing other drivers and going through red lights.

'Slow down,' said Eileen nervously.

'You know,' said Fran, ignoring her, 'I don't think Jason wants to leave Cardiff.'

She overtook at a blind corner and Eileen covered her eyes, her heart leaping up to throttle her.

'I think he wants to stay here,' continued Fran, without so much as a flinch. 'And run the bloody restaurant.'

'Don't be daft.' Eileen took a deep breath to calm her racing pulse. 'He knows that isn't an option. Would you please slow down, Fran?' And all the while a little voice in her head was saying, *And when does anyone ever ask me what* I *want?*

'Does he? Does he know that?' Fran skipped another red light and horns blared all around them. 'All I hear from him are reasons not to leave.'

'He's ill. It's hard to think about that kind of stuff when you're so weak. He's on morphine, for God's sake. He can hardly move . . . Fran, you're driving like a maniac. Stop this car. I want to get out.'

'Sorry.' Fran finally slowed the car down to a legal speed. 'You're right, of course. He needs to get his strength back, that's all.'

They drove in silence down the shady tree-lined Cathedral Road. The leaves were beginning to turn golden. There was change in the air, you could smell it.

After dropping Eileen off, Fran drove straight to the office.

'Managed to stay awake today, have you, Arthur?'

The security guard tried to smile through his shame. 'One time was all, Miss Freeman. Only once in all the time I've been working here.'

'Once too often, Arthur.' Fran didn't look back at him as she headed for the lifts.

She arrived at the seventh floor. 'Any calls, Emily?' she asked the secretary.

'The architects want to come and see you.' Emily was trying quickly to exit the pool game she'd been playing on her computer. 'I've put it in the diary for four o'clock on Thursday.'

'Fine,' said Fran, choosing not to notice the game.

'And Owen called three or four times. He wanted to know when Robbie's coming back. I didn't know what to say.'

'Robbie is out of town for two or three weeks,' said Fran. 'On business.'

'But . . . that's not true, is it, Miss Freeman?'

Fran felt her anger rising. 'Don't interfere in what doesn't concern you, Emily.'

A fat lip quivered. 'Why won't you tell him the truth?'

She was so sloppy, so sluttish in her off-the-shoulder minidress. Another of Jason's bloody fans. 'I'm warning you, Emily, stay out of it.'

Emily looked as though she might cry. 'Is he up to visitors? I'd really like to go and see him.'

Fran struggled to sound kind. 'Not just yet. He's too tired to have lots of people around. I'll tell you when he's well enough. Any other calls?'

'Yes. Detective Inspector Darnley. She said she'd call over later. Five-ish. I told her I might be the only person here but she didn't seem too bothered.'

'Oh, fine.' Fran managed a smile. 'I tell you what, Emily, why don't you slip off early? I know this has all been very difficult for you, and I won't have any more typing today.'

'Really? Thanks, Marsha.' Emily bent down to grab her bag, showing more of her cleavage than Fran wanted to see.

'And Emily, that dress isn't suitable for work. Please don't wear it again.'

Alone in the office, Fran took some papers from her briefcase and crossed to the photocopier. When she was done, she put the originals back in her case and sealed the copies in an envelope. She addressed the envelope to Tony Meredith at the house in Dinas Powys and delved in her desk drawers for first-class stamps

– there were none. She walked over to Jason's desk and began opening drawers. No stamps, but something else caught her attention. A sheet of hand-written paper. Jason almost never wrote things out by hand – he liked to be able to run spelling and grammar checks on everything he set down. She started to read:

Dear Samantha,

I'm in love with you. That is the truth, the honest truth, and I've been holding on to the feeling, to the experience. Another truth is that I've never met anyone like you before – nobody has been so warm, so soft and so open with me . . .

I've been doing some hard thinking tonight. I've been thinking about Jason, lying there in the hospital without his spleen, hallucinating that Samantha Derby was one of the doctors who operated on him, inventing recipes for a restaurant that will never exist. I've been thinking about Fran, prickly with paranoia and distrust, driving through red lights and fretting about how to cover our tracks. And I'm seeing them both in a different light – as a sort of time bomb counting down to zero. I'm frightened about what might become of them – of us – of me.

Standing in Owen's kitchen earlier, washing greasy pans, I found myself wishing I was Meg – for real. And after all I *am* Meg, aren't I? I am her and she is me. Why shouldn't I just stop being Eileen and become Meg permanently? I could stop scamming, stop running, stop looking over my shoulder . . . I could live here with Owen and be happy.

The more I thought about it, the more I *wanted* this life. And I started working it through my mind, thinking there must be a way to make this happen.

I plunged dirty dishes into the grimy water and I scrubbed at them slowly, determinedly as I worked and worked away at this conundrum. I'd miss Jason and Fran of course, but everything has its price . . . Then there were footsteps behind me. Owen's arms came around my waist and he nuzzled the back of my neck.

'Why don't you leave that till the morning and come to bed?'

'I'll just finish off. It won't take more than a couple of minutes.'

'I'll be waiting for you.'

I listened to him going up the stairs. I couldn't bear to think about betraying this sweet man, running off with Jason and Fran and all that money. Breaking his poor battle-scarred heart just when it was starting to mend. But what other option did I have?

And then it came to me. I really *can* stay here with Owen. I'm the only one of us who can choose to remain in Cardiff. Jason and Fran can leave with their money and I'll stay in perfect safety. Tony Meredith may rant and rave and send out the heavies but I'll be untouched because he doesn't know I have anything to do with Robbie Warren and Marsha Freeman. The only way he could ever find out would be if Jason and Fran tipped him off. But if I gave them my share of the money to keep them quiet (– or some of it anyway) – I could buy my safety.

Christ, I could marry Owen. I could have his kids. And perhaps Sîan was right – maybe I *can* reunite Owen and his father. We could open the restaurant together, run it as a couple with Tony's support. I can buy my way out of the scam. I can make this life real. I can do it.

There was a huge bouquet of flowers next to Jason's bed when Eileen and Fran arrived the next day. White tulips, pink carnations, red rose buds, big daisies, lilies with outsized yellow sex parts.

Eileen read the card. 'Best wishes for a good recovery and swift return to work, T.'

'Tony Meredith.' Jason was considerably more chirpy than the previous day. 'It seems we've been forgiven. He's taking us back into the fold.'

'Possibly.' Fran examined the message.

'So maybe we're safe to hang on here for the last instalment after all,' said Eileen, brightly.

'I don't think so.' Fran set the card down on Jason's locker.

'Why not?' protested Jason. '*Swift return to work,* he says. I think the meaning is clear: the deal is back on.'

Fran drew the curtains around the bed with a swish, visibly seething with rage. 'What about your sweet little girlfriend and her investment? What about her, *Robbie*?'

Jason sighed. 'I've written a letter to Samantha. I've even written out the cheque – only I was prevented from posting it due to circumstances beyond my control. Three big ugly circumstances with a total of six fists and six feet!'

Fran leaned closer. 'Sometimes, Jason, you are very slow at

grasping the heart of a situation. Let me give you a little help – who was it that beat you up in the office, my darling?'

Jason made a sound that was half a laugh, half a cough, and then grimaced with pain. 'Keith and two other pieces of shit,' he said, once he was able to speak again.

'And who do you think these two "pieces of shit" were, Jason?' Fran's eyes were full of anger.

'I don't know, do I? A couple of twats who work for Meredith.'

Eileen was beginning to understand.

'OK.' Fran sat back down and folded her arms. 'Tell me something. *Why* did Meredith send his men to beat you up? He's always had us sussed and he thought he had control of us. Why did he suddenly decide we needed to be "warned"? And why such a heavy-handed warning? Why did Eileen see him frothing with rage outside his house? What changed?'

Jason looked pale and tired. 'Fran, who the hell knows how that man's mind works.'

A pattern was forming in Eileen's head. The dots were joining up. 'You think Meredith was tipped off, don't you, Fran? You think someone called him, told him you two were about to rip him off. And Meredith isn't the sort of guy who can stand to have people calling him with this kind of information – telling him about his private business. It made him angry, humiliated. It made him feel he needed to flex his muscles.'

Fran hadn't taken her eyes off Jason while Eileen spoke. 'She's right, Jason. She's a good deal sharper than you, these days. I think you're losing your edge.'

Now Jason was the one to be angry. 'Shut your poisonous mouth, Fran. It isn't you who got beaten to a pulp by those twats. It isn't you who went under the knife, who's lying here now. Jesus, talk about kicking a man when he's down!'

But Fran wasn't ready to shut up. 'What did the men look like? The ones who beat you up?'

Jason rubbed at his head, confused. 'I don't know. I don't remember. I only remember their shoes. *Awful* shoes.'

'I saw them out of the window,' said Eileen. 'I remember a little. They were big, much bigger than Keith. One was dark, the other red-haired. Wearing suits – and quite a bit of gold jewellery.'

'Sadie March's sons.' Fran spat out the words. 'She tipped off Meredith and she lent him her boys for the afternoon. It was your girlfriend's cousins who enjoyed kicking you so much that Keith couldn't call them off! I wonder what makes me think we can't settle this by sending a cheque to Samantha . . . eh, *Robbie*? I wonder what makes me think it's too fucking late for that!'

'Fran—'

'Hello, there, Robbie. We've got a little treat for you.' A face had appeared around the edge of the curtain. It was one of the nurses; small, black and cute with cow eyes. She was accompanied by yesterday's nurse – big hands and too many teeth.

'Hi, girls.' Jason tried to smile.

'Looking a little pale, Mr Warren,' said Big Hands. 'But we'll soon put some colour back in those cheeks.'

Fran rubbed at her head as though it was aching. Eileen took hold of one of her hands, gave it a squeeze, while Big Hands helped Jason to sit up better against his pillows and Cow Eyes handed him a tiny plastic cup.

'Doctor says you can have a little water,' said Cow Eyes. 'Go on. Drink.'

Jason sat for a few seconds just looking at the cup.

'Go on, then,' said Big Hands.

'I'm savouring the moment.' He slowly lifted the cup to his lips and tasted the water, the tiniest of sips. Finally he swallowed. His eyes were filling with tears.

'How was that, then, Robbie?' asked Cow Eyes.

'Heaven!' Jason took a second sip. 'The elixir of the gods.'

'Well, you'd think he was sampling the finest champagne in his restaurant, wouldn't you!' said Big Hands.

Fran twitched visibly. 'His *restaurant*?'

'Oh, he's told us all about the restaurant,' said Cow Eyes. 'Food from all different countries and the statues by that artist – Owen whatsisname. Sounds great to me.'

'He reckons he's going to let a bunch of us have a table on opening night,' said Big Hands. 'On the house. But I keep telling him – the minute he gets out of this place he'll forget all about us.'

'Never!' vowed Jason, emerging from his watery ecstasy. He

handed them the empty cup, triumphant. 'How could I ever forget you, my darlings?'

'Well, we'll see about that, won't we, Trace?' said Cow Eyes. 'Time will tell as they say. See you all later.'

And they strode off down the ward, giggling together.

Eileen tried to give Fran's hand another squeeze, but Fran pulled away.

'You've gone too far, Jason.'

'God, that water was good.' Jason seemed to have recovered himself entirely. Had he forgotten what was said just a few minutes before? 'I wonder when they'll let me have some more.'

Fran got stiffly to her feet. 'We have to be going. I have some work to do and I need Eileen to help.'

'Oh. Pity.' Jason was crestfallen. 'Will you be back later?'

'Of course we will,' said Eileen nervously, wondering what it was that Fran wanted her to do. 'Just as soon as we can.'

'Good.' His face was like a little boy's – helpless, hopeful. 'Listen, you two have been really great. Don't think I don't appreciate it.'

The guilt was taking great mouthfuls out of Eileen and chewing her to a pulp. She tried to sound playful. 'Cut the crap, Jason. We'll see you later, OK?'

'Bye,' said Fran. He looked startled when she leaned over and kissed him on the forehead. He looked vulnerable.

Fran walked quickly down the hospital corridor. Eileen had to trot to keep up with her. Alone together inside the lift, Eileen noticed that Fran was avoiding looking her in the eye.

'What's going on, Fran?'

'We're leaving.' Fran was still staring down at the floor.

'Do you really think Jason will be ready in ten days?'

'We don't have ten days.'

'Well, there's no *way* he'll be ready sooner than that.'

'We're leaving today. Now.'

The lift reached the ground floor and the doors opened. Fran strode ahead past porters, patients in wheelchairs taking exercise, and visitors with flowers and worried faces.

'Fran!' Eileen grabbed her by the arm, made her stop. 'Are you suggesting that we leave Jason behind?'

'It isn't a suggestion, Eileen. I'm telling you. We are leaving – you and me. Today.' Her voice was icy. She made for the nearest exit.

Eileen could almost hear the ticking of the time bomb. 'Fran, stop this. It isn't funny.'

'You're dead right it isn't funny.'

'Come on, let's get a coffee or something. Let's talk about this.' Eileen could hear her voice as though from outside her body – shrill, uncontrolled.

'We don't have time.' The automatic doors slid open and Fran passed through. Outside the sky was iron-grey. The breeze had whipped up into a sharp wind while they were in the hospital with Jason. Fran picked up pace as she headed for the car park.

'What's brought this on?' Eileen was breathless. 'How come we have to go so suddenly? Without Jason.'

'Need you ask?'

'Yes, actually.'

Fran stopped so sharply that Eileen almost bumped into her. 'We're not safe to stay here any longer. Not with Sadie March involved. What's happened to Jason is only the beginning. We're on her patch, Eileen. We could be floating in the River Taff by tomorrow morning.'

'No, Fran. There must be another way.' Eileen struggled to get her thoughts straight. 'Maybe we should go and talk to her. Give her Samantha's money back. In cash. She might be willing to deal with us.'

Fran shook her head. 'It wouldn't work. I know it. She's wise to what we're doing. She's after a lot more than Samantha's ten thousand.'

'But Jason . . .'

'Jason—' Fran spoke the name with contempt – 'has blown it. All the work that you did – that *we* did – in getting hold of that disk – in making everything safe, covering our tracks – it's all worth shit. Because Jason had to follow his dick with that Samantha Derby. It's his fault entirely that we have Sadie March to deal with.'

'But you *love* him.' Eileen's mind was filled with thoughts of that fragile body being kicked and battered until it couldn't hold out any longer. 'Don't you? You love each other. What's going to happen to him if we leave him behind?'

Fran shrugged. 'He can tell them the truth – that his partner ran off with all the money. Anyway, he brought it on himself.' She turned and began to walk again. 'I'm waiting for a call from British Airways. I've asked for two seats on a plane from Heathrow to LA tomorrow morning. One-way. Their computer was down so they're calling me back on the mobile.'

Fran's continuing calm and clarity was making Eileen feel increasingly hysterical. 'How can you be so bloody *cold*?'

'I'd quite like to survive this, Eileen.'

They reached the car. Fran began fumbling with keys.

Eileen thought of another tactic. 'What about the money? You can't just walk into the bank and ask to close your account and withdraw your *one million pounds.*'

'It's already taken care of.' Fran unlocked the boot and opened it up. She lifted out her big old vanity case, her box of tricks, and held it up meaningfully. 'I fixed it up yesterday and I picked up the money on the way to the hospital.'

'How organised of you.' Eileen could feel the energy draining out of her voice.

Fran replaced the vanity case, slammed the boot shut and locked it. 'Get in the car, Eileen.'

Eileen tried to muster her strength. 'I'm not coming with you. I'm staying here.'

Fran laughed. 'Don't be ridiculous!'

'I'm serious,' said Eileen. 'Sadie March doesn't know about me. Neither does Meredith. I could stay here. With Owen.'

Fran stopped laughing. 'You can't mean it!'

For the first time since they left the hospital, Eileen could sense Fran's calm slipping. 'I do mean it, Fran. Go on. You leave. Take the bloody money – all of it – I don't want it any more. I don't want anything to do with it – or with you.'

Fran moved around to unlock the passenger door. 'Just how far do you think you can trust Jason?'

'What does that have to do with anything?'

'Eileen, honey, when I'm safely abroad, sunning myself in California, and they come to visit Jason in the hospital, what do you think he's going to do? Do you think he'll keep his mouth shut? Are you *sure* he'll take the trouble to protect you? Because you'd better be *really sure.*'

Eileen could feel her lip quivering. Could she be sure of anything now?

Fran sighed, irritated. 'Jesus, I don't know why I bother, I really don't. Eileen, you stupid little child, I'm trying to help you. *I'm* the one who cares about you, not Jason. He wanted to marry me, you know – when this was all over. He wanted to marry me and leave you to find your own way. He doesn't give a shit about you.'

'I don't believe you.'

Fran's mobile phone trilled out and she pressed OK to take the call, held it to her ear.

'Hello . . . Yes, it is . . . What?'

Something was wrong. This wasn't the call from the airline.

'. . . How did you get this number? . . . How did you know that I . . . When? . . . OK . . . I understand . . . I'm coming straight over . . . Yes, I remember the address. Bye.' She switched off the mobile. 'Get in the car, Eileen, for God's sake.'

'Who was that?'

'Ted March. They know I took the money out of the bank today. That's why they hadn't come for me already. That's what they've been waiting for.' She swallowed heavily. 'Sadie wants to see me. Now. And she wants me to bring the money.'

Eileen had never seen Fran so frightened. She got in the car without another word.

Fran's driving was even worse than the previous day. It began to rain and the tyres squealed and skidded on the wet tarmac. Eileen felt numb, incapable of doing anything beyond allowing herself to be carried along. Her head was filled with visions of Jason's face, bruised, bleeding, eyes open, fixed and staring.

'They know what my car looks like so we'd better take the train. There's Cardiff airport of course, but . . . no, too risky.'

'What about my things?' asked Eileen in a small voice.

'Forget your things.'

'My passport?'

'I have it in the vanity case. I've been holding your passport for the last year or so, Eileen. It's *so* like you not to have realised.'

'Oh.'

They drove past Llandaff Village. Eileen caught a glimpse of The Black Pig, the pub where Fran had first voiced her worries about Samantha Derby and her aunt, Sadie March. That day seemed so long ago. Then Fran took a sharp and unexpected left turn.

'Where are we going?'

'Newport. We can pick up the London train from there. I daren't risk Cardiff Central.' Fran reached for her cigarettes. 'Light one for me, will you?'

Eileen drew one out of the packet and switched the car's lighter on. 'Surely she couldn't have everything covered already – the airport, the station . . . she can't be that quick off the mark. You're paranoid.'

'Don't bet on it. She knew I went to the bank today. How did she know that, eh? Listen, there's a road atlas in the glove compartment. Take a look at the A48. See if it goes all the way to Newport. I don't want to chance the M4.'

Eileen reached into the compartment and grabbed the atlas. 'We were supposed to be a team, the three of us all looking out for each other.' She spoke faintly, more to herself than to Fran as she flicked to the right page. 'You said we had to trust each other. You said trust was the most important thing.'

'What was that? What did you say?'

'Nothing.'

The cow-eyed black nurse sat on the edge of Jason's bed and passed him another plastic cup. 'Apple juice?'

Jason sipped from the cup. The juice was smooth and golden, simultaneously sweet and acidic. 'God, that is beautiful. There's a hundred different flavours in that juice and I can taste them all individually.'

'You're just easily pleased,' said Cow Eyes, whose name was Jenny.

'I feel as though my taste-buds have been reborn.'

'You sound like one of those evangelical Christians.'

Jason took another sip. 'My senses are alive, more than they've ever been. I'm seeing colours within colours, hearing the sounds behind sounds.'

Jenny laughed. 'D'you know – listening to you now – this is one of those moments that makes all the shitty stuff about my job really worth it.'

Jason smiled at her and took his third and final mouthful of juice. 'I know this will pass,' he said. 'I know it won't be long before apple juice is just apple juice again. But right now – right now it's something else.'

'Great.' Jenny took the plastic cup from him. 'Listen, Robbie, I'd better be off. I've got work to do. I have to go and see Dr Shamir.'

'My girlfriend's a doctor, you know,' said Jason, dreamily. 'In Manchester.'

Jenny looked puzzled. 'I thought that woman who was here earlier was your girlfriend. The older woman.'

Jason shook his head. 'No. She's my business partner. My girlfriend's name is Samantha. Dr Samantha Derby. She's as beautiful and golden as that apple juice.'

Jenny shrugged as she got up. 'I could have sworn you said that other woman was your girlfriend.' She turned to leave.

'Hey, Jenny?'

'Yeah?'

'Is there a phone I can use? I'd like to call her. My girlfriend, I mean. I want to talk to her.'

Jenny raised her eyebrows, still puzzled. 'Sure. I'll sort it out . . . Robbie, that other woman—'

'Fran.'

'Fran. Your "business partner". Did she say she's coming back today? Her and the younger girl?'

'I don't think so,' said Jason. 'I don't think they're coming back.'

The Train

Usually they sat separately, watching, waiting, ready to take advantage of any opportunity that may arise. But today was different. There was no longer any need for scams. They faced each other across the table in a first-class carriage. The vanity case sat on the floor between them. Both women seemed edgy, nervous. Occasionally one or the other would bend down to check on the case, even though they were alone in the carriage.

'Dear oh dear. Cheer up my darlings, it might never happen,' said the greasy ticket inspector with the acne-scarred face.

'It already has,' said Fran, without looking at him.

The inspector gave a wheezing laugh. 'Well, that's one I know I'm not to blame for!' He punched their tickets and staggered on to the next carriage.

'What are you thinking about?' asked Fran after he'd gone.

'Nothing.' It was a lie. She was thinking about what she'd lost. She was thinking about Owen. He'd be coming home from the studio around now. He'd call her name as he walked through the front door, expecting that she'd be there. They were supposed to be going ten-pin bowling tonight. They had joked about the fact that neither of them had ever been on proper dates as teenagers – neither had snogged in the back of the cinema or got candy-floss stuck in their hair on roller-coasters. Neither had ever been to a bowling alley.

Let's do it, Owen had said. *Let's get all togged up in our smart gear and make like it's our first date. We could even pretend to be completely different people for the night – I'll be Mark, the mild-mannered geography teacher. What about you?*

I'll be Eileen, the sandwich-bar waitress.

Owen waiting for her to come in – waiting for hours, getting more and more frantic. Calling her flat, perhaps eventually going round there. Then maybe tomorrow or the day after, finding out the truth or part of it. Marsha also strangely absent, Robbie in the hospital – or worse. The mysterious finances which he'd never thought of questioning suddenly unavailable . . . Would he find out that his father was the source of all the money? Would this ultimately bring them together again or drive them further apart?

First Annie, then Meg. Owen would turn his bitterness inward – blaming himself for being too naive, too trusting. His art would get angrier, more violent. His life would become more lonely. Would Owen ever be able to trust a woman again?

Fran was looking old. There were crows' feet at the corners of her eyes, deep hollows in her cheeks, her neck was thin and scraggy. She seemed to have lost her youth during those final stressful days in Cardiff.

'How old are you, Fran?'

'What? Thirty-four.'

'Yeah?'

'Well, thirty-nine, actually.' Fran smiled. 'But thirty-four's feasible, wouldn't you say?'

'Oh, sure.'

Fran had never admitted her real age before.

'I had this Irish grandmother,' said Fran. 'She always complained like hell about her age – and about the fact that her birthday was on Christmas day. She'd say it was the worst day of the year for a birthday. You only ever got one lot of presents. When she died, the family went through her papers. And do you know what?'

'What?'

'All that time she'd been lying – she was six years younger than she'd made out and her birthday was in May.' Fran chuckled to herself.

'When's your birthday?'

Fran stopped chuckling. 'Christmas day,' she said with a totally straight face.

Eileen gazed out of the window. The train was pulling in at

Bristol Parkway. It was the ugliest station she had ever seen – a bunch of corrugated iron shelters, nothing more. Hordes of people were crowding into second class. She leant back in her comfortable first-class seat and tried to enjoy the privilege. She seemed to have lost her capacity to luxuriate in what she succeeded in taking from others. Try as she might, she couldn't see Owen as some sucker who deserved all he got. Neither could she think of Tony Meredith in that light – even after what he did to Jason . . . what he might still do to Jason if Sadie March didn't get there first.

'What have you done with the papers?' Eileen asked Fran.

'What papers?'

'The Muttar letters.'

'Why do you want to know?'

'Have you posted them to Meredith?'

'Yes.' Fran looked irritated. 'Of course I have.'

'What about Jason? Did you do anything to help him?'

'What do you mean?'

'Well, you could have put a note in to say that if Meredith lays another finger on him, we'll send the papers to the press.'

'What's the point?' said Fran. 'How would we know if he did anything else to Jason? We're gone. Jason's stuck there in the firing line.'

'We could photocopy the documents and send a set to Jason at the hospital,' said Eileen. 'At least then he'd have some kind of protection.'

'It's too late for that.'

She could feel tears forming in her eyes. 'You could at least *try* to help him, you callous bitch!'

'Calm down. You're not thinking straight. There's nothing we can do. Not now that Sadie March is on the case.'

Eileen shook her head. The tears were flowing freely.

'Jesus, Eileen, we're pretty fucking lucky to have got out of Cardiff ourselves. Forget about Jason!'

'Did you ever really love him?'

Fran seemed startled at this question, lost for words.

'Did you?'

'Well, I . . .'

'I knew it.' Eileen gave a deep sniff and wiped her tears

away with the back of her hand. 'You're not capable of loving anyone, are you?' And her head filled up with Owen. With Owen's dark loving eyes. With Owen's smile. Owen's strong hands.

Eileen knew how to love. Or she was learning.

Suddenly, Fran grabbed her right wrist across the table, held it hard.

'Let go. You're hurting me.'

But Fran kept hold. 'Don't you dare lecture me about love, Eileen! Don't you bloody dare!'

'OK, OK. Jesus.'

Fran let go her wrist and turned to gaze out of the window. 'You will never know what that man has put me through. I've had years of shit from him – *years*. And I've stayed with him – waited for him – been there for him. Of course I bloody loved him, but I just can't do it any more!'

Eileen heard the ticking of the time bomb again, glimpsed the new instability in this woman who had previously been an impregnable rock. Slowly she got to her feet.

'Where are you going?'

'To the toilet. I take it I do have your permission to go to the toilet?'

'Don't be dumb. Get me a drink while you're up, will you? Something with a kick to it.'

'Sure.'

The toilet was blocked up with paper and the floor covered in piss. Nevertheless, Eileen took her time. She *had* to find a way of clearing her head of all the worries, the fear and the self-pity. She had to be able to think straight.

I could get off this train at the next stop. And I could go to the police. Tell them everything. Cop a plea. Could the police get to Jason before anybody else does . . . ?

She washed her hands and opened the door. The acne-scarred inspector was in the next carriage, clipping a businessman's ticket.

'How soon is the next stop?'

'About five minutes,' said the inspector, handing the ticket back to the businessman. 'Swindon.'

'Thanks.' Eileen squeezed past him, avoiding looking at his face as her body brushed against his.

She hovered by the doors outside the buffet car. Only three minutes or so and she'd be out of this train and away from Fran. She kept glancing back down the carriage in case Fran came looking for her, but there was no sign of her.

I'll take a taxi. I'll tell the driver to go straight to the police station. Swindon . . . What kind of a town is Swindon?

She tried to imagine herself walking into a police station, sitting down in a small room with two men – or perhaps a man and a woman. Maybe they'd play good cop bad cop – the woman might pretend to be her friend while the man laid into her with the questioning. Perhaps they'd call her a liar, a slut. She could see herself standing her ground against an onslaught of verbal aggression, telling them how urgent it was that they put a guard by Robert Warren's hospital bed. She'd be writing out her statement in all its amazing complexity. Would they ever believe her? She imagined them leading her into a cell afterwards, locking the door behind her.

The train was slowing.

'This is Swindon,' came a voice over the speaker. 'Swindon will be our next station stop. Please remember to take all your belongings with you. This is Swindon.'

She saw herself standing in the dock, and the image began to merge with scenes she remembered from the film *Scandal,* the story of the Profumo affair. She was Christine Keeler, she was Mandy Rice-Davies.

A man in a powdered wig was pointing an accusing finger at her: 'Mr Meredith, in his statement, denies that he ever wrote those letters, Miss Locket. Mr Meredith denies all knowledge of this whole nasty business.'

'Well,' said Eileen/Mandy. 'Well, he would, wouldn't he?'

The train stopped.

A policeman in full uniform was walking down the platform. He was talking into a radio. Eileen noticed the cuffs hanging from his belt, and the truncheon. He glanced up, seemed to see her at the door of the train. He stood there looking at her.

She was about to open the door. She froze. She stared into

his nasty little eyes. He looked rather like Tony Meredith, only taller.

'Excuse me, please,' said a voice behind her, and Eileen moved to one side to allow a woman with an enormous case to stagger past and get off the train. The woman was followed by two small boys who blew raspberries and fired invisible guns at her.

Eileen moved away into the buffet. As she approached the serving counter she heard the doors bang, felt the train begin to move.

'Yes?' said the steward, an officious-looking man with an immaculate side parting. He reminded her a little of that dreadful buffet steward on the train from London to Manchester all those months ago.

'Two large gins with ice and a bottle of slim-line tonic, please,' she said.

'The gin doesn't come in measures. It comes in bottles,' he said unpleasantly, producing a miniature Gordon's.

'I'll take four.'

'Anything else?' He tonged ice into two plastic cups.

I'd like a back-bone, please. I'd like a conscience. Do you have any quick fixes in the fridge? Or perhaps a rewind button that would let me go right back to that day when I got sacked from the Silver Square Sandwich Bar and make a different decision?

'No, that's all, thanks.'

'You took your time,' said Fran, when she got back with the drinks. 'I started to think you'd got off at Swindon. But you wouldn't do a thing like that . . . would you?'

'Swindon looked like a dump so I thought I wouldn't bother,' said Eileen. 'What's the next stop?'

'Reading. Then it's straight on to Paddington.'

'Oh, well, I'm fucked then, aren't I?' Eileen gave a smile of hopelessness and reached for her drink.

'I was thinking about when Jason and I first met.' A dreamy look came into Fran's eyes. 'Have I ever told you about it?'

'No, I don't think you have.'

'I was sitting on my own in a bistro in Islington. My date had blown me out but I thought I'd have the meal anyway. A girl has to eat, after all.'

'Of course.'

'Anyway, he was on his own too. He was on the look-out for someone like me, a well-dressed attractive woman dining alone.' She took a sip from her gin-and-tonic. 'That's a double, isn't it? Thanks. So Jason comes over, asks if he can join me. I say I'd be delighted. We eat dinner together and he starts telling me some bullshit story about himself. Says his name is Hans Peter and he's a fashion designer. Then he spins some elaborate scenario in which he's supposed to be flying to Australia the next day with a load of other designers and a bunch of girls who are going to model his new line for some show in Sydney.'

'Yeah?'

'Absolutely. Jason – or rather Hans Peter – has a problem, though. One of the girls has an inner ear infection and her doctor says she can't fly. He's one girl short.'

'Oh dear.'

'Oh dear indeed. Where can he get a replacement at such short notice? But then – you know what's coming – it hits him like a bolt of lightning – he's sitting there bending my ear with his problems, and all the time the girl he's looking for is right here, just across the table. Me? I exclaim, catching my breath in excitement; surely he can't want little me – me . . . an international model? And then he's laying on the compliments, the flattery. He's pleading for me to go with him on the plane. He even produces an airline ticket from his briefcase which he keeps waving around. He only needs one thing . . .'

'Let me guess,' said Eileen. 'He can't afford to just *give* you the airline ticket. When you arrive in Sydney, money will be no object. The show's already sold out but he doesn't get his share until it opens. Just now he's strapped for cash. He's had to pay the other girl for her ticket and he's invested everything he has in the show – got himself up to his eyes in debt so that he's worried the cheque he wrote her will bounce.'

'Exactly. Has he told you this before? He needs four hundred pounds for the ticket. He needs it now and he needs it in cash. He asks me if I can get that money – if I can get it tonight? Sure, I say. Let's settle the bill and get out of here. When the bill arrives he reaches into his jacket for his wallet.' Fran smiled playfully. 'But he can't find the damn thing. He's fumbling around, looking a little worried, and he's just about to apologise for this embarrassing mishap when I produce said wallet with a flourish from up my sleeve and lay it on the table. Do you know what he says to me then?'

'What does he say?'

'He says, "Wow, you can do magic." And I, of course, tell him there's a lot more magic where that came from – provided he doesn't insult my intelligence with any more of his cock and bull stories. That's when we go off to my hotel together.'

She sat back, smiling, happy. It was impossible to reconcile this nostalgic dreamy woman with the one who walked out on Jason earlier that same day.

'And it was good between the two of you in those early days,' prompted Eileen.

'Oh, it was the best. The very best. I felt like someone who's been trying to sing all their life, doing it really badly, and suddenly I hit the right note. A strong, clear note.' She had a faraway look about her. It made Eileen feel slightly sick.

'And how long did you hold the note?'

Fran shrugged, gulped at her gin. 'I don't know. Let's face it, relationships are always more exciting at the beginning. This was especially exciting because we shared a secret. And we shared a project, right from the start. He always said he knew that I was "the one" the moment I handed his wallet across the table.'

'When did you know he was "the one" for you?'

'Just a moment later. The moment when he said, "You can do magic." There'd never been any "magic" in my life, not until that evening.'

Eileen felt a question coming to the front of her mind – a question that had been nagging away in the background for some time. 'Why did you bring me into it, Fran? I was just some kid, some sandwich-bar waitress. I mean – I know all that stuff about how you needed an extra girl for the scam in Manchester, but why me? What made you think I'd be any good at scamming? What did I have to offer you?'

Fran laughed lightly but didn't say anything.

'Really, Fran. I want to know. It's something I've never understood.' An idea was forming itself. She narrowed her eyes. 'Was I your distraction when the magic was gone – when the initial excitement of the relationship died down and you started to feel like some bored old married couple? Did you bring me in to pep things up, to add another dimension?'

Fran shook her head, smiling. 'What *are* you talking about, you silly girl?'

But Eileen was becoming more sure. 'No, Fran, this is all making sense now. Most couples would just have a baby in those circumstances, but that was far too *normal* for you two. Besides, a baby couldn't earn its keep, could it? A baby's a burden. It costs money, time and attention. With me you still got to play mummies and daddies, you still had the fun of teaching me, showing me how to live. But you didn't have all the mess of bringing up a child; the dirty nappies, the sick-stained bedding, the tantrums . . .'

'Oh, we had the tantrums all right. You were always good at them.'

'I'm right,' said Eileen. 'Aren't I?'

Fran's smile had disappeared. She looked angry now, and hurt. 'Has it ever occurred to you, Eileen, that I wasn't actually thinking of myself or Jason when I asked you to join us – have you even once entertained the thought that maybe I did it for you?'

'Oh, come on, Fran!' Now it was Eileen's turn to give one of those flat humourless laughs. 'You can't seriously expect me to believe that you took me in when you didn't know me from Adam, trusted me, taught me everything you knew – all out of pure altruism? Give me a break! You're the most shrewd person I've ever met. There had to be something in it for *you* – some reason for you to do what you did. You gambled on me and you knew you had a lot to lose. Why did you do that?'

The train was gathering speed. It lurched and suddenly jolted so that they had to grab their plastic glasses of gin to stop them sliding off the table.

'OK. You want the truth. Well, here's the truth, Eileen. That day when I found you in bed with Jason – when I stood at the window and watched you walking away down the street – do you remember what you did?'

Eileen thought back. 'I waved at you.'

'Yes. You waved and you smiled. And I saw something in you

– at that instant. It was an instant of recognition – quite uncanny. I saw myself in you.'

Eileen swallowed her gin down the wrong way and broke into a coughing fit. 'That is such bullshit!'

'No, it isn't. It really isn't.' Fran kept a straight face. 'It was only a hint, of course, only a fleeting glimpse that lasted a fraction of a second. But it intrigued me. I wanted to speak to you, to find out if my instincts were right.'

Eileen was still coughing, struggling to calm her breathing. 'Were they right, then, your instincts?'

'Oh, yes,' said Fran. 'Absolutely. When we talked in the Atlantic, and you told me about your father – then I understood what I'd recognised in you.'

'What was that?'

'Someone who had been a victim but who was determined not to remain one. I saw the hurt and I saw the defiance.'

Eileen had never heard Fran speak like this. 'Where's this coming from, Fran? What are you saying?'

'You're not the only one who had an abusive father, Eileen. You're not the only one who ran away to London and ended up in a mess. Only my mess got darker, nastier. I had to hit the bottom before I was able to pull myself out of it – and believe me, it wasn't easy. When you opened up to me that night, I saw someone just like myself on the downward spiral. And I wanted to help you – I wanted to get you out of it – desperately – I couldn't *bear* the thought of you going through what I'd been through. I knew you were capable of pulling scams. I knew I could teach you how. Jason wasn't keen. He didn't understand – well, after all, how could he! But in the end I persuaded him. I could always convince Jason that I was right.'

Eileen was quiet. She was remembering things Fran had said – and things she hadn't quite said on that first night.

Whatever you do, don't go on the game . . . Just don't do it. The money's good but there are other ways to make money.

She'd said other things since then.

Nobody expects you to do anything you don't feel comfortable with . . . I wouldn't want to do what you're going to do. That's all. Not for Jason, not for anyone . . .

Eileen looked searchingly at Fran. She was trying to see the

Fran who hit the very bottom, trying to imagine how black and nasty it must have been. Looking at Fran now, she could see an intense desperation that she'd never been aware of before – maybe it hadn't been there until this dreadful day, now that they were running together. She was frantic that Eileen should believe what she was saying.

The train reached Reading. The station was teeming with commuters running between trains. Doors were banging, whistles blowing. Eileen caught the eye of a glum teenage girl slouching against the window in a train on a neighbouring platform. She had been staring at the girl without actually meaning to and was somehow unable to stop. Eventually the girl gave her the finger. Reading . . . what did Reading make you think of? Eileen's paternal grandparents, now dead, had lived in Reading. They had a council semi just down the road from an abattoir – there was a hideous stench about the place that coiled inside your gut and caught at your throat. Eileen's grandparents had been there so long they couldn't smell it any more. Reading . . . what else? Oscar Wilde – *The Ballad of Reading Gaol* . . .

'You seem miles away,' said Fran.

'I'm wishing I was miles away.'

'We soon will be, honey,' said Fran. 'This time tomorrow we'll be in LA.'

The train began to move.

'What will we do when we get there?'

Fran shrugged. 'Who cares? Whatever we like. We've got each other, right? That's the important thing.'

'Right.' Eileen couldn't fathom her. So tough but seemingly so needy. She hadn't brought Eileen with her because she cared about her – she'd brought her because she was afraid to be alone.

How dare Fran muscle in on her life in the way she had! How dare she assume Eileen needed to be rescued, guided, manipulated into another way of being. How truly monstrous was this woman's ego?

'You've stolen from me,' said Eileen. 'And I'll never forgive you for that.'

Fran looked crushed. 'What do you mean?'

'You stole the person I was and you reshaped me in your own image. You're some hideous fucking Frankenstein and I'm your monster.'

'Eileen, it wasn't like that. How can you say that?'

'Yes, it was. I was too young and stupid to see it. You and Jason together . . . you weren't offering me some golden future – you were robbing me of my chance of making a good life for myself.' She could feel the pain of it now – the wound had been there for a long time and it had finally started to bleed. 'Find your limits, Jason always said. Find your limits and then break through them. Now I'm beginning to understand what these limits really are. They're the limits dictated by your conscience – the barriers you choose not to cross because you're human and you don't want to hurt other people. You and Jason made me break through those limits. You've made me murder my conscience.'

'Now, just you hold on a second.' Fran seemed to have recovered herself. 'Jason and I never *made* you do anything. You can't dump that one on me. You chose, Eileen. You're responsible for your own decisions and actions.'

'Oh, yeah?' Eileen leant forward and lowered her voice. 'Like I *chose* to come with you today? I had the chance of a new beginning in Cardiff, Fran. Owen showed me real love; he showed me another way to live. I wanted to stay with him and live that life – be that person – *that* was my choice. And you've taken that away from me. You've robbed me again.'

Fran drained her glass. 'Get off your high horse, Eileen. The life you were living with Owen – it wasn't real – it was just a scam.'

'No, you're wrong!'

'Am I? This new beginning of yours, this *real love* – it was based on a lie. Owen was in love with Meg the dreamy little drifter, not Eileen the thieving con artist who was sleeping with him to get some dirt on his father!'

'But he didn't ever have to know about all that.'

Fran smacked her plastic glass down on the table. 'Stop kidding yourself. You're talking about living a lie with this man – permanently. Just how long do you think you'd have been able to keep up the pretence, eh? It'd be like sleeping with your make-up on every night because you're scared of showing your man what your face really looks like. At least with me and Jason the masks come off at the end of the day.'

Eileen hated Fran at this moment, hated her most for speaking the truth. She felt as though she'd been punched in the gut. 'Another drink?' she asked, when she could speak again.

The buffet was closed. The steward tapped at his watch when he saw her coming and gave her a meaningful supercilious look.

'Didn't you hear the announcement?' he said. 'We're only ten minutes out of Paddington.'

He was the sort of man who brought out the kid in Eileen. She pulled a face at him – literally – and wandered over to the pay-phone. As if on auto-pilot, without really stopping to think about what she was doing, she found she was swiping her credit card through the slot and dialling a number. His number. Just to hear his voice. Just one more time.

'This is Owen. I'm busy so talk to my machine.'

Damn! She hung up, beginning to feel the full extent of her grief. Its weight. Her knees were weak.

She dialled again just in case.

'This is Owen. I'm busy so talk to my machine.'

She talked.

5

London

Eileen lay awake listening to the sounds of the city; the buzzing and tooting of cars, the rumble of lorries, the laughing, squealing and drunken-drawling of the hordes waiting for night buses, the wailing sirens. Streetlights and headlamps burned through the thin curtains of the hotel room, casting shadows across the walls. She watched them dance. There was no air in the room – Fran hadn't wanted to open the window because of the noise but it was Eileen who couldn't sleep. Eileen felt as though she would suffocate. She was aware – oh so aware – of Fran's arm flung over her waist, of Fran's deep even sleep-breathing on the back of her neck. How could she sleep so peacefully? Oh yes, of course – she'd murdered her conscience long ago.

She had tried lifting the arm off her but the sleeping Fran had just flung it back over again. She'd tried wriggling away but Fran kept shifting up against her so that now she teetered at the very edge of the bed, clutching at the duvet with tight, tense fingers. She glanced at the clock radio beside the bed. 2.47 – God, it was only ten minutes since she'd last looked! Fran's arm was heavy, crushing her.

On that train journey she'd discovered so many things about Fran and about herself. It was one of those discoveries that was running through her mind now; Fran was afraid to be alone. Tonight she hadn't wanted to sleep alone, had specifically asked the receptionist for a double-bedded room. The middle-aged tweed-skirted hotelier had peered over her glasses at them, raising her thick matted eyebrows ever so slightly. *Lesbians,* her look seemed to say. *A pair of lesbians in my hotel!* Eileen had gone along with Fran's request. After all she was going along with everything else that Fran wanted – why draw the line at something so harmless?

Now she wished she had protested. Fran's presence in the bed was unbearable. What the hell was she going to do? The thought came to her that there may be a further reason for Fran's need to share a bed with her, for the arm around her waist. Perhaps Fran thought she might take off with the money.

It sat in the vanity case under the bed – all those neat little bundles of notes. Maybe . . . just maybe . . . No. That money represented everything she wanted to get away from – that money had put Jason in hospital, had driven her to destroy Owen's life. She wanted none of it. She would go along with Fran as far as LA, and then, anonymous in a foreign country, she would disappear.

Disappear? But you don't just disappear, do you? You move on but you have to move on to something. What would she do? What *could* she do other than stealing and scamming? The world out there was so frightening and so alien – so bloody big! For a long time now she'd had Jason and Fran to guide her through it, to tell her what to do, who to be. She'd wanted to leave them to be with Owen – to have Owen running her life and telling her what to do instead. In truth she was as afraid of being alone as Fran was. The arm that trapped her also protected her.

She tried again to close her eyes and relax her body.

What was it her mother used to say she should do when she couldn't sleep? *Imagine you are walking very slowly towards a wall. A big, black wall, so big you can't see the edges. You're just walking slowly to the wall, reaching out with your hands to touch it, walking slowly, slowly towards the big black wall . . .*

She jerked involuntarily and her heart thudded in her chest. Her eyes snapped open with the suddenness of an overstretched rubber band breaking. Jesus, that wall was so terrifying!

An hour later Eileen was still awake. A man was being sick in the street and she was forced to listen to the terrible retching. She wished she had some cotton wool to stuff in her ears. She was thinking about choice and responsibility. On the train she had accused Fran and Jason of *making* her go along with them, of making her become a degenerate. Fran was right, of course, nobody *made* her do anything. But what were her options? On the one hand a life of scamming with Fran and Jason, on the other a room at the YWCA and no job. And they did their very best to seduce her into this life, that was for sure.

* * *

The light is orange. The light is red. There are hands touching her, unbuttoning her blouse – at first she tries to resist but her movements are clumsy, imprecise. Everything is blurry, moving about. She wants it all to slow down and stay still. The hands are easing her back against pillows, cushions. She knows this room. She has been here before.

Her breasts are bare. There is a mouth against one of her nipples. A tongue is teasing her. It is a woman's mouth. Now there is a mouth against the other breast – a man – he is biting lightly, enough to stimulate but not enough to hurt. She knows his mouth.

'What—' She tries to sit up but they don't seem to want her to.

'Relax, Eileen. Just relax. Lie back and enjoy it.' She recognises the voice. It's that man – Richard. No, that's not his name, is it? His real name is something else.

Someone is pushing her skirt up, pulling at her pants.

'No!'

'Relax, honey.' The woman. All those drinks . . . the spliffs . . . how is this happening?

Her stomach is being stroked and the hand is moving down to her cunt. Then his mouth is there.

'I—'

There is a mouth against hers, a female mouth. Kissing her, pushing a tongue inside. It feels weird – not like kissing a man. It is as though she is kissing herself. It is delicious. She reaches up and pulls the woman closer. Her hair is warm and soft.

The man is pushing his cock inside her.

There's sun coming into the room now. They are unravelling.

'How do you feel?'

'I feel fantastic.'

'We wanted you to have a special night.'

'I did.'

'We want you to remember it.'

'I will.'

'This won't ever happen again.'

'No?'

'No.'

'But if you stay with us, we'll give you other experiences. Other highs. You think this was good, but wait and see what else there is.'

'You broke through your boundaries last night, Eileen. There are other boundaries to break.'

* * *

'Come on, get up,' comes Fran's voice.

I open my eyes. Fran is already dressed. She is sitting at the mirror, brushing her hair.

'It's breakfast time,' says Fran. 'Are you hungry?'

'Oh, Jesus.' I close my eyes again. 'I must have had two hours' sleep maximum.'

'Well, you've been snoring your head off ever since I woke up,' says Fran, cheerfully. She puts the brush away in her handbag. 'Shift yourself.'

She is so cheerful, so brusque. Just as if this was any normal day. It is frightening.

'Come on, move!'

I groan and try to sit up. 'Yeah, yeah, I'm just getting my head together. Look, why don't you go down to breakfast – I have to take a shower. I'll be ten or fifteen minutes.'

'Make it ten,' says Fran.

The shower is strong and hot. I stand under it for longer than necessary – certainly longer than the ten minutes I'd been allowed. I think about Owen getting the message I left. I wanted to tell him how I felt, to try to soothe him, even to apologise – but I wasn't able to articulate clearly and it emerged as a garbled mush of half declarations, half promises. He'll probably hate me all the more for it.

I squeeze shampoo from a hotel sachet and massage it into my aching scalp. I close my eyes as I step back under the shower so as not to get soap in them and my vision is filled with an image of Owen's face – a mess of tears. Shaken, I reach to turn off the water.

'I'm so sorry!'

There is no one to hear. Nobody to respond. Only the steady drip drip from the shower-head. I grab a bath towel from the rail and wrap it around myself.

Rubbing at my head with one of the hand towels, I wander over to the little side window which is all steamed up from my shower. Absently, I begin to write my name on the pane with a finger: E I L – I'm such a fucking kid!

I wipe the letters away with my palm. And then something catches my attention – something down in the street below.

An old silver Jaguar – an XJS pulling up at the kerb. It is familiar, this car. I've seen it somewhere before. Wait a minute …

It couldn't be. There's no way … How could they possibly know …

One of the rear doors is opening. A man is getting out. A big man with ginger hair. From the other side a dark-haired man is emerging. I've seen these men before. At Tony Meredith's house.

I begin to shake uncontrollably. My teeth are chattering as though I am freezing cold. When I try to move my feet can barely take my weight.

Pull yourself together, for Christ's sake!

I am dressing – or trying to – fumbling with my bra-clip, pulling on my knickers inside out, tripping myself up as I attempt to get into my jeans. I am still dripping wet. Glancing out of the window as I try to force shirt buttons into their holes – getting it wrong – I see the top of a shiny bald head. The fat driver is staggering his way onto the pavement. One of the boys is moving to open the passenger door. *No* – I jerk away from the window. I don't want to catch sight of that woman.

Abandoning my socks as a lost cause I dive under the bed for my shoes. There, next to my shoes, sits the vanity case.

I grab it.

The lift takes an age to reach the fourth floor. I stare anxiously up at the green indicator. It sits for what feels like a full minute on floor three. I am on the verge of running for the stairs when a loud ping announces its arrival and the doors slide open. Inside I press 'G' and catch sight of myself in the mirrored interior; hair a bunch of wet rats' tails, shirt all done up in the wrong button holes. No socks, the enormous vanity case dangling from my right hand. I see the fear in my own eyes. I start to shake again.

The lift pings again to announce it has reached the ground floor and the doors open.

I am looking straight into the eyes of the ginger-haired man. The panic hits a crescendo and I am close to screaming. But then – just as I expect the man to raise an arm – to point – to shout, *There she is!* he simply looks down at his feet. He licks a finger and bends to rub a speck of dirt from one of his shoes.

They don't know who I am.

I can hardly believe it.

They've never seen me, of course, but they seem to know everything else. It is such a major thing not to know.

Overcoming the shakes I step tentatively forward out of the lift.

The reception area is dingy and oppressive; heavy flock wallpaper, a huge oak desk, a rack of rusting key-hooks, two old leather Chesterfields and fake chandeliers that tinkle in the wind blowing through the open front doors.

The dark-haired man is standing beside his brother, biting on a nail. The short bald driver is at the desk, shifting uncomfortably in his ill-fitting suit.

She stands beside him, her back to me. Her hair is an immaculately set bouffant, as though she's just stepped out of the hairdresser's. She wears a bright red trouser suit. The jacket sits well on her shoulders. Dressed for war?

'I'm looking for Marsha Freeman,' says Sadie March. Her voice is dry and witchy. She has a strong Welsh accent.

The tweedy receptionist lifts her glasses from where they dangle on a string around her neck and props them on her nose, running her finger down her list.

'I'm sorry, we don't have anyone by that name staying here.'

'Look, we know she's here!' barks the bald man.

'Shut up, Ted!'

I am walking very slowly towards them. I am almost directly behind Sadie March now.

'I'm sorry,' Sadie says to the receptionist, more softly. 'It's possible she may be using another name. The woman I'm looking for is tall and slim, smart, about thirty-five, bobbed reddish hair. Prominent nose, sort of spiky-looking.'

'Oh, I know who you mean,' pipes up the receptionist. 'In fact, that's her companion just behind you. Miss Wilson?'

Sadie March turns around.

I freeze, hardly able to breathe, my mouth so dry I could choke. Sadie is looking into my face. Her heavily made-up eyes are large, green and surprisingly sad.

It's all over.

And then, amazingly, Sadie turns back to the reception desk. 'I don't think so. My friend was travelling alone.'

'Oh, I'm sorry, madam. My mistake.'

It's a miracle. A crazy, tense smile is fixing itself on my face, I can feel it. I nod curtly at the receptionist and quicken my pace.

As I get near the open front doors I hear Sadie's voice again.

'Is breakfast being served at the moment?'

'Yes, madam. But it's residents only.'

I reach the doors.

'I think I'll take a look for my friend in the breakfast room if I may. Through there?'

'Yes, madam.'

Fran . . .

I am through the front doors and out on to the street.

The sky is a cold blue. The wind is sharp and autumnal. The street, which Eileen had barely noticed when they arrived in the dark, is lined with smart, white Georgian houses. A man in a pin-striped suit is strolling down the road swinging an umbrella. A young woman with a soft pink face is pushing an old-fashioned pram. A window-cleaner is whistling as he sets up his ladder against the house next door, a postman is emptying a bright red pillar box, someone is making a phone call in an equally red telephone box. A black cab is humming down the road. Its yellow light is on.

Eileen sticks out her arm to hail it.

Fran . . .

The cab draws up. The grumpy-looking bearded driver asks, 'Where to, love?'

'Heathrow.'

'Hop in.'

She nestles against the hard seat, clutching the vanity case. The cab swings into the traffic.

'Are you all right, love?'

She thinks about Fran, sitting in the dining room, munching on a sausage, mopping up her egg yolk with a piece of toast, reading the paper. She imagines Sadie March stepping casually into the room, followed by her husband and sons, her shadow falling across the table. She pictures Fran looking up, forcing herself to smile . . .

Poor Fran.

She remembers Jason in the hospital bed, sipping at his water, squeezing his morphine drip . . . She stops trying to make herself care what happens to Fran.

She thinks of Owen listening to the message, beginning to cry, to rage, storming up to his study and ripping up the sketches he'd made of her. The thought is awful. Owen has given her so much. He has taught her about the kind of life she could have.

Now she must go out and live it for real.

She has all she needs. The money, the tickets, her passport. She is almost safe now, and yet something is making her uneasy.

'Excuse me,' she says, knocking on the taxi-driver's glass door. 'I've changed my mind. Could you take me to Gatwick, please?'

The driver shrugs. 'Whatever you say, love.' He turns the car too suddenly, throwing Eileen sideways so that she almost falls on the floor.

'Sorry, darling, are you all right?'

Eileen sees her mother falling against the kitchen table, hitting her head, sees Tara the life model crumple to the floor revealing the scars on her arm. She hears Joanne, the smack-head from the YWCA, wailing her way through the long night.

'Yes,' says Eileen, allowing herself the beginnings of a smile. 'I'm all right.'